THE MYSTERIES OF PENDOWAR HALL

THE AUDACIOUS SISTERHOOD OF SMOKE & FIRE
BOOK I

SYRIE JAMES

DRAGONBLADE PUBLISHING, INC.

ARE YOU SIGNED UP FOR DRAGONBLADE'S BLOG?

You'll get the latest news and information on exclusive giveaways, exclusive excerpts, coming releases, sales, free books, cover reveals and more.

Check out our complete list of authors, too!

No spam, no junk. That's a promise!

Sign Up Here

www.dragonbladepublishing.com

Dearest Reader;

Thank you for your support of a small press. At Dragonblade Publishing, we strive to bring you the highest quality Historical Romance from some of the best authors in the business. Without your support, there is no 'us', so we sincerely hope you adore these stories and find some new favorite authors along the way.

Happy Reading!

CEO, Dragonblade Publishing

"There is no fyre without smoke."

The Proverbs of John Heywood, 1546

CHAPTER ONE

Cornwall, England
October 1849

D IANA TAYLOR LOVED the rain. A long ramble across the moors during a gentle shower was one of her favorite pursuits. She was far from home, however, and this was hardly a drizzle. The relentless downpour had been pounding against the roof of the carriage for hours.

Wrapping her woolen cloak more tightly around her, Diana glanced out the rain-splattered window. She had been traveling for four numbing days, accomplishing the first part of the journey by train. But the new railway system in England, although a marvel of speed and technology, was still in development, requiring so many changes at so many stations and involving so many delays that Diana questioned its efficacy—and it did not yet extend as far south as Cornwall. She had been obliged to complete the last leg of her journey by stagecoach and had been met this afternoon at the Crown Inn at Truro by this elegant vehicle. If all went well, they should arrive at Pendowar Hall before dark.

To Diana's mind, she couldn't arrive soon enough. She longed for a good, hot meal by a warm fire and to stretch out in a clean bed.

All at once, a flash of lightning erupted from the heavens,

followed by an ear-splitting clap of thunder. Diana gasped as the bolt struck an ancient oak at the roadside, scattering sparks into the air. With a mighty roar, the uppermost section of the leafy giant crashed down across the road before them. The horses whinnied in terror and the carriage lurched to a halt.

Diana's heart leapt into her throat. Now what?

The coachman descended from the vehicle and approached, his cloak sodden and moisture dripping from his cap. Diana let down the window and blinked back the rain.

"Well, miss, this be a fine kettle of fish. That tree has blocked the road entire."

"We must find another route, then," Diana advised.

"There be no other route, miss."

"Surely, there must be a byway or cart track somewhere?"

"A few, but they're a ways back and I don't dare try 'em, not in this weather. We'd be sunk in mud for sure. Pendowar Hall still be six miles off and there's not much to speak of between here and there. We'd best return to Truro."

"Return to Truro?" It meant backtracking seven miles in the wrong direction and spending the night or even longer at the dreadful Crown Inn. "Oh, surely not."

"Sorry, miss. There's nothing for it. With any luck, the road'll be cleared tomorrow, and you can try again."

Diana was deeply disappointed. "Well, then—" Before she could complete the thought, the drumbeat of the rain was pierced by the tramp, tramp, tramp of approaching hooves. Diana peered out the window at the road behind them. A man thundered up on horseback. His boots and well-made dark cloak pronounced him to be a gentleman. Reining in the animal, he took in the fallen treetop.

"When did this happen?" His voice was cultured, deep, and gruff.

"Only a moment since, sir." The coachman, seeming to recognize the gentleman, crossed to him and touched his cap.

The rider glanced briefly at the carriage from beneath the

low, wide brim of his hat. Through the pouring rain, Diana caught a glimpse of stern features on a clean-shaven face. She guessed him to be in his early thirties. Turning, he exchanged a few words with the driver which Diana could not hear, finishing with:

"If we use the carriage horses, I believe we can clear away that tree. I've done it before."

Nodding, the coachman retrieved a length of rope and set off to begin unhitching the horses.

Through the open window, Diana called out, "Sir, I should be glad to help."

"Stay in the carriage," the newcomer commanded bluntly. "This is man's work."

Man's work? Diana bristled. What exactly did that mean? A proper Englishwoman would not think of participating in an activity so filthy as road-clearing, but these were hardly normal circumstances.

The horseman dismounted, an effort which appeared to cause him pain. When he touched the ground, he grimaced and retrieved a cane affixed to his saddle. Diana's annoyance vanished, replaced by sympathy. This man was either injured or lame. She could hardly sit idle in the safety of the carriage while he rescued her from the road.

Donning her hood, Diana opened the carriage door, stepped down from the vehicle and, braving the elements, hurried towards him down the muddy lane. "Sir!"

The gentleman's horse, no doubt startled by her outcry and rapid approach from behind, danced skittishly and knocked into its rider, causing him to fall to his knees in the muddy road.

Diana, aghast, rushed to him and crouched at his side. "Sir! Are you all right?"

The man's hat remained on his head, its brim preventing her from seeing any of his features but a deep scowl. "I *told* you to stay in the carriage!"

"I'm sorry. May I assist you to a stand?"

"Get away!" he growled.

Ignoring this directive, Diana took his arm and provided what support she could as the man maneuvered to his feet. He was drenched and muddy now, and it was all her fault.

"I'm so sorry," Diana said again, handing him his cane. "May I help—"

"You have been quite enough *help,*" he barked irritably. "Get back in the coach! This is no weather for a lady." Retrieving his horse's reins, he limped to the vehicle and thrust out a hand to assist her to board, his demeanor brooking no refusal.

Diana, beset by conflicting emotions—embarrassment and regret for causing the man's fall, sympathy for the pain from which he suffered, and resentment at his authoritative and condescending manner—grudgingly re-entered the conveyance. She closed the door and window and sat shivering in silence, upset with herself and the entire circumstance.

The rain beat down. The stranger tethered his horse to a tree. The man's debility, although it appeared to give him great discomfort, did not prevent him from organizing and fully participating in the efficient removal of the fallen tree.

When the exercise was completed and the carriage horses returned to their former positions, the horseman took off down the road.

Diana watched him go, annoyed by his attitude, while at the same time, grateful for his help. He could have easily gone around the obstruction via the woods. Yet he had voluntarily undertaken a difficult task under miserable conditions.

The coachman, who more and more resembled a drowned rat, knocked on Diana's window and she lowered the glass again. "Are ye all right then, miss?" he inquired. "We be free to move on now."

"Yes, thank you. We are fortunate that gentleman came this way."

"We are, miss. It just so happens he had business in Truro and was on his way home."

"Home?" Diana recalled the driver saying there wasn't much between here and Pendowar Hall. "Is he a neighbor of the Fallbrooks, then?"

"Why no, miss. That were Captain William Fallbrook himself, the new heir and master of Pendowar Hall."

Captain William Fallbrook? Diana's cheeks burned. What a strange and mortifying way to meet her new employer.

And, if Mrs. Phillips was to be believed … her chief suspect.

As the carriage rattled on, Diana brooded. A Royal Navy captain was no doubt accustomed to giving orders and having them instantly obeyed. No wonder he'd been angry when she'd ignored his directive to remain in the carriage. She was responsible for the man's tumble in the road, for she had startled his horse. She felt terrible about that.

Still, Captain Fallbrook might have been more civil to her. He must have known who she was. She was traveling in *his* coach, after all, and her arrival was expected. Yet he had rejected her offers of assistance, hadn't bothered to introduce himself, and had left without a parting glance.

This lack of acknowledgment stung a bit—but she supposed it was to be expected. The last letter she had received from Captain Fallbrook had been terse and to the point, merely thanking her for her interest in the position and inquiring as to her anticipated date and time of arrival at Truro.

Folding her gloved hands in her lap, Diana sank back against the fine leather seat and reflected on the purpose of her journey, which had all begun two months ago with a visit to her godmother …

"MY DEEPEST CONDOLENCES, my dear Mrs. Phillips," Diana said from her seat by the fire in her godmother's parlor. "I only met your brother once, but he was kind to me."

Diana had been six years old and visiting Rose Cottage in Yorkshire with her family when Sir Thomas Fallbrook, on a trip north, had called on his sister at the same time. He had frightened Diana at first with his gruff and imperious manner, only to delight her and her three siblings by giving them each a sweet, warm from his coat pocket.

"He was a good man." Mrs. Phillips sat across from Diana in a comfortable chair, a formidable black widow's cap blooming around her greying curls. "Although it has been many years since I saw him last, I always look—*looked* forward to his letters." She choked back a sob.

Eliza Phillips had been Diana's mother's best friend, and Diana loved her as dearly as if she were a blood relation. She had been a source of comfort and advice for the better part of Diana's life, and it hurt to see her suffer. "Sir Thomas's passing is a terrible loss."

"Indeed, it is." Mrs. Phillips dabbed at her eyes with her handkerchief, her brow wrinkling. "And I must tell you, Diana: something about it does not sit right with me."

"Oh?"

"It is these letters I received from Thomas's lawyer, a Mr. Latimer." Mrs. Phillips put on her spectacles and retrieved two missives from the drawer in a nearby end table. "He says the parish constable ruled Thomas's death a suicide."

"So you said." Diana nodded in sympathy. "That must pain you greatly."

"It pains me because it is utter nonsense!"

"Why do you say so?"

"Because I knew my brother. We grew up together at Pendowar Hall. I may have left ages ago to marry, but Thomas and I have corresponded regularly all these years. He was a strong, determined man with high principles. He was not the type who would take his own life."

"How can you be certain? You said he had difficulty getting over the loss of his second wife and son."

"Yes. But they died three years ago."

"Grief has no timetable, Mrs. Phillips." Diana knew that only too well. A stab of sorrow, shame, and guilt pierced Diana's chest as the memory came crashing back, still as sharp and awful as it had been more than twenty years ago when her beloved mother had been taken from her. Diana could never forgive herself for what had happened that day.

"Thomas missed Sylvia and little Robert terribly, but he was in no hurry to join them. And he has a daughter still living who needs him."

"Even so, he may have had some reason to end his life. Perhaps he was ill? And in pain?"

"He never breathed a word about illness to me. Indeed, up until a week before he died, my brother was traveling on the Continent and in robust health."

"Might it have been an accident?" Diana suggested.

"Impossible. Thomas and I used to walk that cliff path every morning, rain or shine. We knew every twist and turn so well, we could have walked it blindfolded. There is no way on God's green Earth that Thomas took a misstep and fell to his death." Leaning forward and struggling to take a breath, Mrs. Phillips continued. "This was no accident, Diana. And Thomas would have never deliberately killed himself. He was pushed off that cliff, pure and simple!"

Diana stared at her. "Pushed off? What are you saying?"

"I'm saying: I think my brother was murdered."

Diana pressed her lips together. Her godmother had always been an excitable woman with an active imagination, prone to fears and fanciful thoughts. But she was in mourning, and Diana wished to be respectful. "Who would have wanted to kill your brother?"

"That is what I need *you* to find out."

"I beg your pardon?"

Mrs. Phillips turned her full gaze on Diana. "I need you to go to Cornwall and find out what really happened to Thomas."

"You cannot be serious."

"Oh, but I am. Thomas had money, a great deal of it. Now my nephew, Captain William Fallbrook, has inherited the entire estate—an ancient and valuable property—as well as the title of Baronet of Portwithys. Thomas took that boy in when his parents—our brother, Edmund, and his wife—passed away, sent him straight off to the Royal Navy, and made a man of him. I've never met my nephew. He's been at sea most of his life. But is it a coincidence that he, who spent many holidays as a boy and all his leave from the Navy at Pendowar Hall, and must have understood its value, came home just a few days before Thomas died? Hmm?"

Diana groped for words. "You think Captain Fallbrook killed your brother—his own uncle—to inherit?"

"It's possible, isn't it? I suppose someone else may have done him in. Not everyone liked or understood Thomas as well I did. I will not rest until I learn the truth. But I'm too old to travel. And you are such a clever woman, Diana."

"My dear Mrs. Phillips," Diana began, but her godmother interjected:

"I will never forget that dreadful week when Hortense disappeared. Everyone said my cat had left for good, and I should forget her. Except you. You couldn't have been more than eight years old, but you enlisted your little sisters' aid and made it your business to find her. If not for you, my poor Hortense would have died in that abandoned woodshed."

"Perhaps, but we were just children. I—"

"You and your sisters solved so many little mysteries like that over the years, whenever you came to visit. When I lost the key to the cellar? That time you found my emerald ring? You three are a wonder, my dear, at finding things—and I suspect, at *finding things out.*"

Mrs. Phillips's remarks brought a smile to Diana's lips.

Her mother's favorite saying was *Where there is smoke, there's fire.* "*If you hear a rumor or see signs that something is amiss,*" her mother used to warn Diana and her sisters when they had been small, *"it is probably true."*

Their dear mother was long gone from this world, but her maxim had stayed with them. As little girls, to their father's annoyance, Diana, Athena, and Selena—who were all a year apart—had questioned everything.

They'd called themselves the "Sisterhood of Smoke and Fire." They had been named after goddesses, after all, which made them feel special and powerful. Their older brother, Damon, had also been named after a Greek legend. But, a studious and solemn lad, he didn't share their "predilection for detection," as he liked to call it, and had no wish to join their society.

Boldly, and unapologetically, the three sisters had investigated even the most innocent-seeming domestic circumstance or situation in the parish, determined to discover what terrible truths might have been lurking in the shadows. More often than not, they had turned up nothing. But once in a while, they had uncovered something unexpected. Such as the time when a neighbor's brother had gone missing. They had interviewed practically everyone in the village until they'd learned the truth: he had eloped with a dairy maid.

Those had been childish games, however. They were mature ladies now and long past all such nonsense.

"Mrs. Phillips," Diana said gently, "these circumstances are very different from a missing key or ring, and far more serious. Your brother's cause of death has already been established. The authorities wouldn't have deemed it a suicide without a valid reason."

"Wouldn't they?"

"Did he leave a note or some evidence of his intentions?"

"I have no idea!" Mrs. Phillips waved the letters in the air with a frustrated hand. "I wrote asking for an explanation, but all I got were excuses and platitudes. 'No one could have guessed' ... 'Your brother must not have been in his right senses' ... 'It is the opinion of the parish constable' ... His opinion, indeed! I tell you something is fishy about this whole business. I want proof of what happened, and a reason!"

Diana didn't know how to reply. Her godmother's theories sounded like idle suppositions. And yet this was clearly important to her. "You know I would do anything for you, Mrs. Phillips. But I cannot just show up at Pendowar Hall unannounced and start asking questions."

"Of course not. But an ideal opportunity has just arisen. My only niece, Emma—Thomas's daughter, she's now fifteen years of age—requires a new governess. I have not seen Emma since she was an infant, but I am dreadfully worried about her. Her poor mother died when she was born, you know."

Diana nodded. She had heard the tragic story many times, how Sir Thomas Fallbrook had lost his first wife in childbirth and later, his second wife and son as well. "It is so sad, what has happened to that family. My heart goes out to Miss Fallbrook."

"Mine as well. And now her father is gone! Just think of that poor, orphaned girl! Well, in truth, she's a girl no longer but a young lady. And quite a handful, from what I hear. Thomas once wrote to say that Emma runs wild now and has some kind of learning difficulty. Which is no wonder when you think of all she's been through."

Diana's ears perked up. "What do you mean, a learning difficulty?"

"Thomas never really understood it. He used to say, 'Emma does not apply herself to her studies.' He was at his wit's end with her. Captain Fallbrook is her guardian now—but as a Royal Navy man, he has no experience with such things. He wrote, requesting my advice. He said he prefers to be addressed as 'Captain' rather than 'Sir William,' despite the title he's inherited! What do you make of that?" Without pausing for a reply, she frowned and went on. "Well! I don't trust him! Who knows what the man is up to, or what he did to achieve his position? I can't leave poor Emma in his charge without someone I trust there to look after her." Mrs. Phillips leaned forward in her chair. "I can think of no one as qualified as you for this position, Diana. You could do Emma a world of good. And while there, you can look into my brother's demise. Of course, you would have to be discreet about it."

"I don't know—" Diana began, but once again, Mrs. Phillips cut her off.

"I realize that Cornwall is a great distance away. But I know you've been restless lately and require a new post."

It was true. Diana had been born into a well-to-do family, but eleven years ago, when she'd been eighteen years of age, her widowed father had recklessly gambled away his fortune, and Diana and her sisters had been obliged to find work as governesses. Their circumstances had changed again last year when their father had passed away. He had spent the intervening years haunted by guilt, mending his ways, scrimping, and saving, and due to a good return on an investment, he'd been able to leave each of them and their brother a very small inheritance. The tiny income it produced, however, proved to be not enough to live on, even though Damon had retained the family cottage and allowed Diana and her sisters to stay there rent-free.

Well-meaning friends had pointed out that Diana and her sisters ought to find husbands. But, having spent their most eligible years hidden away as governesses, they were reconciled to the idea that they had missed their chances at marriage. Which, from Diana's point of view, was no loss at all. Before and after her stints as a governess, Diana had suffered too many heartbreaks. She had now fully embraced the spinster state. She and her sisters had been studying German and Latin, with the hope to someday open a school for girls—but that seemed like an unattainable dream. Their home was not big enough to host such an endeavor.

Athena and Selena had already taken positions again as governesses in Yorkshire and Lancashire, respectively. Diana was the last holdout, reluctant to give up this fleeting interval of independence. She had spent the past year struggling to get by, devoting herself to personal study and volunteer work in the community. But the experiment was at an end. She could no longer afford to pay even the modest salary for Martha, their loyal, aging housekeeper. Her brother couldn't help—on his meager income as a curate in a poor parish in London, he could barely afford his own upkeep.

Diana had planned to place an advertisement in the paper next week, seeking a new post. Besides her state of near poverty, however, there had been another motive behind the quest.

Lately, she had found her days unsatisfying.

Teaching—sharing her excitement of learning and overseeing the daily improvement of her students—had given Diana's life meaning and purpose. During her years as a governess, she had endured many challenges, but she had been fond of her pupils, and she had enjoyed the work itself. Without it, she felt like a boat without a rudder.

She was anxious to get away. Away from the pitying looks from the postmistress and greengrocer and ladies at church over her failed love affair last year. She longed to see new vistas ... and to be useful again. To do some good for others.

"If you're looking for work," Mrs. Phillips was saying, "you could find no better place than Pendowar Hall. And you will have one friend nearby in the village of Portwithys."

"Who?"

"Your brother, Damon, asked for my help some two years past to find an incumbency for a college friend of his. I recommended the man to Thomas, and Mr. Wainwright now serves as a curate in that parish."

"How kind of you to arrange that. I remember Mr. Wainwright, although we only met once, years ago."

"It is always nice to know someone when you move to a far-off place. I'm sure you'll love Pendowar Hall as much as I did. It is a magnificent estate in one of the most beautiful spots in Cornwall." Reaching out, Mrs. Phillips took one of Diana's hands in hers and, pausing to take another breath, added meaningfully,

"As for my primary purpose in sending you there ... I will need you to act quickly, my dear."

Sudden foreboding wrapped Diana like a dark veil. "Why is that?"

"It is my heart. My doctor says I may live another five or six months. But likely not much more."

"Oh! I suspected you might be ill but had no idea it was so grave as that." Tears welled in Diana's eyes. "Had you told your brother before he...?"

"No. He had suffered so many losses already. I didn't want to trouble him with my worries, poor man."

"Let us hope the doctor is wrong."

Mrs. Phillips pursed her lips. "I must face reality, my dear. I feel myself fading. Still, I pray, every day, that God will grant me more time." She fixed Diana with an imploring look. "And I pray for something else as well."

Diana squeezed the older woman's hand with affection. "What is that, my dear Mrs. Phillips?"

"Please, Diana. If you love me at all, I beg you to do this for me. Go to Pendowar Hall. Be my eyes and ears. Report to me what you discover. If someone killed my brother—or if he really did take his own life—I need to know the truth before I die."

A HORSE'S WHINNY roused Diana from her reverie. She glanced out the carriage window. They had been traveling for what seemed to be an interminable distance. It was growing dark now and the rain, which had eased to a fine mist several miles back, had ceased altogether.

In the end, Diana had given in willingly to her godmother's request. How could she not? She required employment. And more importantly, it was, for all intents and purposes, Mrs. Phillips's deathbed wish.

Years ago, on the day her mother had died, Diana had ignored another such wish, and her pain and regret would haunt her for the rest of her life. Perhaps, by doing this deed for her godmother, she could begin to make amends for that mistake. And it was the right thing to do, for Mrs. Phillips's sake.

Diana believed her godmother's suspicions to be a figment of her imagination. They appeared to be based on nothing but air. To focus those suspicions on her nephew Captain Fallbrook seemed particularly unlikely. A man who went out of his way to help others by clearing a tree from the road under miserable conditions did not seem the type to commit cold-blooded murder.

If Sir Thomas Fallbrook had died by his own hand, it was heartbreaking. But if Diana could provide some proof of that and set Mrs. Phillips's mind at ease about the matter before she died, it would be worth the time and effort.

The clock was ticking, however. She only had a few months to accomplish it, or Mrs. Phillips might be gone.

Diana's pulse quickened as she thought of the challenge ahead, along with her other reason for going to Pendowar Hall: to teach a girl who was apparently in need of help.

"Emma does not apply herself to her studies," Mrs. Phillips had said. *"She runs wild and has some kind of learning difficulty."*

Diana presumed that meant Emma was often distracted or had trouble concentrating. She had dealt with these problems before and had generally met with success.

Worry, however, overtook her. What if this time, she failed? What if, despite all her best efforts, her new pupil proved to be impossible to teach? What if she couldn't find the evidence Mrs. Phillips was hoping for?

Diana took a deep breath and let it out slowly. She would not fail.

She could not.

Her godmother was counting on her.

They were deep in the countryside now and the glow from

the carriage lamps made ghostly shadows of the dense thickets of trees on either side. The only sounds were the *whoosh* of the wind, the squeak of the carriage, and the steady *thump-thump-thump* of the horses. The road was stony, muddy, and rutted in places, but the vehicle was well made with excellent springs and proved equal to the task. Lulled by the soothing motion of the coach, her mind began to drift, and she fell asleep.

Diana had no idea how much time had passed when she was awakened with a start by the coachman's "Whoa!" and the jolt of the halting carriage.

CHAPTER TWO

B Y THE LIGHT of a feeble moon, Diana saw that they had arrived at the rear entrance of an ancient, immense house built of grey stone.

The coachman opened the carriage door and pulled down the steps. As Diana descended, she was instantly enveloped by a frigid, salty breeze that rang with the sound of distant rushing— evidence that the sea was close by. The driver retrieved her trunk. She followed him through the kitchen yard to the servants' entrance, where a black, wooden door was flanked by two lit lanterns. She thanked him and he departed for the stables.

Diana rang the bell and stood shivering for several minutes, wiping the mud from her shoes on the wrought-iron boot scraper. The door finally opened. A formidable, broad-chested woman of perhaps fifty years of age stared out at her.

"Miss Taylor, I suppose?" she stated abruptly and without a trace of warmth. Her piercing eyes and cheerless expression made Diana feel as though she had given offense by simply arriving.

"Yes. I am Diana Taylor."

"I'm Mrs. Gwynn, the housekeeper. Come in. I'll send the footman out to fetch your trunk."

Diana entered and the woman shut the door. Her severe, tailored dress of black bombazine matched the shade of her cap and the hair peeking out from beneath it.

Diana wondered if the woman's frock was her standard uniform or if it signified that she was in mourning for her former master—perhaps both. Diana had worn black as well, as a sign of respect for the deceased, and because she believed that neat, unadorned clothing best fitted the position she was to fill.

"How do you do, Mrs. Gwynn?"

"Well enough." Mrs. Gwynn led the way down a nondescript hall past several rooms and pantries that belonged to the kitchens.

Diana, of only medium height, towered over the older woman, yet the housekeeper's stern presence was so large and commanding, it made Diana feel small. "I'm sorry to be so late. The weather was awful, and a tree fell across the road. We met Captain Fallbrook along the way. If he hadn't helped clear the tree away, I might not have arrived tonight at all."

"I heard the captain passed you on the road. Got home so wet and filthy—I've never seen the like. Went straight up to his chambers."

Diana flushed at this reminder of her part in the captain's bedraggled state.

"I expect you're hungry?" Mrs. Gwynn's remark seemed to be infused more with weariness at this inconvenience than hospitality.

"I am," Diana admitted.

They entered the servants' hall, where a fire burned invitingly in the grate. A group of domestics sat around a long table engaged in the leisure activities of late evening: darning, sipping tea, playing solitaire, and reading the newspaper. The cozy sight reminded Diana of evenings spent with Athena, Selena, Damon, and their departed father. It wasn't often, in the past decade, that she and her siblings had all been home at the same time, but they were fond memories just the same.

After four days in a carriage, this was a scene she longed to be a part of. These hopes were quickly dashed, however.

"This be Miss Taylor, Emma's new governess," Mrs. Gwynn announced without preamble.

Chairs scraped across the stone floor and the group stood as

Mrs. Gwynn rattled off their names in quick succession.

In an accent Diana couldn't place, Mr. Emity, the butler, a tall, bald Black man with a distinguished air, declared, "Good evening, Miss Taylor," before nodding permissively to the staff. They all resumed their seats and returned to their former activities.

In an adjoining room, Diana heard the clatter of pots and pans and glimpsed two women hard at work, presumably the cook and kitchen maid. Her dream of a hot meal evaporated when Mrs. Gwynn said, "I had the cook put by something cold for you, Miss Taylor. Ivy! Bring that tray upstairs to Miss Taylor's room."

"Yes, Mrs. Gwynn." The maid, a small but sturdy-looking girl who looked to be about seventeen, vanished into the kitchen.

"Sam! Fetch Miss Taylor's trunk from the back door and bring it to her room."

"Yes, Mrs. Gwynn." The lanky young man stood, smoothed back his red hair, and exited.

"I'll show you to your room now." Mrs. Gwynn handed Diana a candle.

Diana followed the housekeeper down a hall and up the narrow servants' staircase. The staff's indifferent reception was familiar. As an educated woman of genteel birth, a governess was considered too much above the servants to associate with them and yet too far below the family to do anything other than teach their offspring. Although that had bothered Diana when she'd first started in the profession, she'd grown accustomed to it. It was just the way things were.

A flash of guilt assailed her, however.

She was here not only to teach, but also, at least for a time, to spy on this household, to learn whatever she could about the demise of its former master and report back to her godmother. But as she reminded herself, her intentions were honorable: to relieve the anxiety of a woman Diana loved. All she sought was the truth.

The door to the first-floor landing creaked as Mrs. Gwynn opened it. They emerged onto a long corridor covered in a low-pile carpet. The walls were painted a dark mulberry and hung with pictures in heavy, golden frames.

"How old is Pendowar Hall?" Diana asked, delighted by the architecture, decorations, and furnishings.

"T'were built over two hundred and fifty years ago, in 1586, if I'm not mistaken." The housekeeper stopped and opened the first door on the left. "This be your chamber."

"Mine?" Diana paused in surprise. "I presumed that I would be housed on an upper floor, either with the servants or near the children's rooms?"

"The baronet who built Pendowar Hall wanted his children and their caretakers on the same level as himself. It's been that way ever since."

"Oh. I see."

They entered the small chamber. It was clean and plainly furnished. A pine wardrobe overlooked a bed, table, chair, and chest of drawers topped by a pitcher and basin. A fire burned in the grate, doing its best to fight off the chill.

Diana immediately felt comfortable and at home. She preferred order and simplicity above all things. A place for everything, and everything in its place. "This will do nicely. Thank you. Is the nursery through here?" She gestured to a connecting door.

Mrs. Gwynn nodded. "No one sleeps there now, ever since Master Robert ..." She paused and pursed her lips.

Diana recalled that only a few years had passed since the boy's death. He had no doubt slept in the nursery. No wonder the housekeeper looked upset. Diana would have to be careful what she said, if she wanted to find answers for Mrs. Phillips without ruffling any feathers.

"Miss Fallbrook has a bedroom of her own a few doors down," the housekeeper went on.

"I should love to meet Miss Fallbrook if she is up?"

"She won't want to be disturbed. She spends evenings on her own."

"I see."

"Beyond the nursery is the schoolroom. You can use it for your sitting room if you like and take your meals there with Miss Fallbrook. All three rooms are joined by connecting doors."

"A sensible arrangement."

The footman entered with Diana's trunk and set it down in a corner. At the same time, the maid—*what was her name? Oh, yes, Ivy*—entered and set a tray on the table. Diana spied a slice of cold meat pie and a mug of dark brew from which arose the tantalizing aroma of hot coffee.

"I don't see a fork," Mrs. Gwynn reproached the serving girl.

"It's right here Mrs. Gwynn," the maid said quickly, unveiling the utensil from beneath the serviette, which hid it.

"Thank you, Sam. Thank you, Ivy." Diana gave them each a smile and was rewarded with a nod and a curtsy before they withdrew.

"You have Sundays and Thursday afternoons off," Mrs. Gwynn announced. "Pendowar Hall be a big house, and some parts be unsafe to tread. Keep out of the north wing. It's closed off on the master's orders. Laundry day is once a month. In the meantime, if you want that gown and cloak sponged and pressed, give them to Ivy in the morning. She'll see to it."

"Thank you."

"Good night." Mrs. Gwynn started for the door.

"Wait." There was no time like the present, Diana decided. Mrs. Gwynn must have known all about the circumstances of Sir Thomas's death. "Before you go, Mrs. Gwynn, I have a few questions if I may?"

The housekeeper's dark eyebrows raised in silent inquiry.

"As I understand it, Miss Fallbrook's father, and your former master, passed away just over four months ago?"

"He did. God rest his soul."

"I am very sorry for your loss," Diana said gently.

Mrs. Gwynn paused, staring down at her folded hands. "Thank you. He were a good man, Sir Thomas." When she glanced up again, pride and affection shone in her dark eyes. "Is it true you're acquainted with the master's sister?"

"Eliza Phillips is my godmother. She was my mother's best friend."

Mrs. Gwynn nodded. "What happened to Sir Thomas were a great tragedy. But then, you'd know, wouldn't you?"

It was the perfect opening. "Actually, I know very little." To test the waters, Diana added: "Was he ill?"

"Ill? Hardly," Mrs. Gwynn scoffed. "My master weren't ill nary a day of his life. Fit as a fiddle he were to the last, 'til the morning that—" She broke off.

So, Diana thought, *Mrs. Phillips was right about that.* "How did he die, if I may ask?"

Mrs. Gwynn hesitated. Then, with a tight-lipped frown, she said, "It pains me too much to speak of it. I'll leave you to your supper, Miss Taylor."

To Diana's frustration, the subject seemed to be closed. "One more thing," she called out to Mrs. Gwynn's retreating back. "What time shall I expect to meet Miss Fallbrook tomorrow?"

"Oh, ach, I should have said." Mrs. Gwynn turned. "I expect nine o'clock will do—that's when the other governesses used to start."

"Have there been many governesses?"

"Too many to count."

"Why is that?"

Mrs. Gwynn shrugged her shoulders, her face unreadable.

"It just occurred to me, when you introduced me to the staff downstairs, I don't recall meeting Miss Fallbrook's lady's maid." Diana knew that although Miss Fallbrook was only fifteen years old, as the lady of the house, it would have been appropriate for her to have a servant of her own dedicated to helping her dress, doing her hair, mending her clothes, and perhaps even chaperoning her if there was no governess present. "Is she about?"

"Miss Fallbrook doesn't have a lady's maid and hasn't for well over two years."

"Oh? Why not?"

"Because when the last one quit, Miss Fallbrook insisted that she didn't want another one. Said she could dress and groom herself. My master got fed up and let her have her way. And who do you think got stuck with all the mending?" Mrs. Gwynn pursed her lips.

Diana took that in. "I see." She could understand it if a young woman of Miss Fallbrook's age didn't yet want a servant grooming and dressing her. Diana and her sisters had never had a lady's maid and had never wanted one—although they had had each other. Taking a breath, she added, "Is there anything else you can tell me about my charge? Something that might be helpful to know before I meet her?"

Mrs. Gwynn seemed to turn the question over in her mind. "I don't like to talk about things that aren't my business. But since you're asking, Miss Taylor: it's my opinion that you've come a long way for nothing. I predict you'll stay a week. Two, if you have real pluck."

"Why?"

"Because Miss Emma Fallbrook would try the patience of a saint. She doesn't listen, won't follow rules, and only learns what she has a mind to. I'm told she's unteachable."

With that, the housekeeper swept from the room.

DIANA HUNG THE few dresses she'd brought in the wardrobe: two additional black frocks and a dress of indigo-blue shot silk to wear to church or on special occasions, should any such arise.

Diana loved the warp and weft of shot silk. Its slightly different colors produced a subtle change of hue depending on the light, and the crisp, fine textile was ideal for shaping a gown's voluminous skirts. She liked the current fashion as well, with its tight sleeves and absence of trim other than piping and a few pleats on the bodice, a style that emphasized the beauty of the fabric itself.

After unpacking her undergarments and accessories, Diana donned her nightdress and climbed into bed, tired after her long journey. As she listened to the unfamiliar creaks and groans of the old house, she thought back on her conversation with the housekeeper.

"You've come a long way for nothing. I predict you'll stay a week. Two, if you have real pluck."

This dire prediction further explained Mrs. Gwynn's—and the other servants'—aloof manner. Why should they waste their time getting to know Diana, whose stay, they presumed, would be so short?

What was it about Miss Emma Fallbrook, Diana wondered, that had caused her previous governesses to bolt? No one, she told herself, was unteachable. Everyone had the ability to learn. While the level of that ability might differ from person to person, it existed in some form. Whether a person *wanted* to learn was another matter ...

"I can think of no one as qualified as you for this position, Diana."

Diana appreciated her godmother's faith in her. She just hoped she was worthy of it. Of that, she could not be certain.

As a child, she'd had a comfortable home, parents who'd loved her, and all the time in the world to pursue her love of books and nature. But when she'd been seven years old, her mother had become ill and died. At the time, Diana had believed it was all her fault because she had neglected to fulfill her duty that day.

Twenty-two years later, reason told her this wasn't entirely logical. And yet she still couldn't shake the guilt that she had contributed to her mother's death.

Since that terrible day, Diana had done everything she could think of to make up for her mistake. She had stepped into her mother's shoes and helped their servant Martha run the house, helped raise her brother and sisters, and assisted her bereaved father as best she could. Doing good for others had become ingrained in her. It was a way of life.

But life continued to find ways to remind Diana of her unworthiness. When she had opened her heart to two different men, they had betrayed her. After her father had lost his fortune at the gaming tables, he'd become a ghost of himself. Her brother's work so consumed him that she rarely heard from him anymore. She and her sisters were obliged to live hundreds of miles apart. Now her godmother was dying. Why was everything and everyone she held dear always taken away from her?

If only she could prove her worth once and for all, perhaps it would make up for her mistake all those years ago. To accomplish that, she must fulfill her godmother's request, get to the bottom of Sir Thomas's demise, and deliver the answer while her godmother was still alive to hear it.

Then, only then, would she be able to feel good about herself.

A MOURNFUL WAIL brought Diana awake with a start. The fire in the grate had gone out and her chamber was pitch black. She sensed it to be the middle of the night.

The high-pitched howl that pervaded the room sent a chill through Diana's bones. Was someone crying? But no. That sound could not be of human origin. When the windows began to rattle, she understood its source: it was the wind.

Pulling the covers up to her chin, Diana listened to the turbulence outside, accompanied by the rush and tumble of the sea. She had just begun to drift off when three more sounds entered her consciousness in quick succession.

The first was the chime of a distant clock sounding the hour of two. The second was a creak from the corridor beyond, a sound she recognized as the door to the servants' stairwell being opened.

This was followed by the soft tread of footsteps in the hall, moving quickly past her chamber.

Diana stiffened. Who would be up at this hour? Although she hated to leave the warmth of her bed, curiosity overcame her.

Rising, she crossed the freezing floor in her bare feet, feeling her way through the darkness to the door, where she stood for a long moment with her ear against the wooden panel, listening. All was silent. She opened the door and peered into the dark hall. There was no sign of anyone. What other rooms lay in that direction? She had no idea.

Presumably, only the family slept on this floor. As far as she knew, the family consisted of only two people: Captain Fallbrook and Sir Thomas's daughter, Emma. Mrs. Gwynn said the captain had retired soon after returning home, but he might have gone downstairs later. In that case, though, wouldn't he have ascended via the main staircase?

Diana shut her door. She considered locking it, but there was no bolt and no evidence of a key. Scolding herself for being a ninny, she returned to bed.

As the wind gusted and wailed, Diana's mind worked on the problem. Who had the mysterious visitor been? And what business did they have on this floor in the middle of the night?

CHAPTER THREE

D IANA AWAKENED TO the cry of a gull. Wrapping the counterpane around her, she crossed the icy floor to the window and, drawing the drapes, gave a gasp of delight.

Mrs. Phillips had described this place in glowing terms, but Diana thought her godmother's memories had been clouded by nostalgia. Not so.

The storm was a distant memory. Before her stood a magnificent view.

Pendowar Hall was situated on an eminence overlooking the distant, roiling sea. Intermittent clouds flitted in a bright, blue sky. The sun, she guessed, had risen a couple of hours earlier.

The manor house, at least what she could perceive from this angle, stood three stories high and was fashioned of grey stone. It was built like a rectangle minus its western side, no doubt to permit sea views from the east wing, where she was housed. The north wing ended in a tall tower. The side wings flanked a rear courtyard landscaped with raised flower beds and a green lawn that sparkled with morning dew.

Beyond the courtyard lay an open area of grass and natural vegetation, which terminated at the cliff's edge. Below, the coastline curved in both directions. Sandy beaches alternated with small coves and steep, rocky cliffs. The sea stretched out in all its glory, the wavy blueness interrupted by thrusting islets of black rock, where seagulls perched and swooped.

Diana was enchanted. She had lived in many fine houses in her former positions, but none as massive or impressively situated as this one. To find herself in this stunning place felt like a gift, and she looked forward to exploring at her earliest opportunity.

After performing her morning ablutions, Diana donned a plain frock and did up her long, dark hair in a simple chignon. She had just satisfied herself that she was neat and presentable when her chamber door quietly opened, and Ivy entered with a tray.

"Good morning, miss. I've brought yer breakfast." Ivy's brown hair looked neat beneath her white cap, but her starched, white apron and black dress were dusted with ash.

"Thank you, Ivy."

"Ye're welcome." She set down the tray, which contained a boiled egg, a bowl of porridge, and a cup of tea. "I thought ye might need help getting dressed, but here ye are, up and ready."

"It's kind of you to think of me. But my frocks are self-sufficient, as you see." Diana indicated the front hooks on her gown's bodice. "My sisters and I make our own clothes and we design them so we can dress ourselves."

"How practical ye are, miss."

"I try to be." Diana brought over the dress and cloak she'd worn the day before, which were muddied at the hem. "Mrs. Gwynn said you might be able to sponge and press these for me?"

"I'd be happy to, miss. I'll take them when I go." Ivy began laying a new fire.

Setting the garments on her bed, Diana sat down and dug into her breakfast. "Pendowar Hall is a beautiful place."

"Oh, it is, miss. Been here four years now, e'er since I were thirteen years old. I like it e'er so much. If they offered me the queen's palace, I'd say, 'No thank ye, I'll take Pendowar Hall any day of the week.'"

Diana smiled at the maid's enthusiasm. "Where does the house's name come from? Do you know?"

"I do, miss. It be from the Cornish *pen*, which is a 'hill' or 'headland,' and *dowr*, which is Cornish for 'water.'"

"Interesting." As Diana sipped her tea, she considered asking Ivy what she knew about Sir Thomas and his untimely demise, but her inquiry with Mrs. Gwynn had gone so poorly, she decided to wait until she knew the girl better. "Ivy," she remarked instead, "I heard something strange in the middle of the night."

Having lit the fire, Ivy stood and wiped her hands on her apron. "What did ye hear, miss?"

"A creaking door. I'd swear it was the door to the servants' stairs. Then I heard footsteps passing this way and continuing down the corridor."

Ivy's eyes widened. "Oh!"

"Might it have been the captain or Miss Fallbrook, returning to their chamber?"

"They never use the servants' stairs, miss. And Miss Fallbrook's not one to be tramping about in the middle of the night."

"Are the master's chambers on this floor?"

"Aye, miss. They be at the other end of the east wing, beyond the gallery. But Captain Fallbrook's never set foot in the master's rooms since Sir Thomas died."

"Where does he sleep, then?"

"In the south wing, in the same chamber as was kept for him since he were a lad, whenever he came on holiday or home from sea to visit."

Diana nodded, recalling what Mrs. Phillips had told her—that Sir Thomas had sent his nephew off to the Royal Navy after the death of the boy's parents. "If it wasn't the captain or Miss Fallbrook I heard ... do you have any idea who it might have been?"

"I do, miss." Ivy came a few steps closer and lowered her voice. "I've heard sounds like that myself in the dark of early morning, while emptying the chamber pots on this floor."

"Have you?"

Ivy's tone was ominous. "It's Morwenna. The ghost that haunts Pendowar."

"A ghost?" Diana fought back a smile. "Who was Morwenna?"

"A mermaid, miss."

"A mermaid?" Every great house seemed to have a legend about a ghost. It amused Diana to think that Pendowar Hall's ghost was a mermaid. "How could a mermaid walk down a hall? I believe they have tails, not feet?"

"When Morwenna's on land, she grows legs and feet like any human."

"I see. Well, thank you for that explanation. I shall keep an eye out for Morwenna."

"I see ye don't believe me, miss, but ye should. It's a frightful tale, and ..." Ivy hesitated, and her brow wrinkled. "Perhaps I ought'nt to tell ye, though. You, of all people."

"You, of all people?" What did Ivy mean by that? Diana had no time to inquire further, however, because at that moment, Mrs. Gwynn entered the room.

"Ivy!" she admonished. "Why are you standing around chatting? The fireplaces on the ground floor await your attention, and did you empty Miss Taylor's chamber pot?"

"I will, Mrs. Gwynn." Ivy withdrew Diana's covered chamber pot from beneath the bed. "I'll come back later for yer dress and cloak," she promised Diana before she scurried from the room.

Diana's heart went out to the young chambermaid. She offered the housekeeper a deliberate smile. "Good morning, Mrs. Gwynn. I hope you slept well?"

"I never sleep well," was her curt, unexpected reply.

"I am sorry to hear that."

"My thoughts plague me at night. So I get up and walk."

"Do you indeed, Mrs. Gwynn? I heard footsteps in the hall at about two o'clock last night. Was that you?"

The housekeeper shook her head. "T'were fierce cold last night, so I kept to my chambers."

"Can you think of who it might have been?"

"Nobody. This old house has strange echoes and there were a

strong wind."

"It wasn't the wind. I heard footsteps. And a creaking door."

"At two o'clock, you say?" Mrs. Gwynn's eyes narrowed, and she waved one hand dismissively. "You must have dreamt it or imagined it, Miss Taylor. By the by, you won't be starting lessons at nine today."

"Why not?"

"Miss Fallbrook's not in her room."

"Where is she?"

"There be no telling. I'll send the hall boy in search of her and tell her to meet you in the schoolroom at eleven."

"Is it common for Miss Fallbrook to miss morning lessons?"

"As common as the tide. You'll get used to it, I reckon."

This did not bode well. "What about Captain Fallbrook?" inquired Diana. "Will I see him today?" After their unfortunate encounter on the road, Diana wasn't looking forward to the meeting, but she knew it was inevitable.

"He's got business with his steward and tenants all day and said he'll see you this evening at seven. I'll fetch you when the time comes."

WITH A BIT of time on her hands, Diana indulged her curiosity by embarking on a self-guided tour of the ground floor of the house.

One grand room opened onto another, the high ceilings ornamented by plasterwork, the walls generously paneled in oak or covered in colorful paper or silk. The furnishings were tasteful and looked to be of recent vintage. Money did not seem to be a problem here. If that was true, however, Diana wondered why Mrs. Gwynn had said the north wing was closed off.

She passed Ivy cleaning out the fireplace in one room while another maid, Hester—a fair-haired woman who looked to be in her late twenties—swept the grand, oak staircase leading to an open gallery landing on the first floor.

Moving on, Diana found herself in a great white hall hung with tapestries and family portraits in gilded frames. Pewter dishes gleamed atop a time-scarred refectory table. Two suits of armor stood at either end of the long room beneath proud displays of weapons from long-ago battles.

Although the chamber, like the rest of the house, was impressive, Diana sensed a palpable sadness in the air. *A mansion like this,* Diana thought, *should echo with the conversations of its inhabitants. The master should be at breakfast in the morning room, downing his coffee and reading the paper while his lady plans menus for the week. Children's laughter ought to ring out from the nursery and a bevy of servants should be rushing to and fro.*

In its place was deathly silence.

Perhaps that was understandable, though. Sir Thomas had died just four months ago.

Mrs. Phillips's words resounded in Diana's brain.

"My nephew, Captain William Fallbrook, who's been at sea most of his life, has inherited the entire estate—an ancient and valuable property—as well as the title of Baronet of Portwithys. Is it a coincidence that he, who spent many holidays as a boy and all his leave from the navy at Pendowar Hall, and must have understood its value, came home just a few days before Thomas died?"

The idea that the captain might have murdered his own uncle sounded fantastic. The product of a vivid imagination. The parish constable had said Sir Thomas had killed himself. It was Diana's job to find out why.

She found a life-sized portrait, elegantly labeled *Sir Thomas Fallbrook, Fourth Bart. of Portwithys*, prominently displayed above the enormous stone fireplace. Diana recognized the imposing figure and commanding features from the one time she'd met him, again recalling his kindness in giving four small children a treat. In the portrait he held a beautifully bound book. A stack of similar books resided on a nearby table. Objects in portraiture, Diana knew, often symbolized the subject's personal interests. Sir Thomas must have been fond of reading—a man after her own heart.

Footfalls echoed on the stone floor. Diana turned to find Mr. Emity, the butler, approaching. A slender man who looked to be in his mid-fifties, he wore a black crepe armband: a tribute to the deceased baronet.

"Miss Taylor." He towered above her, his posture perfectly erect as he gave her a gracious nod.

"Good morning, Mr. Emity."

"I hope your stay with us will be pleasant."

Diana felt an echo of her conversation with Mrs. Gwynn—as if he, too, considered Diana a short-term visitor. "Thank you." She was intrigued by his elegant, unusual manner of speech. "What a lovely accent you have, Mr. Emity. May I ask where you are from?"

"I was born in Guinea, miss."

"Guinea is a long way from England. What brought you to these shores?"

"It is a long story, miss. Perhaps I shall tell you about it some-day."

"I look forward to it." Diana mentioned the footsteps she'd heard in the corridor early that morning.

"The only member of this household who might have been up at that hour is Mrs. Gwynn."

"She said she was awake but kept to her chamber."

"The beat of tree branches against the house can sound like footsteps, miss, and this old place does groan and creak."

Diana remained unconvinced. "Perhaps you are right."

"It has come to my attention that Miss Fallbrook is not to be found. May I suggest, if you are fond of gardens, that you spend some time perusing ours? They were a great favorite of Sir Thomas's. They are not at their peak now, of course, but autumn has a beauty of its own."

"Thank you, Mr. Emity. I am indeed fond of gardens. I shall follow your advice presently." Diana decided to take advantage of this opportunity to learn more about the baronet and his family.

The portrait before them was flanked by pictures of two beautiful and elegantly dressed young women. "Speaking of Sir Thomas," she added, "I was just studying his portrait. The ladies beside him—were they his wives?"

"Yes. On the left is the first Lady Fallbrook, Margaret. On the right is the baronet's second wife, Sylvia."

Margaret looked to be no more than eighteen. Sylvia might have been in her mid-twenties. Diana knew what had happened to both women—Mrs. Phillips had shared the sad stories many times. But she wanted to keep the conversation going, hoping to draw the butler out.

"My godmother, Mrs. Phillips, told me that the first Lady Fallbrook died giving birth to her daughter?"

"She did."

"How sad. And the second Lady Fallbrook?"

A flash of sorrow lit his eyes. "She died in a boating accident some three years past, along with their son."

"I'm so sorry." Diana repressed a shudder. To think that the wife and son had both *drowned*. Of all the ways to die, to Diana, that seemed the most horrible. "Tragedy has struck this poor family many times over."

"It has, miss."

"Their passing must have devastated Sir Thomas."

"The whole household was deeply grieved."

If only she could tell Mr. Emity that she'd been sent to ferret out information on this subject, it would be so much easier. But she must be discreet, as Mrs. Phillips had insisted. "As I understand it," Diana said quietly, "Sir Thomas was still so distressed all these years later, he took his own life?"

Mr. Emity hesitated. As if carefully measuring his words, he replied, "That is one interpretation of the event."

"Is there another interpretation?"

"I—" he began, then he abruptly changed the subject. "Forgive me, Miss Taylor. I have things to attend to. Enjoy the gardens." With a parting nod, he withdrew.

Diana wondered what he'd been about to say. As butler, he no doubt knew everything that went on in this house. She must find a time to question him further.

A clock rang the hour of nine. Two hours before she was to meet with Miss Fallbrook. Diana headed for the servants' door.

Once past the stone wall enclosing the kitchen yard, Diana found herself in the rear courtyard. Birdsong erupted from the trees. The sun warmed her face and shoulders as she paused to take in her first good view of the manor house. The immense, stone edifice rose castle-like to a crenellated rooftop peppered with chimneys, fronted by its verdant lawn and colorful plantings. It was quite a sight to behold.

And yet, taking in Pendowar Hall in the morning light, that same paradoxical feeling of gloom and doom that Diana had experienced in the great hall washed over her. It was as if the house were determined to remind beholders that despite its beauty, the building held secrets, and something dark and sinister was to blame.

Don't be ridiculous, Diana scolded herself. *Buildings can't keep secrets.*

But people could.

Diana had always prided herself on being a practical sort. She laughed at superstitions as pure nonsense. She did not believe in ghosts. But untold generations had lived and died here. She knew of four members of the Fallbrook family whose lives had ended tragically. How many more had similarly suffered? The idea sent a shiver down her spine.

Diana shook off the feeling and set out to explore the grounds.

For the next hour, she meandered. Southern Cornwall—unique in England—was known for its Mediterranean climate. Diana was charmed to find a myriad of impressive gardens ranging from formal flower beds to natural landscapes. Although mid-October, many varieties of flowers were still in bloom and gardeners were at work here and there.

Diana heard the gurgle of water and, rounding a bend, came upon a fast-moving river. Its banks were alive with lush, tropical vegetation including palm trees—a sight so unusual, it took her breath away. An old wooden footbridge spanned the river, leading to a path that crossed through fields on the other side.

The river was pretty, but as Diana stared at the footbridge, the hairs on the back of her neck rose. There it was again—that feeling of impending doom—as if the bridge were a portent for a future evil. This time, though, Diana recognized the source of her apprehension.

It was the sight and sound of the rushing water.

She ought to have learned to swim, she knew it. Living in landlocked Derbyshire, however, it had never seemed important. She admired the beauty of rivers, ponds, and lakes and loved looking at the ocean. But she had never ventured into any of them—and feared to.

The far-off sounds of seagulls and crashing waves caught her ear. Glad to leave the riverbank, Diana ventured through the woods in the direction of the beckoning sea. In time, she came to a dirt path along the cliff's edge. A few feet of scrubby grass and shrubs separated the path from the brink of the precipice. Below, stretches of sandy beach were interrupted by miles of undulating jagged cliffs before the ocean, which pulsed and foamed.

This must be the very path, Diana realized, *from which, according to reports, Sir Thomas Fallbrook fell to his death.*

Was it a deliberate act?

Or was he pushed?

She chastised herself. *Of course he wasn't pushed.*

Diana followed the cliff path, breathing in the tangy air. The scenery was as spectacular as Mrs. Phillips had promised. After a while, she came to a spot marked by dense, high vegetation. A natural break in the shrubbery led to an opening where only a few feet of grass separated the path from the cliff's edge. Urged by some inexplicable compulsion, Diana moved carefully to the brink and glanced over.

It was a long, deadly drop to the rocky cove below. Beset by an uncustomary sense of vertigo, Diana stepped back quickly.

"Good morning."

Diana jerked in surprise. A sturdy-looking man in rough clothing appeared, wielding a pair of shears. The shrubbery had masked his approach. He tipped his cap and began clipping a hedge along the trail.

"Good morning." Diana introduced herself.

"Nice to meet you, miss. My name's Nankervis." He appeared to be about forty years of age, and he introduced himself as the head gardener at Pendowar Hall. "I were born on this estate, miss," he explained, in answer to her query. "My father were head gardener before me, and his father before that. I started in the gardens when I were a sapling myself."

"You must enjoy the work," Diana remarked with a smile.

"I do, miss."

"I can see why. This is a stunning view. And I am quite taken by your gardens."

A crooked smile lit Mr. Nankervis's sun-browned face. "The old baronet, he were right fond of 'em as well. Took long walks every morning, he did, always the same route, in the gardens and along this path."

"Where does this path lead?" Diana asked.

"That way," he said, pointing north, "to the tenants' farms and beyond. To the south, it winds down along the river channel to the beach. At low tide, ye can cross the river by the stepping-stones and pick up the path again farther along at Portwithys."

"How far is the village?"

"Three miles that way. Four by road. But the best and shortest route is by the footbridge over the river." He nodded in the direction of the estate.

"I've seen that footbridge."

"Take care though, miss, won't ye, on this path? The weather can be changeable in these parts. Bright as day one minute and the next, wind or rain or fog can blow in and wrap ye in its grip."

"Thank you for the warning." She paused. "Mr. Nankervis. Is it true what I heard? Did the old master fall to his death from this cliff path?"

He removed his cap, eyes squinting with discomfort. "Aye, miss. As it happens, from this very spot."

"This spot?" Strange, that she had felt a compulsion to approach the edge here, of all places.

"Early morning, it was. They found his body on the rocks below."

"How awful. The poor man."

"A sad day it were for Pendowar Hall."

"I heard that the parish constable ruled it a suicide."

"So he *said.*"

Was it her imagination? Or had Mr. Nankervis placed heavy emphasis on the word *said*? As if there were some debate about the matter? "Did Sir Thomas leave a note behind?"

"No idea, miss. If he did, they wouldn't tell the likes of me."

"Could it have been an accident?" Diana prodded. "Might he have taken a wrong step?"

"Not likely."

"Why is that?"

"He walked this path every day, didn't he? Had done since he were a child, I'm told. He knew the way. It was a fine, fair morning. And he were fit, miss. Not old and feeble."

Diana took that in. Mrs. Phillips had made the same observation.

"What do you think happened, Mr. Nankervis? Do you think Sir Thomas took his own life?"

Mr. Nankervis replaced his cap with a shrug. "I couldn't say, miss. He had his troubles, same as everyone. All I know is I wouldn't put much stock in what the parish constable said." With that, he took off down the path.

CHAPTER FOUR

L IGHT STREAMED IN through the schoolroom windows, casting a golden net across the oak bookcases that lined the walls.

The chamber was generously proportioned and furnished with old desks, two scarred tables, and several upholstered chairs. A blackboard hung on one wall, a framed map of the world on another. Opposite the stone fireplace stood an old upright piano. A cupboard held various supplies: sketchbooks, writing implements, and slates.

As Diana assembled the materials she required for the morning lesson, her mind whirred with the implications of her conversation with Mr. Nankervis.

"All I know is I wouldn't put much stock in what the parish constable said."

The gardener apparently didn't have much faith in the ruling in Sir Thomas's death. Neither, it seemed, did Mr. Emity. *"That is one interpretation of the event,"* he'd said.

Where there is smoke, there's fire … Diana's childhood desire to resolve matters, to unearth the truth, sizzled to the surface of her mind. Was it possible, as Mrs. Phillips suspected, that foul play had been involved? Diana still didn't believe it—but she needed to find the parish constable and speak to him.

Before she could proceed further with that notion, Mrs. Gwynn's voice rang out from the corridor. "Get in there, you!"

A girl stalked into the room and ground to a halt, eyes downcast, her entire body radiating defiance.

"We found Miss Fallbrook," the housekeeper announced unnecessarily, her arms crossed over her large bosom. "Been traipsing all over the beach, she was. Give Miss Taylor a proper greeting now."

"How do you do, Miss Taylor?" Miss Fallbrook stated through clenched teeth.

She looked younger than her fifteen years. A mass of long, light-brown hair, which looked recently brushed and was partially tied back by a black ribbon, cascaded down her back and shoulders, framing a face that might have been pretty if not for the intense scowl that pervaded it. A finely made black crepe dress hugged her slender frame, clean and neat in every respect except for the hem, which was four inches deep in damp sand and dirt. She clutched a small drawstring bag in tense fingers.

"Hello, Miss Fallbrook." Diana stepped forward with a smile. "It's a pleasure to meet you."

Miss Fallbrook kept her gazed fixed on the carpet.

"Be a good girl and don't give this woman any trouble," Mrs. Gwynn commanded. "Good luck, Miss Taylor," she muttered as she spun and left the room.

"So," Diana said cheerfully, "you've been walking on the beach?"

"What of it?" the young woman retorted. "*You've* been walking in the gardens."

"Oh? Did you notice me when I was out and about?"

"No. But it's obvious where you've been."

"How so?"

"Your boots are damp. And there's a blade of grass on your toe."

"So there is." *What a clever observation*, Diana thought. Nodding towards the drawstring bag in the girl's grasp, she added, "What have you there?"

"Nothing." Miss Fallbrook clutched the bag more tightly.

"Well, then. Let's get started, shall we? Please take a seat."

"I'd rather go back outside."

"It is always pleasant to be outside, but our lessons will take place in the schoolroom."

"Why?"

"Because the schoolroom is quiet and conducive to study."

"I don't want to study. I don't need a governess."

"Captain Fallbrook feels differently."

"Cousin William doesn't know *what* I need. Until four months ago, he was almost always away at sea."

"He is here now, and he is in charge of your welfare."

"I have already learned all I need to know."

"We shall see about that. Sit down at this table, please."

Heaving a sigh, Miss Fallbrook plunked down reluctantly into a chair, still clenching the mysterious bag in her lap.

Diana sat down across from her. "I'd like to begin by saying how sorry I was to hear about your father."

Something flickered in the young woman's eyes, hinting at the grief and pain that simmered beneath the surface. But she said nothing.

"I know you're going through a difficult time."

"What would you know about it?" Miss Fallbrook snapped.

"My father passed away last year. My mother died when I was seven." At least Diana had a few cherished memories of her mother. Miss Fallbrook, whose mother had died in childbirth, had none.

The young lady softened a fraction. "How did your mother die?"

"She had a stroke."

"And your father?"

"His heart gave out."

Miss Fallbrook seemed to go somewhere else in her mind for a moment. Was she thinking about her own father, who had, apparently, killed himself? How that must weigh on her! It was not a topic to broach at this meeting, however.

"I have brought you something." From the pocket in her

skirts, Diana brought forth a small object wrapped in silver paper and lay it on the table before her student.

Miss Fallbrook stared at it suspiciously. "What is that?"

"A gift." Diana always liked to bring something to her new charges and had worried over what to bring a girl of fifteen. "If you don't like it, you needn't feel obliged to keep it."

Miss Fallbrook unwrapped the item. It was a white seashell, about five centimeters long and abruptly truncated on one side. "Oh!"

"Your aunt, Eliza—my godmother—said you liked walking on the beach, so I took a chance and brought the only seashell in my possession. I don't know what it's called—"

"A blunt gaper."

"A what?"

"It's called a blunt gaper. I have lots of these, but they're all brown. I have never seen a white one." Miss Fallbrook studied it before placing it on the table. After a brief hesitation, she opened the bag on her lap and withdrew a seashell with dark-brown spirals. "Here's a dogwhelk I just found."

"How lovely." Diana smiled inwardly. Apparently, she had brought her pupil the perfect gift.

"Dogwhelks come in all sorts of colors. They like rocky shores. To get the best shells, you must go when the tide is out. Do you want to see a painted topshell?" One by one, Miss Fallbrook lined up the contents of her bag atop the table, sharing a few details about each.

"Where did you learn so much about seashells?"

"From Miss Darby."

"Was Miss Darby one of your governesses?"

"My second. Miss Emsley was the third. Miss Doré was the fourth. Then came Miss Sullivan, and so on."

"Which number governess am I?"

"Sixteen."

"Sixteen governesses!" Diana inhaled sharply and shook her head. "My goodness."

"Papa said I would win the award for the most governesses of any girl in Cornwall." Miss Fallbrook frowned at this. Her guard, which had temporarily lifted while she'd talked about seashells, went up again. Darkly, she added, "You won't stay long, either."

"Maybe I'll surprise you." Diana struggled to keep her voice matter of fact. "Let's get a sense now of where you are academically. What is your favorite subject?"

"Art," Miss Fallbrook replied instantly.

"Art is a pleasant accomplishment for a young lady. Do you like arithmetic?"

"No."

"Have you learnt any French?"

"*Bien sûr. Bonjour, mademoiselle. Comment allez-vous aujourd'hui?*" She spoke in perfect French.

They exchanged a brief dialogue, which confirmed Miss Fallbrook's facility with that tongue.

"Have you studied music?"

"Of course. I once had a piano teacher, but he quit."

"Why?"

"He brought sheets and sheets of music, but I only play by ear. I've been taught all the other accomplishments required of a young lady: needlework, dancing, and etiquette."

"Have you studied history?"

"Yes," Miss Fallbrook replied impatiently. She launched into a rapid and flawless recitation of the monarchs of England in chronological order, from William the Conqueror to Victoria.

"Bravo," Diana said when the young woman had finished.

"I can do the capitals of Europe, as well." Miss Fallbrook began another matter-of-fact listing of European capitals, which proved just as accurate.

"I see you have an excellent memory," Diana said, interrupting after the tenth city. "But that's enough recitation for one morning. Let's move on to reading and writing."

Miss Fallbrook immediately stretched her arms above her head and emitted a yawn. "I'm tired. I walked a long way this morning. I need a nap."

An odd reaction. The girl had exhibited plenty of energy moments before. "You may nap when our lesson is over." Diana handed Miss Fallbrook a slate and a piece of chalk. "I'd like to assess your handwriting."

The young woman's features tensed. "What do you want me to write?"

"Anything you like."

Miss Fallbrook twirled the chalk between her fingers. Finally, she tilted the slate and covertly inscribed something. The activity took far longer than it should have, so Diana crossed behind the girl to get a better look.

"Miss Fallbrook!" To Diana's dismay, her pupil was not writing, but sketching. She had recreated in chalk the paisley pattern of their chairs' upholstery. "I said to *write* something."

"I hate writing."

"This is merely an exercise. Write a short phrase, please. For example: 'Jane is a good girl.'"

Miss Fallbrook's shoulders coiled. She bit her lip. "Can I just write my given name, Emma?"

"You may."

Miss Fallbrook erased the slate. Slowly and carefully, with furrowed brow, she drew four capital letters that were messy in shape.

What she wrote was: EMAM.

Diana struggled to conceal her surprise. She had never met a girl of Miss Fallbrook's age who couldn't correctly spell her own name. She felt the girl's eyes on her, filled with worry and—was it shame?—and didn't have the heart to correct her. This was, after all, only their first lesson, and they were just getting to know each other. "A fine effort, Miss Fallbrook. I appreciate you doing as instructed. Let's try reading now."

Miss Fallbrook leapt to her feet as if shot from a cannon. "I'm tired."

"This will be our last exercise, I promise." Diana brought

over a book of fairy tales she'd found, which she had read in the original German. "Are you acquainted with *The Children's and Household Tales* by the Brothers Grimm?"

"My last governess read some of it to me."

Diana opened the volume to the first tale. "Sit down please and read aloud from 'The Frog King.'" She gave the book to her pupil.

With obvious reluctance, Miss Fallbrook resumed her seat and stared at the book intently. "'The Frog King. Or The Iron Heinrich,'" she began. "'Once, there was a king's daughter. One day, she went to the woods, where she sat down by a spring-pond. She had a globe with her. A golden globe, and … it was her favorite thing on Earth. She—'"

"Miss Fallbrook, stop," Diana interrupted, puzzled. "How many times have you heard this story?"

"I don't know."

"You are reciting the words from memory, aren't you? Like you did with the kings and queens?"

The young woman's cheeks bloomed pink. "No, I'm not."

"I think you are. Miss Fallbrook," Diana added gently, "do you have difficulty reading?"

"No!" Snapping the book shut, Miss Fallbrook shoved it off the table.

"It's all right if you do. I am here to help."

Miss Fallbrook twisted her hands for a long moment. "All right, *fine*. You'll find out soon enough, I suppose. I can't read! I'm too stupid. There! Are you satisfied?"

So saying, she jumped up and fled the room.

DIANA, RATTLED, STRODE down the hall, carrying her pupil's abandoned bag of seashells. Mrs. Gwynn had said that Miss Fallbrook was "unteachable." But that seemed untrue. Miss

Fallbrook had a head full of knowledge. She was a bright, observant girl with a remarkable memory.

And yet, her handwriting was shaky, she had spelled her name incorrectly, and she did not know how to read. A reading deficiency would not be surprising in a child of five or six. But a young woman of fifteen?

How had this been allowed to happen? Were any of the people in Miss Fallbrook's life aware of the real problem behind the "learning difficulties" that Diana had been warned about? Captain Fallbrook hadn't mentioned it in his letters. According to Mrs. Phillips, Miss Fallbrook's father used to say, *"Emma does not apply herself to her studies."*

No wonder Miss Fallbrook was withdrawn and moody. She suffered from a profound and understandable lack of self-confidence. She thought she was stupid. This explained as well why so many of her governesses had left—perhaps in frustration.

Well, Diana thought, *she* was not about to leave. She had taught plenty of pupils to read. Even after she solved the riddle about Sir Thomas's demise for Mrs. Phillips—presuming she *could* solve it—she would stick to her post and succeed with Miss Fallbrook where others had not. She *must* succeed. She had come here at her godmother's request, after all, and had given her written promise to the captain.

Mrs. Phillips often said that Diana gave too much weight to what she did for others and what they thought of her, but Diana disagreed. How else could a person measure their value? What would they think of her if she failed? What would she think of herself?

The door to Miss Fallbrook's bedroom stood ajar. Diana peeked in, but no one was there. She entered, hoping to gain a better understanding of the pupil in her charge.

The room was spacious and pleasantly furnished in tones of green, white, and pink. Tall, casement windows overlooked the same dramatic coastal view visible from Diana's room. A curtained canopy bed took up pride of place. A bookcase held no books. It was given over to an extensive seashell collection and dozens of small sculptures made of clay.

Diana set Miss Fallbrook's drawstring bag of shells upon the bureau. A stack of sketchbooks lay there. Curious, Diana glanced through one of them. It contained pencil drawings of landscapes, flora, and fauna, many of which resembled scientific illustrations in their attention to detail. There were also several portraits of members of the staff, all of whom Diana recognized. The drawings exhibited an observant eye and a keen talent. Another sketchbook contained watercolor paintings, equally as lovely, executed with far more skill than Diana herself possessed.

After replacing the sketchbook, Diana's attention turned to the small, clay sculptures on Miss Fallbrook's shelves. They represented both animate and inanimate objects but were primarily a collection of animals made of natural clay. They did not appear to have been fired in a kiln. All were charming. A single object carved from wood—a horse about the size of Diana's fist—stood at the center of the collection.

Not wishing to pry any further, Diana quit the room and ventured down to the servants' hall, where she inquired where her errant charge might have gone. No one knew.

"I shouldn't worry, Miss Taylor," Mrs. Gwynn declared flatly. "From what I gather, Miss Fallbrook's only good for a couple of hours of instruction at a time. Tomorrow's another day."

Diana spent the remainder of the day in the schoolroom, putting together a new curriculum.

Later, anxious about her upcoming meeting with Captain Fallbrook, she changed into her clean frock of black silk. As Diana dressed, her pulse raced with worry.

Would the captain still be angry with her for what had happened the day before on the road? She was grateful to him for clearing away that fallen tree and hoped to have a chance to say so.

What, Diana wondered, were Captain Fallbrook's thoughts on the circumstances of Sir Thomas's death? Would there be an opportunity to discuss it this evening, or was it too soon to bring it up? More importantly, she must speak to him about his ward.

As the clock struck seven, Mrs. Gwynn appeared in the schoolroom doorway, carrying a candle.

"Captain Fallbrook will see you now in the blue parlor." Her gaze took in Diana's change of apparel with a frown. "I'll show you the way."

CHAPTER FIVE

DIANA PICKED UP her own candlestick and, shielding the flame with a cupped hand to keep it from blowing out, she followed the housekeeper down the long corridor. "Was it wrong to change my dress before seeing the captain?"

"It won't matter what you're wearing, Miss Taylor." Mrs. Gwynn's tone was thick with discontent. "I used to dress up in the evenings when my old master were alive. But Captain Fallbrook says we're not to stand on ceremony, just to be neat and clean."

"I imagine a great many things are different, now that Captain Fallbrook has taken over?"

"They are." Mrs. Gwynn's lip curled, and she wrinkled her nose. "Used to having command of a ship, he is, and we're expected to obey every order, no questions asked. He be the fifth Baronet of Portwithys, and rightly should be addressed as 'Sir William.' But he'll have none of that! 'Call me *Captain*,' says he. Got his own ideas about plenty of other things as well, which aren't right or proper."

"What kinds of ideas?"

"Well! The master of Pendowar Hall has always come down for breakfast, but the captain wants breakfast in his room on a *tray*. He eats dinner at odd hours—if he wants dinner at all. Twice now, he's gone off to town without a moment's notice and offered no idea of when he'd be back. He sometimes rides to church on Sunday and lets Miss Fallbrook do the same, when there's a perfectly good coach at his disposal."

"These are grave charges." Diana struggled to keep her face impassive.

"Now he's summoned you to the blue parlor." Mrs. Gwynn clucked her tongue with disapproval. "It isn't fitting that a young woman like yourself should meet with her employer without a chaperone. 'I'll sit quiet as a mouse in a corner with my knitting,' I told him, but he'd have none of it. 'I assure you Miss Taylor will be perfectly safe in my company,' says he. That may well be! But it's not right, especially for a man of *his* reputation."

They had reached an open central gallery now and the landing for the grand staircase, which overlooked the great hall below. "His reputation?" Diana repeated, intrigued. "What do you mean?"

The housekeeper lowered her voice. "When a man's unmarried at thirty-two, it tells you something. Clearly, Captain Fallbrook's not the marrying sort. And from what I hear, he's got a woman in every port."

"Does he, indeed?"

"Handsome is as handsome does, Miss Taylor. He might be in a foul humor these days, what with that leg of his, but watch yourself, will you? A leopard doesn't change his spots."

Diana had, over the years, observed any number of men who broke hearts, were unfaithful to their wives, and seduced the chambermaids. Her own experiences with men had also taught her to be wary of them. Men made promises they didn't keep. They professed one thing, when they were after quite another. "I'll keep my guard up, Mrs. Gwynn."

"See that you do."

They proceeded past the gallery to the opposite wing, where Diana glimpsed an immense and well-stocked library. Several closed doors followed. At last, they entered an attractive apartment of moderate size.

The reason for the blue parlor's name was immediately apparent. The walls were covered in smoky-blue wallpaper with an ivory stripe. Elegant couches and chairs were upholstered in accompanying shades from pale blue to cobalt to sapphire. Candles in silver candelabras topped the mantelpiece and several mahogany tables.

Captain Fallbrook sat reading a newspaper in one of two wingback chairs flanking the carved marble fireplace, where a bright fire burned. During their one brief and disastrous encounter, Diana had not gotten a good look at his face. After hearing Mrs. Gwynn's warning, she took him in with interest.

He was attired all in black, from his finely tailored frock coat to his necktie and boots. A reminder that he, like the rest of the house, was in mourning. Mrs. Gwynn had called him handsome—and he was, with his high cheekbones, strong jaw, and shock of wavy, dark hair. But the effect was mitigated by the frown on his face. Indeed, his whole being radiated irritation and choler.

"I've brought Miss Taylor, Captain," announced Mrs. Gwynn as they approached.

"Thank you." Setting down his paper, he grabbed the cane beside his chair and, grimacing, struggled to his feet. His eyes were a startling shade of blue that reminded Diana of the sea at sunset. "Captain William Fallbrook," he said by way of introduction. "I fear our first meeting, Miss Taylor, was not under the best of circumstances."

Diana's wariness was tempered by a stirring of respect. A more egotistical man might have ignored the proprieties and remained sitting, so as not to call attention to his handicap. "It is a pleasure to meet you again, Captain—as you say, under better circumstances."

"Likewise. Have a seat." He indicated the chair opposite. Diana sat. A low table stood between them. Upon it resided a tea service as well as a crystal glass filled with what looked like brandy. "Mrs. Gwynn, pour out before you leave, please."

"Yes, Captain."

With effort, the captain lowered himself back into his chair. Mrs. Gwynn asked Diana how she took her tea, filled two cups, handed one to each, and with a frown quit the room, taking care to leave the door ajar.

Diana sipped the beverage, which was hot and fragrant. There were so many things she wanted to speak to this man about, she hardly knew where to begin. "May I express my condolences, Captain, on the passing of your uncle?"

"Thank you."

"I also wanted to say how grateful I am for your help on the road yesterday. You must know—I had no idea who you were until you'd gone, when your coachman informed me."

He gave her a pointed look. "I was tired, wet, and covered in mud—and in no mood to observe the niceties. My only thought was to get the business over with as quickly as possible so that we could all be on our way."

She expected him to chastise her again for stepping down from the coach. But he did not. "The weather *was* grim and clearing away that tree was a difficult endeavor."

"An endeavor which would have taken half the time, had two able-bodied men been at the task." He scowled at his bad leg. "As you have observed, I am not as fit as I would wish to be at present."

If he is indeed a man with 'a woman in every port,' Diana thought, *it must be a blow to his pride to have been discharged from the Navy with his present infirmity.* "I'm sorry."

Her comment seemed to irritate him further. "I am no object to be pitied, Miss Taylor."

"I did not say it out of pity. I merely meant that I am sorry to see you suffer." She didn't want to pry into the cause of his injury and hoped he would offer the information of his own accord.

But he only said, "Don't be. I was sent home to mend—it has been more like festering—but it is a temporary inconvenience. In six or seven months' time, I should be fit to return to duty. Or so the doctors tell me."

"I am glad to hear it, sir." Diana paused uncertainly. "Forgive me. I understand that you don't wish to be addressed as 'Sir William.' But what about 'sir'? Or shall I always call you 'Captain'?"

"Either 'sir' or 'Captain' will suit."

"Very well." Taking a deep breath, Diana added, "I wish to apologize again for what happened yesterday. My only thought was to be of assistance. Yet in exiting the coach, perhaps ... I did more harm than good."

He waved an impatient hand. "Think no more about it. What's done is done."

His answer set Diana's mind at ease. At least his foul mood wasn't directed at her.

"However," he went on sternly, "I do hope, Miss Taylor, that the next time I give an order, you will take it more seriously. I will not accept being countermanded."

Diana processed that. "Do you mean to say that I must obey your every command without question?"

He stared at her. "Are you truly asking for my permission to be insubordinate?"

"I do not think that term applies." Diana's stomach tensed. She sensed that she was getting into dangerous territory and ought not to proceed with this line of dialogue. But her thoughts veered suddenly to a novel that had come out two years previously that she and her sisters had read and loved, *Jane Eyre*. Diana had felt an immediate kinship with Jane Eyre, not only because they worked in the same profession, but because she admired Jane's passionate insistence that she be valued as a human being, and for her mind, heart, and soul, not just for the rote feminine labors which she was required to produce.

"This is not the Royal Navy," Diana charged, the words tumbling from her lips before she could stop them. "You are my employer, but I am a civilian with a thinking brain and a free will. I should like to think that, if I have a differing view from yours that might, just might, prove a sounder course of action than that which you have ordered, I may be allowed to express it."

His entire body seemed to tense as he stared at her over the rim of his teacup. Finally, with an annoyed huff, he set down the cup, picked up the glass of brandy, and retorted sharply, "Your feelings are duly noted, Miss Taylor."

Well, Diana thought with relief, *that was big of him.* He could have fired her on the spot, she supposed, for "insubordination."

"So. Emity tells me you took a tour of the house and grounds this morning?"

"I did. It is a lovely estate."

"It is, indeed." Oddly, he frowned.

"The gardens are delightful and the house impressive. I like this room in particular."

"Why?"

"I suppose because blue is my favorite color."

"Ah. It was my uncle's favorite room as well."

"It is very comfortable." Diana toyed with her hands in her lap, recalling her godmother's suspicions about the captain. They seemed absurd, but she might as well go fishing. "It must be thrilling to be the master of such a place," she said lightly.

"Must it?"

To her surprise, he sounded disgruntled, as if his inheritance were a burden rather than a source of pride. "Do you find fault with Pendowar Hall?"

"It is a fine place." He took a swallow of brandy then shook his head. "But it should never have come to me."

"Why not?"

"That honor should have gone to Robert, my uncle's son." His jaw set. His dark brows drew together. His voice rang with bitterness. "However, the sweet, young lad perished at the tender age of five."

"So I heard. I'm very sorry."

"Most people, I imagine, would count themselves fortunate—extremely so—to find themselves heir to a property as valuable and ancient as Pendowar Hall. But I never wanted it. A house and fortune were never my aim."

"A house and fortune were never my aim."

Mr. Heyer had said something similar to Diana when he'd come wooing last year. *"I care nothing for houses or fortunes, Miss Taylor. I love you for yourself alone."* Diana had believed him. Oh, how wrong she had turned out to be.

Was Captain Fallbrook's remark equally insincere? If he truly didn't want Pendowar Hall, it put paid to Mrs. Phillips's theory entirely. But there was a peculiar note in his voice and body language that made Diana wonder if it was something he'd felt obliged to say—to appear as the "reluctant heir"—rather than an expression of his true feelings. Or was she reading something into it that wasn't there?

"Uncle Thomas should have lived a great many more years yet." Sighing, he went on. "Did my aunt Eliza acquaint you with the manner in which my uncle died?"

"She did." Diana's heart beat faster, pleased that he'd brought up the subject himself. "Although … I'm not sure I understand what happened."

"I'm still struggling to make sense of it myself. It was so unexpected." He stared into his glass. "And yet … perhaps there were signs I did not recognize." Regret and grief took over the captain's face, tinged by something else. Was it guilt?

Diana understood grief and regret. But why, she wondered, should he feel guilty about his uncle's passing? Unless he'd had something to do with it after all?

Before she could proceed with this line of inquiry, he said, "Enough of that. Let us get back to you. Let me tell you straight out: I have no experience when it comes to the business of a governess. I never had one myself—I attended school until age twelve, when I was shipped off to the Royal Navy. If there is anything you require to do your job properly, I pray you will inform me."

"I do have one request, Captain."

"Go on."

"On my way here this evening, I spied a library that looked quite remarkable. May I make use of it?"

"You are fond of books?"

"Reading is one of my favorite pastimes."

His piercing gaze reflected his approval. "We have that in common. I bring a trunk of books with me whenever I go to sea. I fear I should be lost without them." He took another sip of brandy. "The library and all the books in it are at your disposal."

"Thank you."

"And feel free to use this parlor in the evenings—as blue is your favorite color—or any other unoccupied room in the house that takes your fancy."

"I appreciate that." She was pleased to see that beneath his prickly exterior, Captain Fallbrook was a thoughtful man.

"Pray, avoid the north wing, however, and don't go near the north tower. It has been unoccupied for decades and is in disrepair."

Diana nodded. It was her second warning to avoid the north wing. She wondered again why that part of the house had been abandoned but thought it best not to ask. Perhaps the estate was not as financially sound as it appeared.

"Captain," she said, "there is something else I wished to mention. Last night at about two A.M., I heard footsteps in the corridor outside my room."

"Footsteps?"

"They seemed to come up by the servants' stairs and head in this direction."

"It was probably Mrs. Gwynn. She suffers from insomnia—a plight with which I am all too familiar. She has a propensity to prowl the corridors at night."

"I asked Mrs. Gwynn. She denied any connection to the event."

"I cannot think of anyone else who would have been up at that hour. Unless, perhaps, it was our resident ghost." His mouth twitched slightly. His eyes twinkled as well.

Diana realized that he was teasing her. It was the first time she had witnessed anything other than a serious expression on his face, and he looked even more handsome for the effort. "I heard about your ghost. Apparently, she is … a mermaid?"

"The Mermaid of Pendowar. An infamous legend—also known as the Mermaid's Curse."

"A curse? I should love to hear about that."

"I would not dare tell it to you, Miss Taylor."

"Whyever not?"

"It is a tale that you, of all people, would not wish to hear."

"*You, of all people.*" Ivy had said the same thing. What was it about the Mermaid of Pendowar that was unfit for Diana's ears? "If you say so." It seemed frivolous to spend any more time on the subject. She had more pressing issues to discuss. "Now, I must speak to you on another matter, if I may."

"What is that?"

"My pupil, Miss Fallbrook."

"Of course. I understand that you met today. How did that go?"

"Not as well as I had hoped. At our appointed lesson time, she was nowhere to be found. She was discovered on the beach and arrived in an irritable mood. We had barely gotten started when she got fed up and fled."

He leaned back in his chair with a sigh. "I do not pretend to know or understand my cousin. I have been at sea for the better part of two decades. Until these past few months, I had only seen Emma at brief intervals when I was home on leave. But I did mention in my letters to you that Emma has problems."

"Yes."

"Aunt Eliza recommended you so highly that I hoped—I still hope—you can make some headway with Emma. But perhaps I should have explained further. When Emma was small, my uncle Thomas said, she showed great promise. But when she outgrew her nanny, she began to falter. A pack of governesses has tried and failed. My uncle's second wife, Sylvia, was Emma's governess at one time and she said Emma was difficult in the classroom. That she could not learn."

"That is untrue. Miss Fallbrook is a bright girl. She has learned a great deal."

"Has she?"

"She rattled off the Kings and Queens of England without batting an eyelash. She told me volumes about the seashells she had collected and speaks excellent French. I saw one of her sketchbooks—she is a gifted artist. And she makes delightful sculptures out of clay."

"I am glad to hear it. But rote memorization and artistic prowess do not signify intelligence. Even cavemen could draw."

Diana bristled. "Cavemen may have had far more brain power than we know, Captain. In any case, despite the accomplishments I glimpsed today—which barely scratch the surface of her talents, I suspect—Miss Fallbrook suffers from a serious deficiency, academically."

"What is that?"

"She cannot read."

"I beg your pardon?"

Diana told him what had happened when she'd asked her pupil to read aloud. "She has trouble writing as well. I have not had the opportunity to assess her properly, but when she wrote her name, she spelled it incorrectly."

"How can that be? She is fifteen years old."

"I take it you have not observed the problem yourself?"

"Miss Taylor, I am the new master of Pendowar Hall. I have a great deal on my plate. I do not have time to 'observe' Emma's day-to-day activities."

Irritation prickled through her. "The two ideas are not mutually exclusive, sir."

"I beg your pardon?"

"As the captain of a ship you have, I presume, commanded a vessel as well as hundreds of men. Surely, it is within your capabilities to manage this estate *and* keep abreast of the well-being of one young lady, your cousin."

Captain Fallbrook's jaw dropped slightly. His right eyebrow began to twitch. He slammed down his glass on the side table with a *bang*.

Diana cringed in response. *This time you went too far, Diana.* Was this the moment when he would send her packing? She was debating whether to apologize when he barked his reply.

"You are an impertinent young woman, Miss Taylor." His blue eyes flashed. "But I shall ignore that remark for now. I hired you to manage my cousin. And I expect you to do your job."

"Yes, sir." Diana swallowed in relief.

"Now back to Emma's 'serious deficiency.'"

Diana was about to protest, but he clicked his tongue, reminding her, "Your words, Miss Taylor, not mine."

Diana clenched her hands, silenced.

"I recall some years ago that Uncle Thomas was worried about Emma's eyesight—he took her to an oculist in London, but the man could find nothing wrong."

"There is nothing wrong with her eyesight. I've seen her artwork and witnessed her copy an intricate design in the upholstery of the schoolroom chairs."

He shook his head. "I cannot believe my uncle kept this from me."

"Perhaps he didn't know. Or was embarrassed. Or was being protective of his daughter."

"Do you think her inability stems from a mental defect? Is she intellectually backward?"

Diana's hackles rose again. "No. I do not believe that for a minute."

"Well, I believe in facing reality. If it's true, that Emma cannot read—despite the attentions of any number of governesses— then so be it. Plenty of people are illiterate and get by just fine. Let us concentrate on those skills that Emma does possess." He drummed his fingers on the arm of his chair. "I believe you mentioned in your letter that you can teach all the finishing subjects, whatever those might be, as well as the sciences, arithmetic, history, German, and Latin?"

"Yes, but—"

"Good. I will make sure Emma attends her lessons on time in the future, and I'll trust you to take it from there, Miss Taylor." He waved a dismissive hand. "Thank you. You may go."

Diana nodded, every nerve in her body tense with irritation. Straining to keep her voice even, she replied, "Aye aye, Captain," as she stood and quit the room.

CHAPTER SIX

D IANA'S FINGERS TREMBLED with fury as she undressed for bed that evening.

How had she believed, even for an instant, that Captain Fallbrook was a thoughtful person? In fact, he was self-centered, thoughtless, and prejudiced. It was yet another example of her inability to judge men, on first acquaintance, for who they really were.

For him to talk about how much he had on his plate—as if his duties managing this estate were more important than Miss Fallbrook's care and education! That he had so little interest in his cousin, and so little faith in her intelligence, as to practically wash his hands of her—it was unconscionable!

Miss Fallbrook was not "intellectually backward." Diana would stake her life upon it.

"Plenty of people are illiterate and get by just fine." What a preposterous notion—and this coming from a man who professed himself to be fond of reading. Diana could not and would not condemn Miss Fallbrook to such an existence.

To be unable to read for pleasure or information … to never write or read a letter to a friend or loved one … to be unable to read or write a grocery list … it was unthinkable. Finishing accomplishments and several other subjects would have to wait. More important issues must be tackled first.

She would teach Miss Fallbrook to read or die trying. She

could not live with herself if she failed.

Diana had just finished buttoning up her nightdress when a tentative knock sounded on her chamber door. It was Ivy, carrying Diana's dress and cloak, which were now free of dirt and freshly pressed.

Diana thanked her. After hanging the garments in the wardrobe, she turned to find Ivy studying her with raised eyebrows and a tilted head.

"Is everything all right, miss?"

"Yes. Why?"

The maid knelt before the hearth and began to stoke the fire. "It's only that you seem to be fretting about something."

"Is it that obvious?" Diana sat down on her bed and began brushing her hair. "I suppose I *am* fretting. I have some challenges ahead." She did not think it appropriate, however, to discuss Miss Fallbrook's difficulties with this young chambermaid, no matter how kindly she might be. "I am not ready to talk about it, though."

"I understand, miss. Some things are best not spoken aloud. Whatever's the matter, when the time is right, the solution will come to you. That's what my old granny used to say."

"Your grandmother sounds like a wise woman."

"Oh, she were. My mother couldn't care for me, but she sent a bit of money now and then and Granny raised me like I were her own. Granny said it was important that I learn to read and write, which she'd never been taught to do, so she sent me to school for a year."

"That's wonderful, Ivy." Diana knew how rare it was for a young woman of Ivy's social class to receive any education at all. "I wish every girl could attend lessons. My sisters and I have long hoped to open a school for girls someday."

"Do ye, miss? What's stopping ye?"

"Lack of funds." Diana shrugged. "And lack of a proper location to house a school. It's just a fantasy, really."

"My granny used to say, whatever you dream about, go out

and get it. Never give up. Unless of course there be signs warning you to go another way."

"Signs? What do you mean?"

"Ye know, signs. Omens, like. That if ye follow that dream, a bad fate awaits ye. She were a superstitious woman, my old granny. I can still hear her voice in my head, for all that she's been gone these many years. When she got ill, she said over and over, 'When I die, Ivy, promise me ye won't forget to tell the bees.'"

"Tell the bees?"

"If there's a death, miss, ye must tell the bees about it. Once there was a young man who didn't tell the bees about the death of his father, and what do you think, but he was stung to death himself."

"Oh, no." Diana struggled to keep her face impassive, not wishing Ivy to feel disrespected. She began braiding her long hair into a plait. "Ivy. You mentioned a tale this morning about the Mermaid of Pendowar. Will you tell it to me?"

Ivy stood and wiped her hands on her apron. "I'd better not, miss. I wouldn't want to worry ye."

"What is so terrible about a mermaid's tale that I should be particularly worried?"

"You'll know when ye hear it."

"I'm not the worrying sort."

"All right then, but ... ye won't like it." Ivy took a deep breath. "More than a hundred years ago, the young master of Pendowar Hall, Sir Peter were his name, fell in love with a mermaid called Morwenna, whom he met while swimming in the cove. From the moment he set eyes upon her, his heart was hers. Because she were loved by a human, when Morwenna emerged from the sea, she could walk like any woman. Late at night, when the servants were in bed and all the household were asleep, Sir Peter would light a lantern in the north tower window to signal to Morwenna that it was safe for her to join him. It were there they met in secret and consummated their union.

"When they were together, Sir Peter knew himself to be

madly in love. But when they were apart, he doubted himself. How could a mermaid be real? He began to fear he was going mad, and that he'd just imagined her. So he stopped signaling to Morwenna from the north tower. To end the habit for good, he resolved to marry, and he chose a woman in his employ: his sister's governess. The villagers of Portwithys were shocked that a man of Sir Peter's station would marry a woman so far beneath him. Morwenna were more shocked still and hurt by his betrayal. Every day, her pain and fury grew. A year later, after Sir Peter's bride gave birth to his heir, she were standing on the rocks by the shore as she were wont to do, when a wave rose and swept her out to sea. It were said all around the village that Morwenna killed the governess-bride out of revenge. Sir Peter loved Morwenna 'til his dying day, but he were too filled with grief and shame to go to her—and he killed himself a few years later."

"Oh!" Diana murmured. "What a tragic story."

"That's only the beginning, miss. It became a legend like, and over the years, whene'er the west wind wailed, it were said to be Morwenna's ghost crying out her woe and heartbreak. In time it were said to be a curse: that if any governess and master of Pendowar ever fell in love, she were doomed to die by drowning and he to die of grief." Ivy paused. "Years later, it happened again. My last master, Sir Thomas, fell in love with one of Miss Fallbrook's governesses and married her."

"Her name was Sylvia?"

Ivy nodded. "They were happy until one day she and her young son, Master Robert, both drowned at sea in a boating accident."

"I heard about that. It's so awful."

"It is, miss. After their deaths, a light began appearing now and then in the north tower window. It flashes on and off, the way Sir Peter used to signal to his mermaid love."

"How strange."

"No one can account for it. Sir Thomas checked many a time, I'm told, but there were never anyone in the north tower. They say it's Morwenna, making herself known again. Like a warning and reminder of the curse, which is said to be unbreakable. They say it drove Sir Thomas mad. He never got over the loss of his wife and son and when he killed himself, it were proof of the Mermaid's Curse for all to see."

Diana processed that. "So, you believe that Sir Thomas took his own life? Out of grief over his lost wife and son?"

"I do, miss."

"What makes you think that was the reason?"

"I don't think it. I *know* it. He left a note."

"Oh!" There it was. Sir Thomas *had* left a suicide note. It was the proof Diana had been seeking. It was all so heartbreaking. "What did the note say?"

"I don't know, miss. I never saw it. But I heard the captain and his lawyer speak of it."

"I see." Diana needed to learn more about that note before she told Mrs. Phillips. Her thoughts veered to the last part of Ivy's tale. "Ivy. Have you personally ever seen a light in the north tower?"

"I have, miss."

"Really?" Diana was intrigued. "Have you ever gone up to the tower to see if anyone was there?"

"Oh, no, miss! I wouldn't dare."

"Why not?"

"Because Sir Thomas declared that wing off-limits, and Captain Fallbrook upholds that rule. But mainly because Mrs. Gwynn forbids it. I wouldn't want to get on *her* wrong side. Nor would anyone else on staff."

"I see why you were afraid to tell me this story, Ivy. Because I am the governess now."

Ivy nodded again. Her eyes were alive with concern. "And the new master—he's a single man and ever so good-looking."

"Do you think so?" Diana gave a deliberate shrug.

"Hester, the head housemaid, gets stars in her eyes every time they cross paths. All the girls in the village are half in love with Captain Fallbrook for all that they've only seen him once or twice. Not that he'd notice. He's a gloomy sort, which I guess is understandable with that bad leg of his. But ye'd best be careful not to fall in love with him, miss, or ye might be doomed to an awful fate."

"Don't worry. I don't believe in mermaids or legends or curses. And I do not intend to fall in love with the captain, or anyone else."

It was a disturbing notion nonetheless. Long after she and Ivy had exchanged *good nights* and Diana crawled into bed, one fact from their conversation replayed in her mind, keeping sleep at bay:

Two former governesses at Pendowar Hall had died by drowning.

And Diana could not swim.

MISS FALLBROOK STRODE into the schoolroom promptly at nine o'clock the following morning and, crossing her arms over her chest, dropped down in the chair she had previously occupied.

"I'm only here because William said if I did not come, he would send me away to boarding school."

"I see." Diana gave her a smile. "And you don't wish to attend boarding school?"

"No! Miss Ireland, my seventh governess, told me about the school she attended. She slept in a dormitory with fifty girls, the food was horrid, she froze in winter, boiled in summer, and she was teased, and beaten, and forced to *read aloud*." Miss Fallbrook made a face.

Diana flinched, recalling how dismayed she'd been to read about schools with such harrowing conditions. "Not every school is like that. My sisters and I attended school for a short while, and it was a lovely, wholesome place."

"I don't care. I will never go away to school. I shall live at Pendowar Hall for the rest of my life."

"You may have to leave one day, if you marry."

Miss Fallbrook scoffed. "I shall never marry."

"Why do you say that?"

"Who would want me?"

Miss Fallbrook's lack of self-confidence tugged at Diana's heart. Just because Diana's fingers had been burned where men were concerned, she was not opposed to the idea of marriage for others. Her parents had been happy, after all. "Any man with sense would want you, Miss Fallbrook. Of course, you must exercise discretion in that regard: take your time, choose wisely, and only marry a good and trustworthy man, *if* he can be found."

"You are dreaming, Miss Taylor. My father used to say, 'Emma, you will never amount to anything. You are too odd and too stupid.'"

How, Diana wondered, could anyone speak so heartlessly to a child? Much less a father to his own daughter? "I'm sorry he said that. But it's not true. You are not odd. And you are very bright."

"How can I be bright if I cannot read or write?" Miss Fallbrook shrugged. "It doesn't matter, though. I am fine without those talents."

"Reading is one of life's greatest pleasures." Diana gestured to the books on the schoolroom shelves. "A world of knowledge awaits you inside every one of those books. Curling up in a quiet corner with a novel is like diving into an imaginary world. And what about correspondence? Wouldn't you like to be able to write to and receive letters from your friends and loved ones?"

"I have no loved ones. My relations are all dead."

This assertion cut Diana to the quick. "Not all. What about your aunt, Eliza?" Thinking of that good woman and knowing of her dire illness, Diana's heart gave another twist.

"Papa said that Aunt Eliza came to visit once when I was a baby, but I don't remember her. She used to write to me, but I didn't want anyone else to read her letters. And since I couldn't read them, I threw them away."

How sad, Diana thought. "Did the captain—your cousin William—ever write to you?"

"Never." Miss Fallbrook sighed. "Once, though, when I was four or five years old, William brought me a little carved wooden horse from his voyages. It became my pet, and I made other animals out of clay to keep it company. But … I only see him once a week now when he takes me to church. He thinks me a nuisance."

Diana recalled seeing that little wooden horse on Miss Fallbrook's shelf. She sensed that her pupil admired Captain Fallbrook and craved his attention, although she probably would never admit it. "I am sure the captain cares for you very much." It might have been a white lie, but one which Diana felt was necessary. "And what about friends? Surely, you must have one friend who is dear to you?"

"Papa did not let me play with the children in the village. They were not 'of my station,' he said. When *his* friends came over, I was banished to the nursery."

"Oh, Miss Fallbrook." It smote Diana to think that her young charge had led such a sheltered and lonely life and thought so little of herself. "You will have friends when you get older, and you will be happy to be able to correspond with them, I promise. Explain to me, now, how it is that you have reached the age of fifteen without learning to read and write. Did your governesses never teach you your letters?"

"They tried. Over and over. But I cannot remember them."

Diana needed proof. Crossing to the blackboard, she wrote the word CAT. "Do you recognize this word?"

"No."

Diana erased the A and T, leaving only the letter C. "What about this letter?"

Emma studied the board. She blinked several times. She worried her lip. Her foot tapped against the floor. "Um … is it … an A?"

Softly, Diana asked, "Why do you think it's an A?"

"Because every governess always starts with A." Miss Fallbrook blushed. "I got it wrong, didn't I?"

"Yes, but that doesn't matter. The important thing is that you tried. This is the letter C."

"Oh."

"Do you know what sound the letter C makes?"

"It doesn't make a sound. A letter is not a person or an animal. It is just a squiggly shape."

Diana saw that she had her work cut out for her. "Letters do make sounds, Miss Fallbrook. Every letter has its own unique sound, and when you string them together, they form words, the same words that you hear and speak. That is the nature of written language."

"I don't understand."

"You will, in time."

Diana began as she always did, by patiently introducing the first three letters of the alphabet in capital and lower-case form. Miss Fallbrook inscribed rows of each letter on her slate and on the blackboard, and they practiced the sounds of the letters aloud.

Although Miss Fallbrook dutifully applied herself, her performance was slow and halting. The A-B-Cs she drew were messy. Sometimes she wrote them backwards. Twice, she wrote them upside down. At one point, Miss Fallbrook complained that one of the letters had moved off the blackboard and was sitting on the windowsill.

Diana was perplexed by these irregularities. Every time Miss Fallbrook made a mistake, she was embarrassed, and she grew increasingly frustrated and irritable.

Wanting the girl to have some successes, Diana devoted the remainder of the day to oral instruction in subjects in which her pupil had exhibited an interest the day before: history, geography, and French. When she quizzed Miss Fallbrook at the end of each discussion, the girl's performance was impeccable. She could recall in perfect detail all that she had been told.

When their lesson time was over, Diana said, "You did very well, Miss Fallbrook."

"Did I?" The young woman looked uncertain. "I still cannot read."

"But you shall. We will take it one step at a time. And, as my mother used to say to me when I was a girl, 'Tomorrow is another day.'"

DIANA DEVOTED THE better part of her evening to preparing a new, detailed course of instruction for Miss Fallbrook. She then wrote letters to Mrs. Phillips, Athena, Selena, and Damon to inform them of her safe arrival and her concerns about her pupil.

Since her siblings were aware of the mission Mrs. Phillips had sent her on, Diana gave a brief overview of what she had learned so far about Sir Thomas, reserving further details until she was more certain. With her sisters, she shared the tale of the Mermaid's Curse and the footsteps she'd heard in the night, thinking it might amuse them. She knew her brother would be too busy to reply but hoped to hear from her sisters with news of how they were faring in their governess positions.

As she finished her letters, the clock struck half-past ten. Diana tidied up and was drawing the draperies on the schoolroom windows when she spotted a blinking light in the uppermost window of the north tower.

What in the world? Diana thought. Captain Fallbrook had said that region of the house had been unoccupied for decades and was in disrepair. *Who could be up there?*

The light continued to blink on and off, as if someone were sending a signal beacon with a candle or a lantern. For what purpose? And to whom?

The tale Ivy had told her came to mind.

"It flashes on and off, the way Sir Peter used to signal to his mermaid love ... They say it's Morwenna, making herself known again. Like

a warning and reminder of the curse."

Diana had dismissed the tale as an absurdity. She had dismissed the idea of a light as well. Surely, it was just a figment of people's imaginations, an embellishment to a mysterious, old legend. But the light was there, before Diana's eyes. It was real. Who, Diana wondered, was up in the north tower? She had to find out.

Descending the servants' stairs to the ground floor, Diana followed an unfamiliar maze of corridors until she reached a door that she suspected might lead to the north wing.

The door opened. She entered.

The space beyond was dark and a musty aroma filled the air. Diana's heart pounded as she strode carefully along the corridor, her candle providing the only illumination. This part of the house appeared to date back to the years of its original construction. The floor and walls were of uneven stone, and it was devoid of decoration except for the occasional stuffed and mounted head of a dead animal covered in dust and crowned by cobwebs.

Eerie shapes hovered in the shadows. Diana spied a dark figure and halted in terror, raising her candle, only to find herself face to face with a suit of armor. She inhaled a calming breath, which rippled from her chest like a ghostly chuckle. Why was she so jumpy?

As she moved on, a rustling made her jump again. A mouse froze wide-eyed in her candle-beam, then scampered off. Diana laughed nervously again. This was just an ancient wing of the house, she reminded herself. There was nothing to be afraid of.

The hallway ended in a vestibule, where an ancient door beside a filthy window led outside. A second, more central door constructed of heavy oak and studded with iron fittings sported an iron lock. This, she guessed, gave access to the tower stairwell.

Diana tried the door handle. It was locked.

The clicking of bootheels on stone resounded from the hallway behind her.

"Miss Taylor!" called out a voice sharply from the shadows.

"What are you doing here?"

Diana spun to find Mrs. Gwynn marching in this direction, black skirts swishing. Her indignant face glowered ghoul-like above her flickering candle.

Diana felt like a guilty schoolgirl, caught trespassing by the headmistress. "I saw a light in the tower."

"This part of the house is forbidden," Mrs. Gwynn reprimanded coldly. "I thought I made that clear."

"I know, but I wondered who was up there."

"*No one* is up there."

"There must be someone. I'll show you the light." Diana yanked open the exterior door and hurried out into the cold, night air.

"There's no need for that," the housekeeper insisted, but Diana was ten steps ahead of her.

To Diana's disappointment, when she glanced up at the tower, the light was gone. "There was a light, I swear it. It flashed on and off, as if someone were sending a signal."

Mrs. Gwynn glared from the doorway. "Come back inside, Miss Taylor."

Diana returned to the vestibule and shut the door. "Have you ever seen a light up there?"

"Many a time, for some years now."

So, this *was* a common occurrence, just as Ivy had said. "Does this door lead up to the tower?"

"It does. But the north tower is off-limits, Miss Taylor. Master's orders."

"Which master?"

"The captain. And Sir Thomas before him. He wasn't fond of the place. Locked it up tight as a drum. I'm the only one permitted to go up there now and then, to clean."

"You have the key, then?"

"I do."

"This is our opportunity to discover what is going on, Mrs. Gwynn! Let's go! Whoever flashed that light may be up there still!"

"The best reason I know not to go up."

"What do you mean?"

The housekeeper's hushed voice reverberated in the darkness. "I have no wish to meet Morwenna's ghost."

Diana had hoped the housekeeper would be more sensible than this. "Surely, you do not believe in ghosts?"

"Don't *you*, Miss Taylor?"

"I do not."

"You will when you've lived in this house as long as I have. Now come away, Miss Taylor. Go to bed. Stop fretting about things that don't concern you. And don't let me find you in this part of the house again."

Diana pressed her lips together in frustration as she followed the housekeeper down the silent, gloomy corridor. She may have been turned away tonight, but one of these days, she'd find a way up to that tower to explore.

CHAPTER SEVEN

D IANA SLID A key into the iron lock and pulled the door open. Within, a circular, stone staircase led upwards. She mounted the stairs to what felt like a cloud height, finally reaching the upper landing, where she froze in wonder.

The ghostly form of a mermaid hovered before her, beckoning with an alluring smile and a graceful wave. Mesmerized, Diana stepped forward. But she stepped into thin air. With a cry of terror, Diana plummeted down, down towards the black rocks below. Just before impact, she awoke with a gasp.

What a horrible dream.

As she lay in the darkness, the events of the previous evening raced through Diana's mind. She understood now why Sir Thomas had stopped using the north wing and had locked up the north tower. The legend of the mermaid who haunted it must have haunted *him* after his wife's and son's deaths at sea. When that light had started appearing, recalling the legend of the Mermaid of Pendowar, it was no wonder if it had driven him to madness.

Why the captain continued to keep the area off-limits, however, was another matter. He had claimed it to be in disrepair, but Diana had seen no evidence of that. It just needed a good cleaning. Captain Fallbrook didn't appear to be the superstitious sort any more than she was. There were no such things as ghosts or mermaids. A human being had been up in the north tower last night. Diana would stake her life on it. Whoever it had been, they had flashed a light in the window.

Who'd been flashing the light? And why? How could they enter a tower that had been locked? It could not have been Mrs. Gwynn, for she had appeared after Diana, from the opposite direction.

Who else, Diana wondered, had a key?

MISS FALLBROOK DID not show up in the schoolroom the next morning. Diana discovered the girl in her bedroom, sitting in her window seat with a sketchbook, drawing the scene outside. She was so engrossed in her work that she didn't hear Diana enter.

"Miss Fallbrook. It's time for your lessons."

The girl jerked in surprise and turned. "Sorry." She did not sound sorry in the least. "I forgot the time."

They spent the morning working on three more letters of the alphabet. Although Miss Fallbrook tried, the new material did not seem to be sinking in, any more than it had the day before.

"Can we draw now?" Miss Fallbrook pleaded.

"No."

"May we sculpt, then? I have some clay in my room."

"I saw your clay sculptures. They're charming. The other day when I returned your seashells, I looked at one of your sketch-books as well—I hope you don't mind."

"What did you think?"

"I think art is a fine accomplishment and you have quite an aptitude for it."

Miss Fallbrook's face flushed with modest delight. "Thank you."

"But art will not be part of our curriculum."

"Why not?" Miss Fallbrook gestured wildly with both hands. "Every governess has taught me art! It's my favorite subject!"

"I understand. But you so outshine my own abilities in that subject, I doubt there is anything I could teach you. You may pursue art in your free time. But when we work together, we must concentrate on a more important course of study. You must learn to read and write."

Miss Fallbrook let out a discontented breath. "It is hopeless. The letters look different every time I see them. I can't remember the sounds they make."

"For some reason, this skill is more difficult for you to master than for others, but we shall find a way."

"All my governesses either quit, or Papa fired them. 'You don't try hard enough,' he kept saying. It's why he never loved me."

"I am sure he loved you very much."

"Did you know my father killed himself?"

The question caught Diana by surprise. She didn't know what to say.

"I warned him not to marry Miss Corbett. She was my governess!" Miss Fallbrook went on passionately. "I reminded him of the Mermaid's Curse. He wouldn't listen. Morwenna took her revenge. My stepmother and my brother, Robert, drowned. Then Morwenna drove Papa mad until he threw himself off the cliff."

Diana's throat ached with sympathy. She reached across the table and covered her pupil's hand with her own. "I know it broke your heart to lose your father, and your stepmother and brother as well. These are heavy losses for anyone to bear, and especially hard for someone as young as you. But mermaids don't exist. Curses are not real."

Miss Fallbrook wrenched her hand away. "If that is true ... it just makes everything worse."

"Why?"

"Because if the Mermaid's Curse isn't real, it means Papa knew what he was doing when he killed himself. It means he loved his wife and Robert more than his own life. It means he thought so little of me, his only daughter, that he left me alone forever with no one to care for me but a cousin who spends his life at sea." The young woman burst into tears.

"You mustn't think that way, dear," Diana said soothingly. "If indeed your father took his own life, he may have felt terrible for leaving you but was so sad that he could not help himself."

"There's no 'if.' He shouldn't have done it! He ruined everything! Do you know what the worst part is? Because Papa killed himself, his soul is tainted forever. We couldn't even bury him in the churchyard!"

Diana hadn't thought of that. "Miss Fallbrook," she began.

"Please, miss," Miss Fallbrook interjected with a sob. "Please! May I go?"

Diana did not have the heart to say *no*.

DIANA PACED THE schoolroom floor, eaten up with worry.

There was something different about Miss Fallbrook, something that, despite her obvious intelligence, prevented her from making progress with the alphabet. What was Diana missing?

Some years ago, Diana had served as governess to the family of a highly regarded man at Oxford, a Professor Vaughan, who specialized in English language and literature. Maybe he would be familiar with the aspects of Miss Fallbrook's case.

Diana decided to write to him. Grabbing pen and paper, she composed a missive explaining her charge's difficulties and asking for advice.

As she sealed the letter, Diana sat back with a sigh.

Miss Fallbrook's reading and writing problems were not the only things weighing on Diana's mind. She was equally worried about her pupil's sense of abandonment. The sad fact was, Sir Thomas's death *had* left his only daughter in the lurch, under the guardianship of a man who seemed to be married to the Royal Navy and believed he had discharged his duty to his ward by hiring Diana to look after her.

Was Miss Fallbrook's assertion true—that her father had never loved her? Or had the young woman perhaps misinterpreted his frustration with her inability to read as a lack of love? Had Sir Thomas truly left a suicide note? If so, had he killed himself out of grief, as Miss Fallbrook and Ivy supposed? Or could there have been another reason behind that last, desperate act?

If Diana were to have any hope of helping her pupil—and, of solving the conundrum of Sir Thomas's death—she needed more information.

She went downstairs. The dinner hour had ended, and the servants' hall was nearly deserted. She found Mrs. Gwynn in her sitting room just off the kitchen, doing some paperwork.

"Mrs. Gwynn, may I have a word?"

The housekeeper replaced her pen in the inkwell and gestured silently to the vacant chair beside her. Diana took a seat.

"I wish to speak to you about Miss Fallbrook, if I may."

"What's she done now?"

"Nothing. She worked hard today." Diana gave a brief overview of the girl's achievements and the issues at hand. "Did you know, Mrs. Gwynn, that Miss Fallbrook cannot read?"

Mrs. Gwynn shrugged. "I suspected it."

"I believe she suffers from a debilitating lack of self-esteem. Not only over her reading difficulties, but from her belief that she is … how shall I put it … unworthy of affection."

Mrs. Gwynn discharged a contemptuous breath. "Why should she think that? She was the master's daughter, wasn't she? Had all the best that money could buy. She lives in a fine house, has beautiful clothes, *and* had a father who loved her."

"Did he?"

"Did he what?"

"Did Sir Thomas love his daughter?"

"Of course he did. What father wouldn't love his own child?" Mrs. Gwynn paused, and a faraway look came into her eyes. Whatever it was, she dismissed it with a blink, and pursing her lips, insisted, "He did his best by that girl. She ought to count her lucky stars instead of feeling sorry for herself."

"What was Miss Fallbrook's relationship with her father?"

"She were the apple of his eye. Since the day she were born, he couldn't do enough for her."

This report differed from Miss Fallbrook's, and from what Captain Fallbrook had implied. "As I understand it, he was fond of her as a little girl but became increasingly frustrated by her inability to read."

"Maybe so, but he loved her just the same. Hired one governess after another, didn't he? Always hoping for a miracle."

Diana pondered a delicate way to phrase her next question. "When the second Lady Fallbrook and their five-year-old son passed away, it must have been a great shock to Sir Thomas."

"It were."

"Such a shock and a tragedy that—apparently—he never recovered? And in time, he could not go on living without them?"

The housekeeper's features tightened with visible pain. "So they say."

"*So they say.*" Once again, wording that implied doubt. "Did you have any inkling that Sir Thomas might be about to take his own life?"

"No! None whatsoever!" Mrs. Gwynn's brow furrowed. "He had so much to live for. A grand estate, plenty of money, and ... and ..." She seemed to change her mind about what she was going to say, adding, "He had plans."

"What plans?"

"He spoke about erecting a play area for children in the churchyard as a memorial to his wife and son. Just two days before he died, Sir Thomas showed me a design he'd sketched." From her desk drawer, the housekeeper pulled out a drawing and showed it to Diana. "I've held on to it. I don't know why."

Diana examined the penciled sketch. It was the work of an amateur artist with scribbled notes, but she could discern Sir Thomas's intentions for the play area, which included picnic tables, a rope swing, a rocking horse, and space for croquet, hoops and sticks, and other games. "You say Sir Thomas drew this?"

"Yes. He was excited about it. But he never got a chance to talk to the vicar or curate or a builder about it because …" Mrs. Gwynn's voice trailed off.

"Because he died," Diana finished for her.

Mrs. Gwynn returned the drawing to her drawer with a sniff and a nod. "I were shocked when I heard what happened. But then," she went on emphatically, an undercurrent of grief and resentment in her tone, "you never can tell what another person will do, can you?"

"No, you cannot." Diana paused. The baronet's enthusiastic plans for his wife and son's memorial seemed to indicate a positive state of mind, rather than a depressive one, but did not negate the possibility of suicide. "Ivy said that he left a note?"

"He did, although I never saw it."

Diana was beginning to wonder if the suicide note was real or a piece of fiction or gossip.

"Mrs. Gwynn, I know that you admired your master," Diana said softly. "And again, I am so very sorry for your loss. I feel bad for Miss Fallbrook, as well. I would like to help her, and I would be grateful for your advice on the matter."

"My advice?" She frowned and looked away, rubbing the back of her neck. "I don't know what *I* can tell you."

"It is hard enough to lose one's father. But to lose him in such a manner, and for such a reason! Miss Fallbrook believes her father did not love her enough to stay the course and take care of her. I fear it is a wound that may take a lifetime to heal."

"Well! She'll just have to get over it, won't she?" Mrs. Gwynn's voice rang with bitterness as she turned back to face Diana. "My master weren't responsible for his actions that day."

"Wasn't he? What do you mean?"

"It were the Mermaid's Curse! It's hung over this house for more than a century. It's too powerful a force to reckon with, even for a man as strong as Thomas Fallbrook." Mrs. Gwynn rose from her chair. "Now if you'll excuse me, Miss Taylor, it's been a long day."

Diana left the room, deep in thought. She may not have agreed with the housekeeper's assessment, but she had gained two interesting pieces of information: Sir Thomas had had plans afoot at the time of his death, and his suicide had taken Mrs. Gwynn by surprise.

Diana found Mr. Emity in a room down the hall, polishing a pair of shoes, which she presumed to be the captain's. She poked her head in. "Mr. Emity. Do you have a moment?"

"Yes, miss. If you don't mind the smell of shoe polish."

"I don't mind at all." Diana joined him inside the chamber. "I like the smell, in fact. I sometimes helped our housekeeper, Martha, to make shoe polish and I shine my own shoes."

Mr. Emity smiled as he scooped up a dab of the waxy substance with his cloth and rubbed it into the toe box of a shoe. "It can be a restful occupation, miss. Gives one time to think. And at the end of it, you have a pair of shoes that look almost as good as new."

Diana grinned in return, delighted by this uplifting description of a task that some people might deem tedious. "I quite agree, Mr. Emity."

"So, what can I do for you, miss?"

"It is a rather sensitive subject." Diana reiterated the concerns she had for her pupil, which she had just shared with Mrs. Gwynn. "Miss Fallbrook is deeply hurt to think that her father committed suicide over the loss of his second wife and son."

"I know, miss. I am sorry for it."

"The other day when we spoke in the great hall, I sensed that you are not fully convinced about the ... *circumstances* surrounding Sir Thomas's demise?"

The butler lowered his gaze and busied himself buffing the shoe in his hands. "I'm sure I didn't mean to give that impression, miss."

"You said, 'That is one interpretation of the event.'"

"Did I?"

"Do you think there might be another explanation for his death?"

Still, Mr. Emity said nothing.

Diana tried again. "Perhaps you will say it is not my business. But if there were another reason behind his actions, it might go a long way to helping Miss Fallbrook deal with her grief. And ..." She couldn't admit that she'd been sent here to investigate, but she could allude to the reason. "My godmother, Mrs. Phillips, is also deeply troubled about what happened to her brother. She is very ill. I'd like to ease her mind by relaying the truth if I could before she dies."

Mr. Emity turned to her, an earnest look in his brown eyes. "You ought to speak to Mrs. Gwynn about this. She knew Sir Thomas better than anyone, I expect. Even better than I."

Diana paused. What did he mean by that? Was he simply saying the housekeeper had come to profoundly understand her master as the natural result of her occupation? Or was he implying that Mrs. Gwynn's relationship with the baronet had gone beyond professional bounds? "I have already spoken to Mrs. Gwynn. She blames the whole thing on the Mermaid's Curse."

"Try talking to her again."

Diana frowned. The housekeeper made her uncomfortable. "I think Mrs. Gwynn has shared all she's likely to share. Anyway, I don't think she likes me." Taking a deep breath, she added, "Mr. Emity. Is it true that Sir Thomas left a suicide note?"

"Such a note was apparently found, yes."

Apparently. "Found by whom?"

"Captain Fallbrook."

"What did the note say?"

"I don't know. He doesn't like to speak of it."

"Is Captain Fallbrook certain that Sir Thomas wrote the note?"

"He believed it was in his uncle's handwriting."

He believed. Another implication of doubt. Or was she imagining that? Diana tried another tactic. "How long did you work for Sir Thomas, Mr. Emity?"

"More than thirty years—since before he inherited the title. I started as his valet and for the past twenty years have also served as butler."

"You knew him well, then. Did Sir Thomas behave differently in any way in the weeks leading up to his death?"

"I will tell you the same as I told the parish constable. Sir Thomas seemed upset that week about several things. It was only a week, mind you, for he had just come back from the Continent."

That was right—Diana recalled Mrs. Phillips mentioning that Sir Thomas had been traveling just before he'd died. "Where on the Continent?"

"He had business in Germany. I remained here, as always. Sir Thomas preferred to travel without a valet. The same week that he returned, Captain Fallbrook came home on sick leave, in a bad way with that leg of his. The doctor was not sure if he would ever walk properly again. Sir Thomas was troubled about that. And it was the anniversary as well."

"What anniversary?"

"Of the accident. It had been three years since Lady Fallbrook and young Master Robert drowned at sea."

"Oh! Sir Thomas had a great deal on his mind at the time."

"He did, miss."

"Who is the parish constable?"

"Mr. Beardsley. He owns the grocery and post office in Portwithys."

Diana stored that information in her mind for later use. "Is there anything else you can tell me?"

Mr. Emity opened his mouth to reply then shut it again. It seemed she would get nothing more from him.

"You have been very helpful, Mr. Emity. I appreciate all you have shared. I will think on it. I bid you good night."

Diana turned to go when he blurted out abruptly, "I have always thought there was something wrong about that suicide note."

Diana whirled back to face him. "I beg your pardon?"

Mr. Emity put down his polishing rag. "As I said, miss, I served Sir Thomas for a great many years. He was not the type of man who would leap to his death out of grief—or for any other reason."

"Why do you say that?"

"He was too fond of life for that. But more importantly, he felt suicide was a sin."

Diana took that in. "Did you share these thoughts with the authorities?"

"I tried. But our parish constable is a busy man with no patience to investigate such matters—or to listen to a man like me. Whatever that note contained, he felt it was a clear indication of Sir Thomas's state of mind. He ruled it a suicide and that was that."

"So, what are you saying, Mr. Emity? If you do not believe that Sir Thomas killed himself ..."

The butler's eyes met hers. "Then perhaps ... he was murdered."

CHAPTER EIGHT

WHITE MIST BILLOWED around the shrubbery and colorful leaves dotted the lawn, gifts from the oaks, which were dressed in all their autumn glory. Diana inhaled deeply, appreciating the fragrances of damp earth, grass, and decomposing flora that imbued the morning air.

She had allowed Miss Fallbrook to spend the morning riding and was on her way to the village. At the midpoint of the old, wooden footbridge, Diana stopped to admire the view. The river pulsed with energy, rushing past the tropical plants and trees crowding its embankments. A shiver traveled down her spine as she gazed down at the dark, swirling depths.

Diana hurried on, spooked by the fast-moving water and the ancient bridge, as well as by all that she had seen and heard over the past few days: mysterious footsteps, flashing lights, a legend about a mermaid's ghost—and the butler's revelations from the previous evening.

"He was not the type of man who would leap to his death out of grief—or for any other reason ... But more importantly, he felt suicide was a sin."

It's telling, Diana thought as she passed through a stile and crossed a field dotted with grazing sheep, *that Mrs. Phillips, Mr. Emity, Mr. Nankervis, Mrs. Gwynn, and Captain Fallbrook, people who had known Sir Thomas for years, had all been surprised to learn he had committed suicide.*

"I have always thought there was something wrong about that suicide note."

Had Mrs. Phillips been right all along?

Diana's mother's words also rang in her ears: *"If you hear a rumor or see signs that something is amiss, it is probably true."*

Had someone pushed the baronet off that cliff?

And what about the suicide note? Such notes could be forged. If Sir Thomas hadn't written it, then who had?

THE FISHING VILLAGE of Portwithys was small and quaint. A maze of steep, narrow streets and lanes wound down the hillside towards the wharf past houses and shops that were either whitewashed, half-timbered, or constructed of the local grey stone.

Diana asked a passing farmer for directions to the post office, which was housed at the edge of Main Street in an ancient stone building beneath a sign which read, "A.E. BEARDSLEY, GROCERY PROVISIONS, BUTCHER, AND POST OFFICE."

Its proprietor, she knew, was also the parish constable.

Diana entered the shop and nearly collided with a gentleman on his way out.

"Pardon me," she said, stepping back.

"No, no, forgive *me*." Broad-shouldered and attractive, the man looked to be in his mid-thirties. He was elegantly attired in a bottle-green frock coat, dark-blue jacquard waistcoat, and cream-colored trousers. Coming as Diana had from a house of mourning, it was nice to see a man wearing fashionable colors. Tipping his hat, he said, "John Latimer, solicitor."

Latimer. She recognized the name. He'd been Sir Thomas's lawyer, the one who had written to Mrs. Phillips.

"You must be the new governess at Pendowar Hall?"

"I am." In a village of this size, it was understandable that a newcomer would stand out. "Diana Taylor." She offered him her hand.

He took it and, slowly and ceremoniously, kissed the back of her hand through her glove. The scent of his strong, sandalwood cologne filled her nostrils. "It is a pleasure to meet you, Miss Taylor." As he raked her with his gaze, his tone and smile made Diana feel distinctly uncomfortable.

"And you, Mr. Latimer." Diana tried to edge past him, but he blocked her way.

"Captain Fallbrook said you hail from Yorkshire, I believe?"

"Derbyshire."

"I hope your journey will prove to be worth the trouble. Governesses do come and go from that house as regular as clockwork."

Diana felt a need to defend her pupil. "Miss Fallbrook is a bright young lady and very sweet."

"That's not what I've heard. But then, I have not had the pleasure of seeing Miss Fallbrook in quite a while. Perhaps you see a side to her that others haven't." Mr. Latimer touched his hat again with a parting smile. "Good day, Miss Taylor. I hope we shall meet again."

Diana curtsied silently and was relieved when he departed.

The shop was a lively hodgepodge of fresh produce and other goods on display. The sound of unseen, violent chopping came from somewhere in back. Behind the counter stood a tall woman who introduced herself as Mrs. Beardsley.

As the postmistress processed Diana's letters to her siblings, Mrs. Phillips, and Professor Vaughan, she welcomed Diana to the neighborhood. Diana praised the attributes of the shop, and they chatted amiably about the weather.

"I see you've met Mr. Latimer, our solicitor," the postmistress remarked. "Sir Thomas was one of his biggest clients, or so I'm told, before Captain Fallbrook inherited the hall." She lowered her voice. "Such a terrible business, what happened to the baronet."

"Did you know Sir Thomas well, ma'am?" Diana asked, fishing for information.

"I did not, for all I've lived in Portwithys my entire life. He couldn't have set foot in this shop more'n once or twice. Rarely said a word to me or anyone at church. Had his man of business handle all his affairs. Those what did have dealings with Sir Thomas, his tenants and such-like, say he was a changed man the past few years."

"How so?"

"They say he grew harsh and mean. Rent had to be paid in full and on time, or there'd be hell to pay. Between you and me, there's some as say they aren't sorry he's gone."

"Indeed?" Diana's heart quickened. "Mrs. Beardsley. As I understand it, the parish constable who handled the case is your husband?"

"He is."

"Is he in?"

"Where else would he be?"

"I should like to speak to him, if I may."

"About what?"

Diana hesitated. "About Sir Thomas's death." She decided to leave it at that.

Mrs. Beardsley's eyes narrowed, and her mouth twitched as if she wished to question Diana further. Instead, she turned to the back of the shop and called out, "Mr. Beardsley! You're wanted!"

The sound of chopping ceased. A stocky man emerged from a back room, wiping his hands on his bloody white apron. "What's that?"

"This is Miss Taylor, the new governess at Pendowar Hall. She'd like to speak with you."

Mr. Beardsley strode over with a frown. "Governess, eh? Not interested then in the nice side of beef that's just come in?"

"No, sir, although I'm sure it's very fine."

"What can I do for you?"

Diana plunged in with the questions she had prepared. "You're the parish constable, sir?"

"Aye, that duty's been thrust upon me." He glowered. "What of it?"

"I am entrusted with the care and education of Miss Emma Fallbrook, and I wonder if you could help me. I'm worried about her. She's distraught by allegations that her father, Sir Thomas, took his own life."

"That's no allegation, Miss Taylor. It's a fact."

"Is it?"

"Without a doubt. Sir Thomas was never the same after his wife and son died. Three years that poor man pined. One morning, he could go on no longer. Flung himself off that cliff to kingdom come."

"And yet it's odd, don't you think? His housekeeper, Mrs. Gwynn, maintains that he was excited about upcoming plans to build a memorial to his wife and son in the churchyard. His butler, Mr. Emity, insists that Sir Thomas was fond of life, and opposed to suicide."

"Grief does strange things to a man, Miss Taylor. I've seen it too many times in this damnable job. And he left a note."

"Forgive me for asking, sir—but is it possible the note was forged?"

The man's beady eyes widened, and he let out a scoffing sound. "I beg your pardon?"

"Is it possible that someone wished Sir Thomas harm? That he didn't throw himself off the cliff, but rather was pushed off?"

He crossed his arms over his broad chest and stared at her, cocking his head, and raising a single eyebrow. "Who are *you* to question this matter? Are you a relation of the deceased?"

"No, sir, but my godmother is Sir Thomas's sister. She is curious about what happened to him, and so am I. And as I said, Miss Fallbrook—"

Mr. Beardsley interrupted, his face growing red. "Every morning, I'm up at dawn, running this shop that feeds half the village. But the magistrate had to appoint *me* to this execrable, unpaid position where I'm expected, in my spare time, to not only prevent and solve crimes in the parish but catch rats; impound stray farm animals; attend inquests; collect taxes; keep order in the ale house; whip beggars, vagabonds, and drunks; and punish poachers, fathers of bastards, and church-avoiders. Do I shirk my duty? No, I do not. If a man's been murdered, I do my best to find out by whom and why. But *this* was no murder. It was suicide. I saw the note myself. I saw Sir Thomas's broken body lying in a heap at the base of those cliffs. He killed himself, for sure and certain. Case closed." As if breathing fire, he whirled and stomped out of the room without a backward glance.

Diana stood blushing in his wake. She turned to go, but Mrs. Beardsley motioned with her hand for Diana to stay.

"I don't blame you, miss, for being troubled about this, on account of poor Miss Fallbrook." Leaning over the counter, she added confidentially, "Between you and me, Mr. Beardsley may not always do as thorough a job with these things as he might. Get it over with as quick as can be and back to the shop, that's his method."

Grateful for the woman's reassurance, Diana replied just as quietly, "What do you think happened, Mrs. Beardsley?"

She shrugged. "Perhaps someone did have a grudge against Sir Thomas and forged that note, as you say. But then you can't discount the other theory."

"What other theory?"

"The Mermaid's Curse. Sir Thomas married his daughter's governess, didn't he?"

Not that again.

Before Diana could reply, the postmistress continued with enthusiasm.

"Morwenna still haunts that house and these very seas. Why, Mr. Pritchard, one of our fishermen, was out in his boat one morning when she popped up right in front of him, hovering in the air as large as life. Startled him so much, he nearly fell overboard! Morwenna bides her time, watching every new master and governess, waiting for the next transgression. If she wants her pound of flesh, she'll have it."

Suddenly, as if aware of to whom she was speaking, Mrs. Beardsley bit her lip and added, "Mind you, Miss Taylor, don't go falling in love with the new master, will you?"

THE VICARAGE WAS a crumbling, ivy-covered stone cottage situated on one of the lower streets of the fishing village, not too distant from the wharf. Diana knocked on the front door, hoping to find Mr. Wainwright at home. She had written to him a month ago, reminding him of their mutual connection and letting him know that she had accepted a position at Pendowar Hall.

The housekeeper informed Diana that the curate was not in but could be found in his study at the church. The house of worship, an ancient stone structure that had been battered by weather and blackened by time, stood across from the vicarage, beyond a weedy graveyard enclosed by a wrought-iron fence. Diana found a side door and knocked.

A moment passed. The door opened. A tall man dressed in the black garb of the clergy glanced out.

Diana had only met Marcus Wainwright once, when he and her brother had been in their last year at Oxford, and Diana had been visiting that city. Although he had filled out since then, he was still attractive, with eyes that were a lustrous shade of brown. Diana couldn't hold back a smile. It was so nice to see a familiar face.

"May I help you?"

"Forgive me for calling on you without warning, Mr. Wainwright. I expect I shall see you in church on Sunday, but as I was in the area—"

"Miss Taylor!" Mr. Wainwright gave a gasp of pleasure and recognition and, thrusting out both hands, clasped hers within his own. "How wonderful to see you! I've been hoping you would call. Do, come in."

She followed him into the small office, which was crammed with heavy mahogany furniture buried beneath piles of books, magazines, paperwork, and knickknacks. Sunlight filtered in weakly through a dusty window, as if desperately struggling to cheer up the space.

"Pray, forgive the state of my office." Mr. Wainwright chuckled as he cleared off a stack of reading material from a chair and unceremoniously deposited it elsewhere. "I have so many calls upon my time, I never seem to get around to tidying up. There you go. I can offer you a clean place to sit at least. And a cup of tea, although to my regret, I am out of biscuits."

"A cup of tea will do very nicely, thank you." Diana took the vacant chair. The curate poured out two cups from a pot hiding under a knitted cozy, handed her one, and sat down behind the desk.

"So! Here you are. Exactly as I remember you from that day we spent together at Oxford."

"You are kind to say so, sir, but idle flattery will get you nowhere. You, on the other hand, have not changed much at all."

"Oh, but I have, I have. I am ten years older, and I feel every minute of it. *My* observation, however, was genuine. You look very well. I hope you *are* well and happy?"

"I am." The tea was pale and nearly tasteless. Diana suspected he had been obliged to reuse old leaves. "I hope the same for you, Mr. Wainwright?"

"I am content, Miss Taylor. I am only a curate—the vicar rarely makes an appearance and leaves every duty to me—but I am ever so grateful to Mrs. Phillips for recommending me for this position. And to Sir Thomas, God rest his soul, for hiring me. My time here has been fulfilling."

"I am happy to hear it. My godmother said I would be glad to have a friend in the district and how right she was."

"I cannot tell you how many times your brother mentioned you and your sisters over the years. It's strange, isn't it, that I have never met Miss Athena and Miss Selena? Every time I visited Damon, you were all living elsewhere. How are they?"

"Fine, I believe. They are both working as governesses at present, in Yorkshire and Lancashire."

"And here you are in Cornwall, doing similar good work. I hope it is not selfish of me to say I'm glad you came." He set down his teacup. "How is Damon? It has been ages since I had a letter from him."

"Me, as well." She adored her brother and missed him dearly. "He is so devoted to his parishioners, he rarely takes a moment for himself, much less to write a letter."

"My hat is off to him. I daresay I should never have the nerve to work in the East End of London, what some call 'the worst slum in Europe.' But your brother holds himself to a very high standard."

"He always has."

"I believe myself to be extremely dedicated to my labors—but everyone deserves to have a personal life as well. To this day, your brother considers me too frivolous."

"Surely not, Mr. Wainwright."

"Oh, but he does. I know he does." The curate gave his head a light shake. "In our early days at Oxford, we came to verbal blows over the subject too many times to count. But the university, in its great wisdom, had placed us in a room together, and despite ourselves, we were forced to associate. In time, we found subjects over which we connected, and this built the foundation for our friendship."

"Damon once made a similar observation when he spoke of you."

"Did he? It occurs to me," Mr. Wainwright mused, "that one of the points of connection he and I share is something I also share with you."

"What is that, sir?"

"I lost my mother at a young age."

"Oh—I am sorry to hear it."

"My father passed a few years later. I was raised by an aunt and uncle in Plymouth."

"I hope they provided well for you?"

"They did their best. But they had a house full of children of their own. When I was eleven years old, I gained the respect of the rector in our parish, who financed my education."

"A fortunate acquaintance."

"It is circumstances like these which shape us, I think. We are obliged to grow up more quickly than children who are privileged to have a mother's constant devotion and guidance."

"I know what you mean, sir."

"Remind me. How old were you when your mother died?"

"Seven."

"So young." His mouth curved down in sympathy. "Damon told me that, even as a child, you began managing the household straightaway."

"I did."

"That is a great deal of responsibility for shoulders so small."

"I survived. So did you. And that is all in the past now."

"Perhaps. Perhaps not. Sometimes, these events of childhood haunt us into adulthood."

"Thankfully, I do not feel haunted by ..." Diana's voice trailed off. *No*, she thought. The weight that burdened her was not resentment over childhood duties after her mother's death. It was her part in *causing* that death. Her head felt light as the memory of that day came rushing back, along with all the pain, guilt, and self-recrimination that always accompanied it.

"Are you unwell, Miss Taylor?"

She looked up to find Mr. Wainwright observing her closely, his eyebrows knit together.

"Not at all. I was just ... I was thinking of my pupil, Miss Emma Fallbrook," she lied. "Are you acquainted with her?"

"I know she is Sir Thomas's daughter. I have seen her at church."

"Her situation is similar to what you described. She lost her mother at birth, and now her father is gone."

"My heart goes out to her."

His remark mirrored Diana's own sentiments and was a good opening for the questions on her mind. She placed her empty teacup on his desk. "Mr. Wainwright. I need to ask you something. It might seem impertinent, but I assure you I have good reason for asking it."

"Go on."

"Did Sir Thomas ever speak to you about his feelings on the issue of suicide?"

He stiffened slightly, then went quiet, toying with a letter opener on his desk. "He did come to see me a few times," he said at last. "But I'm afraid our conversations are a private matter."

"I understand. But ..." Diana explained her concerns about both Miss Fallbrook and Mrs. Phillips. "If you know something that might ease their suffering, I should be grateful to hear it."

"Miss Taylor ..." He shook his head.

"I've spoken to the parish constable," Diana persisted. "He's convinced that Sir Thomas took his own life. Case closed. And yet, Sir Thomas's butler and valet, Mr. Emity, seems equally convinced that the baronet would have never done himself harm. That he felt suicide was a sin. You knew him, Mr. Wainwright. Was that true?"

The curate set down the letter opener and sat in silent deliberation.

"The man is gone now," Diana added earnestly. "Anything you tell me cannot hurt him."

He sighed and said, "All right, Miss Taylor. For Miss Fallbrook's sake, and Mrs. Phillips's, I shall tell you what you wish to know. It's true. Sir Thomas confided his fervent belief that life is a gift and suicide is an act against God. When I heard the news that he had taken his own life, I was much surprised—not only because of that, but for another reason as well."

"What other reason?"

He looked at her solemnly across the desk. "It was Sir Thomas's dearest wish to be buried in the churchyard one day beside his wife and son. He arranged with me in advance for a plot for that very purpose. Taking his own life would have made that goal impossible—as it indeed has—and he surely knew it."

CHAPTER NINE

D IANA DREAMT THAT night of the footbridge across the river. Sir Thomas was standing at the rail, a feverish glint in his eyes, as if he meant to throw himself into the rapidly flowing waters.

"Sir, do not do it!" Diana cried.

She raced to the bridge, but when she got there, he said calmly, "Suicide is a sin, young lady. I would never commit such a desperate act."

At which point she awakened with a start.

The dream felt so real, it kept Diana awake half the night. Her mind spun with all that she had learned over the past few days. Mrs. Phillips's assertion resounded in her brain:

He was a strong, determined man with high principles. He was not the type who would take his own life.

Diana had come to Pendowar Hall to prove her godmother wrong. She'd hoped that learning the reason behind Sir Thomas's tragic act of suicide would at least set the good woman's mind at rest.

But would a man so set against self-destruction—a man who wished to spend eternity in the churchyard beside a beloved wife and child—have truly killed himself?

Sir Thomas's body had been discovered at the base of the cliffs. Captain Fallbrook had found a suicide note, which implied it was no accident—but did not absolutely prove that it was suicide. Sir Thomas's early morning walks were apparently a daily ritual. If someone had wanted Sir Thomas dead, they could have followed him or, knowing his typical route, hidden in the shrubbery by the outcropping, pushed him to his death, and forged a note to cover their tracks.

Who would do such a thing? And why? It occurred to Diana that, perhaps, she should not eliminate the captain as a suspect. He'd had motive and opportunity, after all, and he'd been the one who had 'found' the note. *But no. No.* Although she had only spent one evening in the captain's company, something told her that he couldn't possibly be culpable of such a crime.

When dawn broke, Diana rose, dressed, and went downstairs to the great hall, where she stopped and stared up at Sir Thomas's portrait.

"What happened to you?" she whispered to the empty room. "Please tell me. Help me to help my godmother. And your daughter."

There came no answer.

Diana sighed in disappointment. She wished she could speak to Captain Fallbrook about this, but she had not seen him for several days.

On her morning walk, she encountered Mr. Nankervis weeding a grove of palm trees. Diana stopped to admire the graceful wave of the fronds in the breeze.

"Ye're up early, miss," said he.

"As are you." She smiled. "Do you know, I never saw a palm tree in person before I came to Pendowar Hall."

"They be a rare sight in this country, to be sure," the gardener replied, "but they do well in these parts. Captain Fallbrook sent them back ten years ago from his travels—a gift for the baronet. Small trees they were at the time, but they've grown like weeds."

"What a kind gesture."

"The captain *is* kind, miss. And easy to work for. When he took over, he said, 'I'm no expert when it comes to gardening. Just keep up with what ye've been doing, and I'll thank ye for it.'"

Diana was still irritated with Captain Fallbrook for his indifferent attitude towards Miss Fallbrook, but this report spoke well of his character. "I hope Sir Thomas was an equally gracious employer?"

Mr. Nankervis hesitated. "If I'm honest, miss, my old master were a good man, but ... he wanted things done *his* way. If it weren't done to his satisfaction, he let ye know about it. Got very particular in his last few years."

Did such an attitude create resentment among his workers and tenants? Diana wondered. "From what I can see, you've been doing a marvelous job."

"Thank ye, miss."

Another thought occurred to her. "Mr. Nankervis, it has come to my attention that Sir Thomas was not buried in the churchyard. Does he perchance lie here on the grounds?"

"He does, miss."

"Where might I find his grave?"

"In the white garden." He pointed. "It be the last walled garden just before ye reach the river."

"Thank you kindly."

He tipped his cap.

Diana found the designated spot—a rectangular-shaped garden with a gurgling fountain, narrow pebble paths, and leafy beds enclosed by tall hedgerows. She paused uncertainly at the entrance. Captain Fallbrook, his hands resting upon his cane, stood within, in solemn meditation before a marble headstone that sprouted from a small lawn.

Diana was about to leave when the captain turned.

"Miss Taylor. Good morning."

"I beg your pardon, Captain. I have no wish to disturb you. I shall go."

"I was just paying my respects to my uncle, but I am quite at liberty. Join me."

It was more a command than an invitation. But she did work for him, after all. And she wanted to speak with him.

Crossing to the captain's side, Diana studied the headstone.

IN MEMORY OF
SIR THOMAS EPHRAIM FALLBROOK
FOURTH BART. OF PORTWITHYS
BORN 18 FEBRUARY 1790
DIED 10 JUNE 1849
IN HIS FIFTY-NINTH YEAR
A DEVOTED HUSBAND AND FATHER
A LIFE WELL-LIVED
MAY HE REST IN PEACE

"What a fine testimonial," Diana remarked.

"I hope my uncle would find it so." The captain seemed to be in a better mood than he had been the last time they had conversed. "This was one of his favorite spots on the estate. After he …" His brow creased. "Since the churchyard was out of the question, I hoped he would find this an acceptable resting place."

"It is a lovely garden."

"You should see it in spring and summer. He only allowed plants with white flowers here. It is an impressive sight."

"I imagine so. Do you come here often?"

"I try. Did the rounds first thing every morning aboard ship."

"It must be very different for you now." As the words left Diana's lips, blood rushed to her cheeks. She could see in his expression how her comment might be misconstrued. "I only meant," she added quickly, "it must be very different to walk in a garden rather than on the deck of a ship."

He nodded. "There is nothing quite so bracing as the wind in your face on the deck of a ninety-eight-gun ship of the line. But I also enjoy the dew on the grass and the chorus of birds in the trees." He tapped his lame leg with his cane. "It has, admittedly, been difficult of late. My doctor insists that exercise is vital to a full recovery, though, so …" He gestured to a nearby wrought-iron bench. "Sit with me for a moment?"

Again, it felt like a command, not a request. But Diana did as bid, taking a seat as Captain Fallbrook maneuvered his lanky frame onto the bench beside her. It was impossible not to be affected by the pain on his features as he stretched out his bad leg in front of him.

"May I ask how you were injured, Captain?"

"Took a bullet in the thigh last spring as we boarded a pirate vessel. It was touch-and-go for a while there. I spent a couple of months in a Royal Navy hospital and nearly lost the leg."

"How fortunate that you did not."

"I owe a debt of gratitude to the surgeon who removed the bullet, for not chopping it off then and there—and to the nurses who looked after me when the thing got infected. My first month at home I was still stuck in a wheeled chair. Damn nuisance. Forgive my language. I have spent too many years at sea."

"I will not faint at a coarse word or two. I have taught several boys. And I have a brother."

"What does he do?"

"He is a clergyman in London."

"I like London." His voice softened and a pensive smile lit his face. "I wish I could visit more often. But I have spent the better part of my life in the Mediterranean."

"How thrilling it must be to sail from port to port." Diana grinned in return. "Do you have a favorite?"

"There is something unique and memorable about them all. I enjoyed Athens. And I have fond memories of Naples." He glanced at her. "You remind me of a lady I once met there. She had your smile." He went quiet at that, as if absorbed in thought.

His comment brought Mrs. Gwynn's warning to mind—"*a woman in every port.*" "What happened to her?"

"I have no idea."

And there it was. *A man this handsome,* Diana thought, *no doubt broke hearts across the Mediterranean.* "I envy you your travels. I should love to see Mt. Vesuvius, the Acropolis, and the Parthenon."

"Perhaps you shall someday." The sound of birdsong filled

the air. "Does your brother enjoy his work?"

"He does. He is full of energy and devotion, determined to improve the lot of humanity."

"'Choose a job you love ...'" the captain began, and she finished with him, "'... and you will never have to work a day in your life.'"

"You have read Confucius." He sounded astonished.

"He is one of many brilliant philosophers I admire, along with Aristotle and John Locke."

The captain glanced at her, wide-eyed. "I've never met a woman who read philosophy."

"More women would, if school curriculums included it for girls and universities would open their doors to them."

"Did you attend school?"

"For a few years. Primarily, my sisters and I educated ourselves."

"How?"

"In my mother's library."

"Your *mother's* library?"

"My father was a traditional landed gentleman, fond of shooting and farming and such. My mother was different. She loved to read, studied a great deal, and encouraged her children from infancy to do the same. She died when I was young, but I insisted that my siblings and I continue the practice on our own."

Captain Fallbrook shook his head slightly. "You are indeed a most unusual and remarkable woman, Miss Taylor."

"I am not so remarkable, Captain. But I am fortunate—as Confucius would say—to have work that I love."

"As am I."

Under his scrutiny, Diana's cheeks grew warm. To her surprise, she was enjoying his company. A connection seemed to be forming between them.

No sooner had she recognized this, however, than her guard went up. She would not, could not, allow herself to be attracted to this man. For one thing, he was her employer. Diana and

Captain Fallbrook were not of different stations—Diana was the daughter of a gentleman—but still, it would not do.

For another, the captain had a *reputation*.

"Handsome is as handsome does, Miss Taylor ... A leopard doesn't change his spots."

Captain Fallbrook was the last sort of man in whom Diana would be interested—*if* she were interested in a man. Which she was not. She had been down that road twice, and both times it had ended badly. She would never risk her heart again. Men were rarely what they seemed. They kept secrets.

What secrets were Captain Fallbrook hiding?

Is it a coincidence that Captain Fallbrook came home on leave just a few days before Thomas died?

A tiny voice in the back of Diana's mind once again prodded, *what if Mrs. Phillips's accusations had merit?* When the captain had said he'd never wanted Pendowar Hall, could it have been a cover story? Again, Diana told herself, *No.* She couldn't believe that. He seemed to be a good and honorable man.

She was struggling to find a way to direct the conversation back to Sir Thomas, when he said, "So: how goes it with Emma?"

"I have begun a new course of instruction. She is working hard."

"Good. I wish you luck."

"Thank you. Captain, may I make another observation about Miss Fallbrook? Something unrelated to her education?"

"You may."

"She looks up to you."

"To me? I think not. She hardly knows me."

"That can be rectified. Miss Fallbrook told me of a gift you once gave her: a little horse carved from wood."

He puzzled over that. Then the memory seemed to come back to him. "Ah, yes. Picked it up in Sicily, as I recall."

"She treasures that figurine. She has made a whole collection of animals of clay to keep it company."

"Has she? Who would have thought?"

"Miss Fallbrook has never known a mother's love. Now, her father is gone as well. You are the only adult in her life. I suspect that she craves your affection and approval, Captain. If you could find a way to pay her more attention, I know it would mean a great deal to her."

"More attention, eh?" He studied his hands, seemingly uncomfortable. "Duly noted."

"There is something else that worries me. It concerns the manner of her father's death." She explained the problem: that Miss Fallbrook felt abandoned, believed her father had killed himself out of grief over his wife and son, and if that were true, what did it say about his feelings for her?

"You mean how could he leave his only daughter, so cruelly and definitively, in the care of no one but a disabled cousin?"

"I did not mean ..."

"Facts are facts, Miss Taylor." His tone was bitter.

"You are not disabled, Captain. You can walk. And you said yourself, your wound is on the mend."

"So, it seems. But as for the rest ..." He frowned. "Uncle Thomas *did* kill himself and leave Emma in the lurch."

Diana looked him squarely in the eyes. "Did he?"

"I beg your pardon?"

"Is it certain that your uncle committed suicide? Or is it possible that his death might be attributed to another cause?"

His blue eyes flashed. The good will that had been building between them vanished in an instant, as if the air had been let out of a balloon. "What are you saying? Do you wonder if my uncle killed himself for a different reason? Or are you implying he was *pushed* off that cliff?"

Diana hesitated. "Either, I suppose. But—"

"The answer to the first question is: I don't know. As for the second: *unequivocally, no.* My uncle left a suicide note on his desk."

"What did the note say?"

"It was short and to the point: *I cannot go on.* And he signed his name."

"That is short, indeed. Might the note have been forged?"

"I know my uncle's hand as well as I do my own," he snapped.

"And yet isn't it possible that someone familiarized themselves with his handwriting, inscribed those four words, and found a way to drop the note on his desk?"

He stared at her. "A wild speculation, Miss Taylor. What on Earth propels your interest in such a morbid subject?"

Diana realized that she had angered him and was sorry for it, but having brought up the subject, felt compelled to go on—and, despite Mrs. Phillips's warning, to tell him the truth.

"It was ... your aunt."

"My aunt?"

"Mrs. Phillips, my godmother. She asked me to come to Pendowar Hall not only to teach Miss Fallbrook, but also because ... the circumstances of her brother's death did not sit well with her. She asked me to look into it."

His jaw dropped. "Aunt Eliza sent you to *spy* on me?"

"I wouldn't call it *spying*," Diana returned quickly, and less than truthfully, "but—"

"What else would you call it?" He huffed out a sharp breath. "This is unconscionable. I ought to terminate your employment here and now, Miss Taylor."

"I hope you won't, Captain. I think highly of Miss Fallbrook and want to help her if I can."

"Do you?"

"Yes! And with regard to the other matter ... I think your aunt may have a point."

One dark eyebrow arched imperiously. "You think my uncle might have been murdered?"

"I think it's possible."

Silence fell. He still looked incredulous. Finally, he said, "Enlighten me."

Diana shared what Mrs. Gwynn had told her about Sir Thomas's plans to build a play area as a memorial to his wife and son, as well as Mr. Emity's and Mr. Wainwright's assertions about Sir Thomas's aversion to suicide, and his wish to be buried in the churchyard.

The captain frowned. "My uncle never mentioned a play area. As to the rest … I knew about the latter, but not the former." Irritably, he added, "But that proves nothing. People behave in odd and unexpected ways when they're depressed. I once had an officer under my command, a good man with a wife and three children in Bristol, who professed similar beliefs about suicide. And yet one morning at sea, he threw himself off the bridge. I shall always wonder why."

"I am sorry for him and for his widow and children."

"So am I." He glanced away. "In June, when I came home, I sensed my uncle was upset about something. I was in such a dark mood myself, we did not speak much. One night, though, he brought up Aunt Sylvia's and Robert's deaths in such a way, that …" His features tightened with remorse. "I did not understand the depths of his dejection until it was too late. I should have guessed, however. I saw him writing in his journal more often than usual."

"Your uncle kept a journal?"

"A whole series of them, dating back to the days when I visited Pendowar Hall on holiday as a boy and whenever I came home on leave from sea."

"Have you read his journals?"

"Never."

Diana sat up straighter. "The most recent one might give insight into his state of mind at the time of his death."

"I am aware," he shot back. "But I don't know where he kept them. Neither does Emity. I suppose Uncle Thomas didn't want his private thoughts to be read by anyone but himself."

"The journals must be *somewhere* in the house."

"I have made a thorough investigation of the most likely places he would have stored them—his bedroom, the blue parlor, his study—but found nothing."

"Perhaps I could help," Diana offered.

"Thank you but no, Miss Taylor. This is not your business."

"Two sets of eyes are often better than one."

"Keep your eyes on the job for which you were hired: to look after my cousin. And forget this ridiculous notion about my uncle."

"But, Captain. If Sir Thomas wasn't depressed … if he was worried about something or *someone* … if he feared he was in any kind of danger … his morning walking route was apparently well known, and—"

"Miss Taylor," he said, interrupting, "I've never met my aunt Eliza, but she has clearly let her imagination run away with her—and so have you. She sent you on a fool's errand." Checking his pocket watch, Captain Fallbrook labored to his feet. "I must take my leave. I have a meeting with my steward, and you have a pupil to teach. Pray direct your attention to that and stay out of matters that do not concern you. Good day."

CHAPTER TEN

A WEEK PASSED. In subjects that were taught orally, Miss Fallbrook excelled. She conversed well in French, could name all the countries on the globe in Europe and Asia, and could recall a wealth of facts about the natural and scientific world. She was adept and creative when it came to needlework and, although she could not read music, she could dance and sing well, and she played the piano by ear with skill and enthusiasm.

To Diana's regret, however, Miss Fallbrook still did not comprehend the purpose of the alphabet or how it related to the reading process. Diana tried every trick she could think of to help her pupil recognize letters and remember their sounds, but nothing stuck. Her puzzling habit of, on occasion, writing letters backwards or upside down continued.

Diana was discouraged. If she couldn't teach the girl to read and write, what did that say about her tutoring skills? Every time she looked in the mirror, Diana felt like a failure … and a fraud. Every morning, she checked the post, awaiting a letter from Professor Vaughan, hoping he could provide insight into Miss Fallbrook's case, but no answer came.

In the meantime, when Diana ate her solitary meals, visited the gardens, walked the cliff path, or lay in bed on the verge of sleep, her mind worked on the puzzling circumstances of Sir Thomas's demise.

The baronet's suicide note had been so brief. *"I cannot go on."*

What did that mean exactly? *Why* couldn't he go on? What if he hadn't even written that note?

Captain Fallbrook had ridiculed her suspicions and told her to mind her own business. *"People behave in odd and unexpected ways when they are depressed,"* he'd said.

Maybe he was right. Maybe Mrs. Phillips *had* sent Diana on a futile mission.

Diana wrote to her godmother, apprising her of everything she had learned and sharing her doubts and concerns. She wrote similarly to Athena and Selena, adding her worry that her godmother's fears had become so embedded in Diana's mind that all she could see now was murder.

One morning, three letters arrived. The first was a short note from Mrs. Phillips.

Rose Cottage, Yorkshire

Dearest Diana,

You are on the right track. You will get to the bottom of both of these mysteries—one about my niece and one about my brother.
   You are a clever woman. Keep at it.

All my love and thanks,
Eliza Phillips

The second letter was from her sister Athena.

Seven Gables, Yorkshire

My dearest Diana,

Forgive my tardy reply to your letters. My work here requires my every waking moment. By day, when I am not struggling to keep my two charges out of trouble, I endeavor to cram some morsel of learning into their reluctant brains. Every evening until bedtime, I am obliged to sew by the light of a single candle for Mrs. Baldwin, until my eyes fall out. In addition to hemming endless bedsheets and tablecloths and serviettes, would you believe, the dreadful woman has me sewing clothes for the girls' dolls?

I dream of the day when you and I and Selena can be the masters of our own universe, start our school for girls, and choose the pupils we admit to it. How heavenly that would be! By the by, I discovered the ideal house for such a venture, Thorndale Manor, only six miles away. It is an ancient building with lovely grounds, just the right size, and by all accounts has enough bedrooms for us and a handful of servants and ten or eleven pupils, if they share a room.

I accompanied my mistress and her daughters to an estate sale there last week (my presence naturally required in case the little darlings became unruly). It seems the owner has fallen into such bad financial straits that he must sell off many of his possessions and will soon be obliged to unload the entire property. I realize we could never in our wildest dreams ever afford such a place—which is a shame, for the house has the most thrilling reputation. It is said that a murderess once lived there. How exciting it would be to live in such a place! Hopefully, prospective students and their parents would find its history equally enthralling, rather than frightening. The fantasy of owning Thorndale Manor persists and brings me fleeting moments of joy. Meanwhile (can you hear my sigh?), we must soldier on.

Enough about me. I must say, I found your descriptions of Pendowar Hall delightful. How I should love to visit Cornwall! Captain Fallbrook sounds like an interesting man. However, I perceive, from what you wrote, that Miss Fallbrook has more serious learning difficulties than you anticipated. You questioned whether you are up to the task. This admission worries me.

My dearest Diana: you are an excellent, thoughtful, and insightful instructress. When I struggled with our German lessons last year, how patient you were with me! I think back with deep fondness on all our discussions of the great works of literature over the years. Your enthusiasm for your subject is and always has been infectious. The role of teacher fits you to a

"T." (Do you see the joke I made there? Ha ha.) I have always looked up to you. You are so good at everything you do, and you are far more perceptive than me. Whatever is holding your pupil back, in time, you will comprehend its nature and rise to meet it. I know it!

As for the other matters … have you forgotten Mama's old saying: 'where there is smoke, there is fire'? It sounds as though Mrs. Phillips knew what she was talking about. Do not doubt yourself!

With all my love,
Athena

The third letter was from Selena.

Gisborne Park, Lancashire

My dearest Diana,

Hello, sister dear! I think of you often and miss the daily conversations we shared during those precious months together at home, after Papa died. We have a long history of communicating via this method, however, during all the years we have been obliged to live apart. Sharing my thoughts in print and receiving yours in return is the closest thing I have to the pleasure of your company, so please indulge me if I babble on.

How fortunate you are to be in Cornwall at this time of year. To think that a Mediterranean climate exists in England, where tropical plants and palm trees flourish! It is such a departure from all that we have known. The skies here have been grey and stormy. The mistress constantly moans and groans about an ill wind that blows no good. But I love everything about the autumn—the chill in the air, the frost on the ground, the glorious colors of the leaves—and I adore the wind. It's fresh and clean and revives my spirits, no matter how low they may sink.

You asked how I am faring, and my answer is: as well as can be expected. The children have started riding lessons, which allows me a blissful hour of freedom two mornings a week. I subscribed to a circulating library and save my pennies to borrow as many titles as I can afford. Thank you for recommending The Count of Monte Cristo by Alexandre Dumas. I didn't feel confident enough to read it in the original French, as you did, but I found a new English translation and I was absolutely enthralled. It is phenomenal, unlike anything I have ever read before, and such a grand adventure!

Speaking of adventure, it sounds as though you are having one yourself. (The most exciting thing that has happened to me of late was when young Master Ambrose dumped his glass of lemonade down the front of my frock just moments before the vicar came to call. Whether or not this was a deliberate act, I leave for you to judge.) I know you were skeptical about Mrs. Phillips's reason for sending you to Pendowar Hall. Now you mention footsteps in the night, a flashing light in a distant tower, a curious legend about a mermaid, and unexpected circumstances regarding the former master's death. You wonder if you're onto something, or if these things are a series of coincidences.

I know my natural tendency is, as you keep pointing out, to see the best in everything. I still believe that in most cases, things will work themselves out perfectly well if left alone. However, I feel differently about your situation. It puts me in mind of our new favorite novel, Jane Eyre. While serving at Thornfield Hall, Jane also encountered strange circumstances, and was beset by doubts. Critical truths were kept from her, yet Jane blindly trusted Mr. Rochester and accepted all that she was told. This naivete on her part led to a near-criminal act, a breaking apart of all that she held dear—and it very nearly cost Jane her life.

I urge you, Diana, not to make the same mistakes Jane did. You have, my dear sister, a superior mind. I saw it at work all those years ago, when you and Athena and I called ourselves the Sisterhood of Smoke and Fire. We were determined to leave no stone unturned in our "criminal investigations." I know it was mostly childish nonsense—then. But things are different now.

It is in your nature to question things. Mama's words still hold true. If you believe something is amiss at Pendowar Hall, *then perhaps it is. Trust your instincts. All legends have a foundation in truth. Seek the truth before it comes back to haunt you—or harm you.*

Your loving sister,
Selena

Diana read all three letters through a second time, and then a third.

As she paced back and forth in the schoolroom, her godmother's and sisters' words echoed in her brain:

"You are on the right track. You will get to the bottom of both of these mysteries—one about my niece and one about my brother ... Keep at it."

"Have you forgotten Mama's old saying: 'where there is smoke, there is fire'?"

"It sounds as though Mrs. Phillips knew what she was talking about. Do not doubt yourself!"

"If you believe something is amiss at Pendowar Hall, then perhaps it is."

The captain thought Diana's worries were groundless. The parish constable had closed Sir Thomas's case and would clearly never look into it again. But Diana had a gut feeling that her godmother was right. Someone had murdered the baronet and gotten away with it.

Diana recalled her one meeting with Sir Thomas Fallbrook when she'd been a little girl and he'd come to visit Mrs. Phillips. He had been kind. She had come to care about his daughter and was beginning to respect his nephew, two people who were both deeply hurt by the man's purported suicide.

If Sir Thomas had *not* died by his own hand, and it could be proven, it would controvert Miss Fallbrook's idea that her father had deserted her. Either possibility—suicide or murder—would be painful to learn. And yet, wasn't it better to know the truth? If the taint of suicide were removed, the baronet's body could be reburied in consecrated ground, which would no doubt be a great relief to Miss Fallbrook... and perhaps to the captain as well. If

Diana was successful, whatever she uncovered could bring a criminal to justice.

Moreover, Diana had promised to find the truth and report it to Mrs. Phillips. How could she let her godmother down?

Mrs. Phillips only had months to live. Diana must get to the bottom of this mystery. And fast.

To date, she had only asked questions. Now she must *act*. But where to start?

She thought of Sir Thomas's journals. He'd probably kept the most current volume close at hand. Captain Fallbrook had said he'd already searched his uncle's bedroom, the blue parlor, and the study.

How many times, though, had something of her own gone missing—a glove, a handkerchief, an article of clothing—only to turn up months later after repeated searches, in a location she had already checked several times?

The captain simply had not looked hard enough. That journal was somewhere inside this house—Diana felt it in her bones.

She was going to find it.

DIANA'S PULSE HAMMERED with anxiety as she slipped past the first-floor gallery.

Miss Fallbrook was practicing at the grand piano in the music room downstairs. Captain Fallbrook was making the rounds of the property on horseback. The staff was on the basement level, engaged in late afternoon chores or preparing supper. They would not come up to the first floor again until the captain's and Miss Fallbrook's beds needed to be turned down and their fires stoked for the night.

Even so, Diana's nerves were on edge.

The captain had made it clear that he didn't want her prying into this. Diana didn't want to upset him further, but she had to follow through. This morning—fishing for a clue as to where Sir Thomas might have kept his journals—Diana had casually asked Ivy if she'd ever seen Sir Thomas writing in a journal.

"No, miss," the maid had replied, "but then I wouldn't've, would I? The master and I didn't often cross paths. 'Stay out of sight and keep yer head down,' Mrs. Gwynn always says. 'The master likes his staff invisible.' Cleaning his rooms, that were Hester's province. I just tended the master's fire and chamber pot, when he were out or fast asleep."

Diana had decided to begin her search in Sir Thomas's bedroom. By now, she knew which chamber had belonged to him. Pausing in the hallway, her hand on the doorknob, Diana checked to ensure that she was unobserved. She would have to do this quickly and quietly.

The handle turned. Diana slipped within, shutting the door behind her. It was a good-sized chamber, but the air felt close, as if it had not been entered in some time.

A marble hearth stood cold and empty. The heavy, velvet draperies were closed, but late afternoon sun filtered in around the edges, providing just enough light to see. Handsome, carved mahogany furniture filled the space; plush, Turkish carpets covered the floors; and oil paintings enlivened the walls. There was no closet.

Diana started with the writing desk. The drawers contained only blank paper, writing instruments, and an assortment of personal items.

As Diana glanced over the contents, guilt washed over her. What right did she have to see these things—the possessions of a man who had passed away? She almost left there and then. But she reminded herself her intentions were worthy. She must press on.

Diana checked behind the curtains on the four-poster bed and looked beneath the mattress. Finding nothing, she examined the other furnishings, then moved into the adjoining dressing room. The wardrobe was filled with a gentleman's wear: finely made frock coats, waistcoats, and pantaloons. It didn't surprise her that no one had yet disposed of the baronet's clothing. Although her own father had passed away more than a year ago, she and her sisters had not had the heart to donate the contents of his wardrobe to the poor until recently.

A succession of hat boxes and neatly folded neckties and cravats took up an entire shelf. Diana checked the boxes. They contained only hats.

The only other piece of furniture was a tall, elegant, mahogany chest of drawers. Its main drawers contained more assorted clothing, accessories, and personal items. Only three small drawers at the top of the chest remained. Diana glanced inside each one in turn.

A Bible occupied the first drawer. The second held pamphlets about flowering plants and the gardens of Cornwall. Diana slid open the final drawer. A tray within held a gold watch and other masculine jewelry. Diana's stomach sank. There was no journal here.

Another item, however, caught her eye: a metal ring holding a set of keys.

Most were ordinary brass household keys, but some were larger and heavier and made of iron. *Could one of these keys*, Diana wondered, *fit the lock in the north tower door?*

The soft, rhythmic patter of footfalls against carpet echoed in the hallway. Diana's breath caught. She heard Mrs. Gwynn talking to a maid. What if they entered the room to clean? What excuse could she give for being here?

Pulse pounding, Diana shut the drawer, leaving the keys within, and glanced about for a hiding place. She considered slipping inside the wardrobe—but to her relief, the women passed by. Mrs. Gwynn's voice grew fainter until it faded away.

Returning to her own chamber, Diana leaned against the door, her heart still drumming in her ears. She hadn't found Sir Thomas's journals, but there were other places to look. However, she may have—quite literally—found the key to the mystery of the north tower.

The next time a light shone from that window, Diana knew exactly what she would do.

CHAPTER ELEVEN

Charlbury House, Oxford

My dear Miss Taylor,

It is with great pleasure that I received your letter. Celeste and I shall always be grateful for the services you performed as Georgette's governess. You will be pleased to hear that Georgette is married now to an upstanding young gentleman in the banking profession. They are expecting their first child this spring.

As to your questions about the new pupil in your charge—I have taken into consideration all the information you provided. You say the girl has an excellent memory. Keep in mind that a dog can be taught to respond to oral commands, and a parrot can imitate sounds back at you. This is simply a reflex and not a sign of intelligence. As humans, we must rise above the level of the inhabitants of the animal kingdom.

If indeed, despite all attempts to teach her, at the age of fifteen, this young woman cannot recognize letters, read a simple word, or even properly write her name, then she is mentally defective. Do not blame yourself. The creature simply cannot be educated.

My advice is to persuade the girl's guardian to give her a season. My wife assures me that it is common for young ladies to marry at sixteen. Restrict her attention to the feminine accomplishments, which are all that matter to a prospective husband. If she is comely and has a fortune, she will find a good match.

Once this young lady is wed and focused on her womanly

duties—raising children and being a good wife—her husband will handle all her affairs and it will not matter that she cannot read or write.

With all best wishes,

Arthur Vaughan
Oxford University

Diana crumpled up the letter and threw it into the fire. What an insensitive and imbecilic response to her inquiry!

Miss Fallbrook was hardly "mentally defective." On the contrary: Diana was convinced that her pupil was highly intelligent.

And to suggest that Miss Fallbrook be married off at sixteen—to be dependent for life on her husband to read and write for her and handle her affairs! The notion went against every one of Diana's most deeply held principles. Even worse, perhaps, was the insinuation that Miss Fallbrook's only worth was her dowry—the financial assets she would bring to a marriage. *That* concept hit far too close to home.

Suddenly, she was eighteen years old again, whirling about the ballroom floor in her first waltz, in the arms of the handsome, young man who had captured her heart. Her entire life had lain before her, seemingly as rosy as her gown of fine shot silk. Until everything, and every belief she had held about herself and her worth, had come crashing down.

The pain of that betrayal had irrevocably changed her. She could not doom Miss Fallbrook to such a fate. Marriage might be in Miss Fallbrook's future. But if Diana had anything to say about it, her pupil's fortune would not define who she was, and her future happiness would not depend upon her securing a husband. She would have the necessary tools to lead a happy, productive, and independent life as a single woman if she so chose.

Diana didn't know why Miss Fallbrook couldn't read. But every riddle had a solution. She would solve this one. And she would not rest until she did.

HAVING SEARCHED SIR Thomas's bedroom for his journal without success, Diana turned her attention to the blue parlor, a room the captain said had been Sir Thomas's favorite.

She felt guilty exploring places that were not in her assigned domain. But Captain Fallbrook had said she might use the blue parlor in the evenings, or any other unoccupied room she chose, and had not specified a purpose. Taking advantage of the captain's absence—he was having dinner with Mr. Latimer, his solicitor—she made a thorough search of the parlor but found nothing resembling a diary or journal. And thankfully, she didn't get caught.

Once again, to Diana's frustration, Miss Fallbrook did not appear in the schoolroom the next morning. She was not in her bedroom, either. Diana put on her cloak and bonnet and went out in search of her.

It was a bright morning with just a hint of breeze, and the trees flaunted their autumn colors. Aware of Miss Fallbrook's fondness for seashells, Diana thought she might find her on the beach.

But Mr. Nankervis said, "I saw her not half an hour past down by the river, upstream from the old footbridge."

Diana found Miss Fallbrook standing calf-deep in a sheltered pool at the river's edge, her skirts hiked up and tucked in at her waist, her face, legs, and hands streaked with mud.

"Miss Fallbrook!" Diana cried. "What are you doing?"

"Digging for clay." Miss Fallbrook's cheeks bloomed with vitality and her eyes sparkled. "It's a good sort of clay, very pliable, the perfect kind to make things with." She rolled a ball of the natural clay between her palms into a sausage shape and, with a few deft twists, formed it into a rose sprouting from a stem.

Diana recalled the clay sculptures she'd seen in Miss Fallbrook's bedroom and couldn't help but be impressed. Still,

Diana had a job to do. "You were due in the schoolroom more than half an hour ago. Please leave that and come back to the house."

With an embittered sigh, Miss Fallbrook threw the clay flower into the river and did as she was told. By the time she'd gotten cleaned up and taken her place at her desk, most of the morning was gone. Diana had just begun their lesson when the captain appeared.

"Good morning." He stood awkwardly in the doorway, like a statue.

Diana didn't know what to make of it. Captain Fallbrook had never visited the schoolroom before. She and Miss Fallbrook, also evidently startled, returned his greeting. A silence fell.

Did the captain's appearance, Diana wondered, have anything to do with the request she had made, that he pay more attention to his ward? If so, he clearly had no idea how to go about it.

"All is well, I hope?" he managed at last.

"Very well, thank you," Diana replied.

"I trust my cousin is not giving you any more trouble, Miss Taylor? Did she arrive in the classroom this morning at nine on the dot as promised?"

Miss Fallbrook's eyes widened. She stared down at her desk.

"Miss Fallbrook is generally on time," Diana responded. It was the second white lie she had told on her pupil's behalf, but the girl was visibly anxious, and Diana didn't want to cause her any more distress. "She has been working very hard, sir."

"I am glad to hear it." He glanced at his cousin. "Otherwise, it's off to boarding school with you, eh?"

Miss Fallbrook picked at her fingernails but did not reply.

"Well, then, carry on." The captain vanished as quickly as he had arrived.

Only when his departing footsteps indicated that he was out of earshot did Miss Fallbrook let out a heavy sigh of relief. Pursing her lips, she said, "I suppose you didn't tell him because if I'm sent to boarding school, you'd be out of a job?"

"No, Miss Fallbrook. If I lose this job, I can find another."

"Then why ...?"

"I'm here to help you, if I can." *And to find out what happened to your father,* Diana wanted to add. But that was better left unsaid. "Captain Fallbrook doesn't need to know *everything* that goes on between us."

A mix of emotions took over Miss Fallbrook's face. Then she said quietly, "Thank you, Miss Taylor, for not saying anything about ... you know."

"You are most welcome."

DIANA WAS PASSING through the servants' hallway after returning from a late evening walk when she heard music coming from the butler's pantry.

Curious, she proceeded through the open doorway and discovered Mr. Emity within, playing a violin by candlelight. Diana didn't wish to intrude, but she was too entranced to walk away. Pausing outside the door, hidden, she hoped, from his view, she stood and listened.

Diana could not name the piece nor the composer. She only knew that the music was divine, and it carried her away. When the song ended, Mr. Emity cleared his throat.

"Miss Taylor, please do not tarry in the hallway. Come in."

Embarrassed at being caught, Diana entered the room. "Forgive me for eavesdropping. I heard you playing and was quite overcome. You are very talented, Mr. Emity."

"Thank you for saying so, miss."

"I don't believe I've ever met a butler who played the violin."

"My first master taught me to play the fiddle."

"Did he bring you to England?"

"Not exactly, miss."

"You once promised to tell me the story of how you came to

this country, Mr. Emity. I am most interested in hearing it if you are inclined to share."

"Well then, miss, I shall tell you." He set down his instrument and bow and gestured for Diana to sit. Taking the chair opposite, he began. "I was captured as a child off the Guinea coast by a Portuguese slaver and spent my early years in Brazil as a house slave, where I learned to play the fiddle. My master took me with him to Lisbon and obliged me to perform for others—I was an oddity, an amusement. While there, a British admiral heard me play. He had me kidnapped to serve as his valet and play aboard his ship."

"Oh!" Diana replied. He recounted all this so matter-of-factly and yet every word cut at her like a knife.

"He kept me for six years until 1807 when the slave trade was abolished in this country. Although the admiral had been keeping me as his 'indentured servant' rather than a slave, he got skittish and decided to set me free. He dumped me in Falmouth, where Sir Thomas found me playing music for pennies on the streets. I was just twenty-two years of age then, and Sir Thomas not much older himself, but he hired me to serve as *his* valet. And here I have been ever since."

Diana burned at the injustice that this man had suffered. "That is a remarkable story, Mr. Emity."

"I don't know how remarkable it is, miss, but it is my story, and it is true."

"What happened to you is most unfair and cruel."

"It was, and I know it." The shrug he gave was at odds with the tightness of his pressed lips. "But I cannot change the past."

"Do you miss home, Mr. Emity?"

"If you mean Guinea, miss, I do think of it sometimes, and the family I left behind. But it was so long ago, it is a shadow in my mind now."

"Sir Thomas was fortunate to find you on that street in Falmouth, Mr. Emity."

"I believe myself to be the fortunate one, miss. I love Cornwall. It is now my home. Sir Thomas became my friend, I think. He was a good man at heart."

"I am glad to hear it." Diana thanked him for sharing his story, adding, "I wanted you to know—after what you told me about the circumstances of Sir Thomas's death, I spoke to the parish constable. He may be satisfied with his verdict, but I am not."

Mr. Emity's eyebrows lifted. "What do you intend to do, miss?"

"I intend to learn the truth."

"A bold endeavor. Please let me know if I may be of any help."

She glanced at him. "I do have one question for you, Mr. Emity: did you ever see Sir Thomas writing in a journal or a diary?"

"Every now and then, miss. But every time I entered the room, he hid it from my view."

"Do you have any idea where he kept his journal?"

"I do not."

"Where was he when you saw him writing in it?"

Mr. Emity rubbed his chin and glanced away, as if lost in thought. "Different places, miss. Sometimes in the blue parlor. Sometimes in the gardens. Most often, as I recall, I found him scribbling in his study."

His study. Instinct told Diana that Sir Thomas would have hidden his journal there. She would have to look herself when the opportunity arose.

Diana thanked the butler again.

As she turned to go, he said, "You will be careful, won't you, miss?"

"Careful? Why?"

"If someone did murder Sir Thomas, they might not take kindly to the idea of someone looking into it. You might be putting yourself in danger."

Diana gave him a little smile. "Don't worry, Mr. Emity. I am just the governess. No one takes any notice of what the governess says or does."

ONE OF DIANA'S jobs was to prepare Miss Fallbrook to enter society.

When Diana had first entered the social scene at age eighteen, she had made the mistake of taking people at face value. But men—and women—were not always as they seemed. They did not always follow through on their promises or say what they were really thinking.

Diana didn't wish Miss Fallbrook to suffer as she had. So, she decided to begin introducing her charge to others now. Since Diana was unacquainted with any people of their class in this parish, she determined that they would undertake charitable work. The activity would benefit the community. It would introduce Miss Fallbrook to the joys of giving and give her insight into the way others lived. It would improve her ability to communicate. And it would allow her to see the foibles and inconsistencies of others firsthand and learn from them.

Mrs. Gwynn arranged for the cook to prepare three baskets of food and gave Diana directions to several farms where she felt the offerings would be most appreciated. Diana was disconcerted when, on the morning of their first excursion, Miss Fallbrook put up a fuss and refused to go. It was only after a great deal of cajoling that Miss Fallbrook relented and, with slumped shoulders and a pinched expression, accompanied Diana from the house.

The morning sun had just broken through the clouds as they set out. The colorful offerings from the trees danced on the breeze and scattered across the lawns as Diana and her charge crossed the grounds towards the edge of the estate. A salty tang enlivened the air, accompanied by the sound of the distant sea. Despite the beauty of the autumn day, however, Miss Fallbrook's face was still troubled, and her steps were slow and halting.

"You needn't look so worried, dear," Diana told her. "I think you will enjoy this."

"I won't," Miss Fallbrook insisted. "And it's not as if I've never done this before."

"Oh? You never said."

"You didn't ask."

With a twinge of guilt, Diana realized this was true.

"My stepmother made me accompany her when she brought baskets to the poor. I didn't mind at first. It is always nice to be outdoors, and the tenants were appreciative. But then ... I didn't want to go anymore."

"Why not?"

They were crossing the footbridge over the river and, running a hand over the old, wooden railing, Miss Fallbrook said idly, "Be careful not to lean on the railing here, Miss Taylor. It has wood rot. Papa said he would have it replaced, but he never did."

"Do not change the subject," Diana scolded as they proceeded side by side along the dusty path. "*Why* didn't you want to go anymore?

Miss Fallbrook sighed. "My stepmother made me read to the children."

"Oh." Diana's chest filled with compassion. She could guess what was coming next.

"I couldn't do it. The children laughed at me. My stepmother kept insisting that I try again, always with the same result. She said I was a spoiled young miss and just because the children were poor and dirty, I shouldn't turn up my nose at them. But I wasn't! I like children. I would have read to them if I could."

"I know you would have." Diana gave her pupil a sympathetic look. "I would never put you in that position, Miss Fallbrook."

"Do you promise?"

"I promise. I hope, someday, that you will be able to read. But until that day comes, and you feel comfortable and confident, I will never ask you to read to anyone but myself."

Miss Fallbrook's face brightened. There was a newfound skip to her step. "Thank you."

They first visited the Bartons, a white-haired couple whom Diana recognized as regular attendees at the Sunday service. The small farmhouse was humble, cold, and redolent of bacon grease and smoke. Mrs. Barton beseeched her guests to take seats on mismatched chairs by the hearth, where a weak fire burned in the grate.

"Ye'll forgive me for such a poor fire," Mrs. Barton said. "I keep asking Mr. Barton to fill up the coal scuttle but can't get him to rise from that chair."

"May I help?" Diana offered.

"Oh! No, no," Mrs. Barton answered quickly, as her husband's face reddened. "He'll see to it after ye're gone."

The Bartons asked after Captain Fallbrook, whom they fondly recalled from his visits to the area when he was a boy. They were quietly grateful for the fresh bread, cake, apples, cheese, and marmalade bestowed upon them. Diana and Miss Fallbrook declined anything on offer other than a cup of weak tea, knowing it would be a sacrifice for the elderly couple to share what little food they had.

Miss Fallbrook was reluctant to speak at first, but Mrs. Barton drew her out. They soon discovered a common interest in seashell collecting. The old woman brought out a few of her favorite shells and a pleasant conversation followed.

"Why do you think," Miss Fallbrook pondered after she and Diana left, "that Mrs. Barton wouldn't allow you to fill up her coal scuttle, if her husband couldn't be bothered?"

"Perhaps her husband isn't the problem. Perhaps in truth, they were too low on coal to add any more to the fire."

Miss Fallbrook's forehead wrinkled. "Then why didn't Mrs. Barton say so?"

"Perhaps she was too embarrassed to admit it."

"Oh." Miss Fallbrook's eyes widened. This was followed by a troubled frown. "Do you think we should bring them some coal?"

"An excellent idea. I'll talk to the captain about it."

The next stop was much the same. The recipients were hardworking people who expressed their thanks for the offerings and were disposed to make their circumstances seem better than they were. After a brief but cordial visit, Diana and her pupil went on their way.

Their final visit was to Greenview farm, which Diana had learned was run by a Mr. Trenowden. Passing through a wooded area, they came upon a ramshackle stone cottage, where a sturdy, rosy-cheeked woman in an old cotton dress hung washing on a line. Although the paint on the front door was peeling, the windows looked freshly scrubbed, and the shrubbery was neatly trimmed.

A man was mending a fence, assisted by a lad of perhaps sixteen years of age. Miss Fallbrook took in the boy with interest, but he took no notice of her. A half dozen younger children played in the dirt yard. Three girls wore dresses that were too small for them, all made from the same faded green fabric.

"I hope they never made fun of you here?" asked Diana quietly.

"No. I've never been to this farm," Miss Fallbrook confided.

A little boy with tousled hair and scabbed knees ran up to them. "What ye got there?"

Diana smiled. "A basket of goodies."

"Can I have one?"

"Me! Me!" A girl in an ill-fitting pinafore rushed over with excitement.

"Let us see what your mother has to say," Diana answered.

"Mum! Mum! They brung goodies!" cried the boy.

Their mother pegged a pair of wet trousers and dried her hands on her threadbare apron as Diana and her charge approached.

"Good afternoon, Mrs. Trenowden," Diana greeted her. "I am Diana Taylor, the governess at Pendowar Hall, and this is my pupil, Miss Emma Fallbrook."

"I know who ye be." Mrs. Trenowden dipped in a curtsey. "Ye've grown up into a right pretty young lady, Miss Fallbrook."

Off Diana's encouraging nod, Miss Fallbrook twisted her hands together and responded in a low, faltering voice, "Thank you. We have brought you a little something, ma'am. The bread and cake were baked fresh today, and the marmalade is our cook's specialty."

"How kind." Mrs. Trenowden accepted the basket with a grateful smile. "There ne'er be enough food to go 'round in this house, no matter how many hours my husband labors in the fields." She called out to the man working on the fence. "Jack! Come say *hello* to Miss Fallbrook and her governess, Miss Taylor!"

The man pocketed his hammer and crossed the yard to them. He was powerfully built with a broad chest and muscular arms that his shabby coat did nothing to hide. Touching his cap, he said through tight lips, "Miss Fallbrook. Miss Taylor."

Miss Fallbrook's brow creased at this frosty reception. "Mr. Trenowden."

"I am pleased to meet you, sir," Diana said, equally confused by his unreceptive attitude. "You have a lovely farm."

"T'isn't my farm," he shot back, darting a glance at Miss Fallbrook. "It be *her* people's farm. For all that my family has worked these lands for four generations."

An uncomfortable silence followed. Mrs. Trenowden rescued the moment with a laugh. "Aw, Jack, these ladies mean no harm. Be off with ye if ye can't be civil."

Mr. Trenowden marched off around the side of the house, motioning to the lad who had been working on the fence to follow him.

The oldest girl, who looked to be about twelve, asked Miss Fallbrook, "Would ye like to play tag with us?"

"I've never played tag."

"Never? Well, come on, then. We'll teach you."

Miss Fallbrook glanced at Diana, as if seeking permission. "Go ahead," Diana told her.

The girls ran off with the other children, who conversed boisterously before starting the game. Diana smiled. Her pupil seemed to be enjoying herself. Mrs. Trenowden returned to her duties, two overflowing baskets of wet laundry at her feet.

"May I help you, ma'am?" inquired Diana.

"I wouldn't wish to trouble ye."

"It's no trouble. And it looks like you could do with a hand."

"Suit yourself." Mrs. Trenowden reached into her apron pocket and gave Diana a handful of clothes pegs. "Forgive my husband for his rudeness just now, won't ye? Most times, he be as gentle as a lamb. This past year, howsoever, he's been as hot-tempered as a wrongly shot boar."

"I'm sorry." Diana pegged a pair of trousers.

"I suspect it's the drink. Jack ne'er used to take more 'n a pint every now and then. But we've had a run of bad luck of late. One day about five or six months back, he got into an argument with the baronet after church. Got so bad, I feared they'd come to blows."

This information piqued Diana's interest. Sir Thomas had died about five months ago. Could there have been a connection? "What were they arguing about?"

"I've no idea. Jack would ne'er tell me."

"Was your husband well-acquainted with Sir Thomas Fallbrook?"

"Not at all. The baronet didn't talk much to folk like us, Miss Taylor." Mrs. Trenowden hung a wet sheet on the line. "The new landlord, howsoever, be nothing like his old uncle."

"Oh? Have you known Captain Fallbrook long?"

"E'er since he were a boy. Knew him as Master William then. A good-looking lad and grown up into such a handsome man. Never took a wife, and more's the pity—probably never will, now."

"Why do you say that?"

"No need to, I expect. He's got mistresses across the seven

seas, is what I hear." She sighed. "Such a shame, what happened to him—his injury and all. He didn't deserve it. He's always been such a kind and generous soul."

"Has he?"

"Went off to sea at age twelve, but whenever he got shore leave, he'd stop in every now an' again. 'How are ye today, Mrs. Trenowden?' he'd say with a smile. If there were a chore to be done, he'd chip in. Did as much for my neighbors as well. I'll ne'er forget the kindness he did us, must be six or seven years back. I were laid up with a newborn and the children were all ill wi' fever. The captain heard about it and didn't he stop by wi' a jug of new milk and bread and cheese and coal for the fire? And three year ago, he brung me a piece of fabric from one o' his travels. A right pretty shade of green. Enough to make dresses for all my girls, and a waistcoat for Jack as well."

Diana had heard good reports about the captain from several parties now, and this information only added to the mix.

"He'll make a better landlord than Sir Thomas Fallbrook ever did," Mrs. Trenowden added, "for all that he'll be away at sea most of the time." She paused at that, a sudden, odd look coming into her eyes. Blinking, she continued rapidly, "Of course, it's awful what happened to Sir Thomas. Losing his wife and son and taking his own life like that. We all feel terrible about it."

Diana nodded, studying the woman as they said their goodbyes. Was it Diana's imagination, or was Mrs. Trenowden hiding something?

CHAPTER TWELVE

As Diana and Miss Fallbrook made their way back to Pendowar Hall, Diana's mind whirred as if in tempo with the breeze fluttering the tall grass and cow parsley at the lane's edge.

She was not surprised by Mrs. Trenowden's account of Captain Fallbrook's popularity with women. She *was* intrigued, however, by the farmwife's anecdotes about the captain's nature. To learn that he had been so generous with his uncle's tenants ever since he'd been a boy was a real tribute to his character.

On the other hand, here was yet another report about the popularity—or rather, the *unpopularity*—of the former baronet. The only people who seemed to have a high opinion of him were Mrs. Gwynn and Mr. Emity. What was it the postmistress had said about Sir Thomas?

"He was a changed man the past few years. They say he grew harsh and mean. Rent had to be paid in full and on time, or there'd be hell to pay. Between you and me, there's some as say they aren't sorry he's gone."

Was it just a coincidence, Diana wondered, that Mr. Trenowden had had an altercation with Sir Thomas just before the baronet's death?

"Got so bad, I feared they'd come to blows."

What had they been arguing about? The farmer clearly resented that his family had worked Greenview Farm for centuries but didn't own it. Could that grudge against the Fallbrook family have been a motive for Mr. Trenowden to commit a heinous act? If so, did Mrs. Trenowden know about it? Could that have been the reason behind the odd look in her eyes at the end of their conversation just now?

"Mrs. Barton has some pretty seashells." Miss Fallbrook's remark drew Diana from her thoughts.

"She does, indeed."

"And Mrs. Trenowden is nice."

"I like her, too. Did you enjoy playing with her children?"

"I am far too old to *play*," Miss Fallbrook insisted, "but it was … diverting."

Diana's lips twitched. Miss Fallbrook had clearly enjoyed that game of tag. But if she wanted to make less of the experience, it was perfectly all right. Their visits today had done her good.

"Their elder brother is called Harry," Miss Fallbrook went on tentatively. Her cheeks grew rosy and she ducked her chin, avoiding Diana's gaze.

Diana suspected that her pupil was sweet on the boy. "He looks like a hard-working lad."

"A hard-working lad who paid me no notice." Miss Fallbrook sighed. "Not that it matters. Papa said I must never speak to a farm boy."

Diana understood why. There would be social harm for a young lady of Miss Fallbrook's standing to associate too closely with a farmer's son. And yet, her response to him was very natural for a young lady of her age, even though nothing could come of it. Diana chose her words carefully, not wishing to discourage her charge from making new acquaintances. "There'd be no harm in speaking to him with a chaperone present. I'd be happy to accompany you if you wish to visit Greenview Farm again. Harry Trenowden might make a good friend."

Miss Fallbrook eyed Diana as if she'd just said that Harry Trenowden might fly to the moon. "Boys can't be *friends*. They can only be *beaux*."

"That's not true. Anyway, you are too young to be thinking about beaux."

"I am not. My thirteenth governess, Miss Potter, said her sister married at fifteen and was very happy."

"I am happy for her. But, Miss Fallbrook, you won't even put your hair up for another three years. Most girls do not come out until eighteen."

"Eighteen seems such a long time to wait! Did you come out at eighteen?"

"I did."

"Have you ever had a beau?"

Diana hesitated. It was not a subject she cared to discuss—yet neither did she wish to lie. "Yes. Two beaux, in fact."

"Two?" Miss Fallbrook clasped her hands together. "When? What happened?"

"One question at a time." Diana laughed to cover her anxiety. The recollections were like stabs to the heart. "I met my first beau at my coming out ball."

"You had your own coming out ball?"

"I did."

"But—I thought governesses were too poor to have their own balls."

"I wasn't always poor. My father was a gentleman, and when I was young, we were well-to-do."

"Oh."

"A young man who was visiting from Cheshire attended my ball at the last minute. His name was Mr. Graham. He was the second son from a prominent family. We were only allowed to dance together twice—that is the rule for what is seemly—but he asked me to dance five times."

"Five times!" Miss Fallbrook's mouth fell open. "What did you do?"

"I said *yes*."

"All five times?"

"All five times."

Her pupil giggled. "How shocking!"

"I know."

"Was Mr. Graham a good dancer?"

"He was."

"Was he handsome?"

"Very."

"Did he propose?"

"After asking me to dance five times, I should think so."

A gasp escaped Miss Fallbrook's throat. "Are you saying that he made you an offer the *same night you met?*"

"No, of course not. But he came to call the very next day, and every day thereafter for a fortnight, and *then* he proposed."

"After only two weeks!" Miss Fallbrook's eyes sparkled. "Tell me about the proposal. Where did it happen? And how?"

Diana smiled grimly at her charge's enthusiasm, recalling her own sense of excitement at the time, and how quickly things had changed.

"Mr. Graham came to our house with a bouquet of pink roses. He asked my father for my hand. Papa was impressed with the young man and his family connections, and he wanted me to be happy. So he gave his permission and then left us alone together in the parlor."

"Did your suitor go down on one knee?"

"He did."

Miss Fallbrook let out a long sigh. "That is *so* romantic!"

"I thought so too at the time." It was Diana's turn to sigh. "I thought we were madly in love."

Her pupil's smile faded, as if suddenly recalling that this story didn't have a happy ending. "But you weren't?"

"I have learned since that true and lasting affection, and the admiration that is required to sustain it, takes longer than a fortnight to develop. I didn't know that then." Her godmother had written and cautioned her to take things slowly, but Diana hadn't listened. She had already made her choice. "And I didn't know that his regard for me was not founded on affection at all, but on something else."

"On what?"

"My money."

"Oh!" Miss Fallbrook's steps seemed to become slower and heavier as they strode along. "How did you find out?"

"In the worst of all possible ways. We had set a wedding date, and I had ordered my wedding gown and trousseau from the dressmaker, when my father lost most of his fortune in a single night at the gaming tables."

"Oh, no!"

"Upon discovering that my dowry was gone, my betrothed vanished as well."

Miss Fallbrook's face fell. "Did you ever hear from him again?"

"Not a word. I later learned that he had married a woman with ten thousand pounds. He was a second son, after all. He would never inherit, so he had to marry money." Even so, the betrayal still smarted after all these years, making Diana feel ... *less.* Less desirable. Less worthy of love. Less deserving of respect.

"I'm so sorry," Miss Fallbrook whispered. They walked on in silence for a while. "What about your second beau, Miss Taylor?"

Diana stiffened. All at once, she was back in that moonlit garden as if under a spell, listening to promises that had held no more weight than air. The memory jabbed like a blade. "I should prefer not to talk about him."

Miss Fallbrook struggled to hide her disappointment. "All right. But wait. What happened after your father lost his fortune?"

"I went to work as a governess, which I've done ever since. Well, I took the past year off after my father passed away. But I need employment. And I discovered that idleness doesn't suit me."

"So, when my aunt Eliza told you that I needed a new governess ..."

"I applied for the position straight away." One day, if her

quest went well, Diana would tell her pupil her other reason for coming to Pendowar Hall. But not yet.

Miss Fallbrook glanced up at her and said quietly, "I am glad you came."

Diana clasped her charge's hand in hers and gave it an affectionate squeeze. "So am I."

THE CLOCK STRUCK twelve. Diana brushed her long, dark curls and plaited them, looking back on the day with satisfaction.

Her relationship with Miss Fallbrook seemed to be entering a new phase. Today, a sweetness had emerged, and in their conversation, she felt they had formed a kind of bond. Doing good for others, Diana believed, had done Miss Fallbrook good. She had learned a bit about human nature. And the experience had, for the moment, taken her mind off her frustrations in the schoolroom.

Those frustrations still preyed on Diana's mind, however. They had gone over the entire alphabet twice now, but what her pupil seemed to have learned one day was undone the next. Sometimes, Miss Fallbrook saw letters in words in a different order than everyone else did. Why? And what could be done about it?

Diana was about to climb into bed when she paused.

It had become a practice, ever since she discovered that set of keys in Sir Thomas's bedchamber, to peek out her window every night just before she retired. She had never seen the light in the north tower window again and had begun to think she had just imagined it. Why on Earth would someone have been up there, anyway? It was all silly nonsense.

And yet, compulsion propelled her to rise and part the curtains slightly. A full moon bathed the grounds in its silvery glow. She glanced at the north tower.

There it was again! A light in the uppermost window was blinking on and off.

Diana's pulse began to race. Mrs. Gwynn and the captain had both warned her to stay out of the north wing. She didn't wish to countermand a direct order by her employer or to incur the housekeeper's wrath, but something strange was going on. Could the light be linked in any way to the footsteps she'd heard on her first night at Pendowar Hall? And could either—or both—of those incidents have had anything to do with Sir Thomas's death? Probably not.

But Mrs. Phillips and her sisters had urged her to follow her instincts.

She *had* to investigate.

Captain Fallbrook generally kept to his rooms at this hour. Miss Fallbrook and the staff had long since gone to bed. Surely, Diana could visit the north wing—and if she was lucky, the tower—just this once without anyone knowing.

First, she needed those keys. And there was no time to lose. On her previous attempt, by the time she'd reached the north tower, the light had gone out. Donning her dressing gown, Diana thrust her feet into her slippers, grabbed her candle, and rushed down the corridor to Sir Thomas's bedchamber.

To her relief, the keys were exactly where she'd last seen them. Diana grabbed the keyring in such a rush, she fumbled. They fell and hit the floor with a clatter.

Diana froze, every nerve on alert. How far would the sound carry? *This is madness*, she told herself. She must stay at Pendowar Hall until she discovered who murdered Sir Thomas—and could prove it. There was so much she longed to do for Miss Fallbrook, but she had barely gotten started. Was she risking everything in this one foolish endeavor? If the captain found her here, he might well give Diana her walking papers. *Go back to your room. Give this up.*

But all was silent. Regaining her courage, Diana pocketed the keys and hurried down the hall, protecting her candle flame with one hand as she made her way downstairs. Her pulse beat hard and thick as she navigated the north wing's dark, twisting passageways until she reached the vestibule where the massive, oak door waited.

Diana slipped one of the iron keys into the ancient lock. It did not turn. Nor did the next. Her heart sank. Were they the wrong keys, after all?

She tried the third iron key. With a satisfying click, the tumbler turned, and the bolt slid open. Diana's excitement mounted as she pulled the heavy door ajar.

A circular, stone staircase stood before her, similar to the one she had seen in her dream. As Diana made her way up the stone steps, a sudden chill settled over her. She hoped that whoever was behind that flashing light was still up in the tower. But was she placing herself in danger in this pursuit? Mr. Emity's words came back to her.

"If someone did murder Sir Thomas, they might not take kindly to the idea of someone looking into it."

Nevertheless, one foot slowly moved forward and then the other. Diana's body seemed to be working of its own volition as it carried her up the stairs.

The flight ended at a narrow landing with another aged, oaken door. It was locked as well. Half-trembling with anticipation, Diana tried each key in succession until she found one that fit. A thrill ran through her as she felt the lock unclasp.

Was she in time? Was someone within? If so, what would she say to them? She had not thought it through, she realized. But she had come too far to stop now.

Diana opened the door.

Within, it was dark as pitch. By the light of her candle, she made out a small, furnished chamber.

Diana entered and cautiously took in her surroundings. Her spirits deflated. Whoever had been here had come and gone. Her frustration, however, was quickly replaced by curiosity and a sense of wonder.

Against the far wall stood a massive four-poster bed, its wooden headboard elaborately carved in the shape of a mermaid. The bed curtains stood half open and matched the coverlet and draperies, which, although faded and thick with dust, were fashioned of an intricately woven fabric in shades of blue, green, and gold, featuring mermaids under the sea.

Tapestries decorated the walls, depicting mermaids with long, flowing hair surrounded by sea creatures and seashells. Interspersed with these coverings were oil and watercolor paintings of mermaids. But the theme did not stop there. Art objects of mermaids in a variety of poses occupied the furniture and shelves, all coated in the same layer of dust.

Diana gaped in amazement. Who had built this chamber and why? To make certain no one was hiding in the shadows, she conducted a thorough search of the room.

She was alone.

Not for long, however. The thud of footfalls on the stairs broke the silence. Diana's pulse hammered in her chest. Had Mrs. Gwynn come to lecture her again? Would she be very angry? It was not the housekeeper who burst into the room, however.

It was the captain.

CHAPTER THIRTEEN

C APTAIN FALLBROOK WORE a dressing gown over black trousers and a half-buttoned shirt. "Who goes there?" he bellowed, candle in hand, relying on his cane for every halting step. Catching sight of Diana, he froze several paces inside the door, blinking in apparent surprise. "Miss Taylor?"

"Captain."

"How did you get in here?"

"I … found these." Hesitantly, she brought forth the ring of keys from her pocket.

"*Found* them? How? Where?"

Diana's face flamed. "In your uncle's chamber."

"What were you doing in my uncle's room?" He looked fit to be tied. "And how dare you come up here when I told you this wing, and this tower in particular, were expressly forbidden?"

"I'm sorry. I know it was wrong. You would be within your rights to dismiss me, sir. But I hope you will not." Diana swallowed hard.

His blue eyes blazed with a fury he visibly struggled to hold in check. "Don't tell me this has something to do with our earlier conversation? About my uncle?"

Her cheeks grew even hotter. "I can explain, if you will allow me."

"Pray go on, then," he said through gritted teeth.

"I was thinking of your ward," she began. "I went to your

uncle's room in search of his missing journal."

"His journal?"

"I still hope that its discovery will help explain the circumstances of his death."

"I told you to give that up!"

"I know. Forgive me, Captain. My curiosity got the best of me. I didn't find a journal—but I came upon his keys. I never touched them until tonight when I saw a blinking light in the window of this tower. Did you see it?"

"Yes." His features remained taut, and his tone abrupt.

"Do you know the person and the motive behind it?"

"I do not."

"I had to know. I hoped one of those keys might provide access to the tower, so I borrowed them. But the room, as you see, is empty."

He fell silent, brooding. "I suppose you expect me to forgive you for *borrowing* what does not belong to you and expressly *disobeying* my orders?"

"I expect nothing."

"Hand them over." He held out a hand, palm upward. Diana gave him the keys. He placed them in his dressing gown pocket. "This is the second time you have flouted a directive of mine, Miss Taylor."

"The second time?"

"The roadside? The carriage? The storm?"

Diana bit her lip, remembering. "I'm sorry."

He heaved a sigh. His anger seemed to ease slightly. "You have done no harm this time, I suppose. But take care not to do so again. I have my reasons for wishing this room to remain undisturbed."

"Yes, sir."

She wanted to ask him what those reasons were but thought it best not to test him in this mood. She became aware, suddenly, that he was only half-dressed, and so was she. The sight of his unbuttoned shirt and the resulting exposed flesh caused a heat to rise to her face and her pulse to quicken.

The impropriety of this meeting was not lost on her. She was alone in an isolated tower with a handsome reputed womanizer. The description seemed appropriate, for as his gaze took in her own state of *deshabille*, a sudden glimmer lit his eyes. She ought to go at once. But despite herself, her feet remained rooted to the spot.

"You're certain no one else is here?" the captain asked.

"I am. Is there any other means of exit from this room, other than the tower stairs?"

"No."

"Well, it is a great distance from the east wing to this part of the house. Whoever it was must have fled down the stairs and exited outside into the night before I arrived. I think they were sending a signal."

"A signal? For what purpose?"

"I could not say. Or someone might be playing a trick. I cannot help but wonder if this is somehow connected to the other unexplained events at Pendowar Hall."

His forehead furrowed. "What unexplained events?"

"Well, for one thing, the footsteps I heard in the hall on my first night here."

"You mean the footsteps you dreamt?"

Her stomach tightened. "I did not dream them any more than we dreamt the light in that window."

"No, we did not dream that. But I think I understand what happened now. The moon is full tonight. When it achieved the optimum angle, its brilliance was reflected in the window."

Diana frowned. "But the light flashed."

"Clouds must have passed intermittently before the moon. I admit, I was curious, and I made my way here to investigate. But I see now it was simply a trick of the light. What else could it have been? The tower was locked. The only person other than myself—and *you*, on this occasion—who has the key is Mrs. Gwynn, and I trust her implicitly."

Diana could think of no rebuttal. "Perhaps you are right. Perhaps it was a trick of the light."

"I'm sure it was. It is late, Miss Taylor. Allow me to show you back to your room."

They left. He locked the door.

As they made their way down the stairs, Diana asked, "Captain, who decorated that chamber?"

"An eccentric and deluded ancestor more than a hundred years ago."

"You mean the baronet who fell in love with the mermaid?"

"The same. After his wife's death, it is said that Sir Peter furnished the north tower room to appease Morwenna. Others believe it is a shrine to his 'one true love.' He carved the bed himself and slept there every night until his death."

"What a fascinating tale. It's a beautiful room."

"It's an embarrassment," he argued.

"It's a tribute," she insisted.

"To what? A madman's folly? A vengeful spirit?" They reached the ground floor. Captain Fallbrook locked the door behind them. "Those who followed have not proven any more discerning," he said as they made their way down the long, dark hall. "That chamber has been unoccupied for over a century, and yet no one has changed a thing."

"You haven't changed it, either," Diana pointed out.

"When would I have had time?" he shot back, his tone once again harsh and irritable. "I have only been here four months and I have either been recovering or occupied every moment."

A hot flush crept up Diana's neck. "Forgive me. I shouldn't have said that."

"I assure you it is on my list to redecorate that room from top to bottom and repair this wing. Why it hasn't been done before is a mystery to me."

"Perhaps the former baronets were afraid of upsetting Morwenna's spirit."

He glanced at her as they continued down the hall. "That's

ridiculous. Tell me you don't believe it."

"I don't. But others do. It is not ridiculous to those who believe the Mermaid's Curse to be unbreakable."

"But it is *not* unbreakable."

"Isn't it? Ivy implied otherwise."

"Then Ivy has forgotten the codicil."

"There is a codicil?"

"Every worthy curse has a codicil, Miss Taylor." Despite the lightness of the remark, his tone was still embittered. "This one is truly extraordinary."

"Enlighten me."

"According to the legend," the captain explained, "there is one way the curse can be broken: a Master of Pendowar must once and for all pledge his love to a maid who comes from the sea. However, this time, he must not only love her, but agree to spend all the rest of his days with her."

"Presumably *under* the sea?"

"Presumably."

"A rather difficult pledge to enact," Diana remarked. "If he did so, 'the rest of his days' would last no more than a matter of minutes under the sea."

"Indeed," he agreed.

"Is that the entirety of the codicil?"

"There is one more part, which, upon its occurrence, will supposedly prove the curse has been broken. It is said that on the day that Morwenna's spirit is appeased, she will express her approval in two ways: by causing the ocean to rise to the top of the cliffs and by turning the beach itself green."

"Oh, my. I should like to see that."

"It is madness! All of it. And to me, that tower room is just an awful reminder of the horrible day when Aunt Sylvia and Cousin Robert ..." A haunted look swept across his face.

"What happened to them, Captain?" Diana asked quietly. "All I know is that they died at sea."

They had reached the main part of the house now, where

they would part ways. He stopped. His features hardened, as if a mask had dropped into place.

"That is a conversation for another time, Miss Taylor. I bid you good night."

DIANA AND MISS Fallbrook spent a good portion of the following day visiting the poor. Her pupil's initial shyness had faded, and in its place a gregarious nature blossomed. She was initiating conversation now and taking a real interest in the people they met and the help they were providing.

"The other day, when we visited Greenview Farm," Miss Fallbrook remarked as they walked home that afternoon, "I couldn't help noticing how old Mrs. Trenowden's apron was, and her girls' dresses fitted them so poorly. Can we get them some new things?"

"I don't know about *getting* them," Diana replied, "but perhaps we can make them."

"*Make* them?" Miss Fallbrook frowned. "My needlework skills are limited to embroidery."

"That is a good start. I can teach you the rest."

"Where would we get the fabric and thread?"

"We shall need money for that."

Diana wrote a note to the captain, and a meeting was scheduled for the following evening at seven o'clock. At the appointed hour, Diana paused on the threshold of the study. She had never visited this chamber but had been curious about it.

The manly room, which was situated on the same level as her own chamber but at the opposite end of the building, was not overly large. A fire gleamed in a stone hearth, casting a reddish glow on walls covered in dark wooden paneling, bookcases, and built-in cabinetry. French doors led to a narrow balcony. Captain Fallbrook sat behind a polished desk, writing. Boxes, stacked at both sides of the desk, were open and filled with what looked like ledgers and paperwork.

"Captain."

He looked up from his work. "Miss Taylor. Enter. Take a seat." He gestured to the empty chair facing his desk. She sat.

They had exchanged no more than cursory greetings in passing over the past two days, since he had found her in the north tower room.

She wondered if he would mention it, but he said, "Please forgive the state of this chamber. It was my uncle's study and he left it in disarray." He replaced his quill in the inkstand. "You wished to see me?"

"Yes." Diana explained the charitable work she and her charge had been doing. "All the tenants we met with would benefit from a new delivery of coal."

"Thank you for bringing this to my attention. I've been distracted by other matters of late—replacing roofs and improving drainage in the cottages—and this escaped my notice. I will see to it immediately."

Diana was gratified by this proof of the captain's dedication to his tenants' welfare. "I have another proposal, sir." She explained her idea to sew clothing for the poor. "I believe we can purchase the fabric and notions in the village, but we need funds."

"A worthy project." His features reflected his approval. When they had settled the details, he remarked, "There is something I wish to discuss with you as well."

"Oh?"

"These past few months, to gain a better understanding of the affairs of the estate, I have been going through my late uncle's papers and correspondence. It turns out I require your help."

"*My* help?"

"Uncle Thomas kept all the letters he received as well as early drafts of many—or perhaps all—of the letters he sent." He gestured to the boxes surrounding them. "The sheer quantity of paperwork is voluminous."

"Do you wish me to help organize it?"

"No, nothing so prosaic as that. I have a system and I am making slow but steady progress. However, this afternoon, I came upon drafts of letters he wrote to a company in Germany, along with correspondence and other documents that I cannot read. I presume they are in German." He slid a folder to her across the desk. "Am I correct?"

Diana examined the contents of the folder. "These are indeed in German."

"I didn't even know my uncle was familiar with that language." He shook his head. "I know he went to Germany this past spring, just before he died. I thought he had gone abroad on holiday, but this appears to be about a business matter. I need you to tell me what these documents contain."

Diana hesitated. She and her sisters had been studying German for the love of the language and its literature, and a view to teaching it one day. But she still considered herself a novice. "Although I have a facility with the German language, I am not fluent. It will take me some time to translate these."

"There is no rush. Just do the best you can. As this doesn't fall under the scope of your usual duties, I will pay you an additional fee."

"That is unnecessary."

"It *is* necessary, and there will be no further discussion about it."

Diana expected him to issue some parting words. Instead, he stared moodily into space. "If that is all, sir ...?"

"Actually," he replied abruptly, "there is another matter."

"Sir?"

"The other night when we returned from the north tower, you posed a question which I put off answering." A distant look came into his eyes, an expression rooted in pain. "You asked me what happened to my aunt Sylvia and cousin Robert."

"I understand if you'd prefer not to talk about it."

"I should prefer, if I could, to never think or talk about it again. But it preys on my mind every waking and sleeping moment, and I expect it shall for the rest of my life." He leaned back in his chair with a sigh. "What happened is no secret. I should rather you heard it from me than from one of the servants or local gossips. In the wrong hands, these things tend to grow and change, blending fact and fiction and supposition until they scarcely resemble the truth."

Diana waited silently for him to continue.

He took a deep breath. "Three years ago, the last time I was home on leave, my cousin Robert wanted to go sailing. Aunt Sylvia wanted to go as well, but Uncle Thomas wasn't feeling up to it, so I offered to do the honors."

"*You* took them sailing?"

His lips tightened as he nodded. "The weather was clear when we set out. But we had not been gone fifteen minutes when the boat started taking on water. To this day, I have no idea why. I'd taken that boat out the day before and it had been sound. I had no time to figure out the problem, however, for a strong wind suddenly blew up. I was busy bailing and adjusting the sails, and before I knew it, it had turned into a gale. Despite the weather, I could have brought us back to shore safely, if the boat had not filled so quickly. It became engulfed and turned over. Aunt Sylvia was not a strong swimmer. Robert could not swim at all. Both were swept away, along with the vessel. I don't know how long I remained out there, battling the waves, desperate to find them, but ... they disappeared. At last, I returned to shore, too exhausted to move or think. My aunt's and cousin's bodies and parts of the fractured boat washed up on shore the next day."

"Oh." Sadness seemed to creep into Diana's every pore. "What an awful tragedy."

"My uncle grieved for his wife and son. But he was also angry—at me. He saw the whole thing as my fault, and I could not blame him. If only I had not agreed to take them sailing that day. If only I had taken more time to examine the boat. Surely, *he* would have done so. His accusations cut me to the quick. I returned to my ship and vowed that I would never darken his door again."

"I am so sorry."

"We exchanged only a handful of letters over the last three years. Then I was injured and obliged to go home. I had no home but this one— my father was a clergyman and when he died, the vicarage went to the next incumbent, as usual. In June, when I returned to Pendowar Hall, I thought my reappearance and my uncle's animosity towards me might be the reason behind his distracted, distant mood. I asked no questions. We kept to our separate corners of the house. When his body was found on the shore below the cliffs—well, you know the rest. Knowing that he killed himself over the deaths of his wife and son is a burden of grief and guilt I carry with me every moment of every day."

Diana's soul ached as she absorbed this tale and observed the captain's sorrow in relating it. "You have suffered grievous losses. But you cannot be certain that is the reason behind your uncle's death. And you cannot blame yourself for what happened to your aunt and cousin."

"I can and I do."

"The boat was faulty, not you."

"I am a sailor, Miss Taylor." Taking a deep, pained breath, he briefly closed his eyes. "I should have known the boat was unsound before setting sail."

"How could you have suspected as much? You said the boat had been fine the day before."

"That is no excuse." He clasped his fingers tightly, then loosened them. "I should have checked it more carefully. I should have known better than to take them out that day at all."

"How could you have foreseen the turn in the weather? You said it blew up out of nowhere."

He glanced at her across his desk. "I appreciate your attempts to ease my conscience, Miss Taylor. But I accepted my part in this debacle long ago. I killed my aunt and cousin. And now my uncle, too. These are facts I cannot escape. I wish with all my heart that

I could bring them back. But I cannot. The guilt and regret will haunt me all my life."

Diana's heart twisted with compassion. "Guilt and regret are like a cancer, Captain. They can eat one away from the inside if we let them. I know that all too well."

"Do you? How?"

Hot tears burned behind Diana's eyes. The words escaped despite herself.

"Because I killed my mother."

CHAPTER FOURTEEN

THE CAPTAIN STARED at Diana across his desk. Quietly, he said, "Tell me."

Diana swallowed down the lump in her throat. She had never talked about this with anyone except her siblings. But the guilty burden had weighed on her for years. The overwhelming need to share it was met by a concern and empathy in his gaze so compelling, she found herself pouring out her heart.

"I was seven years old. My mother had been ill for a year and was now thin, pale, and bedridden. One morning, she asked me to go to the apothecary and fetch a tonic that had helped her before. She didn't want the staff to know because my father disapproved of the tonic. I put the money in my pocket and dashed off to the village. But when I got there, my friends Nancy and Beatrice, the vicar's daughters, invited me to play with them. I didn't think my mother would mind if I played for just a few minutes. But before I knew it, it was growing dark, and by then, I had forgotten all about my errand. When I got home, I learned that my mother had had a stroke while I'd been gone. She died that night."

"Dear God." The captain shook his head. "And you blamed yourself?"

"If I had not been so selfish ... if I had brought my mother the tonic ... she would have lived."

"You must know that isn't true. It sounds as if your mother

was very ill and would have died that night or soon after in any case."

"Perhaps. Perhaps not." Diana wiped at the tears that streaked her cheeks. "No one blamed me. No one knew my mother had asked for a tonic. And yet … *I knew.* I kept the secret to myself, confided in no one except my brother and my sisters many years later."

Ever since, like a heavy book that'd been placed upon a wrinkled paper to flatten it out, the weight of Diana's guilt had pressed down on her, day after day, year after year, until it had become a part of her that was impossible to extract. She wasn't sure why she was telling the captain now. Maybe it was because they shared the same sense of guilt—the belief that they had inadvertently killed someone dear to them.

"Since then," Diana continued, "I've spent every day of my life trying to make amends for that mistake."

"Amends? How?"

"By being the best person that I can. By serving others. By helping people to manage their lives, trying to prevent them from making mistakes like I did."

"You are a good woman, Miss Taylor, and your goals have merit. But you were just a child when your mother passed away. It was not your fault. You are not responsible for what happened that day. You must forgive yourself."

Diana shook her head, knowing this to be impossible. Her voice wavered. "I could say the same for you, Captain, with regard to your aunt and cousin."

He took that in and fell silent. His forehead creased. "A good reminder," he answered quietly, "which I shall try to take to heart. But as you have discovered, that is easier said than done."

DIANA SPENT ALL her spare time over the next few days translating the documents Captain Fallbrook had given her with the help of a German dictionary she'd found on the schoolroom shelf.

As she worked, Diana couldn't stop thinking about her last conversation with the captain. Admitting to her part in her mother's death had been like ripping open an age-old wound. Her heart felt raw. Her soul felt bare, all her guilt and shame on view for him to see. And yet, the captain hadn't seemed to judge her. His response had been compassionate.

"You are not responsible for what happened that day."

If only she could believe that.

She knew the reverse to be true for Captain Fallbrook. On the day that Lady Fallbrook and Robert Fallbrook had been lost at sea, the captain hadn't neglected his duty and selfishly indulged his own pleasures. He had struggled valiantly to find them, and in so doing, might have drowned himself. It had obviously been an accident. He was wrong to blame himself.

Diana may not be able to fix her own situation, but she could do something about *his*. If she was correct—if Sir Thomas had not killed himself out of grief for his lost family or for any other reason—although murder was a dark and terrible alternative, knowing the truth might ease one portion of the captain's guilty burden.

She had promised to keep her eyes and ears open for her godmother, and she would keep that promise. Not only for her, but now for her pupil and Captain Fallbrook as well. Someone might make a telling remark that would open a new door. If she had heard nocturnal footsteps once, she might hear them again. Who knew where they might lead? When she had time, she would resume her search for Sir Thomas's journal.

With that settled in her mind, Diana returned her focus to the letters she was translating. The drafts of Sir Thomas's letters were in imperfect German, had numerous words crossed out, and were peppered with ink blots. Diana agreed with the captain's theory that Sir Thomas must have rewritten clean versions before sending them.

By contrast, the letters from the German company were neat and businesslike. However, she had noticed a pattern in the paperwork that filled her with unease. As Diana translated the final document in the folder, an alarming notion suddenly struck her.

Was this, she wondered, the answer to the riddle about Sir Thomas's death?

She must speak to the captain at once.

Taking the folder with her, Diana hurried to the opposite wing, recalling that Captain Fallbrook sometimes worked in his study in the late afternoon. She reached that chamber and paused in the open doorway. Captain Fallbrook was seated at his desk. Before him sat a gentleman she recognized.

Apprehension tightened her stomach. This man's name had come up several times in the paperwork she had just translated.

The captain glanced up. "Miss Taylor."

"Forgive me, sir. I didn't realize you had a visitor. I'll come back later."

"We have finished our business. Allow me to introduce you." He and the gentleman rose as Diana entered the room. "Latimer, may I present Miss Taylor, my cousin's new governess. Miss Taylor, this is my solicitor, Mr. John Latimer."

"Miss Taylor and I have met. At Beardsley's in the village, a fortnight ago, I think it was?" Mr. Latimer appraised Diana with his steady gaze, a look that once again sent a slight chill rippling up her spine.

"How nice to see you again, sir." Diana dipped in a polite curtsy.

"It turns out Miss Taylor has some facility with the German tongue," the captain remarked. "I asked her to translate the documents I mentioned."

Latimer's eyebrows raised. "Is that right? I thought governesses taught little more than the three Rs and a bit of needlework."

Did Diana detect a note of anxiety in his voice and features?

"I am lucky to have found one so skilled," said the captain. "How have you been progressing, Miss Taylor?"

"Very well, sir. I have finished my translations."

"I look forward to your report."

Captain Fallbrook exchanged a few additional words with his solicitor, they shook hands, and with a parting bow, Mr. Latimer exited. Diana took the vacated chair, and the captain resumed his own seat.

"So, what did you find?"

Diana set the folder she'd brought on his desk. "As you suspected, these letters and legal documents are all related. They pertain to a financial investment Sir Thomas made with a German company called Franke and Dietrich, to build a new railway line in Germany."

"A railway line? That surprises me." The captain rubbed his chin. "When the so-called 'Railroad Mania' started up in this country five years ago, my uncle told me he suspected stock prices were inflated and he was leery of investing. How right he was."

Diana knew about the recent crash in railway shares in England. It had been a major topic of conversation both upstairs and downstairs. The debacle had cost its speculators millions. "However, based on this correspondence, he *did* make such an investment in Germany."

The captain nodded. "Well, from what I've read, railroad shares are a safer bet on the Continent."

"Perhaps. However, I don't think this one was quite so safe after all. I have little experience when it comes to financial matters, but something about this deal seems fishy to me."

His eyebrows rose. "How so?"

"The first letter is dated March 1847, two and a half years ago. Franke and Dietrich promised investors an excellent return on their investment after the railroad was in operation and turned a profit. A flurry of correspondence went back and forth until the contract was signed, and the stock certificates delivered. Eighteen months ago, the company reported that production had begun. Since then, letters from Germany have dwindled. As far as I know—as far as the letters I have goes—the last one is dated nine months ago."

The captain shrugged. "A new railway line must be an enormous undertaking. The company has no doubt been busy overseeing matters more pressing than correspondence with investors."

"What could be more important than keeping their investors happy? And yet, despite many attempts on your uncle's part to reach Franke and Dietrich—it seems as though he kept an early draft of every letter he sent, seeking information about progress on the line and requesting a tour of the area where the track was being laid—it appears that they never replied."

The captain took that in. "Did anyone oversee the deal from this end?"

"Yes. His solicitor, Mr. Latimer. His signature is on several of the documents."

"And you think … what? That something went wrong with the deal?"

"It may have. Perhaps the company encountered problems building the railway line."

"If that happened, surely, Latimer would have informed me, since it would presumably represent a loss to the estate I was inheriting."

"Perhaps he isn't aware of the issues involved."

"I suppose that's possible."

"That's not all. You said your uncle had just returned from a trip to Germany the week before he died, and he was distracted and depressed. You theorize that he was still grieving for his wife and son. But might his disquiet have been due to a speculation that went bad?"

The captain considered the notion, then shook his head. "My uncle was a rich man. One bad investment, if that is indeed what happened, would not seriously impact this estate—certainly not enough to drive him to suicide."

"That's not what I'm suggesting."

He crossed his arms over his chest, studying her. "What *are* you suggesting, then?"

"What if, during your uncle's trip to Germany, he discovered that this financial scheme had gone wrong? What if he met with the men behind the project—and threatened to reveal what he had learned? Might that be a motive for them to want him dead?"

He stared at her long and hard, then let out a disbelieving laugh. "Allow me to be certain I understand you. You are implying that"—he glanced at a document in the folder—"Franke or Dietrich—or Franke *and* Dietrich—sailed across the North Sea to England with the express object of pushing my uncle off a cliff? Or hired someone to do the dirty deed for them?"

"It is possible, isn't it? If Franke and Dietrich absconded with the money, they might have been desperate to preserve their secret."

The captain's lips twitched as if he were struggling to repress a smile. "An interesting conjecture. I do appreciate your efforts in executing these translations, Miss Taylor, and I thank you for bringing this matter to my attention. I am afraid, however, that you are letting your imagination run away with you. As I said before: my uncle wasn't murdered. He took his own life."

"Captain—"

"I'm sure Franke and Dietrich are perfectly respectable businessmen. John Latimer's father was my uncle's solicitor for decades. When the old gentleman died the son took over. John is a good man. He has patiently gone over the estate accounts with me these past few months. I will speak to him about this railway scheme. Hopefully, there is a simple answer for all of it."

Diana bit back a response, forcing herself to nod respectfully. She didn't believe in simple answers. And she didn't like being doubted.

"Where there is smoke, there is fire."

Something untoward was going on here. Somehow, she

would get to the bottom of it.

Pendowar Hall, Cornwall

My dearest Mrs. Phillips,

I hope you received good news from the doctor on Wednesday and that you are feeling better this week than the last. I promised to send regular notes about my progress at Pendowar Hall, and here is my latest report.

I want to begin by saying that, based on all I've learned about Captain Fallbrook, we may remove him as a suspect. I don't believe he is connected in any way to his uncle's death. Were you to meet the captain again today as a grown man, I know you would like him.

In my last letter, I told you about the documents I translated for the captain, along with my suspicions. Captain Fallbrook has relayed to me that his solicitor, Mr. Latimer, insists that the investment in the German railway company is sound and will provide an excellent return in time. Mr. Latimer said he has never met the financiers of the project, but his father did some years ago and, before his passing, encouraged his son to get involved in what he believed was an exciting opportunity. Mr. Latimer has received written assurances from the company that excellent progress is being made on the railway line. Unfortunately—and rather frustratingly—he has misplaced that correspondence. So he can provide no proof.

I still think it possible that the railroad scheme was a fraud. If I am right, and if Sir Thomas found out, it isn't out of the question that one of the financiers would wish to keep him quiet. They could have come to England, done their nefarious deed, and vanished like the wind—or sent or hired someone to do it for them.

I intend to write to the company myself and make inquiries. In the meantime, I feel certain that Sir Thomas's journal will shed light on the matter. I made a thorough search of the captain's study the other night but found nothing. I shall go through the house room by room, if need be, to find that diary, even though I must do it all by stealth. Captain Fallbrook thinks the idea is folly.

Speaking of the captain, I am frustrated by his lack of connection with Miss Fallbrook. They live in the same house yet rarely see each other, except when he escorts her to church by coach or on horseback. Determined to improve this relationship, I organized an outing yesterday after church—a picnic. Miss Fallbrook was excited by the prospect. She idolizes her cousin, although she would never admit it. He maintained that he had no time for such a diversion, but after a bit of powerful persuading on my part, he gave in.

Our cook was away at the time, visiting a friend, and a temporary replacement was performing her duties. I ordered a basket of picnic delicacies (all my favorites and yours): cold chicken, hardboiled eggs, cheese, bread, pickles, and lemon tarts. A few clouds had gathered, but we felt confident it would not rain. I chose a pretty spot in the garden where we laid out a blanket to enjoy the feast.

Everything went wrong. It turns out Miss Fallbrook won't eat hardboiled eggs, Captain Fallbrook doesn't like cold chicken, they both hate pickles, and neither is fond of lemon tarts. If only our cook had been here, she could have warned me about their preferences! We ate bread and cheese in awkward silence. Every time I tried to start a conversation, it led nowhere. They have no clue how to talk to each other.

I admit, the captain made a feeble attempt: he asked Miss Fallbrook if she liked boys. The girl turned beet red and looked as though she wanted to die on the spot. What an awkward question for an older male relative to pose! Could he not have asked about her horse or seashell collection? Thankfully, he dropped the subject and doesn't seem to be in league with the dreadful Professor Vaughan, who insists that we not bother with Miss Fallbrook's education and marry her off at the earliest possible juncture.

We had only been picnicking for about an hour when the sky darkened, and a sudden, hard rain poured down. We gathered everything up and made a run for it. By the time we'd reached the house, we were all drenched to the bone and we went our separate ways.

Oh, Mrs. Phillips! Everything I have tried to do lately seems to fail. What does that say about me? The picnic was a fiasco. Despite my best efforts, Miss Fallbrook still struggles with the alphabet. I discovered a new possible lead in Sir Thomas's case, but the captain dismissed it outright. Still, I shan't give up. I promised you to make inroads on these last two fronts, and I shall make good on that vow.

I send you a heart full of love and wishes for your improved health. I look forward to your reply more than I can say.

With all my love, your goddaughter,
Diana

Rose Cottage, Yorkshire

Dearest Diana,

I am sorry your picnic did not turn out as you had hoped. May I say, however, that your description of the event was most amusing. One day, I trust you will be able to look back on it and laugh as heartily as I did.

In the meantime, reflect on this: things rarely go as we plan or expect. When life's circumstances are not what we wish them to be, we have no alternative but to make the best of what is. We might be obliged to change our thinking and move in a new direction—and that is all right. For if we stand still in one place too long, we might find ourselves stuck at that point forever.

I know you went to Cornwall as a favor to me—you could surely have found gainful employment closer to home—and I am grateful for all you are doing. But something you said in your last letter troubles me. You wrote:

"Everything I have tried to do lately seems to fail.

What does that say about me?"

You must cease this kind of thinking, Diana. I believe you will solve the mystery of my brother's death. I believe you will find a way to help Emma learn to read. Even if you don't, you are putting in the effort, which is all that matters. I perceive that my niece and nephew have already benefitted from your presence. If you are not yet making the progress you desire, perhaps you might reexamine your methods.

What do I mean by this? Indulge me when I say: I have been watching you these many years, my dearest, and here is what I have observed: ever since your mother passed away, you have been the responsible child, the compulsive server. You stepped into your mother's shoes and never took them off. Your father came to rely on you to run the house and take care of your brother and sisters. Oh! How I wish I could have been of more help in those early years, but I had my own responsibilities, and you lived so many miles distant.

At such a young age, you took your duties in stride, and they became second nature to you. But I wonder now if it wasn't an unhealthy thing. For today, you seem to measure your self-worth only in terms of what you can achieve for others, determined that they should benefit from your experience and advice.

But did it ever occur to you to ask Emma and the captain what they might prefer to eat, rather than devising a picnic menu of your own favorites? Did you bother to ask if they even liked the idea of a picnic? Perhaps they would rather do something else!

Everyone, I believe, has a valuable and accurate inner guide. Let people think for themselves and make their own choices. Step back and listen more. You might be surprised at what you hear. I hope you will not take offense at what I have said but rather, take it in the light in which it is intended: one loving heart speaking to another and wishing you only the best.

You asked about my health, but as I have run out of room, I will only say, every day is a bit harder than the one before, but I

*am doing the best I can. Pray forgive my penmanship—my
hand is not as steady as it once was.*

*I send you hugs, kisses, and thanks over the miles. Do write
again soon. I eagerly await every new revelation.*

I love you dearly,
Eliza Phillips

Diana finished reading the letter and heaved a frustrated sigh.

She appreciated Mrs. Phillips's good intentions. But her godmother lived hundreds of miles away. She had not seen Miss
Fallbrook since she'd been very young, and she had never even
met the captain. How could she know the best course of action
for Diana to take?

The very nature of Diana's position required her to manage
things for Miss Fallbrook. She couldn't leave important decisions
up to a fifteen-year-old girl. As for the picnic—everyone liked
picnics. The idea that Diana ought to have bothered a busy man
like Captain Fallbrook about menu choices—it was ridiculous.
She had wanted to surprise him and Miss Fallbrook with a lovely
afternoon. It was not her fault that they were so picky about what
they ate, or that the cook who knew their tastes had been away at
the time.

Her godmother had meant well, but she was off the mark.
People often had difficulty making decisions. It was Diana's duty
to provide a guiding hand. It fed her soul to be of assistance to
others. And how else was she to make amends for neglecting her
mother in her hour of need?

Diana studied the letter again, this time, though, with rising
worry. Mrs. Phillips's handwriting *was* shakier than in the past. In
some sections, it was almost illegible. Clear signs of her failing
health.

"Every day is a bit harder than the one before."

Tears pricked Diana's eyes. The clock was ticking much too
fast.

The answer was not to step back.

To achieve her goals, Diana must work even harder.

To TEST HER theory about the German railway scheme, Diana wrote to Franke and Dietrich, introducing herself as a woman of means temporarily residing in Cornwall, and giving the Portwithys post office as her return address. She explained that she had heard about the financial rewards of the project from Mr. Latimer. Would they please reply at their earliest opportunity with details of the investment?

When Diana posted the letter in the village, she asked Mrs. Beardsley if she recalled Sir Thomas corresponding with a company called Franke and Dietrich a couple of years ago.

"He did," Mrs. Beardsley affirmed. "Letters went back and forth for quite a while."

"Do you remember if, perchance, a gentleman—or gentlemen—from Germany visited this area about four months ago, around the time that Sir Thomas died?"

"I can't say that I recall anyone of that description. We don't get many people here from abroad."

"What about strangers from *this* country?" Diana prodded, believing that Franke and Dietrich could have sent money and hired a local person to commit the deed. "Did you see anyone unfamiliar in Portwithys at the time? A rough-looking man, perhaps?"

The postmistress pursed her lips, as if thinking, and then shook her head. "No, miss. Not that I recall, anyway. Why do you ask?"

Diana gave a quick shrug. "Just curious, that's all. Thank you." As she left the shop, she felt Mrs. Beardsley's inquiring gaze on her.

Diana made a similar inquiry in the pub, the inn, and the bakery. No one remembered a visitor from Germany nor an outsider at all at the time, either of whom would surely have been an object of curiosity in Portwithys.

She left the village disappointed.

Her theory was beginning to sound less and less likely.

CHAPTER FIFTEEN

T HE WIND TUGGED at Diana's bonnet as she made her way across the grounds. It was the second morning in a row that Miss Fallbrook hadn't turned up on time for lessons. It was a bad habit and Diana would have to break her of it.

She had checked the riverbank first, thinking Miss Fallbrook might be digging for clay again, and was now on her way to investigate the beach. In all honesty, she could not blame her pupil for avoiding the schoolroom today. Their last reading lesson had ended with them both in tears.

Diana reached the edge of the bluffs and paused to take in the view, her bonnet ribbons flapping in the breeze. The air was so crisp and salty, she could taste it. The sea stretched to eternity, the vast blueness broken up here and there by rocky, black islets. Seagulls screeched over the foaming waves, which rushed up on the sandy beach. The scene felt vigorous and alive, a marked contrast to Diana's inner anguish and doubt.

She zigzagged her way down the narrow path along the scrubby hillside. The tide was out. On the stretch of sand near the water's edge, she noticed a trail of footprints disappearing around the cliffs at one side of the cove. Were they Miss Fallbrook's?

Following the trail around the bend in the cliff, Diana found herself in a smaller, shallower cove. The beach here was only about a dozen feet deep. The footprints led to an immense cave cut into the rocky cliffside.

A shallow saltwater channel connected the cave with the sea. A ribbon of sand edged the channel, permitting entry to the cave. The footprints continued along it.

Diana entered the cave and waited for her eyes to adjust to the darkness. The interior was damp and gloomy, the wet, sandy floor strewn with rocks and pebbles. Moss clung to rocky walls. At high tide, Diana suspected, this part of the cave might fill with water. She moved further inward.

Rounding a bend, Diana found herself in a cavern that resembled a small indoor harbor at low tide. A sailboat that looked to be of recent vintage was beached and tethered to an iron post. Across the way, Diana spotted Miss Fallbrook on her knees, making a sand sculpture of a giant mermaid. So intent was she on her undertaking that she didn't hear Diana's approach.

Diana gently cleared her throat to announce her presence. Miss Fallbrook jumped and leapt to her feet. Her face flushed with guilt as she brushed sand from her skirts. "I'm sorry." She seemed to be truly remorseful this time. "I got carried away and I guess I forgot the time."

Diana felt bad now. It was a shame that her pupil had to sneak down here and sculpt in secret. "Your sand mermaid is lovely."

"Thank you." Miss Fallbrook smiled hopefully. "Unfortunately, she won't last. When the tide comes in to Smuggler's Cave, it will wash her away."

"Smuggler's Cave? Why is this called that?"

"Because smugglers used it years and years ago to import things from France."

"Whose boat is that?"

"Ours."

Diana suddenly understood why the sailboat looked so new. It would have replaced the one that had been destroyed three years ago, when Lady and Robert Fallbrook drowned. "Did the masters of Pendowar Hall know about the smuggling?"

"Oh, yes. They were part of it." Apparently sensing that she wasn't going to be chastised for her truancy, Miss Fallbrook warmed to her subject. "My great-great-I-don't-know-how-many-greats-grandfathers all made lots of money off it, by allowing smugglers to unload their wares on our beach. But then the revenue men found out, so my ancestor arranged for the smugglers to drop off their goods in secret here and pick them up again when the coast was clear."

"What an exciting piece of history."

"It is rather. But that's not the best part."

"What is the best part?"

"There's a secret passageway that leads from these caverns all the way up to the house."

"A secret passageway?" Diana was fascinated.

"They carved a tunnel and masses of stairs right into the cliff. It starts over here." Miss Fallbrook motioned for Diana to follow her to the back of the cave, where a shadowy opening yawned. "It ends at a hidden doorway near the green parlor on the ground floor of the house."

Diana had read about such passageways but had never seen one in person. "Can we go up it?"

"We could, but we would need a torch."

"Another time, perhaps. Let's go home the usual way, shall we?"

Miss Fallbrook's smile evaporated. "All right." As they started back towards the mouth of the cave, she sighed. "Can we skip our reading lesson today?"

"We mustn't."

"I cannot bear to go over the alphabet *again*."

The frustration in Miss Fallbrook's eyes mirrored Diana's own. If only there were a way, she thought, to transfer the girl's delight in sculpting with sand to reading and writing ...

An answer came to Diana like a bolt from the blue. "Wait. I have an idea."

"What?"

Diana crouched down and beckoned for her pupil to join her.

"I want you to sculpt a letter out of sand."

"Why?"

"Just try it." Diana drew the letter S in the sand with her fingertip. "This is an S. Remember? Use the sand like you did with your mermaid sculpture and make the letter S."

Miss Fallbrook hesitated. Then, biting her lip, she scooped up sand and molded it into the designated shape.

"Does the S shape remind you of anything? An animal, perhaps?"

Miss Fallbrook seemed to think about it. "A snake."

"Yes! What sound does a snake make?"

"Sssss?"

"Exactly! As it happens, the letter S makes the same sound as a snake. Can you say it with me?"

They pronounced the sound aloud together.

"Good work, Miss Fallbrook. Make another S out of sand. This time, while you shape it, think of a snake and say the sound aloud."

Miss Fallbrook repeated the sound as she molded another S out of sand. Diana employed a similar tactic for the letters A, N, and D, emphasizing the sounds of each letter, and comparing the shapes Emma molded to things she could visualize—an apple wedge for A, a noodle for N, and a dog's snout for D.

"The marvelous thing about letters," Diana enthused when her student had completed these exercises, "is that they not only represent individual sounds, but when the sounds are put together, they form *words*. The same words that you use and recognize in speech." She moved to a fresh section of sand. "Now, I want you to mold these letters again, one at a time, in this order: S-A-N-D."

The young lady performed the requested task. Diana told her to touch each molded letter in order from left to right, while pronouncing the sounds each letter made. Miss Fallbrook's attempt was awkward. They were just four separate sounds to her.

Diana gently took her pupil's hand in hers and coaxed her to scoop up a handful of sand. "What do you call this?"

Miss Fallbrook blew out a disgruntled breath. "*Sand.* Obviously."

"Yes, it's sand. Sand is a thing. You can see it. You can touch it. Sand is also a word. Look at the letters you made, *touch* the letters you made, and *read it.*"

Miss Fallbrook stared at the letters she had molded out of sand. Hesitantly, she touched them and sounded them out again but did not yet seem to make the connection.

"Listen to the waves crashing on the beach," Diana said with fervor. "Smell the salt in the air." She scooped another clump of sand into her charge's palm. "Feel the sand with your fingers. Now read the word again. What does it say?"

"Ssss-Aaaa-Nnnn-Dddd ..." All at once, Miss Fallbrook's face lit up with understanding. "Oh! Oh! Sand! *Sand!* I see it. I feel it. The letters make the word *sand!*"

"Yes! Yes!" Diana exclaimed. They both leapt to their feet with excitement.

"I read it. I read it! Oh, Miss Taylor. I can't believe it. I read a word!" Miss Fallbrook embraced Diana tightly.

Diana returned the hug, her heart swelling. "This is just the beginning, Miss Fallbrook. But now you have the key."

DIANA WAS THRILLED by Miss Fallbrook's sudden and significant advance. Why she had required such a unique methodology to make the reading connection was unclear to Diana. But if the young woman needed to visualize letters in three dimensions to grasp their meaning, then so be it. Since Miss Fallbrook's first love of sculpting had begun with clay, Diana decided to utilize that medium to keep the momentum going.

The next morning, Diana brought her pupil to the riverbank,

where they dug up a quantity of natural clay. Miss Fallbrook wanted to hold their lesson there. Diana hesitated at first, thinking the classroom was best, but—recalling Mrs. Phillips's advice—she gave in to her charge's request. And right there on the grassy riverbank, beneath the autumn sky, Miss Fallbrook sculpted all twenty-six letters of the alphabet out of clay and sounded out the letters for each. For the first time, she conducted the exercise with enjoyment and a sparkle in her eyes, for she understood the purpose behind it.

And for the first time, the lessons began to stick.

The next few days flew by as they traded off working with clay and sand, returning one more time to the beach, and studying in the schoolroom when the weather demanded it. As Miss Fallbrook molded letters with her hands, she finally came to recognize them, and their sounds came readily to mind.

Since her student thrived on visualizing things in three dimensions, Diana devised new techniques in other subjects to emphasize the real rather than the abstract. Things that could be touched and felt, rather than imagined.

When the supplies for their sewing projects arrived, Miss Fallbrook was delighted to discover an activity so much more rewarding than embroidery. A flat bolt of fabric could be re-imagined, designed, cut, and sewn and into a three-dimensional object—a garment that could be worn and appreciated.

For science and nature, they searched for beetles under leaves, held ladybugs in their hands, and dug in the dirt for worms. To make mathematics problems more accessible, Diana employed sticks, pebbles, and reeds. One night, when a thunderstorm rattled the rafters, they shivered under the covers while Diana read aloud from *Frankenstein* by Mary Shelley.

They touched the old, stone walls and battlements of Pendowar Hall while discussing its ancient status and history. With lanterns in hand, they explored the passageway from Smuggler's Cave all the way up to the house, marveling at the steps chiseled into the rock and dirt, all brought about by the Fallbrook ancestors' ingenuity and cunning.

"Just think of all the riches brought up via this route and hidden in the house," Miss Fallbrook told Diana when they arrived at the end of the tunnel, a seldom-used parlor on the ground floor, where a secret door had been fashioned to resemble a bookcase.

"Who knows about that passageway?" Diana asked her pupil.

"I don't know. Everyone in the house, I expect. Cousin William said he used to play down there when he was visiting Pendowar Hall as a boy."

Did anyone else know about it? Diana wondered. The passageway, she realized, would make it easy for someone to sneak into the house in the dead of night and get to the north tower without being noticed. She filed away that notion in her mind for later examination.

In the meantime, she focused on her pupil, who was flourishing in this new educational environment. Miss Fallbrook could hardly wait for each new study session to begin.

And Diana could hardly wait to tell the captain about it.

A HEAVY RAIN had been falling all day, but at last, the clouds parted slightly and a weak sun peeked out. Finished with their studies, Diana and Miss Fallbrook decided to take a walk.

Donning heavy cloaks, gloves, and boots, they strolled across the grounds, inhaling with pleasure the earthy fragrance of damp leaves and grass. It was cold but refreshingly so. They wandered along the cliff path, drinking in the sight of the sea. In time, they came to a place where the path diverged.

Diana knew that one direction led to a promontory with an impressive ocean view, while the other continued inland until the two forks met again some distance beyond. A sign was posted on the inland fork: PATH CLOSED.

"I wonder what's wrong?" Miss Fallbrook remarked.

"It must be due to the rain," Diana theorized. "Perhaps there's a pothole or a muddy pool."

They followed the outer fork to the edge of the cliff, where they paused to take in the scene. Waves crashed onto the rocks below, spouting billowy foam high into the air. A strong gust of wind blew up and blasted them full in the face, threatening to knock them off their feet.

"Let's go!" Miss Fallbrook cried, rushing ahead.

Diana hurried after her. But the path was very narrow. As she rounded the bend, she stepped into a hole near the cliff's edge, where the ground had crumbled away. Diana's heart lurched in terror as she stumbled and wavered. Beside her lay a sheer, deadly drop. Somehow, she managed to direct her tumble onto the sturdy portion of the path, where she fell to her knees and dug her gloved hands into the mud and dirt.

"Miss Taylor!" Miss Fallbrook rushed back. "Are you all right?"

Diana's pulse pounded and her limbs trembled with relief as she regained her equilibrium. "Yes, I'm fine."

"I leapt over that hole—I'm so sorry, I didn't think. I should have warned you!" Miss Fallbrook helped Diana rise, took her arm, and they returned to the safety of the gardens. "Do you think someone put the warning sign on the wrong side of the path?"

"It's possible." Diana's heart thundered in her chest. *I could have died just now.*

Her cloak and gloves were soaked with mud. She looked forward to returning to the house and warming up by the fire, but it was quite a way off.

In a thickly wooded area, they came upon a small outbuilding, where dead leaves clustered wetly on the pitched roof. Diana had passed the structure before, but it had always been closed and dark. Now, a light burned in the mullioned windows and smoke billowed from the chimney.

"What building is this?" Diana asked.

"The shop." Miss Fallbrook darted to the window. "Look! It's William."

Diana joined her, shivering, intending to draw the girl away. She paused upon observing Captain Fallbrook within. They'd had little contact since their unfortunate picnic over a fortnight ago, for the captain had been busy overseeing repairs to several tenant properties. He had never been far from her thoughts, though. She had often found herself wondering where he was, and how he was.

She took him in now as he stood, coatless and tieless, at an ancient, scarred workbench heaped with tools and wood, focused on something he was making. The sleeves of his linen shirt were rolled up to reveal muscular forearms, a sight pleasing to her feminine sensibilities. But it was the unexpected look on his face, when he glanced up and spotted them through the window, that caused butterflies to dance in Diana's stomach.

His brows lifted with delight. His mouth widened in a smile. He made no disguise of his pleasure in seeing her. She was, she realized, equally glad to see him.

Covering whatever he was working on with a cloth, the captain crossed to the door. Although he still relied on his cane, Diana was pleased to observe that his limp had eased somewhat, and his injured leg appeared to give him less pain.

"Miss Taylor! Emma, good afternoon," he called from the small front porch.

Diana and her charge moved in that direction and returned the salutation. He took in the state of Diana's bedraggled cloak with alarm.

"What happened?"

"I fell on the cliff path."

"It's crumbled away at the outer fork," Miss Fallbrook explained. Her shyness around her cousin seemed to be forgotten in the excitement of the moment.

"I'm so sorry. I'll speak to Mr. Nankervis about it. Are you all right?" he asked Diana.

"No harm done, except to my pride—and my cloak and gloves." Diana couldn't repress another shiver.

"But you're cold. And muddy. Both of you, please come in and warm yourselves by the fire."

Diana was grateful for the invitation. "Thank you, Captain." Before she could say more, her pupil dashed past them into the shop and disappeared.

Diana joined the captain on the porch, intending to follow Miss Fallbrook inside. But the captain moved in close, blocking her entry. He smelled delightfully of Pears soap and the faint fragrance of wood dust that rested on his clothes.

"Allow me to assist you with that." He cradled the hook of his cane over one arm and gestured to Diana's sodden, dirty cloak. "We can lay it by the hearth to dry."

"Thank you," she said again.

As Captain Fallbrook helped her to remove the garment, their faces nearly collided. Diana's breath quickened and sped up even further when he took one of her gloved hands in his. "Your gloves?"

He assisted her to tug off first one wet glove and then the other. For a moment, their bare hands touched, sending a jolt like lightning through her.

"Welcome to my workshop, Miss Taylor," the captain said softly, his blue eyes meeting hers before he released her hand and stepped back.

Diana's pulse drummed in her ears. She couldn't remember when she had ever experienced such a visceral physical reaction to a man.

Oh, yes, she could. It was the night she had been alone with the captain in the mermaid's room in the north tower.

What was it Mrs. Trenowden had said?

"He's got mistresses across the seven seas, is what I hear."

Diana could see why. He was intensely charming when he wanted to be.

You have no business, Diana scolded herself, *feeling jolts of lightning or anything similar for Captain Fallbrook.* He was her employer. Besides, she was not interested in becoming involved with him or with any man.

She would definitely have to be on her guard around him.

CHAPTER SIXTEEN

T HE WORKSHOP WAS of a good size.

As she entered, Diana was immediately conscious of the pungent fragrance of freshly cut wood and the wood shavings that peppered the floor. Dozens of saws, drills, and other tools hung on racks affixed to the walls, nestled amongst chests with small drawers and shelves piled high with lumber of various shapes and sizes. Miss Fallbrook was across the room, exploring. A door at the back was ajar, leading to what looked like a small chamber.

Captain Fallbrook crossed to the hearth, where he draped Diana's cloak and gloves over a chair to dry. She moved close to the flames and held out her hands, relishing the warmth that spread through her body. "What a marvelous shop."

"It was built over a hundred years ago by the same ancestor who, as the story goes, fell in love with a mermaid."

"The one who carved the mermaid bed?"

He nodded, moving to stand beside her and spreading out his own hands towards the fire.

Despite herself, Diana's stomach fluttered at his proximity. *Stop that*, she warned herself. *There will be no stomach fluttering.* "I still hope to catch a glimpse of the ghost of this infamous mermaid," she teased.

"Perhaps you shall. Heard any more footsteps in the night?"

"Sadly, no."

"As the legend goes," he said, eyes twinkling as he glanced at her, "the Mermaid of Pendowar walks on two legs when she appears on dry land."

"So I've heard."

They shared a smile.

He glanced at his ward, who hummed as she investigated the woodworking projects on display across the room. The captain lowered his voice to just above a whisper. "Emma looks happy."

"I think she is," Diana replied just as softly. "We've had a new development in her reading and writing."

"What kind of development?"

Diana briefly told him what had happened at the beach and the progress Miss Fallbrook had made since.

"Do you mean to say that Emma can read now?"

"She finally understands the *concept* of reading now—the idea that letters make sounds and join in patterns to form words. There is still a disconnect at times between what is written and what she sees, but I believe she has finally started down the right path."

"And this all came about by having her mold letters of the alphabet out of sand and clay?"

"It did. I don't understand why—it is most unusual, I think. But we happened upon an activity that your cousin already enjoyed, and it helped her make the connection."

He shook his head while grinning. "You more than *happened* upon it. It was a stroke of genius."

Diana took a step back from the fire, suddenly growing too warm. "It is only the beginning," she said, still whispering, "but Miss Fallbrook is starting to believe in herself now, which is so important."

The captain stepped back to again stand beside her. "Since the day you arrived, I have felt ... that is to say, I have known that Emma was in good hands. Thank you."

He gave her a look so appreciative and full of admiration that Diana felt a blush bloom in her cheeks. "You're welcome."

Lowering his head to hers, he whispered, "Would you like to see what I am making for Emma?"

"I would."

Diana joined him at the workbench, where he covertly lifted a cloth and showed her his work in progress. It was a small, wooden box. The hinged lid was expertly carved with images of seashells. "For her keepsakes," he whispered.

Diana was awed by his handiwork and touched that he was making his ward a gift. "It's beautiful," she returned discreetly. "When did you learn how to do this?"

"My father taught me. He learned from his father. And I whittled a lot at sea. It is a sailor's second trade, you know." He gave her a wink and a smile.

Despite herself, his nearness, and the expression on his face, made Diana's insides quiver—*again*—and her heart beat double-time. She wanted to smack herself.

Was he flirting with her? If so, he was very good at it.

Had the captain given the same wink and smile to that lady in Naples, whom he had mentioned? Did he smile this way at every woman he met in all those ports of call? No doubt he was used to having ladies swoon at his feet.

Diana refused to swoon.

"How long have you been working on this?" she whispered, willing her pulse to resume its normal pace.

"Ever since you pointed out so diplomatically that I ought to pay more attention to my cousin."

"I am sure Miss Fallbrook will love it."

"I hope so." He sighed. "I never know what to say to her."

"That will come more easily with time."

"I am afraid I made a dreadful mess of that picnic you worked so hard to plan."

Diana recalled what her godmother had said about that affair. "Perhaps it was not as well-planned as it might have been," she acknowledged.

"I understood the thought behind it. I should have been

more … open and accepting."

"*I* should have asked you and Miss Fallbrook what you might like to eat or do, rather than forcing my idea of a picnic upon you."

He caught her eye. They shared a laugh. *There, that's better*, Diana thought. Things had settled down between them to something more manageable, something resembling friendship.

He was about to say something when Miss Fallbrook called out to them from across the room, "What are you talking about?"

Diana felt her pupil's eyes on her, as if silently questioning.

"Carpentry," was the captain's quick reply as he stowed the carved wooden box in a drawer.

Miss Fallbrook made her way to them, carrying a small, wooden figurine of an elephant. "William, did you make this?"

"Yes. Ages ago."

"May I have it?"

"That old thing? It is not one of my best efforts."

"I think it's sweet."

He went very still and then bowed his head. "Take it. It's yours."

"Thank you." The young woman cradled the little elephant to her chest. Captain Fallbrook returned her smile. In that moment, Diana glimpsed a connection between the two that warmed her heart.

They decided, in time, to return to the house. Miss Fallbrook requested permission to go back on her own and flew off ahead of them.

"You said your father taught you woodworking," Diana remarked as she and Captain Fallbrook headed down the path together. "I take it that was a hobby, since I recall you mentioning that he was a clergyman?"

"Yes. 'The truest and most worthy occupation for a second son,' he used to say."

"The clergy is a noble profession. It is my brother's entire life."

"It was my father's as well. He poured his energy into writing sermons and tending to his *flock*, as he called them. My mother was the perfect clergyman's wife. As a boy, I used to accompany one or the other on their visits to our parishioners."

That, Diana thought, *must be where the captain developed his habit of assisting the less fortunate.* "How old were you when your parents passed away?"

"Twelve. They perished within days of each other from typhoid, which they contracted from a poor family in our village. How the scourge bypassed me, I shall never know."

"It is difficult enough to lose one parent so young. But to lose both at once—it is unthinkable."

"My uncle became my guardian. Within a fortnight, he arranged a commission for me in the Royal Navy."

"So soon?"

"I had no wish to go to sea. I had hoped to enter my father's profession. But that would have required further schooling and attending university. I suppose Uncle Thomas didn't want to be bothered raising me. He just wanted me gone."

"How cruel."

"I felt that way for years. But in time, I was grateful."

"Were you?"

"There is much to be said for a career in the Royal Navy. I love my occupation now and cannot imagine my life any other way."

They emerged from the woods into an open space with gravel paths and manicured, dormant flower beds. Pendowar Hall rose majestically beyond, smoke escaping from the chimneys atop its grey, stone battlements.

"I too was thrust into a profession I did not expect," Diana said as they navigated the final stretch together. She told him about the young man to whom she had been affianced, who had dropped her as a result of her father's loss of fortune.

The captain's features hardened. "What a cad. I'm sorry that happened to you."

"I do not seek sympathy. I only wish to point out that like you, my life—and my sisters' lives—changed suddenly and irrevocably into something we could not have imagined. Yet looking back, I have no regrets. I love my work."

"Yet another of the many things we have in common, Miss Taylor." He glanced at her. "Are your sisters in the same occupation?"

"They are."

"I hope they enjoy it as much as you seem to?"

"Well, to be honest, although Athena and Selena love teaching, they have never been terribly fond of governessing. I don't blame them. Every household is different. It can be a difficult and lonely life. For some years now, we have harbored higher aspirations."

"Such as?"

"We dream of opening a school for girls."

His brows lifted with interest. "A school for girls?"

"Yes. Such institutions are few and far between, and the curriculum at those that do exist leaves much to be desired. Girls are every bit as intelligent as boys! Why should the male of the species benefit from a wide and varied education, encompassing everything from science, mathematics, and literature to history, philosophy, and beyond, while the female is taught nothing but needlework, music, sketching, a smattering of foreign language, and deportment? It is a travesty!"

"You make a fair point," the captain mused.

"If girls could only learn what boys do from a young age, think how it would expand their minds!" Diana declared passionately. "They could understand and participate more fully in the world. And someday, perhaps, the professions that men guard so assiduously will open to women and they won't be stuck at home. But it must begin with education. Which is why my sisters and I dream so fervently about opening a girls' school."

"It is an admirable goal."

"But an impossible one, I'm afraid." Diana took a breath to

calm herself. "For it would require a venue. Which is not within our means."

They had reached the house now and paused. "Nothing is impossible, Miss Taylor. The word itself says: 'I'm possible.'"

Diana laughed at that and, mimicking his earlier phrase, replied, "A fair point, sir."

"Who knows? Your fortunes might change. For your and your sisters' sakes, I hope they do," he said as they shared a parting smile.

"YOU LIKE MY Cousin William, don't you?"

Diana's spoonful of ham and potato soup froze halfway to her mouth. "What do you mean?"

It was another cold, blustery day, and they were having lunch in the nursery while Ivy stoked the fire.

"I mean, he likes you, and you like him." Miss Fallbrook's tone was serious, and her face solemn.

The remark caused a flush to creep up Diana's throat. "Of course I like him. And I should be glad if Captain Fallbrook does not *dislike* me."

"It is more than that. I saw the way you looked at him yesterday at the shop. And the way he looked at you." Miss Fallbrook buttered a piece of bread. "You could not keep your eyes off each other."

"I enjoy talking to the captain. We have become friends. But I am in his employ. A relationship between us would be inappropriate."

"Yes," agreed Miss Fallbrook, "but not because you work for him. I shouldn't care about that. It would be wrong— inappropriate, as you say—because you are my *governess*."

"What is the distinction?"

Her pupil regarded her with pained disbelief. "Have you

forgotten the Mermaid's Curse?"

"Oh, *that*. Miss Fallbrook …"

"If you and William fall in love, you are both doomed!" Miss Fallbrook's voice rang with concern.

Ivy rose from the hearth, her face alive with equal worry. "She's right, miss. If you two fall in love, Morwenna will see to it that you die from drowning, and that the captain dies of grief."

"I could not bear it if anything happened to you, Miss Taylor!"

"Calm yourselves, girls." Diana struggled to hold back a smile. "I am happily single and intend to remain so. Anyway, the Mermaid's Curse is just a legend." As she said so, a remark in Athena's last letter came back to her:

"All legends have a foundation in truth."

Ivy shook her head, her face grave. "It's more than a legend, miss. It has happened twice, and it could happen again."

Miss Fallbrook gasped. "It almost *did* happen again. Yesterday! That hole on the cliff path. You might have fallen into the sea!"

"Don't be silly," Diana replied. But it was true. She *had* very nearly lost her balance and fallen to her death.

"It was Morwenna," Ivy whispered.

Diana knew that no mermaid's ghost was responsible for her near-accident. But was it possible that someone who'd known she'd been out for a walk that day had arranged the circumstances?

Mr. Emity's warning came back to her again.

"If someone did murder Sir Thomas, they might not take kindly to the idea of someone looking into it."

Had the PATH CLOSED sign truly been placed on the wrong side of the fork?

Or had someone deliberately moved it?

THE CLOCK IN the hall had long since chimed the hour of two, but Diana couldn't sleep.

The captain had spoken to Mr. Nankervis, who'd admitted that he'd set the warning sign on the cliff path. But hearing about Diana's fall, he'd become upset and worried that he'd inadvertently put it in the wrong place.

Which, Diana realized, proved absolutely nothing.

Someone, aware that Diana was questioning the circumstances of Sir Thomas's death, might have moved that sign after Mr. Nankervis had placed it, hoping to get rid of her. It was a frightening thought but not an impossible one. It had also put her pupil in danger.

Diana wrestled with this idea for some time before finally concluding that she was overthinking the matter. It had been pure chance that she and Miss Fallbrook had taken the path that day. Bad luck that Diana had stumbled, and nothing more.

Miss Fallbrook's question from the day before, however, still rang in Diana's ears, driving all thought of the cliff path incident from her mind.

"You like my Cousin William, don't you?"

At their first meeting, Diana had been irritated by the captain's attitude. He had viewed Diana's position as a necessary evil and had written off his ward as a lost cause.

So much had changed since then. She now saw that he was a good and thoughtful man. The sort of man who sent palm trees from the Mediterranean to his uncle and fabric to needy tenants, who took care of the people on his estate and was struggling to improve his relationship with his young cousin. Diana and Captain Fallbrook had many things in common, from a love of reading and doing meaningful work to their desire to help the poor. She couldn't help but *like* him.

But for Miss Fallbrook to think those feelings went anything beyond a calm and proper *admiration*—to even consider that Diana might like him in *that way*—it was unthinkable.

"I saw the way you looked at him yesterday at the shop. And the

way he looked at you."

She couldn't deny the way her stomach had fluttered the day before when he had gazed at her. Or the way her heart had jolted at the mere touch of his hand. But these had been mere physical responses to his innate masculinity and charm. Hadn't they?

It was true, the captain *had* looked at her several times with warmth, as if he'd thought her someone special. But what did that signify? Nothing. Diana's history had taught her better. Men had never liked her for *her*. When the truth came out, they had always been after her money—or money they *thought* she possessed.

It was different with the captain. He was a wealthy man now. He wouldn't care if Diana had a fortune. In fact, he knew that she did not. But he had no reason to care *about* Diana, either.

"A leopard doesn't change his spots. When a man's unmarried at thirty-two, it tells you something."

Who was Captain Fallbrook really, deep within his soul? One day, he might discover that she was still sleuthing and send her packing. Or *she* might discover that he had been deceiving her from the start, keeping a secret like that of Mr. Heyer, the second beau who had left her soul in tatters, or one as nefarious as Mr. Rochester's in *Jane Eyre*. If so, the truth would come out. The man behind the mask would be revealed. And when it happened, Diana would be ready, with her heart intact, unbroken.

Even if the captain *were* the rare exception to the rule—and truly the generous and personable man he appeared to be—it was no consolation. For according to reports, he was *not the marrying sort*.

And neither was she.

When he recovered his health—hopefully in a matter of months—he would return to his duties at sea. One day, when Miss Fallbrook had made sufficient progress with her reading, Diana would return to Derbyshire. Perhaps they would keep in touch by post—but she would probably never see either of them again.

This idea made her unaccountably sad. She quickly brushed it aside.

Often, new people came into one's life for a moment and then moved on. It was the way of things. She and Captain Fallbrook could be friends, but nothing more. And it was just as well, considering the legend that loomed over this house.

The Mermaid's Curse, Diana thought defiantly, *will have to wait for another victim.*

She had just rolled over in bed and taken a deep breath, willing herself to go to sleep, when two sounds made her freeze.

The creak of the door to the servants' stairs.

And footsteps.

Diana sat up, her pulse thudding in her ears as the footfalls passed her doorway. She had only heard that sound once before, on her first night at Pendowar Hall. She wasn't dreaming it. It wasn't the wind. And it was no ghost. Someone with two very real legs and feet was traversing the halls again in the middle of the night.

Diana quickly lit a candle, threw on her dressing gown and, eschewing slippers, quietly opened her chamber door. The corridor was dark, but she heard footfalls moving fast at the far end of the corridor. Whoever it was had entered without benefit of candle—or else they had blown out the flame.

Diana followed as swiftly as she was able. Who could the intruder be? Was it a member of the household staff? Or had they gained entry via the passageway from Smuggler's Cave?

Whoever it was, what did they want? Diana had wanted to mention her theory about the passageway to the captain, but he already knew of its existence and had dismissed her other suspicions so emphatically, she had seen no point in bringing up the subject until she had some kind of proof.

The carpet prickled Diana's bare feet as she made her way down the hall past the gallery to the opposite wing. The blue parlor was dark and silent. The library was similarly empty.

As she approached Captain Fallbrook's study, Diana thought

she heard a noise. Was it coming from within that chamber or without? She entered. To her disappointment, the study was dark—but she detected the scent of a recently snuffed candle. She touched the candle on the desk. Its wick end was soft and warm.

Someone has just been here.

A slight chill infiltrated the room. One of the casement doors, she noticed, was slightly ajar. Had it been the perpetrator's mode of exit? Diana slipped through the French doors onto the narrow balcony.

The night was cold and so dense with fog that not a star shone in the heavens. The balcony's paving stones felt like ice as Diana crossed to the balustrade and gazed down. The walls below, she recalled, were covered in thick vines, but she could make nothing out in the fog. If someone were climbing down that way, they must indeed have been a ghost, for they made no sound.

Frustrated, Diana returned to the study. Who had been here at such an hour? What had they wanted? Her gaze turned to the desk, where she noticed folders and papers in disarray. Captain Fallbrook was generally neat and organized. Had the intruder been going through these documents when he'd heard her approach and fled with haste?

Curious, Diana set down her candlestick and glanced through the paperwork. She immediately recognized Sir Thomas's handwriting from the letters she had reviewed previously. Several folders contained more early drafts of the baronet's correspondence. As with Sir Thomas's letters to the railway company in Germany, he must have rewritten these before sending because they included crossed-out words and ink splatters. They related to mundane matters: repairs for a tenant's leaky roof, the sale of a horse, the requisition of a new set of clothes from a London tailor.

One letter, however, caught Diana's eye. It was addressed to Mr. Jack Trenowden at Greenview Farm.

Pendowar Hall
24 May 1849

Mr. Trenowden,

As you have paid no rent these past four quarters and every letter my steward sent has remained unanswered, I am taking matters into my own hands. Despite your family's long tenancy at Greenview Farm, I cannot go on ignoring the situation.

Consider this your final notice. The entire amount owed is due in full by 1 July of this year, or you must vacate the premises.

Yours,
Sir Thomas Fallbrook, Bart.

Diana stared at the letter, her heart beating a staccato rhythm in her chest.

No wonder Mr. Trenowden had been so cold to Miss Fallbrook when they'd met. No wonder he held such a deep resentment towards the Fallbrook family. Several generations of *his* family had lived and worked at Greenview Farm. It was his home and livelihood. And Sir Thomas had been about to evict him.

Sir Thomas's death had apparently granted the Trenowdens a reprieve since they still lived there.

Could this letter be a motive for murder?

Diana's gaze fixed on four words in the first paragraph, and her breath caught in her throat.

"I cannot go on."

The same four words that had comprised Sir Thomas's suicide note.

CHAPTER SEVENTEEN

T HE HEAVY FOG from the night before had vanished, leaving a cloudless blue sky in its wake. From the garden bench where she and Miss Fallbrook were seated, practicing French, Diana caught sight of Captain Fallbrook returning on horseback to the stables.

"Miss Fallbrook, you have earned some time off. Would you like to go riding?"

"Yes! Thank you, Miss Taylor." The young woman leapt up and dashed back to the house to change into her riding habit.

Diana waited outside the stables until the captain emerged. "Sir."

"Miss Taylor." He looked dashing as always in his black frock coat and pleased to see her. Tenting a hand over his eyes against the sun, he took in his ward across the way. "Were you holding a lesson *en plein air?*"

"We were—and do so now whenever the weather permits. Miss Fallbrook prefers the out-of-doors."

"How is her reading coming along?"

"She makes new progress every day."

"Excellent. I am heading back to the house. Will you walk with me?"

"Yes, thank you. I was hoping to have a word with you."

"About what?" They started back towards Pendowar Hall.

The best approach, Diana had decided, was a direct approach.

"I heard footsteps last night."

His face fell. "Not *this* again. I thought we agreed you had dreamt that."

"Pray hear me out. I had trouble sleeping and—"

"Welcome to the club. I have not had a decent night's rest since I returned to shore," he said, interrupting testily. "I miss the rocking of a boat at sea."

"I'm sorry, Captain."

He heaved a sigh. "You were saying?"

"It was well after two o'clock. I heard footsteps in the hall and followed them. Someone was in your study."

He eyed her sharply. "How do you know?"

Diana told him about the snuffed candle, the papers in disarray, and the French door that had been ajar.

"That is easily explained. I was in my study working last night, until about half-past one. I must have left the candle burning when I retired. That's why you smelled a snuffed candle."

"But, sir, who blew it out?"

He shrugged. "The wind. I often leave the French doors partially ajar—I enjoy the night air. It would explain the dispersed papers as well."

"What about the footsteps?"

"As I have said before, it must have been Mrs. Gwynn doing her nightly rounds."

"If it was Mrs. Gwynn, I would have encountered her in the hall."

"Not if she went down the south stairs."

"The south stairs?"

"There are two servants' stairwells, one at either end of the house, to the north and south."

Diana hadn't realized that. It helped explain how the trespasser had vanished so quickly—perhaps he hadn't gone over the balcony at all. "I still believe there was an intruder. Anyone could gain access to Pendowar Hall via the passage from Smuggler's

Cave."

He considered that. "True. But unlikely. You didn't actually see anyone, did you?"

"No. But I found something."

"What did you find?"

"An early draft of a letter from your uncle to his tenant at Greenview Farm." Diana stopped, withdrew the letter from a folder, and gave it to him. "Mr. Trenowden was seriously in arrears in his rent."

The captain read the letter. "Yes, I know about this. Jack Trenowden has had a hard time of it these past few years. His horse died—he's had to pull the plow himself. He loaned a substantial sum to a brother who never paid him back. And then a blight destroyed most of his crops."

"Oh!"

"When I inherited the estate, I forgave the greater part of the debt and am allowing Trenowden to pay back the remaining sum, when he's able, in small installments."

"That is kind of you."

"I only did what I thought was right." They continued on across the rear courtyard, on their way to the house. "Forgive me, but I don't see a connection between this letter and the footsteps you say you heard last night."

"I'm truly sorry for all that the Trenowdens have been through. They seem like good people. But ... the man has a large family to feed. Do you think he might have been driven to take extreme measures to hold on to his farm?"

The captain stared at her. "Are you asking if Jack Trenowden killed my uncle to avoid eviction?"

"Sir Thomas died on the first of June, a week after that letter was written. Knowing of your generous nature and perhaps hoping, once you inherited Pendowar Hall, you would erase his debt, Mr. Trenowden might have been driven to take Sir Thomas's life."

"Miss Taylor—"

"The suicide note said, '*I cannot go on.*'" Diana gestured to the draft of the letter in Captain Fallbrook's hand. "In his letter to Mr. Trenowden, Sir Thomas wrote '*I cannot go on ignoring the situation.*' It would be an easy phrase to trace or copy."

His forehead furrowed. "Even if what you say is true—and I assure you, *it is not*—if Trenowden received a copy of this letter, he would have been able to trace and copy it at home. Why would he have snuck into the house last night?"

"To search for and retrieve this early draft. If found, it could prove the suicide note to be a forgery."

"How would Trenowden have known that my uncle had kept a draft of this particular letter?"

"Perhaps it was general knowledge that Sir Thomas kept drafts of all or most of his correspondence. The perpetrator couldn't take a chance of its being discovered."

The captain shook his head, straining for calm. "Miss Taylor. How many times must I say it? I beg you to give up this nonsense. Jack Trenowden could no more have killed my uncle than the Man in the Moon."

"Why not?"

"Because he was out of the county at the time and did not return for weeks. I remember that distinctly because he was unable to attend my uncle's funeral."

MR. TRENOWDEN'S WHEREABOUTS at the time of Sir Thomas's death were verified by his wife a few days later, when Diana and her pupil delivered the apron and pinafores they had made for the family.

After church on Sunday, Mr. Wainwright further confirmed that fact.

"Mr. Trenowden was indeed away then," the curate told Diana. "In Shropshire, I believe, helping his widowed sister."

They stood beneath a giant yew tree in the church's courtyard, where parishioners milled about after the morning service. "Why do you ask?"

Her theory had been so far off the mark, Diana was embarrassed to discuss it now. It had further occurred to her that if someone other than Mr. Trenowden had used that draft in the study to forge the suicide note, why wouldn't they have taken the draft with them then and there? Why leave it to be discovered?

At the same time, she remained unsatisfied.

"Please keep this between us," she said, lowering her voice, "but I believe someone has been sneaking into Pendowar Hall late at night and looking for something in Captain Fallbrook's study."

"Looking for what?"

"I wish I knew. You told me, Mr. Wainwright, about Sir Thomas's wish to be buried in the churchyard, and it has gotten me thinking." She mentioned the enigmatic suicide note. "Did Sir Thomas seem depressed to you in the months leading up to his death?"

He pursed his lips and glanced away. "I would say he appeared more distracted than depressed. But that is merely an observation."

"Can you think of anyone who might have wished Sir Thomas harm?"

"I cannot."

"An excellent sermon, Mr. Wainwright."

The sudden appearance at the curate's elbow of Mr. Latimer, the captain's solicitor, made Diana start. He shook hands with Mr. Wainwright, and they entered a cordial conversation. Moments later, Mrs. Gwynn came up to pay her respects, followed by Mr. Emity and several other servants from the manor house.

It was Diana's cue to leave.

DIANA DECIDED TO try a new route back to Pendowar Hall along the shore. She wound her way down the path from the village to the beach, where the tide was at its lowest ebb.

It matched her spirits.

Someone had gotten away with murder. Mrs. Phillips had suspected it, and Diana knew it now as surely as she knew the sun would rise the next morning. She'd exchanged several more letters with her godmother, who seemed to grow weaker by the day, and continued to encourage Diana to learn the truth.

To Diana's frustration, all her theories so far had come to nothing.

With a sigh, Diana pressed on, the briny wind assailing her cheeks. Golden pebbles crunched beneath the soles of her half-boots as she crossed the beach to the ocean's edge. The hard-packed wet sand there was strewn with damp seaweed, drift-wood, and other debris from the previous night's storm. A few feet away, waves bubbled up in frothy whiteness. A seagull swooped down to splash and grab a tidbit from below the surface of the sea beyond.

Diana was so entranced by these sights, sounds, and smells, she didn't notice the board until she'd almost tripped over it.

About five feet in length, the piece of driftwood looked to have been manufactured of good quality wood. Flecks of white paint clung to its smoothly planed surface, but it was ragged at both ends, as if the victim of a violent rupture. Had it come from a boat?

Curious, she bent down to examine it. The hairs stood up on the back of Diana's neck.

The plank was peppered in one spot with a series of tiny holes—holes that didn't look as if they'd had anything to do with screws or nails but had been drilled to deliberately inflict damage.

"IT APPEARS TO be from a boat's hull," conjectured Captain Fallbrook from astride his horse.

Diana had brought the plank up from the beach and encountered him and his ward on the estate grounds as they rode home from church.

"What kind of boat?" Diana inquired.

"My guess is a sailboat. A small, white one. One that was dashed to bits on the rocks, from the looks of it."

A white sailboat. Dashed to bits on the rocks.

"Why did you bring that home, Miss Taylor?" Miss Fallbrook, astride her own steed, wrinkled her nose with distaste. "It's just a nasty piece of driftwood."

"It's the holes," Diana explained. "It looks to me as though someone drilled them deliberately."

"Holes?" Captain Fallbrook dismounted. Holding on to his horse's reins, he asked, "May I?" He examined the plank. "I see what you mean. It is curious."

"How old do you think this is?" Diana asked.

"It could be from a vessel that sank a few years ago or half a century ago. It's hard to say."

Just then, the contingent of servants they'd seen at church rounded a bend in the path. Everyone issued courteous greetings and paused to examine Diana's discovery.

"Why would someone drill holes in the hull of a boat?" asked Mrs. Gwynn.

"Perhaps they were trying to scuttle it," Mr. Emity suggested.

"I'll bet it was a smuggler trying to get rid of the evidence," exclaimed Miss Fallbrook, her interest evidently renewed, "and to avoid capture by revenue men."

Diana had a very different possibility in mind.

THE WIND HOWLED. Angry waves rose to man height as Diana gripped the mast of the small, white sailboat, terrified.

At her feet, water bubbled up through tiny holes in the hull. Quickly, the flow became a torrent that engulfed the boat. The vessel overturned, hurling Diana into the surging sea. She flailed and struggled. If only she had learned to swim!

Diana watched in horror as the boat was swept away. And then she was sinking, sinking, her heavy skirts a leaden weight that dragged her down. Was she going to die? With a gasp, Diana came awake, her heart pounding.

She stared into the darkness, struggling to calm herself. It was no mystery why she had dreamt of holes in the bottom of a boat and drowning. The subject had occupied her thoughts all afternoon and evening, ever since she'd found that piece of driftwood on the beach.

Might that plank, she wondered, have belonged to the boat that sent Sir Thomas's wife and son to their deaths? Diana's blood ran cold at the thought. If it were true, it meant that more than one murder had taken place at Pendowar Hall.

But who would have wanted Lady and Robert Fallbrook dead? And why?

CHAPTER EIGHTEEN

T HE IDEA OF a scuttled boat still preyed on Diana's mind as she headed down the hall the following evening, looking for the captain.

She found him in the library, up on the ladder. An elegant chamber with a high, carved ceiling, the library was filled with books all beautifully bound in similar shades of brown, tan, and burgundy. The sight of him made her pulse beat double-time. She did her best to ignore it.

"Good evening, Captain," Diana called up to him. "What are you looking for?"

He glanced down at her. "A novel I once borrowed as a boy: *Ivanhoe*. I am inclined to read it again."

"An excellent choice."

"I'm dashed if I can find it, though."

"I've been looking for one of my favorites, *Jane Eyre*."

"Oh? I've heard of it, although I haven't read it."

"It came out two years ago. I couldn't afford a copy, of course, so I borrowed it from a circulating library. It was so popular, I had to wait months to get my hands on each of the three volumes in succession. In between, I held my breath, desperate to know what would happen next."

"Indeed? Who's the author?"

"Currer Bell. It's a pseudonym, apparently. No one knows who it is. Some critics think the book was written by a man, but

I'm certain it was a woman, for some of the ideas expressed are quite revolutionary. It would be a thrill to read it again, if perchance it is here—but I am puzzled by the shelving system."

"The system is simple." He descended from the ladder with a sigh. "The books are shelved by size and color. My grandfather and my uncle were fond of book collecting, but all that mattered to them was that the volumes looked pleasing on the shelves."

"It does make for an impressive sight."

"But an exasperating one." He crossed to her. "Unfortunately, Portwithys doesn't have a circulating library or bookshop. You said you want *Jane Eyre*? May I help you search for it?"

"I wouldn't wish to put you to the trouble. I am here for another reason. I need to speak to you about something."

"Let us sit, then." He made his way to two wingback chairs that stood side by side before the marble hearth.

"Your leg seems to be troubling you less of late," Diana was gratified to observe.

"It is getting better, I think, slowly but surely. I am heading to London the day after tomorrow to consult with a specialist."

Despite herself, Diana was sorry to hear that he was leaving. "I feel certain his report will be encouraging. How long will you be gone?"

"A fortnight."

Two weeks? It sounded like forever.

They both sat down. "It's been years since I was last in London. I plan to see a couple of friends," the captain was saying, "attend the theatre, lectures, and visit art galleries and museums."

"How lovely that sounds. I hope you have a wonderful time." Diana was happy for him, although she knew she'd miss him dearly. She enjoyed their conversations and had found herself looking forward to the next time she'd see him. "It has been ages since I've been to London as well. I loved the British Museum and the National Gallery."

"Two of my favorites." He turned to regard her. "Now, you have my full attention. What is it you wanted to speak to me about?"

Diana gathered her thoughts. "Captain, you know that plank I found yesterday, from a sailboat we surmise was scuttled?"

"What of it?"

"Might it have come from the boat in which Lady Fallbrook and Master Robert perished?"

A sharp breath escaped his lips as he stared at her. "I beg your pardon?"

"You said you hadn't been out long when your boat began taking on water rapidly. What if someone sabotaged it?"

He blinked rapidly. "You *cannot* be serious?"

"Captain. I am aware that my conjectures about your uncle's death annoy you, and I hate to try your patience further. But this is different. What color was the boat in which you sailed that day?"

"Miss Taylor—"

"Was it white?" Diana persisted.

"Yes," he acknowledged. "It was white. But if there had been holes in the hull, I would have noticed them."

"Not if they were drilled in a concealed spot. Under one of the seats, perhaps. And those holes were tiny. Whoever drilled them might have plugged them up with something—mud for example—that washed away not long after you set sail."

His face drained of color, but he made no reply. Her statement hovered in the air between them, casting a pall over the room.

"Can you think of anyone who might have wanted to kill Sir Thomas's wife and son?" Diana asked.

"*No.* They were liked by everyone."

"You were aboard that boat as well. Might you have been the intended victim?"

He raised a hand to his temple and shook his head. "No. If someone wanted to do away with me, I should hope they would have done so in a very different manner, without injuring my aunt and cousin."

"Who stood to profit if all three of you had perished that day?"

The captain stared at her. "No one," he replied emphatically.

"Is that true, Captain? You and Robert were the heirs to Pendowar Hall. Who's next in line?"

"A distant cousin who resides in the West Indies and has no interest in the estate whatsoever, nor any desire to return to England."

"Oh."

"The only one who *profited* from the tragedy that day was *me*, when I inherited this estate." He huffed out an exasperated breath. "You have the most outlandish notions, Miss Taylor. Forged suicide notes? People sneaking into the house at night? A tenant wreaking revenge? And now murder on the high seas? White is the most common color for boats. Furthermore, do you have any idea how many boats have been lost on those rocks over the centuries? Hundreds. Perhaps thousands. The odds of that one piece of driftwood coming from the boat in which I sailed three years ago are so minute as to be inconsequential."

"Sir," Diana began, but he grabbed his cane and rose from his chair, eyes flashing.

"You have tried my patience to the limit, Miss Taylor. I keep telling you, there has been no murder at Pendowar Hall. Please stop looking for something that isn't there. One more *conjecture* of this kind and I will ask you to quit the premises at once for home. Do we understand each other?" With that, he quit the room.

Diana rose and headed back to her own chamber, burning with frustration and ... other feelings that were much deeper and infinitely more painful. *Worry. Sorrow. Regret.*

On the one hand, the captain was right. The plank she'd found could have come from any one of a thousand different boats. But she couldn't *stop looking* any more than she could stop breathing. She didn't want to lose her position. She had so much more to teach Miss Fallbrook, a promise to keep to her godmother, and a mystery to solve. She would just have to proceed with discretion, and keep her thoughts to herself, until she had evidence that proved incontrovertible.

On the other hand, it hurt Diana to the quick to see Captain Fallbrook so angry with her. Tears welled in her eyes as she replayed his angry remonstrance in her mind. They had been getting along so well of late, and she felt as though she had ruined all that.

Was there some way, she wondered, that she could placate him? He was leaving for London soon.

All at once, an idea came to her for a peacemaking gesture.

DIANA'S QUEST BROUGHT her back to the library later that afternoon. To her surprise, she found Mr. Latimer reading the newspaper by the fire and smoking a cigar.

"I am early for my meeting with Captain Fallbrook," Mr. Latimer explained as he stood, and they exchanged courtesies. "I hope you have not come to the Pendowar library in search of a particular book?" he added.

Why did that smile of his always make her feel so uncomfortable? "In fact, I have," Diana admitted. "Two books, in fact."

Mr. Latimer glanced at the sea of similarly bound volumes on the shelves surrounding them. "That may prove to be a futile effort, I fear, for both Sir Thomas and his father before him were more concerned with appearance than practicality."

"So, I see." It suddenly occurred to Diana that the man's presence here was opportune. She had a question for him. "Mr. Latimer, as I understand it, you worked for Sir Thomas for many years?"

"Since I was a lad." Mr. Latimer puffed on his cigar. "I helped in my father's office to learn the trade."

"Were you aware that the baronet kept a series of journals?"

"Journals? No. Why do you ask?"

"I should like to find them. For my pupil's sake," Diana added quickly. "I wish to understand him better."

"I'm sorry I can't be more help."

Mr. Emity entered. "Captain Fallbrook is at liberty to see you now, sir," he informed the solicitor, with a courteous nod for Diana.

"I would appreciate it," Diana confided quietly to Mr. Latimer, "if you would not mention my purpose here to anyone, particularly the captain. One of the books I seek is meant to be a surprise for him, and he doesn't want me wasting my time looking for the journals."

"Your secret is safe with me," Mr. Latimer vowed under his breath as he followed the butler from the room.

DIANA STOOD ON the library ladder, facing a sea of brown leather.

It was Thursday, her afternoon off, and the house was quiet. She had spent the previous two evenings combing the library, working her way along the shelves by candlelight.

Diana loved the smell of old books. The familiar scent of wood polish, with its notes of beeswax, turpentine, and white soap, made her nostalgic for home and the concoction Martha made to dust their own furniture.

As she searched for *Ivanhoe* and *Jane Eyre*, she'd kept an eye out for Sir Thomas's journals. It seemed unlikely that he would have stored them in such a public place, but one never knew. Endless works of history, science, geography, and fiction had whetted her appetite. She wished she could take them all down to a comfortable chair and disappear inside their pages.

As Diana moved up to one of the higher rungs of the ladder, the scent of furniture polish became more pungent. All at once, her foot slipped out from under her, she lost her grip on the rail, and with a gasp, tumbled backward.

For a second, Diana was airborne, plummeting through space. Then she felt a hard impact.

And everything went black.

TICK TOCK. TICK *tock*. *Tick tock.*

The rhythmic sound invaded the darkness, mirroring the throbbing that resounded inside Diana's skull.

Slowly, she opened her eyes and struggled to get her bearings. She lay awkwardly on the floor beside a turned-over chair. *That's right. I'm in the library.* She'd slipped and fallen from the ladder. She must have lost consciousness.

Her head hurt. She touched her temple. Her fingers came away red and slick with blood. Shock and fear vibrated through her, and she passed out again.

"MISS! MISS!"

Diana awoke to find Ivy and Hester, the head housemaid, crouched over her with wide eyes and pale faces.

"Miss!" Ivy cried again, gently stroking Diana's cheek with one hand. "Oh!" Her lips trembled as she clasped her hands together. "Thank goodness, she's come to."

Hester's mouth was agape. "Can you sit up, miss?"

Diana found her voice. "I … don't know."

"We'll help you," Ivy offered. Working together, the two maids gently scooped Diana to a seated position.

Diana's head and body ached and something warm dripped into one eye. *Blood.* The same sticky substance that was splattered across her dress. Sweat broke out on Diana's brow. Her stomach was besieged by nausea. The room spun.

"Hold this to your forehead, miss, and press hard." Ivy produced something white and cottony—Diana later learned it was a pillowcase from a pile of clean linens she'd been carrying.

Diana pressed as directed, wincing from the pain. "Thank you."

"Do you think she needs a doctor?" asked Hester.

"I'll fetch Mrs. Gwynn."

A doctor was summoned. Diana was brought back to her chamber. She wanted to ask for the captain—*oh, how she wished he were here to comfort her*—but she recalled that he was on his way to London. Miss Fallbrook learned what had happened, appeared, and refused to leave Diana's bedside. For the next hour and a half, the young lady pressed on Diana's wound and Mrs. Gwynn fetched water for Diana to drink while they waited for the medical man to arrive.

He announced that Diana had a cut on her forehead that would require a few stitches. "Head wounds bleed more than injuries to almost any other part of the body," he explained.

Diana struggled not to cry out as the doctor stitched the wound. He prescribed a sleeping draught along with something to ease her pain.

"You must rest now," the grey-haired doctor said with fatherly concern. "No physical exertion of any kind for the next three days."

"Three days? That is quite impossible, Doctor," Diana told him, glancing at her pupil, who was wringing her hands nearby. "I have duties to perform."

"You've had a serious accident, Miss Taylor."

"It's a wonder you didn't break anything," Mrs. Gwynn muttered, shaking her head.

"You're lucky that chair broke your fall," the doctor pointed out, "and that the maids found you. Had they not, you may well have bled to death on that library floor. You have suffered a mild concussion. Bed rest is essential."

Mrs. Gwynn wanted to write to Captain Fallbrook to inform him of Diana's accident, but Diana pleaded with her not to.

"He's there to see a physician, and he has plans in the city. I don't want to disturb him." *Surely*, Diana thought, *the captain would be too busy to care about what was happening at home with her. And the thought that he might* not *care, and would ignore such a letter, was too painful to consider.* "I'm fine. Or I will be in a few days. The doctor said so."

The three days passed quickly, as Diana slept a great deal of the time. The doctor called every morning. Miss Fallbrook and Mr. Emity came to see her frequently. Mrs. Gwynn, Ivy, and Hester took turns changing Diana's dressing and bringing her meals. On the third morning, Diana awoke to find her pupil at her bedside again.

"I've been so worried, but you look much better," Miss Fallbrook noted.

"I *feel* better." Diana's forehead was still tender, but her head and body aches were gone. "How have you been faring without me?"

"All right, I suppose. I've been practicing French and music *and* handwriting, and ... I made you something." Shyly, she handed Diana a notecard.

On the front of the card, Miss Fallbrook had sketched a delicate rose in bloom. Inside, she had scrawled in pencil: GET WEL SOON. LUV, EMMA

"I don't know if I spelled everything right—"

Tears welled in Diana's eyes. "It is perfect, Miss Fallbrook. Thank you. I shall treasure this."

THAT MORNING, THE doctor removed Diana's stitches and pronounced her well enough to get up. After lunch, Ivy helped Diana style her hair to cover the small wound on her forehead.

"There now, miss," Ivy pronounced with satisfaction as she completed her handiwork, "ye look good as new."

"Thank you, Ivy. I still don't understand what happened the

other day. I am generally quite sturdy on a ladder."

"They'll never get me to dust those library shelves." Ivy shuddered. "Afraid of heights, I am."

A sudden thought occurred to Diana. When she'd slipped on the ladder, she recalled being aware of the strong scent of furniture polish. "Who *is* responsible for dusting the library?"

"Hester. And the maids we bring in once a year for spring cleaning."

"Did Hester dust the library earlier this week?"

"No, miss. She couldn't have even if she'd wanted to."

"Why is that?"

"She ran out of wood polish. I would have loaned her my jar, but it went missing."

"Missing? When?"

"A few days ago. I looked everywhere, but it was nowhere to be found. Right upset I was. Hester and I had to make up a new batch."

Sudden dread prickled Diana's spine. She had presumed her fall from the library ladder to have been another simple accident. But what if that had not been the case?

CHAPTER NINETEEN

D IANA SIPPED HER morning coffee, her thoughts drifting to the captain, as they so often did these days. She hoped his appointment with his physician had gone well, and that he'd received a good prognosis about his injured leg.

She wondered what he was doing right now. Having breakfast with a friend? Did he plan to visit a museum or gallery today? If so, which one? She hoped he was making the most of his stay in London. After all that he had been through, he deserved this time away.

Even so, she found herself counting the days until his return—another ten days to go. Diana's heart felt heavy. The house felt so quiet without him.

Her last conversation with the captain still weighed on her mind. It pained her that she had upset him with her theories and suspicions. But she'd felt that she'd had no choice—and she still wondered if something foul was afoot.

When she'd spoken to Mr. Wainwright in the church courtyard on Sunday, she had, perhaps foolishly, shared with him her concerns about Sir Thomas's death, in earshot of everyone who had attended services that day.

The doctor said that fall from the library ladder could have killed Diana—if not from internal injuries, she might have bled out on the floor if Ivy and Hester had not arrived in time and brought her around.

She had explained away her fall on the cliff path as bad luck. But what if it hadn't been? And what about her "accident" in the library? Had someone staged it?

The maids' jar of furniture polish had gone missing. Anyone, Diana reasoned, could have snuck into the house via Smuggler's Cave, stolen that jar, and deliberately applied an extra coat of polish to the upper rungs of the ladder, making it extremely slippery—and dangerous.

For that to be true, and assuming she was the intended target of such an attack, the perpetrator would have had to know about Diana's quest in the library. The only person she'd told had been Mr. Latimer. She'd asked him to keep that information to himself. But what if he hadn't? Or if he had? Might *he* have been culpable? Or—had someone else observed her labors in the library? She'd been at it for several days, after all.

No, no, no. Once again, she was—as the captain would say—letting her imagination run wild. Accidents happened. She'd simply taken a misstep on that library ladder, that was all.

Diana rose and checked the clock on the schoolroom mantel. It was half-past nine. Lessons should have begun half an hour ago, but as usual, Miss Fallbrook was nowhere in sight.

Glancing out the window, she observed her pupil sitting on a bench, drawing. She looked blissfully engrossed. A lump rose to Diana's throat. Miss Fallbrook was always happiest when engaged in an artistic pursuit.

Diana ventured outside and crossed the courtyard. Miss Fallbrook glanced up at Diana's approach, slammed her sketchbook shut, and stood. "I'm sorry. I know I'm only supposed to draw on my own time."

"May I see your sketchbook?" Diana asked.

The young woman's cheeks went crimson. "Please don't take it away."

"I won't. I'd just like to see what you've been drawing."

As Miss Fallbrook waited in silence, Diana studied each sketch with attention. She had seen some of them before but had only given them a quick perusal, and there were new additions: a spray of oak leaves and acorns. The white garden with its bubbling fountain. Waves crashing upon the shore. A stray cat on a wall.

Diana paid particular attention to the portraits, all of the people whom she recognized: Mr. Emity. Mrs. Gwynn. Ivy. Hester. Bessie, the kitchen maid. There were even portraits of Mr. Wainwright, Mrs. Trenowden, and a self-portrait of Miss Fallbrook. The drawings were all lifelike in their detail.

"When did you sketch these portraits?"

"At different times over the years. Sometimes, the subject sat for me. Other times, I drew from memory. I did the self-portrait before my looking glass."

Miss Fallbrook's face was still flushed with what seemed like guilt, a sight that caused a heat rise to Diana's own cheeks. A comment in one of her godmother's letters surfaced in Diana's mind.

"Everyone, I believe, has a valuable and accurate inner guide. Let people think for themselves and make their own choices. Step back and listen more."

When Diana had first read those lines, she hadn't truly understood them. But now she did.

Miss Fallbrook loved to draw. Her progress in reading and writing had come about entirely through art. It was only with the best of intentions that Diana had removed drawing from their curriculum. But by insisting that art was less worthy of their time than the subjects *she* deemed to be important, had she squelched the girl's creative outlet?

"Miss Fallbrook, I owe you an apology."

"For what?"

"You have a gift for art. There may not be much I can teach you on the subject, but we will add it back to our course of study."

"Oh, Miss Taylor!" Miss Fallbrook threw her arms around Diana. "Can we start now?"

Diana hugged her back. "Yes, we can."

THAT MOMENT MARKED a new beginning. Diana invented creative lessons that combined reading, writing, and art.

In addition to their exercises with clay and sand, she directed her pupil to draw the letters of the alphabet as illustrations. Miss Fallbrook threw herself into the activity with glee. A capital "A" became three blades of seaweed in formation. "B" the right half of a butterfly. "C" a curved caterpillar. Focusing on the sounds that letters made, Diana instructed Miss Fallbrook to string them together to form words, which she was able to read and write.

She encouraged Miss Fallbrook to dictate stories, which Diana transcribed and Miss Fallbrook illustrated. Afterwards, they read the story aloud together. With renewed confidence, Miss Fallbrook drew cartoons, adding captions. She still struggled with spelling, and words sometimes still appeared to the young woman in a scrambled order. But more often, she could make sense of them now.

The crowning glory was to be an activity for the captain's return in a week's time.

"I should like us—that is I should like *you* to spend more time together," Diana said.

"Not another picnic," Miss Fallbrook declared dubiously.

Diana laughed. "No. I hope I have learned a thing or two since then. If you could do anything with your cousin, what would it be?"

"Anything?"

"Within reason. Flying to Mars would be beyond my help."

Miss Fallbrook's brows drew together. "I suppose … I should like to go horseback riding with him on the beach."

"What a lovely idea." It was something Diana would never have thought of. "Anything else?"

"I have always wanted to draw his portrait."

"You never have?"

Miss Fallbrook shook her head. "The last time William came home on leave, I was twelve. He treated me like a child. Then my stepmother and brother died ..." Her face grew grim. "Last summer, right after he returned, my father died. Something bad always seems to happen when William comes home. And he was so badly injured himself, I didn't dare to ask."

"His health is greatly improved, I think, and these are both reasonable requests. I cannot guarantee he will sit for a portrait, but let us ask him, shall we, when he returns from town?"

Miss Fallbrook nodded. She bit her lip and glanced at her hands. "There is one more thing I should like to ask him, if I may?"

"Oh? What is that?"

Miss Fallbrook whispered her request in Diana's ear. Diana smiled.

DIANA WAS WORKING on lesson plans in the schoolroom that evening when she heard some bustle downstairs. Was that Captain Fallbrook's voice? *It couldn't be.* He wasn't due to return for another week.

She stood, her heart pounding in confusion, as the tread of boots echoed up the stairwell. She recognized that footfall. *It was him. He was here!* A sense of pure joy flooded her chest.

Diana struggled to gather her thoughts. What was it she had planned to say and do when she finally saw him again? She couldn't remember. All at once, Captain Fallbrook strode into the schoolroom. He looked cold and dusty from travel, his brow was wrinkled, and he had circles under his eyes. He halted a few feet away, regarding her.

"Miss Taylor," he barked. "How are you?"

"I am well, sir." She had never been so happy to see anyone in her entire life. "How are *you?*"

He waved an impatient hand, still studying her. "Fine, fine. You are well, then?"

"Yes. What are you doing here, Captain? I understood you were to be away another week."

"I was. Emity wrote to say that you'd been in an accident in the library. You are certain that you're well?"

It was the third time he'd posed the same question. "I am. I'm sorry, Captain. I didn't want anyone to disturb you. I hope you didn't cut your trip short because of me?"

He hesitated, fidgeting with his hands. "No, no," he said, glancing away, as if to avoid her eyes. "I had grown tired of town and was … ready to leave."

Diana sensed that he was being less than truthful. To be back so soon, he couldn't have spent more than a couple of days in London. To know that he had come back early because of her—her heart turned over at the thought. "I'm sorry," she said again. "I know it was a visit you had been looking forward to. Please don't think twice about what happened in the library."

"Emity said you fell from the ladder, hit your head, and required stitches?" His eyes were filled with worry.

"It was clumsy of me."

"Have you suffered any headaches since? Lightheadedness? Or any other ill effects?

"No, sir, I am recovered." Self-consciously, Diana's hand went to her forehead, where her hair covered the wound.

"Are you?" He stepped closer and reached his own hand up towards the spot she was protecting. "Pray, allow me to see."

"Captain, no," Diana demurred. "It's not a pretty sight—"

"I've seen more injuries on board ship than I can count, Miss Taylor," he said, interrupting. "I won't rest until I see for myself that the wound is healing."

His nearness set every nerve in her body atingle, a sensation that intensified when his fingers lightly brushed aside her hair and touched her forehead. Diana's thoughts scattered as he made his assessment.

He nodded, as if satisfied. "Yes. It is healing quite well."

Diana took a step back, her heart thumping like a runaway locomotive. "The doctor seems pleased with my progress." She swallowed hard, adding hastily, "What about you? Did you see a physician in London?"

"I did."

"What did he say?"

"That I should be well enough to return to duty in the spring."

The idea of his departure from Pendowar Hall gave her a sharp pang. "I am relieved to hear it."

"As was I."

Diana struggled to rein in her racing pulse. "Did you get to see any sights, I hope, while in London, even though your visit was so short?"

"A few." He shrugged. His gaze was full of warmth. "I'm happy to be back."

I'm happy, too, she wanted to say. But before she could voice the words, he continued. "What were you looking for in the library, may I ask?"

Diana gave a little gasp. She had almost forgotten. "I'm so glad you asked. I have something to show you that I think may be of interest to you." From a cupboard, Diana retrieved the three volumes she had finally found the night before and handed them to him. They were beautifully bound in brown leather with gilt edges and gold lettering on the spines.

He inhaled a sharp, elated breath. "*Ivanhoe!* Where on Earth was it?"

"Tucked in between an eleven-volume set of *The Diary of Samuel Pepys*, some travel books, and several volumes of English poetry."

He flipped open the first volume, smiling. "It is just as I re-membered it."

"I hope the book gives you as much pleasure on the second reading as it did on the first."

"I'm sure it will." Gratitude lit his charismatic, blue eyes. "Thank you. I appreciate this more than words can say."

"You're welcome."

"I can only imagine the effort that was required to find this. It is yet another example of your most salient quality, Miss Taylor."

"What quality is that?"

"You have a good and kind heart."

The expression on his face caused that heart to turn over in its chest. "So do you, Captain. Were our positions reversed, I'm sure you would have done the same for me."

He took that in and laughed. "Would I, indeed?"

"I have heard of many kindnesses you've performed for the tenants on this estate."

He took a step closer and spoke in a low tone. "Don't believe everything you hear, Miss Taylor. I may be a wolf in sheep's clothing." He stood so near that for the second time in as many minutes, Diana found it hard to think.

"My opinion stands," she managed to say. "You cannot convince me otherwise."

He grinned affectionately. "You see the good in people, Miss Taylor. I like that about you. And I like it that you see good in me." Reaching up, he touched her cheek with gentle fingertips.

Once again, sparks shot through Diana's body from this intimate contact. She found herself powerless to reply. Time seemed to be suspended as they gazed at each other. Did he intend to kiss her? Did she want him to?

Suddenly, his expression altered, as if thinking better of the situation. His hand left her cheek. He cleared his throat and took a few steps back. "I'm glad to see that you're recovering from that fearful accident."

"Thank you." Regret streamed through her at the absence of his touch.

"Take greater care in the future, will you? That's an order."

"Aye aye, Captain." Diana's heart continued to pound as she struggled to keep her face impassive.

He seemed to search for words. "How is … Emma faring?"

It was another reminder of a subject she needed to broach. "Well, sir. She looks forward to seeing you. In fact, she has made two requests of your time."

He smiled, his eyebrows lifting. "Oh? What does Emma want?"

"DON'T LOOK SO serious, William," complained Miss Fallbrook from behind her easel.

"I don't believe in smiling for portraits." Captain Fallbrook sat relaxed and complacent in the rear courtyard, with one arm draped lazily over the back of his bench.

Diana watched from a nearby chair. Could it only have been two days since their encounter in the schoolroom? She willed herself to draw a curtain over it. *Stop thinking of the captain in a romantic light.* Just because his touch had made her pulse race, it didn't mean she wanted him in *that* way. Based on his reaction to their almost-kiss, he apparently felt the same. They were friends. It was all they could be, and it was enough.

"I can give you a mysterious glint in the eye if you like." He fixed the artist with a look so comical, it sent Miss Fallbrook into a fit of giggles. Diana couldn't help but smile.

The previous day, her pupil and Captain Fallbrook had returned from their horseback ride on the beach in high spirits. It had pleased Diana to observe the interaction between the two, which had evolved in a most natural way into something rather sweet.

Diana tilted her head back to catch the sun on her face. In Athena's latest letter, she had mentioned snow showers and ice storms in Yorkshire. Yet here in Cornwall, it was a bright-blue

December day, the temperature reminiscent of early autumn. "I can't believe Christmas is only twelve days away," she remarked.

Miss Fallbrook paused, rolling her pencil between her fingers. "William, may we have a party on Christmas Day?"

He looked at her with narrowed eyes. "A party? Whatever for?"

"We used to have a party every year. Papa liked it when we decorated the house, and it was the only day of the year, other than my birthday, when I was allowed to dine downstairs. We had presents in the drawing room after breakfast and Papa invited a few friends over for dinner. It was heavenly! But ever since my stepmother and Robert died, Papa wouldn't celebrate Christmas at all."

The captain frowned. "There isn't much time to plan a party."

"I can help. Please?" Miss Fallbrook leaned forward and seemed to be holding her breath.

"I shall discuss it with Emity and Mrs. Gwynn and see what we can do."

"Oh, thank you!" Miss Fallbrook's delight shone like a beacon.

"Captain," Diana ventured. "There is one more thing Miss Fallbrook has been wanting to ask you." She gave her pupil an encouraging smile.

The words burst from Miss Fallbrook's throat, as if she'd been holding them back for ages. "May I have a new gown?"

The captain studied her, rubbing his chin. "What's wrong with what you've got on?"

"I've worn black for nearly seven months now. It is time for third-stage mourning. It's permissible for you to wear other colors as well, William. And I should *so* love to wear a white gown at Christmas."

He hesitated, his glance darting to Diana, his raised eyebrows requesting confirmation. Diana, pleased that he valued her opinion, gave him a subtle nod.

He gruffly replied to his cousin, "All right then. A new white gown it is. I presume there's a dressmaker in the village?"

"Yes! Of course there is!" Miss Fallbrook leapt up from her stool, crossed to the captain's side in three quick strides, and wrapped her arms around him. "Thank you!" she cried again. "Thank you so much!"

Captain Fallbrook's cheeks grew rosy as he gently patted his cousin's back. "Don't thank me. Thank the poor woman who has only twelve days to make you a brand-new gown."

Miss Fallbrook laughed, and Diana, her heart warmed by the burgeoning closeness between these two, couldn't help but join in.

AS THE DAYS ticked by until the holiday, the house was abuzz with plans. Mrs. Gwynn was tasked to plan a small dinner party for Christmas Day. Captain Fallbrook, Diana had learned, had arranged to have baskets of food sent to every tenant on the estate. On Christmas morning, Miss Fallbrook and the captain were to exchange gifts, another treat.

There was trouble, however, in paradise.

"This is the most boring present in the world," Miss Fallbrook moaned as she and Diana sat over their needlework one morning.

They were hemming handkerchiefs. Diana had thought them sensible gifts for her pupil, Captain Fallbrook, and the staff. "What is on your wish list?" Diana asked.

"I don't have a wish list. If I receive a gift, I should rather be surprised."

Diana pondered as she stitched. An idea came to mind for a different gift for Miss Fallbrook. Hopefully, she could find the items in a village shop and the cost wouldn't exceed the money she'd saved from her earnings to date. Captain Fallbrook presented a greater challenge. "What do you think the captain would like, if not a handkerchief?"

"I don't know. Can you help me think of something?"

Diana recalled a remark he had once made, and a notion presented itself. It would be an unusual gift—but it might suit him perfectly.

If she could find one.

CHRISTMAS EVE DAWNED cold and bright.

The house had been cleaned from top to bottom. A team of farmhands brought in an enormous, freshly cut yule log and established it in the drawing room hearth. Deliveries arrived from the butcher, fishmonger, and grocer, and the kitchen was busy preparing a feast. Diana and her charge helped the maids to decorate the house with boughs and garlands of local evergreens, holly, ivy, hellebore, and rosemary, adding ribbons and bows in festive colors. That afternoon, they wrapped gifts.

Miss Fallbrook had been enthused by Diana's idea for the captain's Christmas gift. Diana had found a retired sailor in the village who'd possessed the exact item they'd required. When she'd explained its intended recipient, the man had refused payment, insisted on remaining anonymous, and quietly delivered it in the same wooden trunk in which it had been stored. Diana and her pupil had just begun to wrap a ribbon around the trunk when Captain Fallbrook unexpectedly appeared in the schoolroom doorway.

"Forgive me for intruding. May I have a word, Miss Taylor?"

Diana and Miss Fallbrook faced him in a united effort to hide the trunk from view. "Yes, Captain?"

So focused was he on his errand, he didn't seem to notice their apprehension. "It's about Christmas dinner." He stood straight and tall, hands clasped behind his back, addressing them as he might the crew on board his ship. "It's going to be a small affair, but I need more ladies at the table. I should be gratified, Miss Taylor, if you would join us."

Diana's breath hitched. "It is not customary for a governess to—"

"I don't care what is customary."

"What will your guests think?"

"They will think what I tell them to think."

"I appreciate your invitation, Captain, but—"

"It is not an invitation. It is an *order*. I will thank you to follow it." He started for the door, then turned back. "One more thing. Emma: didn't you say you always had breakfast downstairs on Christmas morning?"

"Yes." Miss Fallbrook's single word resounded with hope.

"I shall see you in the morning room tomorrow at nine A.M. sharp. Miss Taylor, you will accompany her. That is all."

CHAPTER TWENTY

"**Y**E LOOK A picture," Ivy proclaimed.

It was Christmas morning. Diana had donned her best frock of indigo-blue shot silk, and Ivy had done wonders with her hair. Ringlets framed her face and the ropes of braids looped around a chignon at her nape looked particularly nice. "Thank you, Ivy."

"Thank *ye* for the handkerchief, miss."

"It was my pleasure."

The evening before, at a gathering in the servants' hall, Diana had handed out the handkerchiefs she'd made to members of the upper and lower household staff, as well as to Mr. Nankervis, the coachman, and the groom, who had all been appreciative.

Once Ivy had left, Diana retrieved the last letter she'd received from Mrs. Phillips, wishing her a Happy Christmas. She reread it with a heavy heart. Her godmother was bedridden now and reduced to writing in pencil. She'd been very pleased to hear about Miss Fallbrook's progress but had peppered her missive with questions about Sir Thomas's death. Had Diana learnt anything new?

To Diana's disgruntlement, she had not.

Diana reviewed in her mind all that she had gleaned so far. Whether or not the baronet's distracted mood when he'd returned from Germany had been caused by an investment scheme gone wrong was still in question. She had never heard back from Franke and Dietrich.

She agreed with Mr. Emity that there was something wrong about Sir Thomas's suicide note. Its wording exactly mimicked the phrase in his letter to Mr. Trenowden. Her suspicions about Mr. Trenowden had not held water, but the baronet had apparently not been a popular man. Had he written a similar threatening note to someone else, giving them a reason to want him dead?

What about the footsteps she'd heard late at night, and the papers she'd found in disarray in the study? What of the light in the north tower? Did these things have anything to do with Sir Thomas's death?

Diana thought about the driftwood plank she'd found on the beach. She had been so certain it had come from the sailboat in which Lady Fallbrook and her son had lost their lives. The captain had discounted that theory as improbable, and he might have been right. But if their boat *had* been deliberately scuttled, it would be an important finding. If only there was a way to prove it.

Diana's earlier stumble on the fork in the cliff path and her fall from the library ladder pricked at the back of her mind as well. She hadn't mentioned either incident in her letters to her godmother and her sisters and brother, not wanting to worry them unnecessarily. She had told herself they had just been accidents. But what if she was wrong? Both times, she could have died. What if someone *had* orchestrated the incidents hoping to get her off the scent? She had suffered no other mishaps since then, however …

It's Christmas Day, she reminded herself with a shake of her head. *A day for celebrating and rejoicing, not wallowing in worry.*

She had just determined to sweep all this from her mind when Miss Fallbrook rushed in, setting the bell-shaped skirts of her new white, silk gown aswirl. "At last, I get to wear a pretty gown again!"

A modest dress fashioned with a pleated bodice, low pointed

waist, and just a dash of lace, it fit the girl perfectly.

"I asked Hester to help me dress and put up my hair. What do you think?"

Miss Fallbrook's tresses were drawn up in the latest style, like Diana's. The new look made her appear several years older than her fifteen years—almost a different person. Diana believed the girl was too young for such a hairstyle, but she didn't want to dampen her pupil's enthusiasm. "You look very nice," was her matter-of-fact reply.

"So do you."

They hurried to the morning room. A fire leapt in the grate, bringing cheer to the chamber. The captain, already seated at the head of the festively set table, rose as Diana and Miss Fallbrook entered. Diana's heart tripped over itself. He stood stiff and regal in a tailored, navy-blue frock coat and cream brocade waistcoat. It was the first time Diana had seen him dressed in anything but black, and the shade of blue brought out the mesmerizing color of his eyes.

His brows lifted as he took them in. "Happy Christmas."

Diana and Miss Fallbrook returned the greeting and sat down at the table. A delicious-looking breakfast was laid out before them, everything from ham, kippers, and sausages to eggs, cheese, toast, scones, butter, cream, marmalade, tea, and coffee. After months of porridge, Diana's mouth watered at the sight.

"What a feast," Diana remarked as they helped themselves and began to eat. "It reminds me of Christmas breakfast at home."

"You have never spoken of your home, Miss Taylor," returned the captain as he skewered a piece of ham with his fork. "Tell us about it."

"Well, it was built over two hundred years ago. It sits on a rise at the edge of a moorland, which spreads out as far as the eye can see."

"Is it as big as Pendowar Hall?" Miss Fallbrook spread butter on a scone.

"Nowhere near as big and nothing like it. But I love it just the same." Nostalgia rose within her as Diana thought of the cozy cottage with its latticed casement windows and front door overhung with ivy. Memories of home, and all the Christmas mornings she had shared there with her family, overwhelmed Diana in a rush, and tears sprang to her eyes. She felt Miss Fallbrook's and the captain's questioning glances and dashed the moisture away. "What about you, Captain? How did you celebrate Christmas aboard ship?"

Captain Fallbrook gamely regaled them with tales of his holidays at sea, some of which were so amusing, they had Diana and his cousin laughing into stitches.

"I shall never forget one Christmas some years back," he told them. "We were anxious to arrive at Barcelona. I sensed that land was not far off, but the fog was so dense, there was no sign of it. A canny, old sailor had taught me in my youth that sometimes, if you close your eyes for a moment and then stare again long and hard at the horizon, the sight you seek will emerge from the gloom. I tried it. And there it was! 'Land ho!' I cried and all on board rejoiced. We had a hearty Christmas dinner that day, one which I shall never forget."

"I have read about a similar technique," Diana commented, "called steganography."

"Steganography?" repeated the captain. "What is that?"

"It is the practice of hiding an image or message within another image. For example, you might look at a picture and see a tree. But when viewed from a different angle, the picture is something else entirely, such as the image of a cat's face."

"I should like to see such a picture," Miss Fallbrook remarked.

"I have only seen a few myself," admitted Diana, "but they were cleverly done."

Before they knew it, the clock was striking ten and it was time to move into the drawing room to open their gifts. They took seats by the fire, where the captain gaped at the trunk that had a tag with his name on it.

"Youngest goes first," Miss Fallbrook announced. "That was Papa's rule." She began by opening her gift from her cousin.

It was the box with a seashell-carved lid that he'd been working on in the woodshop, now completed, stained, and varnished. Miss Fallbrook adored it. Diana went next. Her pupil had painted a watercolor for her of the old, wooden footbridge over the Pendowar River, surrounded by colorful tropical foliage on the banks. As Diana studied it, the strangest sensation came over her. The painting felt … menacing, somehow. It made no sense. It was just a picture. Yet Diana wanted to wrap it back up in the brown paper in which it had been shrouded and hide it away in a dark corner to never look at again.

Determined not to reveal her disquiet, Diana thanked the giver profusely.

Miss Fallbrook was delighted with her presents from Diana: a set of colored pencils and a new sketchbook. "I was so afraid you were going to give me a handkerchief!"

Diana didn't admit how close that prediction had come to being true.

The captain handed Diana a package. "Miss Taylor."

Diana opened his gift and fell silent in awe. He had made her a wooden keepsake box equally as lovely as his cousin's. The carved lid on hers depicted a woman sitting beneath a tree, reading a book, and it was lined in blue velvet.

"I recalled that your favorite color is blue. Do you like it?" he asked gruffly.

"I love it. It's beautiful. Thank you."

He handed her another package. Diana protested that she couldn't accept two gifts, but he insisted, "You earned this one."

Diana unwrapped the parcel and let out a gasp of shock and delight. It was *Jane Eyre*, the three volumes bound in reddish-brown decorative cloth, which elegantly embossed and gilded.

"I found it in a London bookshop," the captain explained.

Diana shook her head. *Such an expensive gift!* "This is too much, Captain. You must keep it. It will make a fine addition to your library."

"It's Christmas, Miss Taylor. Gifts must be accepted in the spirit in which they were given. It is a rule." He glanced at his ward. "Is that not so?"

Miss Fallbrook laughed. "It is!"

"Well, then … thank you," Diana said again, hugging the volumes to her chest. It had been many years since she'd had a new book to call her own. "I cannot wait to reread it."

"Good. And now," the captain said with a grin, turning to the trunk at his feet, "I want to know what *this* is." As he untied the ribbon, he teased, "Is it a ball? A bagpipe? A hat rack?" Upon opening the lid, he exclaimed in surprise, "Well, I'll be blowed. It's a hammock!"

Diana and her pupil beamed as he unfolded the hanging canvas bed and studied it in wonder. Miss Fallbrook bubbled over as she related the story of the retired sailor who had willingly parted with it.

"You said you missed the rocking motion of your boat at sea," Diana explained. "I thought it might help you sleep."

"I don't know what to say," replied he, proving that motto untrue as he proclaimed his thanks. "I am grateful to the man for his generous donation, and to you for thinking of it. I look forward to trying it."

Their gift-giving completed, Captain Fallbrook called for the carriage, insisting that Diana accompany them to church. As the coach rattled along, and Miss Fallbrook and the captain chatted animatedly, their interaction revealed a new and open affection that made Diana's heart swell.

I may be far from home, Diana thought as a deep contentment settled over her. *I may miss my sisters and my brother and my godmother. But this has been a perfect Christmas morning.*

THE GUESTS GATHERED in the drawing room, where the Yule log burned brightly, and the sight and scent of Christmas greenery filled the chamber with festive cheer.

It was a small party but no less lively for it. Mr. Latimer, dressed in a black velvet frock coat and drenched in his familiar, sandalwood cologne, complimented Diana's gown in a tone that made her stomach churn. Mr. Wainwright was also in attendance, along with one of Captain Fallbrook's old friends from the Navy, Lieutenant Commander Keating, a ruddy-faced man of short stature who looked to be in his mid-forties, and his wife, a petite woman in a fashionable gown of Christmas plaid.

"Miss Fallbrook is so improved, I hardly recognized her," Mr. Wainwright said, taking Diana's arm and leading her across the room. "I used to think, *There is a wild, young thing who can never be tamed.* But she has grown up in the months since you came. Why, she looks quite eighteen."

Diana frowned. It bothered her to think that people might perceive Miss Fallbrook as being more mature than she was. Diana didn't want the young lady to grow up too fast, to find herself in an awkward position, or to be hurt.

Dinner was announced. In the dining room, silk brocade covered the walls and an elegant chandelier hung over a large, mahogany table. A centerpiece of evergreens, nuts, apples, and blazing candles presided festively over fine china, an array of silver flatware, and a formidable number of crystal glasses. A row of servants, some hired especially for the occasion, stood behind every chair with clasped hands and eyes cast forward, ready to assist the diners to their seats.

After everyone sat down, the staff brought in the meal, a lavish affair that began with soup and moved on to boar's head, mince meat pies, fish, and roast goose. Mr. Emity poured the wine, a different bottle for every course. Miss Fallbrook asked if she might have a glass and was disappointed by the captain's quick refusal.

The meal was delicious, and the conversation flowed congenially. Diana became uncomfortable, however, when she noticed Mr. Latimer murmuring something in Miss Fallbrook's ear. The young woman blushed and toyed with the food on her plate, a dazzled expression on her face.

Perhaps Mr. Latimer was just being kind to a young lady—but he was in his thirties! Miss Fallbrook was only fifteen years old. She had spent no time in society. *I should have foreseen this and better prepared the girl*, Diana chastised herself.

A footman ceremoniously brought in the plum pudding, flaming, and topped with holly. As everyone enjoyed the treat, the group discussed its history, from its roots in medieval English sausages to its shift from savory to sweet.

"They say the first records of plum pudding date to the fifteenth century," Mr. Wainwright remarked, "but is it such a noble tradition, I daresay it goes back to the days of King Arthur and Camelot."

"There is no proof that King Arthur or Camelot ever existed," Captain Fallbrook pointed out.

"Never discount a fine legend," Mr. Latimer replied with a laugh. "Have you heard of King Arthur's Lost Land of Lyonesse?"

"Never." Emma looked fascinated.

"It stretched from Land's End at the tip of Cornwall to the Isles of Scilly," Mr. Latimer explained. "But one night after a mighty storm, it was engulfed by the sea and never surfaced again."

"Your very own Atlantis in Cornwall," Lieutenant Commander Keating observed.

"If you travel down the back road between Truro and Tresillian," Mr. Latimer declared, "beware of the old Devil's Arch Bridge."

"Why?" Diana asked, amused.

"It is said that if you dare walk under the bridge, you must hold your breath or the Devil himself will possess your soul and drag you to hell."

"And," exclaimed Miss Fallbrook with enthusiasm, "that road

is haunted by the ghost of a highwayman."

"He dangles a noose from the top of the bridge to hang passing coach drivers," Mr. Latimer added mischievously, "before stealing the belongings of the passengers within."

Captain Fallbrook shot him a glance of barely veiled irritation. "Don't tell me you believe this nonsense."

"There is more truth to Cornish legends than you think, Captain," commented Mr. Latimer. "You and Miss Taylor ought to be wary of one in particular: the Mermaid of Pendowar."

"I've been thinking about that." Mr. Wainwright glanced at Diana with concern.

"I know about the Mermaid of Pendowar, gentlemen." Diana scoffed. "She does not worry me."

"Perhaps she should," Mr. Latimer replied. "You and the captain seem to get along, Miss Taylor. Who knows how Morwenna might interpret that?"

"Morwenna's wrath is a fearful thing," Miss Fallbrook agreed, her brow wrinkling.

"Mermaids, ghosts, and curses are not real," Diana insisted.

"I hope for your sake, you are right. And," Mr. Latimer added, eyes twinkling, "that you know how to swim, Miss Taylor."

Diana's smile fell away. Despite herself, her chest constricted, and a feeling of dread enveloped her.

Mr. Wainwright gasped. A hush fell over the room. Diana felt everyone's eyes on her.

"I was only teasing," Mr. Latimer asserted. "Do not tell me, Miss Taylor, that ..." He paused suddenly, as a thought seemed to occur to him. "Forgive me," he added quickly, glancing at the tabletop. "Perhaps that was insensitive of me. In view of how ..." His voice trailed off.

Diana guessed that Mr. Latimer—and everyone else—was thinking of how Lady and Robert Fallbrook had died. The captain's face constricted. He turned to Diana.

"Do you truly not know how to swim?" the captain asked quietly.

"I never learned," Diana admitted. "I never needed to."

"Let us hope," Mr. Wainwright intoned solemnly, "that you never shall."

CHAPTER TWENTY-ONE

"**W**AS IT NOT wonderful?"

It was Boxing Day, the day after Christmas. The captain had distributed gifts to the staff early that morning and had given them the rest of the day off.

Diana and her pupil had taken the day off from studying as well. The weather was so fair that after breakfast they had stretched out a blanket on the riverbank, where for the past hour, Miss Fallbrook had been going over the delights of the festivities the day before.

"Breakfast was delicious. But Christmas dinner … to dine at table like a proper grown up with … with you and everyone was divine!"

Diana was still troubled by the interactions she had witnessed between her pupil and Captain Fallbrook's solicitor. "You seemed to enjoy chatting with Mr. Latimer."

Miss Fallbrook's cheeks grew pink. She shrugged and picked at the blanket. "It was nice to *be* talked to by such a kind and good-looking gentleman. Papa never talked to me like that. As if my thoughts and opinions on things mattered."

"I'm sure he would have, Miss Fallbrook, had he lived longer, and seen the young lady you are becoming."

"But he *didn't* live longer. He killed himself. Because he couldn't bear to live without his darling wife and son."

Diana frowned. Miss Fallbrook hadn't spoken on this subject

in a while, but her inner wound was clearly still as fresh as it had been the day Diana had met her. "We don't know that he killed himself, Miss Fallbrook, or if he did, if that was the reason."

"We do know it. He left a note to say so. Oh, if only Papa had never married Miss Corbett!" Emma's expression darkened. "If only our guests had not been obliged to leave so early last night. But the moment the sun went down, everyone got their coats. Why cannot Christmas always fall on a night with a full moon?"

"That would certainly be convenient." Diana sat up. "Shall we go in now?"

"Wait. I have something to show you first." Miss Fallbrook grabbed her sketchbook from her satchel and opened it. "I drew this last night."

It was a black-and-white sketch of hills and dales. "Very nice," Diana pronounced.

"Keep looking at it," Miss Fallbrook prodded.

"Why?"

"It's a hidden picture. Can you see the cow?"

Diana studied the drawing again. "I only see a landscape."

"Try again. Remember what William said about searching the horizon? Close your eyes for a moment and then stare at it long and hard."

It took a few tries, but finally, uncannily, the drawing seemed to realign itself in Diana's brain to form a completely different picture. "I see the cow! You are very clever, my dear."

"I would never have thought of it if you hadn't told us about hidden pictures."

"I would never have thought to tell you, had the captain not shared his 'Land ho!' story." Diana beamed as they shared a laugh. "Speaking of stories, I just had a thought. Do you have a pencil I can borrow and a spare piece of paper?"

Miss Fallbrook fetched a pencil from her satchel and opened her sketchbook to a blank page.

Diana wrote a sentence and handed the sketchbook back to her pupil. "Read this, will you?"

Miss Fallbrook sounded out the words. "The ... blue ... boat ... has a ..." She paused. "I don't know that word."

"You do know it. Spell it out for me."

"H-W-I-T-E."

Diana bit her lip. The word was *white*. Miss Fallbrook now remembered the sounds that letters made. But sometimes, the letters still appeared to her in a scrambled order. If only there were a way to help her *see* the word that everyone else saw.

And then it came to her.

"Miss Fallbrook, think of this word like a hidden picture."

"What do you mean?"

"If you could make a cow emerge from a landscape, you ought to be able to make this word appear to you. Close your eyes and then stare hard at the word again."

"I'll try." On her third attempt, Miss Fallbrook cried, "Oh! Oh! It's *white*, isn't it, Miss Taylor? The blue boat has a white sail!"

"Land ho!" Diana exclaimed, and, laughing, they wrapped each other in a hug.

THAT AFTERNOON, DIANA took a walk along the cliff path.

It was hard to believe it was December. The sun shone in an azure sky. Beneath the sun's rays, the dark-blue sea glittered as if a giant had scattered handfuls of diamonds across its cresting surface. Diana came to a familiar open spot surrounded by a cluster of shrubbery and paused, keeping her distance from the cliff's edge. Sudden unease rippled through her. It was the point from which Sir Thomas had met his death.

Below, the sea surged, rushing up in great sprays of foam on the rocky shore.

What happened to you, Sir Thomas? Diana wondered yet again. *How did you die?*

She knew that Miss Fallbrook and the captain were still

haunted by what had happened to him. Her godmother was patiently awaiting word. They deserved to know the truth. Diana sighed, disheartened. She had gathered a lot of evidence, but she had not solved the riddle.

She continued on. It was a lovely afternoon and she wanted to enjoy it. After following the cliff path for a while, she turned inland onto a trail she had never explored that delved into a wood.

Entering the quiet, tree-lined grove, she paused in wonder. Sun beamed down in brilliant shards through the leafless canopy, casting a golden glow on a parade of daffodils in bloom. Hundreds of yellow heads spread out before her beneath the trees, nodding with every touch of the breeze.

As she took in the exquisite sight, she heard snapping twigs. Moments later, Captain Fallbrook appeared from around a bend in the path.

"Miss Taylor."

Although he still carried a cane, he walked with newfound agility and looked so jaunty that Diana's insides flipped as usual. "Hello."

He stopped before her. "A glorious sight, eh?"

Yes, you are. "To think that daffodils should bloom in late December, in England! It seems incredible."

"One of the many gifts of our Cornwall climate." Returning her smile, he quoted, "'I wandered lonely as a cloud, that floats on high o'er vales and hills …'"

"'When all at once I saw a crowd,'" they recited in unison. "'A host of golden daffodils. Beside the lake, beneath the trees, fluttering and dancing in the breeze.'"

"One of my favorite poems," he said.

"Mine as well."

They discussed the final stanza, in which the poet, at home, gets pleasure from recalling the sight of the daffodils.

"Wordsworth is a genius," the captain remarked, "to be able to capture a scene like this so perfectly in words."

Diana agreed. The path was just wide enough for them to stroll side by side. She was glad of the company and yet keenly aware of his proximity, which made her heart thump.

"I wanted to thank you again for the hammock."

"Have you tried it?"

"I had it hung last night from the beam in my bedchamber with a rope to make it swing. I enjoyed my best night of sleep in months."

"I'm glad. Miss Fallbrook will be happy too."

His voice dropped as he gave her a hesitant smile. "She seemed to like the box I made her?"

"She loves it! And I love mine. It was thoughtful of you to make them. *Jane Eyre* was a most generous gift as well. I started reading it again last night. I don't know how to thank you."

"You have already thanked me." He paused. "I was tempted to read the book before I gave it to you, to better understand what you love about it. But I worried about damaging it."

"I'd be happy to lend it to you, Captain, once I've finished."

"Marvelous," he replied. "I look forward to discussing it with you afterwards."

Diana grinned anew at that. "That makes two of us. By the by, Captain, I have something to report."

"Oh?"

She told him about the hidden picture his ward had drawn, and her success that morning in unscrambling a word. "We call it the *Land Ho Method*."

"I'm delighted that my old seafaring tale should have had such a positive consequence." He gestured with his cane to a fallen tree at the side of the path. "Do you mind if we sit a moment?"

"I could do with a rest myself."

He settled beside her on the log. Mere inches separated them. Her thoughts veered to the day she'd given him *Ivanhoe*. She could still feel the gentle pressure of his fingers against her temple, and the way he had stroked her cheek.

"I've been wanting to tell you," he said, as if reading her thoughts, "I am enjoying *Ivanhoe* even more than I did the first time I read it."

"I think we read books from a different perspective as adults than we did as children."

"So we do. As a boy, I was transported to the Middle Ages and the world of jousting. This time, I am more interested in the romance." His eyes met hers.

Diana's pulse began to drum even louder in her ears. Could he hear it? "That's my favorite part of the story as well."

"You remind me of Rebecca. You are both strong, smart, impassioned, and devoted women of principle."

"A true compliment." Warmth spread throughout her chest. "Thank you."

"How did you feel about the ending?"

"Do you mean, should Ivanhoe have married Rebecca instead of Lady Rowena?"

He nodded.

"Rowena was the safe choice."

"Does that make it right?"

"Not necessarily. But I like to think it was the right choice for Ivanhoe and Rebecca. Despite everything, they were not destined for each other."

He went quiet at that. "Tell me, Miss Taylor, why did you never marry?"

"I suppose because … I never found the right man."

"You told me about the scoundrel who vanished when you lost your dowry. Was there ever anyone else?"

Reluctantly, she admitted, "Yes."

"What happened?"

Diana hesitated. She had rarely told this story to anyone. But he already knew about her first failed romance. And she had shared her most deeply held secret with him—her culpability in her mother's death. He might as well know this, too.

"Last year, not long after my father passed away, I met a

gentleman who courted me in earnest. He pressured me to marry quickly. Something did not feel right, so I made inquiries. I discovered that he was deeply in debt. When *he* discovered that he'd been wrong about my financial situation—that the competency I'd received from my father was in fact quite tiny—he disappeared in a puff of smoke."

"I'm so sorry."

"I didn't know him long enough to form a very deep attachment. But … it was humiliating. It still feels like an open wound that will never heal."

"And yet it will, in time." He leaned forward earnestly. "Those men were not worthy of you. They hurt you, and you did not deserve it. But don't carry that pain and resentment forever, Miss Taylor. You must forgive them."

Diana considered that. "I think my pain has become too much a part of me to let it go. If I do, I fear all that will be left is a gaping hole."

"You're much stronger than you think. Forgive them," he said again. "Not for their sakes, but for your own. For your peace of mind. It's the only way forward."

"Forgive them." He made it sound so simple. But it wasn't. Not for her. For a long moment, there was no sound but the breeze ruffling the daffodils and the trees. Diana returned to their earlier subject. "What about you, Captain?"

"Me?"

"Why have you never married?"

His blue eyes bore into hers. "I suppose because … I never found the right woman."

"With all those women to choose from?" Although she strove for a light tone, there was a catch in her throat.

"All what women?" His voice was soft and deep.

"They say you have a woman in every port."

"Do they?"

A tension seemed to vibrate through the air between them, as if they were two magnets being drawn closer by an invisible force. His lips were a hair's breadth away. The sensation of wanting to feel those lips on hers was so strong that Diana's insides began to tremble.

"What else do they say?" he added quietly.

"That you … are not the marrying kind."

He reached up to brush a lock of hair off her forehead. It was the third time his fingers had touched her face and the effect was just as scorching as the first two times. "Do they, indeed?"

He kissed her. The kiss was soft and gentle. As his lips touched hers, sparks seemed to race through Diana's body, igniting a flame at her core.

"I have been wanting to do that for weeks now," he confided when the kiss ended. "I could not help myself. I got carried away. Forgive me?"

All Diana could manage was a nod.

He propelled himself to a standing position. Extending a hand to help her rise, he advised, "I shall stay here a while longer. Go home, Miss Taylor, before I get carried away again."

DIANA STRODE BACK and forth within the confines of her bed-chamber like a tiger in a cage.

The clock had just struck one. She had tossed and turned in bed for hours then had gotten up again, wrapped herself in her blanket, and begun this ceaseless pacing, the captain's kiss still burning upon her lips.

She had told herself that she and Captain Fallbrook could be no more than friends. She had worried, at first meeting, that she couldn't trust him—but he had given her no reason for that distrust.

Over the past few months, she had come to see the man he was. He and his young cousin had grown closer. He had gone out of his way to do thoughtful things for his ward and herself. She and Captain Fallbrook had shared confidences. She delighted in their conversations. For weeks now, he had been her first thought upon awakening and her last thought before falling asleep. His guilt over what had happened to his family tore at her heart. He had become a part of her in a way she could never have anticipated. When they'd kissed, she had felt as if her soul were connected to his.

Diana paused at the window, wrapping her arms around her chest. The night sky was inky black. Clouds obscured the stars. An owl hooted and the wind sang in the trees.

She had been betrayed twice and had vowed to never trust or love a man again. But one could not direct the heart, could they?

What she had felt among the daffodils … what she was feeling now … was *love*.

Despite every warning, and all her efforts to shield herself, she had fallen head over heels in love with Captain Fallbrook.

She was aware that there was no future in it. Not for the same reasons her romantic liaisons had failed in the past. The captain had plenty of money. But he was *not the marrying sort*. When she had brought up his reputation, he hadn't even tried to deny it. His reply had been a kiss. And then:

"I have been wanting to do that for weeks now. I could not help myself. I got carried away. Forgive me?"

He had, earlier, called himself a "wolf in sheep's clothing" and when it came to his relations with women, no doubt he was. Hadn't she just melted at his very touch? To him, she knew, she was merely the woman conveniently at hand in his current port. When he returned to sea, he would forget all about her.

She, however, would never forget him. She would feel his absence deeply—no doubt forever. But she would have to put it behind her. After he left Pendowar Hall, hopefully she could …

She had no time to complete the thought, for a sudden creaking sound broke the stillness.

Diana froze, every nerve alert. The staccato patter of footfalls echoed in the corridor.

It had been weeks since she'd last heard them. This time, she vowed, the interloper would not evade her.

Grabbing her candle, Diana rushed from the room and down the corridor, her heart thumping with every step. She passed the open gallery, saw a flicker of light approaching from the opposite direction, and paused. Wait—what was this?

Mrs. Gwynn emerged from the gloom.

"Miss Taylor." The housekeeper's broad form blocked the way. "Why are you up?"

"Did you just pass this way?" Diana whispered urgently.

"No, I came up the south stairs."

"I heard someone. He may be in the study."

"I have just come from there. I saw no one."

"He may be hiding. Pray, allow me to pass."

"You have no business going into that room at any time, but especially at this hour. Go to bed, Miss Taylor."

Diana argued the point futilely. The housekeeper stood her ground. Finally, Diana had no choice but to return to her chamber. *Insufferable woman.* The intruder had been within Diana's grasp, and now the moment was lost.

She would not let this stop her, however. Someone had traipsed down that hall. She was going to find out who—or at the very least why.

Diana got dressed and waited. Twenty minutes passed. She listened in the dark corridor to make certain the housekeeper had left the floor and then made her way to the study. The door was closed. She put her ear to it. No sound came from within. Quietly, she opened the door and entered.

To her disappointment, no one was there. But the scent of sandalwood cologne imbued the air. *Captain Fallbrook didn't wear cologne.*

Diana quit the room and hurried down the south servants' staircase, but she didn't encounter a soul on the stairs nor in the servants' hall or kitchen yard. With a sigh, she returned to the study. Nothing looked out of place on the desk. And yet, she knew a man had been in here, and recently. She had an idea who it might have been. Why? Had he come in search of something?

Diana recalled her own search of this chamber some weeks previous. She had hoped to find Sir Thomas's journal but had come up empty. The captain had said he had looked here as well. Had they missed something? It struck her that she was here now with no one the wiser. *It wouldn't hurt*, she thought, *to take another look for that journal.*

Diana checked the drawers in the desk again, as well as a cupboard that held maps and miscellany. She made another, careful overview of the titles on the bookshelves. A journal, she reasoned, might be differently sized than a book or novel, and have no markings on its spine. The cases held only books, however.

A childhood memory surfaced in her mind. Once, embarrassed about a schoolgirl crush she had admitted in her own diary, she had hidden the volume *behind* some books in her chamber. Perhaps the baronet had done something similar?

The fireplace was framed by mantel-height bookcases. Diana set to work on the shelves to the right side of the hearth, glancing behind the books in groups of three or four. At the far end of the top shelf, she noticed something odd and paused. A small, wooden knob had been installed at the back of the case.

Diana tugged on the knob. Nothing happened. She tried the opposite motion.

Diana gasped as, with a slight clicking sound, the bookcase swung inward like a door on hidden hinges.

CHAPTER TWENTY-TWO

D IANA HELD HER candle to the opening and peered within.
Behind the low bookcase door lay a small, dark room.
She ducked beneath the jam and entered. The concealed chamber
had a bare floor and unfinished walls. Its ceiling was high enough
for her to stand upright. The air was almost unbearably stuffy. An
ancient cot with a broken leg stood against one wall, its rope bed
rotted and moldy. Nearby, several open crates held dusty bottles
of wine and brandy.

This must be a priest hole, Diana thought.

She had read about priest holes, constructed during Eliza-
beth's reign or shortly thereafter to conceal Catholics, often in
attics and cellars or behind fireplaces and staircases. The dusty
cases of wine and brandy suggested that this one had been used
more recently to store smuggled goods. *Is that*, she wondered,
what brought the intruder here—something to do with smuggling? But
no. The room was too closed off, the air too fetid. No one had
entered this space in months.

A small trunk stood just inside the door. The hasp was old
and rusty. It bore no lock. Diana lifted the trunk's lid—and froze.

The trunk was full of books. Dozens of volumes of varying
sizes, shapes, and colors, some of which looked decades old,
others much newer. Diana dropped to her knees and opened one.
It was not a book at all. It was filled with handwritten prose in a
messy style she instantly recognized.

Sir Thomas's handwriting. These were the baronet's journals.

The diary pages featured occasional crossed out words and ink blots, similar to the drafts of Sir Thomas's letters that she'd seen. Atop the pile lay a volume bound in burgundy leather. She snatched it up. The entry on the first page began:

4 January 1849

A cold wind has blown up from the east, but it did not prevent me from taking my walk this morning. For breakfast, I had ...

Diana's stomach seized with excitement. It was Sir Thomas's diary from the current year.

Bringing the journal and her candle back into the study, Diana sat down beside the cold hearth and began to read.

THE FIRST MONTHS of Sir Thomas's journal were mainly a recap of weather conditions, the food he had consumed that day, the state of the crops, and his irritation with the news he had read in the paper that day.

These entries were interspersed with an occasional rant about an expense he was obliged to incur for a tenant, or his dissatisfaction with his daughter's governess, whom he called "an idiot with no more sense than the pupil she fails to teach."

This jab at Miss Fallbrook's mental prowess was painful for Diana to read, but also telling. How sad that father and daughter had been at such odds over an issue that had never been the young woman's fault.

More interested in Sir Thomas's state of mind in his final weeks, Diana flipped to a later entry. Apparently, he had taken the journal with him when he'd traveled abroad. Diana's breath caught in her throat as she read what he had recorded there.

Sir Thomas had indeed attempted, while in Germany, to meet the officers of Franke and Dietrich—just as she had suspected. But the company had moved and left no forwarding address. He further wrote:

> *I hired a carriage to convey me to the location where the railway line was supposed to originate. Latimer had assured me time and again that the project was under construction and great progress had been made.*
>
> *Upon arrival, I was met with a sight that made my heart sink. The land had been cleared for about a mile, and perhaps two hundred feet of track had been laid, but no more. Not a soul was to be seen, nor was there any construction equipment on hand. The site was abandoned.*
>
> *The entire investment seems to have been a deception. I fear the worst—that Franke and Dietrich have absconded with the cash. Did Latimer know of this?? Was he paid off for procuring trusting and foolish investors, like myself? I have never been so angry in my life.*

So, the railway investment *had* been fraudulent.

Diana read through the next few entries in the journal, after Sir Thomas had returned to Pendowar Hall. He matter-of-factly recorded his nephew's coming home from the Royal Navy and the severity of his leg wound but gave away nothing of his feelings for the captain or for his deceased wife and son. His thoughts were focused almost entirely on the financial matter that had distressed him.

Diana's candle sputtered. It was spent and about to go out. Quickly, she grabbed another candle from the desk, thinking to light it from her own—but moved too hastily. The candlestick slipped from her grasp and fell with a clatter. Her heart pounded. Had someone heard? But silence reigned. Retrieving the fallen candlestick, she lit it seconds before her own wick disappeared into the molten wax.

Sir Thomas's final journal entry, the night before his death, concluded with:

> *I have written to Latimer. We are to meet tomorrow. I shall tell*

him what I discovered in Germany and inform all the men I know who invested in this swindle. If Latimer is indeed guilty—and something tells me that he is—I will prosecute him to the full extent of the law. I'll see to it that his license is revoked and send him and all the men behind this to prison. I would send them to hell if I could.

"I thought I heard something."

Captain Fallbrook's deep voice so startled Diana that she nearly dropped the journal. He stood in the open doorway, half-dressed and his hair disheveled, as he had been that night many weeks ago when he had found her in the north tower room.

Diana leapt to her feet. Her heart thundered at the sight of him. Despite herself, she felt again the memory of his kiss. She banished it. "Captain."

"What are you doing?" he demanded, raising his candle. Before she could reply, he caught sight of the open bookcase door that revealed the cavity beyond. "And what on Earth is *that*?"

"A bookcase door, like the one that leads to the tunnel to Smuggler's Cave. There is a secret room behind the fireplace."

"A secret room?" He crossed to it.

"I think it was a priest's hole that may have been used later to hide smuggled goods. And more recently: your uncle's journals."

"His *journals*?" He stared at her.

"I found them, Captain." Diana couldn't hide the excitement in her voice. "There's a chest in there full of them."

"Is there, indeed." His expression changed. He looked uncomfortable now, as if he were about to come face to face with something unpleasant.

What, Diana wondered, was worrying him? And then she remembered: he believed his uncle had hated him. Did he fear that proof of that rancor would be found within those pages? Frowning, he ducked through the doorway into the hidden room. She followed.

"Well, I'll be blowed." He shook his head in wonderment.

"My uncle was a crafty devil. He never said a word about this to me." His gaze fell on the trunk. "You're certain these are his journals?"

"I am."

"How did you know to look here?"

"I didn't. It was just a wild guess." Diana held up the volume she carried. "This is the journal he kept before he died. I've read some of it."

"Have you?" His matter-of-fact tone did not disguise the anxiety and censure in his eyes. "My uncle's private journal—which he went to great effort to keep hidden. Yet you felt *you* had the right to read it?"

Diana's cheeks flamed. "Forgive me, Captain. I should have come to you first. But ..." Wanting to appease him, she thought fast. "Do you remember yesterday in the daffodil field ... when you kissed me?"

His voice went quiet. "It is a moment I am not likely to forget. But what has that to do with this?"

"You said, 'I could not help myself.' Well. I felt a similar compulsion. My curiosity overcame me."

He let out a sudden laugh, a sound that instantly eased the tension in the tiny room. "An excellent argument, Miss Taylor. You would have made a fine barrister."

"If women were allowed to enter that profession, I should be the first to sign up."

"Good for you." He laughed again. "And now *my* curiosity overcomes me." He nodded towards the book in her hands. "Did you find anything of note in that journal?"

"I did."

"I suppose ... there are pages full of regrets for having ever laid eyes on me, and diatribes about my failure to save his wife and son?"

"No. Sir Thomas's thoughts at the end of his life were taken up by something else entirely: his worry over the railway scheme in Germany."

"The investment Latimer arranged?"

"Yes. As I feared, it was a hoax."

Captain Fallbrook brought the trunk of journals into the study, lit several more candles, and asked Diana to tell him everything.

After sharing what she had learned and reading out relevant passages, she said, "I believe your uncle was about to reveal his findings about the railway investment but never got the chance—because he died the next morning before his scheduled meeting with Mr. Latimer."

"Hmm." The captain drummed his fingertips on the desktop. "So, what are you thinking? That Latimer may have silenced my uncle before he could spread the word?"

"It's possible."

"A serious accusation."

"Fraud is a serious crime. If Sir Thomas had gone to the authorities, and Mr. Latimer was found guilty, he might have lost his ability to practice law—or worse yet, gone to prison. I think Mr. Latimer knew Sir Thomas kept a journal and worried that it might incriminate him. I suspect he's been sneaking into the house late at night and searching the study, hoping to find and destroy Sir Thomas's journal, as well as any paperwork related to the investment."

"Again, an interesting theory. But what proof do we have?"

"None, I suppose … except for the cologne."

"What cologne?"

"The scent of a man's cologne lingered in this room when I arrived. I recognized it. Mr. Latimer wears that scent."

"Does he?" The captain sat back in his chair. "You never cease to surprise me, Miss Taylor. I will get to the bottom of this."

THE FOLLOWING AFTERNOON, Mr. Emity brought a summons

from Captain Fallbrook. He wished to see Diana in his study without delay. Miss Fallbrook giggled and teased Diana from behind her geography book. As Diana left the school room, she assured her pupil that this 'summons' was purely of a business nature. To her frustration, her student remained unconvinced.

Diana arrived to find Mr. Latimer seated across the desk from the captain, his face scarlet, his eyes downcast.

"Miss Taylor, I apologize for interrupting your school day, but I felt this could not wait." The captain gestured to a chair. When she was seated, he resumed. "Since the discovery and idea originated with you, rather than give you the information secondhand, I should like you to hear Latimer's confession from his own lips."

His confession? Satisfaction shot through Diana like lightning. He was guilty. He would own it.

"Go on, Latimer." Captain Fallbrook pulled the bell cord to summon a servant. "Tell Miss Taylor what you told me."

Mr. Latimer ran an agitated hand through his hair. "When I proposed the railroad project to Sir Thomas and the other investors, it was with the best of intentions. Franke and Dietrich came highly recommended. My father believed that railways are the future of transportation for both goods and people, and I saw it as a means of getting in on the ground floor of a burgeoning industry. I did not get wind that anything was amiss until after Sir Thomas's death."

"*After* his death?" Diana repeated.

Latimer nodded. "I received a letter from Sir Thomas asking me to call about an urgent matter. He was vague about the details. When I arrived that afternoon, I learned that he had died. About a month later, when I found out what was going on ... that no railway line was being constructed and the firm had vanished along with the money ..." Latimer heaved a sigh. "I worried that Sir Thomas had learned of this while in Germany—that that must have been what he had intended to tell me that day. I recalled him mentioning that he kept a journal. I could not take the chance of someone finding it in case ..." Latimer's cheeks flushed with shame.

"And so," Captain Fallbrook continued for him, his eyes flashing with disgust, "this reprobate has been sneaking into the house, hoping to destroy any evidence that might incriminate him." He quirked a brow at Diana that seemed to say, *Precisely as you suspected.*

"I cannot tell you how sorry I am," Mr. Latimer said. "Ever since I learned the truth, I have been working to raise funds to pay back my clients. I intended to tell them everything. I just needed more time."

Diana could not read the look in Mr. Latimer's eyes. He appeared to be sincere. But was it all an act? This was the same man who had flirted so cavalierly at Christmas with Miss Fallbrook. In the library that day, when she had asked him if he'd known the baronet had kept a journal, he had lied to her face. If he could lie about that and sneak into this house repeatedly in the dead of night, what else might he be capable of?

"I am afraid you have run out of time, Latimer," the captain said firmly. "You will, without delay, contact every man who invested in that fraudulent enterprise at your direction, and divulge the truth of the matter—or I shall tell them myself."

"I shall, sir."

"I won't bring charges against you—but you may from this moment consider your services in all my affairs to be terminated."

"Sir!" Mr. Latimer's face fell. "If you will only reconsider. My family has served yours for more than three decades. Again, I offer my deepest apologies. I promise to be transparent about every matter going forward, be it legal or financial."

"And so you should—with any clients you are fortunate enough to keep after this—*if* you manage to retain your license."

Mr. Emity appeared in the doorway. "You rang, sir?"

The captain stood. "We are finished here. Emity, please escort Mr. Latimer out."

As Mr. Latimer turned for the door, the beseeching look vanished from his face, replaced by a penetrating scowl. Diana stood and was about to follow when Captain Fallbrook spoke.

"Miss Taylor, stay a moment."

She turned back. He picked up several letters from his desk. "I know you often take early morning walks. Please deliver these letters to the post office tomorrow morning. They must go out first thing. The hall boy usually takes them, but I heard he's laid up with a cold. I would do it myself, but I promised to call on tenants in the opposite direction."

"Of course." Diana took the letters. They were alone in the room now.

"All this business with Mr. Latimer—I would appreciate it if you would keep it to yourself. I don't want our affairs to become a source of gossip, or to disclose how easy it was for an intruder to gain access to Pendowar Hall."

"Yes, sir."

"I will have a lock installed on the door to the smuggler's tunnel at the earliest opportunity."

"An excellent idea."

The captain toyed with a pencil on his desk. "And ... one more thing."

"Yes?"

"I wanted to thank you."

"For what?"

"For finding my uncle's journals. I intend to read them."

"I hope they provide you comfort, Captain. Or at the very least, useful insight."

"We shall see. Meanwhile ... I'm glad to know about that hidden room. I expect it has been here for centuries, a secret passed down from one baronet to the next."

"I'm sure your uncle would have told you about it, had he lived."

"I expect so."

"Captain," Diana couldn't help but add, "do you believe

everything Mr. Latimer said?"

"I have no reason to disbelieve it."

"What if he was not entirely candid? We don't know what Sir Thomas wrote to Mr. Latimer that day. What if the baronet admitted that he knew the railway investment was a hoax? It might be just as we theorized: that Mr. Latimer came here that morning to silence him. Sir Thomas may have kept an early draft of that letter, as he did so many others. I could look if you like."

Unexpectedly, the captain's face clouded. His features became as hard as marble.

"Leave it be, Miss Taylor. You have done your duty in bringing this to me. Latimer is a coward and a charlatan, but I do not think him capable of murder. He will never darken my door again."

DIANA HEADED DOWN the corridor, perplexed by Captain Fallbrook's reaction at the end of their meeting. He'd become similarly angry some time ago, when she'd brought up the possibility of the scuttled sailboat. Why?

This worry was replaced by a new one when, upon arriving in the schoolroom where she had left her pupil, Diana found the chamber empty. Miss Fallbrook wasn't in her bedroom, either.

An awful suspicion overcame her. Racing down the main staircase to the front hall, Diana glanced out a window and gasped in dismay. Outside on the gravel sweep stood Miss Fallbrook and Mr. Latimer. The girl was gazing up at him adoringly. The groom waited with Mr. Latimer's horse nearby.

Diana bolted out the front door and down the steps. "Miss Fallbrook! Come inside at once."

The young woman's cheeks grew rosy, but she didn't move.

Mr. Latimer smiled down at her. "I fear I must take my leave."

"It was nice to see you again, sir," Miss Fallbrook replied sweetly.

"And you, my dear." He kissed her gloved hand. "I bid you *adieu*."

Diana's blood boiled. Mr. Latimer climbed upon his horse, tipped his hat to Miss Fallbrook, and trotted off down the drive.

"What were you thinking, little miss?" Diana scolded once she and her pupil were back inside the foyer.

"Do not call me *little miss*. I am a woman now."

"You are not a woman. You are fifteen years old. And that man is more than twice your age."

"I have heard of couples with a greater age disparity who are very happy."

"You two are not a couple, Miss Fallbrook, and never can be."

"Why not? He is the only man who has ever treated me like a grown-up."

"That is only because you have not been around any other men."

"I have!"

"Where?"

"At church."

"That's not the same thing."

"Mr. Latimer says that on Christmas Day, he saw me differently."

"I do not doubt it. He saw your fortune." The words were out before Diana could stop them. Hurt bloomed in her pupil's eyes and Diana added, "Forgive me. You are too young to understand this yet, but money is a great motivating factor." Diana knew that better than anyone. "You have a substantial dowry and Mr. Latimer knows it."

"He doesn't care about my dowry. He is a respected solicitor with money of his own."

"Not as much money as he would like, perhaps." Diana thought of the man's current financial woes. "He might be feeling rather desperate at the moment."

"Desperate?" Miss Fallbrook's nostrils flared. "How cruel you are. Do you think no man could like me for my own sake?"

"I didn't say that."

"Papa admired him. So does Cousin William."

"Not any longer. The captain just severed their relationship."

Miss Fallbrook stared at her. "What do you mean?"

If only Diana could tell her about Mr. Latimer's newly discovered crimes. But Captain Fallbrook had asked her to keep mum on the subject. "Mr. Latimer betrayed your father's trust on a business matter," she replied vaguely.

"I don't believe you," countered Miss Fallbrook heatedly. "You are just saying that because you are jealous. You don't want me to find love because *you* never did."

The shocking words were like a slap to Diana's face. "Miss Fallbrook. That's not true."

"I feel sorry for you, Miss Taylor. I see the way you look at William. But that can never lead anywhere, can it? Because of the Mermaid's Curse. And because he's a determined bachelor. You are a spinster whose failed love affairs have left you bitter and alone and afraid to trust a soul. I don't want that to happen to me." With that, Miss Fallbrook turned and fled up the stairs.

Diana stood frozen in place for some long minutes before she sank down on a nearby chair and began to weep.

As Diana crossed the grounds early the next morning, a swirling fog hugged the lawns and shrubbery, obscuring everything but the tops of the tallest trees. The cold, dank air made her shiver despite the protection of her woolen cloak.

Diana hadn't wanted to venture out in this weather, but she had promised Captain Fallbrook to post his letters. She had breakfasted earlier than usual to complete her errand and slipped a note under her pupil's door to say that lessons would begin at ten instead of nine. Although, after their fractious encounter, Diana could not be certain the girl would even show up today.

She was still shaken by the cruel things Miss Fallbrook had said. Diana thought they had grown close by now. But, she realized, she had provoked the young woman's outburst by calling Mr. Latimer a fortune hunter. That had been a mistake. Miss Fallbrook was a young girl in the throes of her first romantic attachment—however inappropriate it was.

Diana cast her mind back to her own first experience of love. If her father, instead of supporting her and Mr. Graham's courtship, had forbidden her from seeing him, would Diana have obeyed? She doubted it. After all, she didn't heed her godmother's advice.

Love could, at times, be a force too strong to be reckoned with. It could blot out common sense. Miss Fallbrook was not thinking straight. Given time, Diana hoped she could help her see reason. She just hoped she *had* time. If Mr. Latimer's license was revoked, he would lose his means of earning income and might see Miss Fallbrook's fortune as his only way to survive.

A familiar grove of palm trees loomed up out of the fog. Diana had reached the riverbank, although it was difficult to see much of the river itself. An eerie quiet surrounded her, the world hidden by heavy, low-lying mist. The path was familiar, however, and with practiced steps, Diana found access to the footbridge.

The planks made their usual creaking sound as Diana made her way across, holding tight to the railing. An unseen bird squawked. Diana heard the distant flap of wings. Halfway across the bridge, she became aware of the creaking of planks behind her.

Was someone following her? She stopped and glanced in that direction but couldn't see more than a yard before her face.

"Who's there?" she called out. The creaking ceased. Not a breath stirred the air.

Don't be silly, Diana reprimanded herself. Old bridges sometimes creaked. She was alone. Who else would have been mad enough to go out in this fog?

Diana walked on. The creaking resumed, faster now. Diana's stomach tensed.

Before she could turn to look again, she felt a jarring impact against her back, thrusting her forward against the wooden railing. With a splintering sound, the railing gave way.

Diana cried out in horror as she plummeted into misty whiteness. A second later, she hit the river and was engulfed by freezing waters.

CHAPTER TWENTY-THREE

"**H**ELP! HELP ME!"
Diana flailed frantically in the fast-moving river. She gasped as an enormous rock appeared before her. Just as she was about to bash into it, the current swept her around the obstruction and spit her out the other side.

"Help!" The frigid waters rushed along at a breakneck pace. Diana knew the river's destination: its wandering course eventually wound down through a cleft in the cliffs on its journey to the sea. She was doomed.

She struggled to stay above the surface, but her long skirts, heavy cloak, and half-boots weighed her down. Kicking and thrashing, she rose, gulping air, only to be pulled down yet again.

Diana wrenched at the clasp on her cloak, ripped it from her body, and watched the garment float away. It made no difference. The merciless current pulled her along and down again, holding her in its grip beneath the water until she was desperate to breathe.

No, no, no ... Was she going to die?

All at once, a rush of sound and motion surrounded her. Urgent arms grabbed her around the waist and chest. She was being pulled up, up, up, until she broke the surface and with a great gasp inhaled the sweet taste of air.

"YOU'RE LUCKY TO be alive, Miss Taylor," said Mrs. Gwynn.

Diana lay in her bed, shivering beneath the covers as the housekeeper and Ivy looked down on her.

"It's a miracle Mr. Nankervis happened by and heard you call out," Ivy exclaimed.

Diana had expressed her profuse gratitude to Mr. Nankervis, who had insisted on accompanying her back to the house and refused to leave until he felt certain she would be well cared for.

Captain Fallbrook was still away, visiting tenants at the far edge of the estate. The doctor had come and gone. Worried that Diana might have caught a chill, he'd insisted that she keep to her bed and had given her something to help her sleep.

"Such a terrible accident." Mrs. Gwynn clicked her tongue. "But it's no wonder you fell. The footbridge can get wet and slippery in the fog, and that old railing should've been fixed ages ago."

"It wasn't an accident," Diana insisted. She had been trying to tell them that for hours, but no one was listening. "Someone pushed me off that bridge. Whoever it was, they knew I planned to walk to the village this morning."

"There, there, Miss Taylor," Mrs. Gwynn said calmly. "You're overwrought and imagining things. After all, you nearly drowned."

Ivy placed a bell on Diana's bedside table. "Just rest now, miss. Ring if ye need anything."

Diana tried to protest again, to make them understand. *Someone wants me dead. The same someone who killed Sir Thomas.* But the medicine stole her power of speech, and she drifted off into a heavy sleep.

Time passed in a feverish haze. She was cold. So cold. Her teeth chattered. People appeared and disappeared, hovering over her. Mrs. Gwynn. Mr. Emity. Hester. Ivy. Was that the captain?

She recognized Mr. Nankervis's kind but worried face.

"If he'd come a minute later, it would have been too late," someone said.

"The doctor fears she might die," whispered someone else.

"She will not die," asserted another deep voice.

A cup was forced to Diana's lips. "Drink this." She swallowed something hot and salty, choked, and fell back to sleep.

Diana lost all track of time. What day was it? Was it even day or night? One moment, she felt as though she were being consumed by a volcano and then next as if she were immersed in an arctic bay.

When she slept, she was besieged by dreams. On the beach with Miss Fallbrook, sculpting letters in the sand. Climbing up the tunneled passageway from Smuggler's Cave by lamplight. Strolling through a field of golden daffodils with the captain. He took her in his arms, a molten look in his eyes. *I have been wanting to do this for weeks.* He pressed his lips against hers.

Diana awoke, her heart pounding in her chest. She lay still for a long moment, savoring the dream, before she opened her eyes. Her bed chamber was lit by a single candle and the glow from the hearth. Rain pelted the windows. Ivy and Hester sat beside her bed.

"Ye're all right, miss." Ivy gently dabbed Diana's perspiring forehead with a cloth.

Hester brought a teacup to Diana's lips. "Drink this. It's beef tea."

Parched, Diana took several sips. The hot, meaty brew was delicious and quenched her thirst. "Thank you."

"I'm so glad ye've come to, miss," Ivy said.

"The doctor weren't sure ye would. But we never gave up hope."

"How long have I been asleep?"

"Two days," Ivy replied.

"Two days!" Diana couldn't believe it. "Have you been taking care of me all this time?"

"It was mainly Mrs. Gwynn," Hester replied. "But Ivy and I and others filled in."

Diana was surprised to learn that the housekeeper had taken such interest in her. "You are so good to me, all of you. Thank you." Diana's thoughts turned to the gardener who had saved her life. "Is Mr. Nankervis all right?"

"He be fine, miss," Ivy answered.

"I hope he knows how grateful I am to him."

"He does. Came to see ye twice now," Hester said.

Had Captain Fallbrook come? Diana didn't want to betray her feelings by asking. "Was Miss Fallbrook here?"

The two maids exchanged a glance. "We haven't seen her, miss," Ivy replied.

Diana wasn't surprised, considering their last, heated conversation. Somehow, she had to smooth that over.

"I best return to my duties now." Hester rose. "I'll leave ye in Ivy's capable hands." Diana thanked her again. Hester left.

"Ye're lucky, miss." Ivy clasped her hands and shook her head. "If not for Mr. Nankervis, Morwenna would have had her revenge again."

"Morwenna?" Diana looked at her. "What do you mean?"

"Well," Ivy replied gravely, "ye're in love with Captain Fallbrook, aren't ye?"

Heat infused Diana's face. "No," she lied. Were her feelings for Captain Fallbrook so obvious?

"He's in love with ye, miss. I can tell."

"He is not." As she said it, Diana questioned her own words. She had told herself there was no future for her and the captain. That she was only a dalliance, the woman at his latest port of call. But what if that weren't true? What if …

I have been wanting to do that for weeks now. I could not help myself.

He had kissed her. He had, many times, regarded her with what could be interpreted as affection. Was it possible that Captain Fallbrook *did* have feelings for her? Could they … might they ...

Hope rose within her, a hope she had never allowed herself to consider.

Perhaps, she thought, *it is time to put the past behind you.* She had spent far too long, she realized, being afraid to care for or trust a man—so worried that she would be hurt, she hadn't allowed herself to *feel.*

"Sometimes, folk are in love and don't even know it," Ivy was saying. "But Morwenna knows. It's a good thing Mrs. Gwynn were never a governess, or she would have drowned a long time ago."

Diana reeled in her thoughts and redirected her attention to the housemaid. "Mrs. Gwynn? What do you mean?"

Ivy hesitated, as if the remark were something she hadn't meant to reveal. "Well," she went on hastily, "Mrs. Gwynn worshipped the ground Sir Thomas walked on. She and the baronet were ... close, is all I'm saying. If she'd been a governess, Morwenna might have put an end to her, same as she tried to do to you."

Diana *had* noticed Mrs. Gwynn's reverence for her former master. Had the housekeeper been in love with Sir Thomas? Was it possible that they'd had a love affair? It was an intriguing thought.

"Ivy, listen to me: Morwenna is not real. Neither is the curse you keep going on about."

"They *are* real, miss." Ivy leaned forward with a worried frown. "The light in the north tower—it came back."

"When?"

"Last night. I didn't see it, but Mrs. Gwynn and Mr. Emity did."

Diana didn't know what to make of that.

"It's a sign, miss. Morwenna knows about ye and the captain, and she tried to drown ye."

"What happened at the river has nothing to do with my relationship with Captain Fallbrook, nor with mermaids or curses. I did not slip and fall off that footbridge. Someone pushed me."

"Ye keep saying that, miss, but ..." Ivy tilted her head skeptically. "Why would someone do such an evil thing?"

"Because I have been questioning the circumstances of Sir Thomas's death. I don't believe he took his own life. I think someone may have killed him."

Ivy looked shocked. "Who would have wanted to kill the baronet, miss? Unless ..." She broke off and frowned.

"Unless what, Ivy?"

"Never mind. It's nothing."

"Ivy. Do you know of someone who might have wished Sir Thomas harm?"

"I'm sure I'm wrong. I don't want to say."

"This is important, Ivy. If you know something, please tell me."

Reluctantly, Ivy sighed. "It's a terrible thought, miss. But all these months, there's something I haven't been able to get out of my mind."

"Go on."

"The night before Sir Thomas died, he and Captain Fallbrook had a row. I didn't mean to listen, but they spoke so loud and all. The baronet were fearful angry with the captain. He said some terrible things, blamed Captain Fallbrook for what happened to his wife and son and then ... he said he was going to change his will and disinherit him."

DIANA STRODE ALONG the cliff path. A seagull flapped along beside her—but strangely, it was flying upside down. Captain Fallbrook approached. He carried no stick. His leg was perfect—miraculously healed.

"I love you," Diana told him, hoping to hear him say the words back and yearning for him to take her in his arms.

Instead, his eyes flashed with fury, and his tone was menacing. "I told you to leave it alone. But you will not give up. You have to die."

Diana fled in terror. His footfalls pounded on the path behind her. She felt the impact of strong hands as, with a mighty shove, he pushed her off the edge of the cliff. Diana screamed as she plunged towards the jagged black rocks below.

With a gasp, Diana awoke.

The curtains were parted, revealing an early morning sky that poured down with rain. A fire burned in the grate, doing little to ward off the chill. A teacup sat on her bedside table. With effort, Diana propped herself up, took several sips, and lay back down again. She sensed that her fever was gone.

The awful nightmare haunted her. In her mind, she saw again Captain Fallbrook's malevolent glare and heard again the angry words he had hurled at her in her dream:

"I told you to leave it alone. But you will not give up. You have to die."

She could feel the impact of his hands when, in her dream, he had shoved her off the cliff. It was exactly like the impact she'd felt when she'd been pushed off the footbridge.

The footbridge.

A sudden cold dread filled Diana's every pore. The idea that Captain Fallbrook would try to kill her ... it was absurd.

Or was it?

It was the captain, after all, who had sent her on that errand to the post office, insisting that it be taken care of first thing in the morning, when the fog was always at its worst.

Could it be that ... *No!* Captain Fallbrook would never wish her harm.

But Diana's stomach clenched as she recalled his anguished remarks about the boating accident that had taken Lady Fallbrook's and her son's lives.

"I killed my aunt and cousin. And now my uncle, too. These are facts I cannot escape."

Diana had dismissed them as the misguided beliefs of a deeply troubled man. But what if they were *not* misguided beliefs?

What if they were admissions of guilt?

The captain had maintained that he'd had no interest in inheriting Pendowar Hall—but what if that wasn't true? What if, as she'd suspected when he'd first uttered the words, it had just been a ruse, to present himself as the reluctant heir?

Diana sat up in bed, her mind reeling with disbelief. *No, no,* her reason countered. *Do not go down this path. It leads to madness.* Captain Fallbrook was a good man. He would never murder anyone in cold blood.

But she could not help it.

His father, a second son and a clergyman, had had no home to leave his son when he'd died. Pendowar Hall was an ancient and valuable estate that had been in the Fallbrook family for centuries. Had the captain secretly coveted it all along? If so, what might he have done to obtain it?

Other than his uncle, Robert Fallbrook had been the only person standing in the way of his inheriting Pendowar Hall someday. Was it possible that the captain had been behind that boy's death as well?

Had her instincts been right about that plank she'd found on the beach? *Had* it come from the sailboat that had met its horrific end three years ago? Captain Fallbrook had access to the woodshop and all its tools. Counting on his own strong swimming abilities, he could have deliberately sabotaged that boat and set sail before an impending storm.

Diana covered her face with her hands. *It can't be true. It can't be.* And yet ...

"Something bad always seems to happen when William comes home," Miss Fallbrook had said.

The tragedy that had killed young Master Robert had claimed the life of his mother as well. With horror, Diana recognized: it was an ingenuous touch. Lady Fallbrook's death by drowning called back the Mermaid's Curse. It explained away the incident in the eyes of every superstitious person in the parish. That it also drew his uncle's ire—that he blamed the captain for the accident—was a pill he'd had to swallow to achieve his prize. And oh, how beautifully he had played it, feigning to be guilt-stricken, a man who "could not forgive himself" for the very deaths that he had orchestrated!

What about the lights in the north tower? They had begun after Lady Fallbrook's and her son's deaths, stopped for three years, and started up again after Sir Thomas's death. Whenever the lights had flashed, Diana suddenly realized, Captain Fallbrook had been at home. Was he behind that as well? Had it all been a ploy to keep the Mermaid's Curse alive, to deflect suspicion from himself?

With Robert Fallbrook out of the way, perhaps the captain, secure of his future inheritance and occupied by his naval duties, had been content to bide his time and wait for his uncle to die a natural death. But then, Captain Fallbrook had been injured. There was no guarantee that he would return to sea again. He had come home to face an uncle who blamed him for the deaths of his wife and son ... *and had threatened to disinherit him.*

That must have been the breaking point, Diana thought. *The captain couldn't risk losing everything then.* Perhaps he'd learned that his uncle had had an appointment with Mr. Latimer the next morning. He'd had no choice but to get rid of his uncle before he could revise his will.

Captain Fallbrook was the one who had "discovered" the suicide note, which—having access to all the drafts of Sir Thomas's correspondence—would have been easy to forge.

And so, he had risen early, and knowing Sir Thomas's customary walking route, had lain in wait—and pushed him off the cliff.

Just as—fed up with Diana's dogged determination to find the truth—he had pushed *her* off the footbridge to silence her.

Diana reeled with horror. The signs had been there all along, staring her in the face.

Captain Fallbrook was a murderer three times over. Nearly four times, for he had tried to kill her as well. Not long after her arrival, she'd told him that she'd come to Pendowar Hall to learn the truth about Sir Thomas's death! The day she'd had her near accident on the cliff path, *he* could have moved the warning sign. He could have also staged the accident in the library—she'd slipped and fallen from the ladder just hours after he had left for Town.

Mrs. Phillips, she saw now, had been right all along. She'd fingered the captain from the start. Diana should have listened—and followed her own instincts. How many times had she warned herself not to trust Captain Fallbrook? Just as she'd feared, he *had* been keeping a secret—and a monstrous one at that.

How could Diana have been so blind?

How could she have ever thought she loved him?

Heart pounding, Diana got up and hastily dressed.

Ought she to go to the parish constable? No, that would do no good. Why should Mr. Beardsley listen to her? She had not been here when any of this had happened and she had no proof of anything, only theories.

But she couldn't do nothing. She wasn't safe. Having failed to kill her this time, the captain would try again. She must get away. But where?

She could go to the vicarage. Surely, Mr. Wainwright would provide her shelter. A glance out the window, however, told her that getting to Portwithys would be no simple matter. It had been raining all night and was still coming down in buckets. The courtyard was nearly floating, which meant that the road and every path would be deep in mud.

Still, she had to try. She looked for her cloak, but it was gone. Then she remembered: it was probably lying on the bottom of the river. All she had was a lightweight jacket. It would have to do. Diana shrugged into it and grabbed her umbrella when a light knock sounded on the door.

The door opened and Captain Fallbrook strode in.

CHAPTER TWENTY-FOUR

D IANA FROZE, HER blood seeming to go cold in her body and her pulse pounding in her ears.

Captain Fallbrook stopped a few steps inside the doorway. "You're up."

Words failed her. Diana felt like a mouse trapped in a cage. She couldn't let him know what she had deduced. Not until she had gotten safely away.

"Mrs. Gwynn told me you were feeling better. I wanted to check on you myself. You do seem much improved. I ..." His gaze lingered on her face, and his brows wrinkled in confusion. "Is something wrong?"

She swallowed hard. "No."

"You look as if you've seen a ghost."

"Oh?" Her voice was so high and strained, she hardly recognized it. "Perhaps I ... got up too quickly."

He took in her jacket and umbrella. "Are you going somewhere?"

"I ... thought I might take a walk."

"In this weather? Don't be mad."

The door stood open. Should she try to dash past him into the hall? But he was stronger than she. He could easily stop her.

"You're trembling. You had best lie down." He stepped closer and gestured towards the bed.

Her heart leapt in fear. She took two steps back and rammed

up against her dressing table. "I don't need to lie down. I've been in bed for days."

"Because you've been ill. You had a frightful accident."

"It was no accident! You pushed m—" The words shot from her mouth despite herself. Heat crept up her neck.

He stared at her. "What?"

"Nothing."

"Do you still think what happened on the footbridge was no accident?"

She hesitated. Somehow, she had to gain his trust sufficiently to leave this room and the house. She needed help. Knowing what he'd done, she couldn't leave poor Miss Fallbrook in his care. "I don't really remember what happened."

"And yet, just now, you seemed to remember perfectly." His features tightened. "The doctor claimed you were hallucinating when you said it wasn't an accident. But it seems you still believe that it wasn't. And you are looking at *me* as if *I* had something to do with it."

Diana's whole being tightened with apprehension, but she couldn't bring herself to deny it.

"You think *I* pushed you off that bridge?" He squinted at her with a slow, disbelieving headshake. "Why on Earth would you think that?"

"Because you killed th—"

Although she did not complete the statement, he seemed to read her thoughts—and the terror she tried to hide. The color drained from his face. "Ah." He stumbled back a step. With a disbelieving headshake, he continued quietly. "You're the one who said I must not blame myself. That it was not my fault, any more than—as I pointed out—you were not to blame for your mother's death. But … now you think *I killed them*? My uncle. My aunt. My cousin? You think I murdered them all in cold blood? Why? To inherit Pendowar Hall?"

Afraid that he might strike or grab her, Diana raised an arm to protect herself. But instead of coming after her, his shoulders drooped. He gave her a long, disappointed look and then broke eye contact.

"Had I truly wanted to kill my cousin Robert," he pointed out, "would I have put my own life in danger in the process? I very nearly drowned that day." He heaved a deep, wavering sigh. "Moreover: at the time my uncle died, I had just returned from the Navy, bound to a wheeled chair and in such a state, I could barely walk two paces. I could not have pushed my uncle off a cliff that morning even if I had wanted to."

His expression was so deeply pained, and his words rang with such sincerity, that Diana felt the first stirrings of doubt.

"As for you, Miss Taylor … I just spent two sleepless nights walking the corridors, worried that you might die. I sat by your bedside to spell the maids. At the time, so strong were my affections for you, I believe I would have given my own life to save you." He frowned and repeated quietly, "At the time."

Without another word, he turned and quit the room.

DIANA STARED OUT the schoolroom window at the rain, a mournful battering that mirrored the weeping within her soul.

The doctor had called again and pronounced Diana much improved but insisted she not return to work for a week. On no account could she venture out until the weather cleared.

Ivy had left lunch on the table, but Diana could not bring herself to take a single bite.

She felt like an utter fool. How could she have been so wrong? How could she have ignored the physical limitations imposed by Captain Fallbrook's injury when he'd returned home all those months ago?

More importantly, how could she have ignored her own heart?

Everything she had learned about Captain Fallbrook over the

past months told her that he was a good and generous man. She loved him. How could she have ever imagined him to be capable of murder?

Experience had so predisposed her to the idea that people lied, Diana had jumped to an erroneous verdict. The captain was deeply hurt by her allegations. That had been all too evident.

"At the time, so strong were my affections for you, I believe I would have given my own life to save you.

"At the time."

So, he'd had feelings for her after all. *Had*, emphasis on the past tense. By accusing the captain of murder, Diana realized, she had lost him forever. Lost his trust and destroyed any chance she might have had for a relationship with him. She had done it to herself. There was no undoing it. It was over.

Diana sank down onto her bed and wept bitterly, the tears choking her, until her chest and jaw and throat and teeth ached. Finally, as limp as a rag doll, she wiped her eyes and blew her nose, filled with despair.

Now what? Diana wondered. She had been about to run to the vicarage when Captain Fallbrook had come in. But from what had she been fleeing? The captain meant her no harm.

A knock sounded on the schoolroom door. Diana looked up to find Mr. Emity standing hesitantly in the open doorway.

"Beg pardon, miss. I have been worried about you. I came up to see how you were faring. I heard weeping. May I?" At Diana's nod, he entered, eyeing her with concern. "Are you all right?"

"Not really, Mr. Emity." Diana crushed the handkerchief in her hand. "But thank you for asking."

"You are still ill, then?"

"Physically, I'm much improved. I fear my ailment now is more of the mental variety."

"I see." He indicated an empty chair at the table where Diana sat. "Will you permit me to join you?"

"Of course. I cannot promise I'll make fit company, though."

"Perhaps I can be company to you." He sat down and folded

his hands on the tabletop. "What troubles you, Miss Taylor?"

Diana sighed. "I have committed a terrible folly, Mr. Emity."

"A wise woman like yourself? I do not believe it. You are incapable of such a thing."

"I think that is the problem. I dared to think myself wise. But I drew false conclusions about someone."

"About whom, miss?"

"About Captain Fallbrook."

"In what regard did you draw these conclusions?"

"I thought ... and you will laugh at this ... that *he* was responsible for the murder of Sir Thomas, Lady Fallbrook, and their son."

Mr. Emity's brows arched. "You think all three of them were murdered?"

"I did for about a minute. All the facts seemed to fit. And so ... I accused Captain Fallbrook of those crimes to his face."

Mr. Emity blinked rapidly and gave a subtle nod. He lowered his voice. "How did the captain take it? Was he very angry?"

"It might have been better if he had been. But ... no. He looked at me with such disappointment, Mr. Emity. And such pain. If I had struck him with a knife to the heart, I could not have inflicted a deeper wound."

"I'm sure that's not true."

"If I ever meant anything to him at all, I have ruined it."

"I doubt that, miss. Since Sir Thomas's death, Captain Fallbrook has not been in the most wholesome frame of body or mind. But he is a different man since you came. I believe you have been good for him. The captain has a high regard for you. He has told me of it many times."

"Has he?" This was another blow to Diana's soul. Confirmation of what she'd almost had but lost. "Well, if that was once true, it is no longer. He despises me now."

"No one could despise you, Miss Taylor."

"You didn't see the look in his eyes. And he's not the only one who hates me. Miss Fallbrook does, too."

"No, miss."

"She does. I tried to come between her and … someone she admires."

His nose wrinkled. "Mr. Latimer?"

She glanced at him. "You know about that?"

"I know more about what goes on in this house than you might think."

Diana sighed again. "I failed that girl, Mr. Emity."

"You did not, miss. You have taught her a great many things. She is a confident young woman now. She can read because of you."

"What good is that if she throws her life away on a scoundrel like Mr. Latimer? I have an idea that it might have been he who pushed me off the footbridge."

"I suppose it could have been."

Diana darted him a glance. "You believe me about that?"

"That someone pushed you off the footbridge? I do. That is hardly something you could have imagined."

Tears burned in Diana's eyes. "No one else believes me, Mr. Emity."

"There are none so blind as those who refuse to see."

"If only I knew who committed that heinous act—it would answer the riddle of Sir Thomas's death. You and Mr. Latimer were leaving the study the other day when Captain Fallbrook asked me to mail those letters. Did you overhear his request?"

"I did, miss. Mr. Latimer would have heard the same."

"He was present at Christmas dinner when I admitted that I can't swim. And he has reasons to wish me dead."

"You mean, because you alerted the captain to the railroad investment in Germany?"

"You really do know everything that goes on here, don't you?"

"I have only just become acquainted with the newest details.

And may I say: I do not trust that man."

"Neither do I."

"But," Mr. Emity reflected, "that does not make him guilty of murder. There may be others who knew you were going to the village that day."

"But who?" Diana suddenly remembered: she had told her pupil that their lessons would start later that morning. She and Miss Fallbrook *had* quarreled … But no! That was ridiculous. It couldn't have been Miss Fallbrook! Could it have?

"Have you spoken to Mrs. Gwynn?" Mr. Emity asked.

"Mrs. Gwynn?"

"She knows what goes on at Pendowar Hall as well as I do. And she knew Sir Thomas better than anyone."

It was the second time, Diana realized, Mr. Emity had pointed that out to her. "I have never felt comfortable talking to Mrs. Gwynn."

"That is no reason not to speak with her. You might be surprised at what you hear."

His last remark gave Diana pause. Where had she heard that before? She sighed. "What have I been doing all these months, Mr. Emity? Everything I've attempted seems to have been a waste of time. I failed my pupil. I failed the captain. I failed to solve the mystery of Sir Thomas's death." *In so doing, I failed my godmother*, she thought.

"You must not think that way, Miss Taylor. You have not failed. You've done great things here. You have made a difference in both Miss Fallbrook's and the captain's lives. You have helped the poor in this community. You boldly tried to solve a mystery. Be proud of these accomplishments."

Diana let out a bitter laugh. "I have nothing to be proud of."

"How can you say that?"

"I made a mistake many years ago, Mr. Emity."

"Everyone makes mistakes."

"This was a big one. I've been paying for it ever since."

He lay a hand over his heart, then quickly lowered it. "You still feel bitterness, guilt, and regret over this mistake?"

Fresh tears trickled down Diana's cheeks. She nodded.

"I cannot believe that whatever you did was unforgiveable. You have recognized your mistake and feel sorry for it. Now, it is time to let it go. To forgive yourself."

Captain Fallbrook had once said something similar. "How do I do that?" Diana whispered. "How do I forgive myself?"

"By believing in your heart that you are deserving of it."

As Diana processed that, Mr. Emity gave her a gentle smile across the table.

"I recall something my father once told me, back in Guinea when I was a small boy. 'You are a worthy and unique person just for being you. Take care of yourself, for this is the only life you have.' It is time now, Miss Taylor, to not only forgive yourself … but to *take care of* yourself."

"What do you mean?"

"Someone made an attempt on your life. They might make another attempt, and soon. You are not safe here anymore, Miss Taylor. You must give up this search and go home."

DIANA PULLED OUT the trunk from beneath her bed. Her eyes were wet with tears as she retrieved a dress from the wardrobe, folded it, and placed it in the trunk.

Diana still couldn't forgive herself. But she could follow Mr. Emity's other advice—to go home.

It was impossible to leave today. It was still raining cats and dogs. But if the weather cleared, she could ask Captain Fallbrook to provide a ride to Truro tomorrow. She might as well get ready now.

Her heart ached at the thought of leaving Pendowar Hall. This place, and the people in it, had become as dear to her as her own home and family. But Miss Fallbrook wasn't speaking to her. The captain would be glad to see the back of her. And someone wanted her dead. She didn't dare wait around to find out who.

As she folded up another garment, though, she recalled something else Mr. Emity had said, and paused.

"You have made a difference in both Miss Fallbrook's and the captain's lives."

Diana hadn't done anything remarkable for Captain Fallbrook, except to hurl accusations in his face. She *had* achieved some success with Miss Fallbrook, though. Her pupil had finally acquired the tools to understand the reading and writing process. But her command was tenuous. If Diana left now, Miss Fallbrook might fall back into her old patterns and all their progress would be lost. Worse yet, the young woman was embroiled in an infatuation with an unsuitable man, a situation that could only lead to no good. Three days had passed while Diana had been ill. Who knew what had transpired in that time? How could she leave until that was resolved?

She thought about her promise to Mrs. Phillips, who seemed to be fading with every passing day. Her godmother had put her trust in Diana to find Sir Thomas's killer. How could she let her down?

"You are not safe here anymore," Mr. Emity had insisted.

Diana believed that. There was no longer a shred of doubt that someone had murdered Sir Thomas. Otherwise, they wouldn't have tried to get *her* out of the way. But if Diana did not bring that villain to justice, evil would triumph.

Diana would not flee. Difficult as it might be to encounter Captain Fallbrook again, she would remain and finish what she had started. If only she could solve this mystery, maybe, just maybe, Captain Fallbrook would find it in his heart to forgive her for her unfounded suspicions against him. That alone was reason enough to take a risk and stay.

With newfound resolve, Diana dried her eyes and returned her clothing to the wardrobe. She would have to be careful. On the alert at every moment. But somehow, she would learn the truth.

"Miss Taylor?"

Miss Fallbrook's voice startled Diana from her reverie. She entered and stopped a few feet away, twisting her sketchbook in her hands. "May I have a word?"

CHAPTER TWENTY-FIVE

"Y OU MAY." DIANA was relieved to see her pupil.
Miss Fallbrook's gaze was downcast. "How do you feel?"

"Better. Thank you."

"I offered to sit with you while you were ill, but William insisted that he or one of the staff must do it."

"It was kind of you to think of me. But I am recovered, as you can see."

"I'm glad. Although Mrs. Gwynn says you may not return to work for a week?"

"So the doctor ordered. I hope you have been enjoying your time off?"

"It has been … all right." Miss Fallbrook shifted uncomfortably. Her gaze darted to the window. "Will this rain never stop?"

"It is rather grim."

Miss Fallbrook still didn't seem able to look Diana in the eye. "Miss Taylor, I … I owe you an apology."

"Oh?" Diana waited.

"The last time we spoke … I said some awful things. I feel horrible. I was unkind and I didn't really mean it."

"Thank you for apologizing."

"Can you ever forgive me?"

"I can and I do. Miss Fallbrook, I owe you an apology as well. When I saw you outside with Mr. Latimer that day, I reacted without thinking. I was too harsh. I think I embarrassed you."

The young woman's eyes lifted at last to meet Diana's. "You did."

"I'm sorry. I should have handled that better. And I'm sorry as well if I made you feel bad when I mentioned your dowry. Not every man is after a woman's fortune. I hope Mr. Latimer *does* like you for *you*—as well he should, for you are a lovely and likeable young woman."

A smile lit Miss Fallbrook's face. "Do you really mean it?"

"Of course, I do. But—Miss Fallbrook, I also meant it when I said that you are still very young. Mr. Latimer has far more experience of the world than you do. You are not even out yet, dear."

"That doesn't matter." Miss Fallbrook's eyes looked dreamy, and she took a long, savoring breath. "I *love* Mr. Latimer."

"I know you *think* that now. And what you feel is real to you, at this moment. But it is a first love."

"So?"

"First love is special. But unfortunately, it is often founded on unstable ground and does not always last. *I* know that better than anyone. Mr. Latimer might seem to be all that is good and amiable today, but I urge you to tread carefully. He may not be the right man for you."

Miss Fallbrook's smile fled. She bit her lip. "How can I know if he is the right man for me?"

"By taking the time to get to know him better. Be patient. Give yourself a couple of years—"

The young lady gasped. "A couple of *years*! But *you* got engaged after only two weeks!"

"Yes, but it didn't work out, remember? *And* I was eighteen years old at the time."

"Still. I can't possibly wait *two years*."

"You can and you must. You have so much to learn. Let me teach you. There is no rush. I see such great things ahead for you, Miss Fallbrook. If you and Mr. Latimer are meant to be together, you will know it in time."

Miss Fallbrook averted her eyes again. "If you say so, Miss Taylor."

"Patience is a virtue, my dear. You do not see it now, but one day, you will thank me for giving you this advice." *If only I had heeded Mrs. Phillips's advice,* Diana thought, *I might not have had my own heart broken in those early years.*

"Actually ... that is another reason I'm here. To thank you for all the advice you have given me and all you've taught me. And ..." She held out her sketchbook. "I wanted to give you this."

"Your sketchbook? I cannot take that."

"It's one of my old ones. I have the new one you gave me for Christmas. I know you like my art, Miss Taylor. I'd like you to have it."

"Well then, I shall accept with grace. Thank you." Diana wrapped her arms around her pupil, who returned the hug with vigor. When the embrace ended, Diana asked, "What are you going to do on this rainy day, since I am not to recommence lessons yet?"

"I thought I might ... draw in my room," Miss Fallbrook returned vaguely.

"An excellent plan."

"What will you do, Miss Taylor?"

"I haven't decided yet. But I will see you later."

"Yes." On her way out, Miss Fallbrook paused to glance back and added, "Thank you again, Miss Taylor. For everything you have done for me."

There was a hint of finality about the remark that struck Diana as odd. Or, as she had done so many times of late, was she reading something that wasn't there?

AFTER MISS FALLBROOK had left, Diana sat down at the lunch tray Ivy had left for her. The food was cold now, but Diana's appetite had returned, and she was grateful for the nourishment.

As she ate, she pondered her next move.

Mr. Emity would disapprove of Diana's decision to stay at Pendowar Hall. But she couldn't leave now, not with so much at stake, and so much still undone.

Diana revisited their conversation in her mind. He had asked, for the second time, if she had spoken to Mrs. Gwynn, insisting that she knew this house and Sir Thomas better than anyone.

Ivy had also said something intriguing about Mrs. Gwynn:

"She and the baronet were ... close, is all I'm saying. If she'd been a governess, Morwenna might have put an end to her, same as she tried to do to you."

Diana had perceived the remark as just another example of Ivy's superstitious nature. But she found herself wondering, again, if Mrs. Gwynn had been in love with Sir Thomas. If that were true, might it figure into all of this somehow?

Diana felt as if the answer to this riddle was dangling right in front of her nose, but she hadn't grasped it. She had avoided Mrs. Gwynn as a rule because the woman always made her feel uncomfortable.

"That is no reason not to speak with her," Mr. Emity had said. *"You might be surprised at what you hear."*

Diana suddenly remembered where she'd heard that last phrase before. Mrs. Phillips, in one of her letters, had counseled Diana to listen more. It had proven to be good advice where Miss Fallbrook was concerned.

Perhaps, Diana thought, *I haven't listened hard enough.*

DIANA FOUND THE housekeeper downstairs in her sitting room. A hearty fire added warmth to the otherwise cheerless room.

"Mrs. Gwynn, may I speak with you?"

Grunting her assent, Mrs. Gwynn waved Diana into the empty chair across from her. "Thought I'd rest my feet a minute, seeing as how Captain Fallbrook's away."

A sharp pain speared Diana's chest at the mention of the captain. "Where has he gone?"

"Don't know. He just said he was going out, which is madness in this frightful weather. Would you like a cup of tea?"

"Yes, thank you." Diana sat down.

"I'm glad to see you up and about." Mrs. Gwynn's features looked strained, and her voice lowered as she poured two cups of tea from an elegant porcelain teapot. "You were so ill. I—we— were all worried about you."

It was the first time the housekeeper had spoken so cordially or expressed concern for Diana. To think that she'd almost had to *die* before the woman viewed her as a worthy human being! Better late than never, however. It might help with the conversation Diana had in mind.

"I understand that you watched over me while I was ill, Mrs. Gwynn. I wanted to thank you."

"It's part of my job."

"All the same, I'm grateful."

The housekeeper shrugged. "You're welcome."

Diana took a sip of the hot brew. "This tea is excellent—just what the doctor ordered. And that is a lovely teapot."

Mrs. Gwynn tenderly touched the teapot with a nostalgic smile. "It were Sir Thomas's favorite. Always wanted his tea served from this pot. I like to borrow it now and then."

It felt like the perfect lead in. "You served Sir Thomas a long time, did you not Mrs. Gwynn?"

"Came to this house at age eighteen as a housemaid and never left."

"Is that when you and Sir Thomas met?"

She nodded. "His father, the old baronet, used to call Thomas his baronet-in-training. Took him everywhere. To London, to meetings with his steward, to call on all the tenants and such. When the old man passed, Sir Thomas were still young, but he took over as smooth as glass. Loved Pendowar Hall, he did, and served it well to the end of his days."

"You have great affection for Sir Thomas."

Her voice softened again, and a faraway look came into her eyes. "Best master that ever was."

"And yet, I have heard that he could be a harsh, uncompromising man."

"That only happened after … after he lost his second wife and son. You should have seen him before that, Miss Taylor. He were everything upright and good. Such a handsome man, and such a smile! When he walked into a room, he quite took it over. You couldn't look anywhere but at him." She fell silent and stared down at her teacup.

"Mrs. Gwynn … I know we call you 'missus,' but … did you ever marry?" Diana asked, aware that "Mrs." was often an honorific title for women in the housekeeper's position.

"No, I never did."

"Did you ever think of marrying?"

The housekeeper's cheeks bloomed pink. "I might have, once or twice. But I was that fond of … of Pendowar Hall. I didn't want to leave."

"Was it the house you were fond of?" Diana asked gently. "Or was it Sir Thomas?"

The question seemed to startle Mrs. Gwynn. "I don't know what you mean."

"Ivy told me that you and the baronet were very close."

Mrs. Gwynn glanced up sharply. "Ivy said that?"

"She also said if you had been a governess, you would have fallen victim to the Mermaid's Curse. Which can only mean one thing. Did you love him, Mrs. Gwynn?"

The housekeeper's teacup dropped to its saucer with a clatter. "Who do you think you are to ask such impertinent questions?"

Diana paused. Had she gone too far? "Forgive me," she said quickly. "I did not mean to upset you." If Mrs. Gwynn had loved Sir Thomas, only to watch him marry two other women, it must have broken her heart. Diana was no stranger to heartbreak.

Perhaps she ought to try another tactic.

"I only asked because I thought we might have something in common. I loved two men—or thought I did—but they betrayed me in one way or another." She related the story of her failed romances.

"The rascals!" exclaimed Mrs. Gwynn. "But it's their loss, Miss Taylor, not yours. Those men don't know what they gave up. You have a goodness about you. I've seen how you are with Miss Fallbrook. I didn't think you'd last a fortnight, and yet here you still are. You've done more for that girl than all her previous governesses put together."

"It means a lot to hear you say that."

"I've seen a change in the captain as well. He's a happier man for knowing you."

Diana stared down at the tabletop. Was that change what Mr. Emity had been referring to? "If there ever was anything between me and Captain Fallbrook—it is over."

"Is that why he stomped out the door this morning with a face as grave as death? Well, I suppose it's for the best, given the Mermaid's Curse and all." With a sigh, she refilled their teacups. They sipped in silence for some minutes. At length, she said, "You're right, you know."

"About what?"

"About Sir Thomas." The housekeeper leaned back in her chair and glanced up at the ceiling. Taking two long, shaky breaths, she murmured, "Lord forgive me, but I did love him. And he loved me."

Diana's pulse quickened. "When did it start?"

"The moment we first set eyes on each other. It were my first day at Pendowar Hall. He were twenty-seven then—nine years older than me and as handsome as could be. I were setting a fresh pitcher of water on his dresser and he walked in and ... that were that."

Diana's mind worked on the implications. "You had a love affair?"

She nodded, her face flushing an even brighter shade of pink. "Thomas said his father would never allow a union between us, and he couldn't go against him. I didn't care. As long we could be together now and then, it were enough for me. For many years, it were pure heaven. But then Thomas's father died, and he still said we couldn't marry. I were a servant, he said. He were the new baronet. What would the world think? It wouldn't be right. We should just go on as we were. And so, we did for five or six more years, until I ..." She frowned. Her eyes grew misty.

"Until?" Diana suddenly guessed where this was going. Delicately, she asked, "Did you have a child by him?"

Mrs. Gwynn bit her lip and nodded. "I never told him. How could I? He'd said time and again that he would never marry me. Every woman I knew in service who got in the family way was sacked on the spot. I couldn't take that risk. But I couldn't raise a child on my own, either. How would we live? So, I went away for six months, said I must care for a sick relation. And—" A sob escaped her throat. "I left my baby to be raised by another."

"Oh! How difficult that must have been."

"You can't imagine it if you've no child of your own. But it fair broke my heart." Mrs. Gwynn wiped tears from her eyes. "I came back to Pendowar Hall and became the housekeeper. I worked hard and tried not to think about the child I gave away. Soon after that ... he met and married the first Lady Fallbrook."

"Miss Fallbrook's mother?"

Mrs. Gwynn nodded. "His first wife were the daughter of a wealthy gentleman, a good woman of his own class, and they seemed to be a good match. I thought, *That's it. He's done with me now.* I weren't bitter about it. I knew our relationship would have to end someday. But marriage or no, things went right back to the way they'd been between us."

"Did his wife know?"

"I don't think so. We were discreet. We met in the wood-shop—there be a room in back with a little bed, where he slept sometimes. When Miss Emma were born, and the first Lady

Fallbrook died, Thomas came to me for comfort and I were proud to give it to him. But having married once, I think he grew accustomed to it. When Miss Emma was five, she outgrew her nanny, and he hired her first governess: Miss Corbett. Pretty as a picture, she was. I warned him to keep his distance—the Mermaid's Curse and all—but did he listen? No. He fell head over heels. Said she made him feel young again, and he couldn't live without her. But Miss Corbett were the daughter of a seamstress and a blacksmith with only a few years of schooling behind her." The housekeeper scoffed bitterly. "She barely qualified to be a governess."

"And yet, he married her."

"All that claptrap about it being beneath him to marry a servant, and she were no better than me! 'We can carry on like always,' he told me. 'She'll never know.' Oh, how I wanted to say *no*, Miss Taylor. To walk away from this house and never come back. But where could I go? This was my home. And I still loved him."

Diana nodded, an ache in her throat. "I understand."

Mrs. Gwynn's tone deepened as she went on. "The thought of them together made me so angry, I could see red. More governesses came and went as the years went by, all of them frustrated by Miss Emma. But Miss Corbett were now *Lady Fallbrook*. And she were *my mistress*! I had to do her bidding! Every time she gave me an order, I wanted to scratch her eyes out. When Master Robert were born, I thought of the child I'd been obliged to give away, and my heart broke all over again. Sir Thomas simpered over Master Robert like he were the most marvelous creature who'd ever drawn breath." Her own breath came in gulps now, and her face turned purple. "Sometimes, I wanted to slap Thomas's face and wring that little boy's neck."

Diana stifled a gasp. This was a side to the housekeeper that Diana had never seen. The words were all the more shocking by the venom with which they were spewed. "I can see where that … might have been difficult to bear."

"It fair near killed me."

"So … what did you do?"

Mrs. Gwynn pressed her lips together. "*Do*? What could I do? I kept my head down and I carried on. And then one day, *Lady Fallbrook* and Master Robert died."

Diana's stomach knotted and her mind reeled from the vehemence Mrs. Gwynn had just expressed. However, part of her understood it. *How difficult it must have been for Mrs. Gwynn to see the man she loved marry twice, while continuing to see* her *on the sly*, Diana thought. *And how awful that Mrs. Gwynn had been obliged to give up her child at birth.* It appeared that the housekeeper had never gotten over it.

And who could blame her? Diana couldn't imagine the agony of such a separation. Had Mrs. Gwynn ever seen her child over the years? Diana was about to ask, but their conversation was cut short when the kitchen maid, Bessie, darted in crying and announcing that she'd cut her finger.

Mrs. Gwynn instantly rose to see to it.

Diana took her leave, rattled and full of questions.

CHAPTER TWENTY-SIX

T HERE WAS A break in the storm.

A pale afternoon sun filtered through the rain-streaked windows of Diana's chamber, illuminating Miss Fallbrook's sketchbook, which lay open on her lap.

Diana turned a page in the sketchbook. It was a portrait of Mrs. Gwynn. The excellent rendering captured the stern but even-keeled expression of the housekeeper Diana had thought she'd known. Now, she questioned the veracity of that image.

Mrs. Gwynn's resentment over everything that had happened with Sir Thomas appeared to have simmered for years. His refusal to marry her, despite their decades-long affair, was reason enough to be hurt. When he'd first wed and had his daughter, not long after Mrs. Gwynn had secretly given birth herself, it must have compounded the injury. But when he'd fallen in love and married a second time—to a mere governess, an employee not much more elevated than herself—it seemed to have been the last straw.

"Every time she gave me an order, I wanted to scratch her eyes out."

"I wanted to slap Thomas's face and wring that little boy's neck."

Diana pressed her fist to her mouth, a dreadful notion shocking her to the core. Did Mrs. Gwynn's efficient exterior hide the soul of a woman gone mad?

The lovers' secret meeting place had been the woodshop where the drills were stored. Had Mrs. Gwynn sabotaged the boat that had sent the second Lady Fallbrook and her son to their deaths? Had she killed them hoping that Sir Thomas would marry her at last? It wouldn't have been an unreasonable expectation. After all, his excuse about not marrying a servant no longer held water.

When the years had passed, and Sir Thomas had not married her—but had wallowed in grief instead—had Mrs. Gwynn finally lost all reason?

Had she given in to her rage and murdered *him* as well?

If Mrs. Gwynn was behind all of those deaths ... had she tried to kill Diana as well? The housekeeper, Diana realized, could easily have moved that sign on the cliff path and added extra polish to the library ladder. But what of the footbridge incident?

Diana suddenly remembered: the morning she had gone to post the captain's letters, she'd asked Mrs. Gwynn to send up her breakfast early. Mrs. Gwynn had known Diana would be crossing the footbridge in the fog.

This could be the answer to the mystery! Diana's heart thudded as she turned a page in the sketchbook, grappling with these ideas.

Another portrait met her gaze. Diana paused. The artistry of the sketch revealed something that she had never noticed before. She gasped aloud. All at once, it was as if a cloud had been lifted from Diana's mind. The pieces of the puzzle fell into place.

I know, Diana thought, her heart thundering. *I know who murdered Sir Thomas.*

And she could guess why.

If only she could tell the captain! But he was away. Even if he were here, why should he believe her? After this morning, he probably despised her. Diana must find a way to inform the parish constable. Mr. Beardsley might be equally dubious, but she had new information now and these sketches to accompany her theory.

Diana glanced out the window. Clouds were regathering. It might rain again at any minute. Every route to Portwithys was no doubt swimming in mire, but she would have to chance it. The footbridge was out of the question. The cliff path could be dangerous in the rain, but it was either that or the road.

She was about to grab her jacket when there was a faint tap at her door. Diana opened it to find the hall boy, a shy lad of eleven, holding a note.

"If ye please, miss. I'm to give ye this." Without ceremony, he thrust the note into Diana's hand and raced away.

Diana unfolded the note. She recognized the block letters and shaky writing style at once as her pupil's. Filled with a sudden sense of dread, she read it through.

MISS TAYLOR,

I AM LAEVNIG WITH MR. LATIMER. WE AR TO MARY. WE SHALL GO BY BOAT FORM SMUGLERS CAVE. THN BY CARIGE AND TRAYN TO SCOTLND.

DONT WURRY. WISH ME WELL.

EMMA

Diana was aghast. She thought she had talked Miss Fallbrook out of this! Panic seized her. When had this note been written? Had Miss Fallbrook and Mr. Latimer already made their escape? There was no time to lose. She must try to prevent this calamity.

Diana raced down the servants' stairs. Fetching a lantern from the storage closet, she lit the candle and dashed to the hidden door to the tunnel to Smuggler's Cave. The new lock had been left unbolted. Had the would-be lovers escaped this way? Diana heaved open the door.

The stairs were as steep and narrow as she remembered, the passage just as musty and dank. Diana plunged down into the twisting darkness, grateful for the lantern that lit her way. The sound of dripping water grew louder as she descended. At several spots, the steps were crumbling, and she had to press a hand against the wall to steady herself as she slipped by. The tunnel's rocky surface was dry to the touch at first but grew increasingly damp.

A salty tang invaded the air now as well as the roaring sound of the distant ebb and flow of the sea. At last, the stairs ended, opening onto a wider, sloping space—the first of several connecting caverns. Diana raced through one cavity into the next. Turning a bend, she found herself at the rear entrance to Smuggler's Cave.

A dim light filtered in from the unseen mouth of the cave, illuminating the craggy, dark walls and the sandy floor strewn with rocks and pebbles. The tide was higher than it had been on Diana's previous visits and rushing in fast. The cave was already more than half filled with seawater.

The Fallbrooks' sailboat, she saw with relief, was still there, chained to its mooring beside the boat's storage cupboard. She had arrived in time. Miss Fallbrook and Mr. Latimer hadn't left yet!

Another thought came on the heels of that one: what if this sailboat had not been their object? What if Mr. Latimer had come for Miss Fallbrook in his own boat? They could be long gone by now.

As Diana wrestled with the awful implications of this, she felt a sudden, sharp blow to the back of her head and fell in a faint.

THE SHOCK OF freezing water brought Diana back to consciousness with a start.

She opened her eyes to find an ocean wave receding and then surging up again around her prone body. The cavern's ceiling towered high above. Her skull throbbed as if it might split in two, keeping pace with the thrum of the water that lapped over her thighs.

Grimacing in pain, Diana maneuvered to a stand. The tide had risen further and now almost filled the cave. Across the away, the tethered sailboat bobbed on the roiling sea.

What on Earth had happened?

She was in a different place, she realized to her dismay, than she'd been when she'd passed out. She was now trapped on a tiny, shrinking, rocky outcropping backed up against the cavern wall on one side and surrounded by sea on all the others. The ledge dropped off sharply into water that looked deep and perilous. Violent waves crashed in and out. She dared not cross that watery void.

Someone must have dragged her here after hitting her on the head. Who?

A tremor of fear crept up Diana's spine. She had the strangest sensation, as though she were being watched.

She turned.

Ivy stood on an embankment, safe from the rising water. She was smiling.

Diana stared at Ivy as understanding dawned. "Miss Fallbrook did not write that note, did she?" Her voice echoed across the cavernous space.

Ivy's grin became a smirk. "Her handwriting weren't hard to imitate. She writes so bad."

For the second time that day, Diana felt like a fool. There had never been any elopement. She should have known Miss Fallbrook would never have left like that. It had been a ruse on Ivy's part, to get Diana down to this lonely, dangerous place.

How ironic, Diana thought. She had deduced who the murderer was, just in time to fall into her malevolent hands.

"Ivy, help me," Diana pleaded. "There's a rope in the storage cupboard. Throw it to me."

"Not on your life." Ivy chuckled, a low, wicked sound.

"Don't do this, Ivy. What would your mother think if she knew?"

"My mother?" Ivy glowered. "What do ye know about my mother?"

"I know you are Mrs. Gwynn's daughter. I know that Sir Thomas was your father."

Ivy hesitated. "How do ye figure that?"

"I saw your portraits in Miss Fallbrook's sketchbook." For the first time, Diana had observed that Ivy's and the housekeeper's noses were similar, and that they had similar expressions—when they smiled, their left eye crinkled. There was something about the shape of Ivy's face, as well, that had reminded Diana of Sir Thomas. Why had she never perceived these things before? "I guessed who you were," she added. And she'd guessed what Ivy had probably done.

"You're a clever one, miss. No one else has ever noticed a resemblance. But then, who looks twice at a chambermaid?"

Diana's heart pounded with trepidation. She had to keep Ivy talking, get on her good side while trying to figure out an escape plan. "How long have you known about your parentage?"

"Since I were thirteen. My mother sent for me when I were old enough to earn my keep. She said how sorry she was that she had to give me up. Made me promise to keep it a secret from my father, as she had."

The water had risen above Diana's ankles. "It must have been hard, to keep that secret all this time."

"It weren't fair. I were his child, and *he* didn't even know! Miss Fallbrook is so stupid, he didn't like her. But to see him simper over that boy and his wife, a *governess! If only those two were out of the way*, I thought, *he could marry my mother.*"

"Sir Thomas could have married your mother long before he met Miss Corbett, but he didn't," Diana pointed out. "What made you think this time would be different?"

"I weren't working here *then*. He didn't know anything about me. But after I came to Pendowar Hall, I were sweeping the workshop one day when he came in. He were nice to me. He showed me how to use some of his tools. I thought, if Mama told him who I am, he would love me. And when he were free and single again, we could be a family."

"I see." Diana swallowed hard. "And you knew the captain planned to take them sailing?"

Ivy nodded. "I got a drill from the woodshop and bore holes in the boat beneath one of the seats. But I needed the boat to get far out to sea before it took on water. I remembered something my granny once taught me—a way to fix a damaged pail by plugging the holes with mud. It worked, but not for very long, and I thought that was perfect." A smug gleam lit Ivy's eyes. "Not long after the boat were put out to sea, a lucky storm blew up. And just as I hoped, Lady Fallbrook and her brat drowned."

Diana struggled to remain calm. "I will never tell anyone, Ivy, I promise. If you will just fetch the rope and throw it to me."

"I heard drowning is not so bad. It'll be over quick."

Should I take the risk? Diana wondered. *Jump into the water and try to make it to the embankment where Ivy stands?* But the deep pool rushed and foamed between them like an angry beast. The memory of the river water closing over her, and her clothing dragging her down, kept Diana frozen to the spot.

"Captain Fallbrook might've died that day as well," Ivy was saying, "which would have served him right. He only be the baronet's nephew. He didn't deserve to inherit Pendowar Hall. *I'm* the oldest living child. By rights, the house should be *mine.*"

Diana knew this wasn't true. By law, the estate could only go to the next male heir. Otherwise, Miss Fallbrook would have inherited as a legitimate daughter. Surely, Ivy must have known this? But there was no point in arguing with her—she was clearly deranged—and there was no time.

Fighting down her panic, Diana said, "If you help me, Ivy, I'll help you. I'll tell the captain who you are. He'll be happy to know you're his cousin. And he'll do right by you."

"No, he won't, no more'n my father did. I waited three years after Master Robert and Lady Fallbrook passed for him to get over his grief. But he never did. Finally, I could wait no more. I told him. I said, 'Sir Thomas, I'm yer daughter.' I hoped he'd accept me as his flesh and blood. But no! At first, he were too shocked to speak. Then he grew angry and said, 'Keep this idle suspicion to yerself, or I'll sack ye *and* yer mother.' Oh, how I hated him then. I was nothing to him, invisible, just the girl who lit his fires and emptied his chamber pot. While my mother suffered in silence, in love with a man who would only take her to bed in secret."

The water splashed at Diana's knees. Terror spiraled through her. "What did you do, Ivy?" But she knew the answer.

"The next morning, when he set off on his walk, I hid in the shrubbery at the point where he always stopped to admire the view. Then I crept up and shoved him off the cliff. Just like I shoved ye off that footbridge."

"And you forged Sir Thomas's suicide note, 'I cannot go on'? Just like you forged the note from Miss Fallbrook?"

"A little bit of schooling can go a long way." She smirked. "I should've taken and burned Sir Thomas's letter after I copied from it, but I didn't think of it 'til later. It's not my job to clean his study. I feared it'd be suspicious if I went back looking for it." Ivy glared at Diana across the churning waters. "And I never thought anyone would figure it out."

"The lights in the north tower … was that you?"

"I had to keep Morwenna alive in folks' minds so they'd blame the Mermaid's Curse. I borrowed my mother's ring of keys when she were sleeping and it worked like a charm. No one suspected a thing. And no one ever would have if *ye* hadn't come to Pendowar Hall, poking yer nose into everything." A wave rushed up against the embankment and Ivy stepped back, shaking her head. "Ye were too close to discovering the truth. Ye had to die."

"You don't need to kill me. I'll go home tomorrow. I'll never set foot in Pendowar Hall again. And I will never tell a soul."

"What, and leave me looking over my shoulder for the rest of me days? Not likely. Ye're like a dog with a bone. Ye'll never keep quiet."

The freezing water slapped at Diana's waist. "That day in the library when I fell. You were so good to me, Ivy. Remember? You may have saved my life. You can save me again."

"Do you think I *wanted* to save ye?" Ivy sneered. "When that sign on the cliff path didn't work, I had to try again. I saw ye were on a mission to find some book, so I put extra polish on that ladder. Ye would have bled out for sure if that stupid Hester hadn't come by and started shrieking. What could I do then but help ye?"

Diana shivered, both from cold and shock. "Please, Ivy," was all she could think to say.

"Ye should have drowned in the river, but the sea is better still. When yer body washes up, everyone will know it were Morwenna who came for ye. The captain, he be next on my list." Ivy let out a spiteful laugh. "He'll meet with an accident one day. And once again, they'll say it were the Mermaid's Curse."

Just then, a massive wave crashed in. The heaving waters grabbed hold of Diana, threw her up against the cave wall, and dragged her away again. In seconds, she was hurled the entire length of the cave and then spit out into the violent, open sea.

The wind howled. It was raining again, a heavy downpour. Diana choked and thrashed, panic-stricken, tossed about by angry whitecaps. Waves crested overhead and thrust her down, then up again. With each dunking, she struggled frantically to rise to the surface, where she gasped for air, only to be pelted by the deluge from the skies before she sank again.

A strong current seized her and propelled her onwards. Diana managed one more long breath before it pulled her down, down, down, cartwheeling head over heels into the watery depths.

Was this the end? Diana stared up at the surface far above, powerless to reach it. Oh, how desperately she needed to breathe.

Suddenly, a figure swam up and hovered before her: a beautiful young woman with long, flowing red hair. No. Not a woman. A *mermaid*. Her upper body was bare, her breasts wrapped in seaweed. Her glistening, greenish-blue tail undulated softly.

Morwenna.

She regarded Diana with a cunning, malicious smile. Diana knew she was hallucinating. *I must be on the edge of death*. Still, she couldn't help but silently appeal to the apparition.

I must breathe, or I shall die.

The mermaid's mocking expression seemed to say, *Then die. You asked for it.*

Perhaps the mermaid was right. Perhaps Diana *had* asked for it. She had dared to belittle the legend's power, had loved a man despite every warning.

Captain Fallbrook's face swam before her eyes. She had lost him. And yet it hurt to know that she would never see him again. She thought of Athena, Selena, Damon, and Mrs. Phillips ... sorry that her death would cause them pain.

She hated to leave this world and all the beauty in it. But her lungs felt as if they might explode. It was as if the entire universe were about to burst its way out of her chest.

Do it. Breathe in, Morwenna taunted.

Terror ebbed, replaced by surrender. Morwenna wanted her and would just keep coming for her. Diana was ready to give in. Just as she was about to open her mouth and inhale the freezing water, a voice resounded in her mind.

No. You cannot drown. Not today. Fight. Fight!

It was the captain's voice. She heard it loud and clear. As if he were calling to her not in her mind, but across the ocean's depths.

Once again, Diana knew she was hallucinating. But it struck her suddenly that if she died, Captain Fallbrook and her godmother would never learn the identity of Sir Thomas's killer. Mrs. Phillips would go to her grave full of anxiety and doubt. Captain Fallbrook would continue to blame himself for the deaths of his aunt and uncle and cousin. Miss Fallbrook would forever believe that her father had committed suicide without a thought for her. Their lives would be ruined, while that scheming vixen Ivy continued to work right under their noses. And then ...

"The captain, he be next on my list. He'll meet with an accident one day. And once again, they'll say it were the Mermaid's Curse."

Diana couldn't let that happen. *Oh, Captain! I cannot die*, she thought desperately. The truth would not change anything between them, but she loved him. She could not give up now. *I must survive so I can tell you. So I can save you.*

Diana dug down for all her strength and fought against the churning sea, kicking her legs and moving her arms. She knew no swimming strokes and made little progress, but it was just enough, for she reached a region where the current swept her up and carried her the rest of the way. Breaking the surface, Diana desperately filled her lungs with air, just as a wave caught and rushed her forward. With a painful jolt, she struck something hard and sharp. A huge, black rock. Diana spun, reached out, and clung.

She had, she realized, reached one of the tiny islets offshore. The heaving tide kept tugging and drenching her, and the rain kept pouring down. But Diana persevered, crawling forward on hands and knees over the craggy surface until she was free from the ocean's grasp.

She had made it. She was safe. For several minutes, Diana lay in a heap, too fatigued to move or care about the rain that assaulted her. All at once, a bolt of lightning illuminated the grey skies, followed by a boom of thunder. Diana almost laughed. She was already drenched to the bone. What did thunder and lightning matter?

But they did.

Propping herself up on one wearied arm, Diana saw through the rain that the islet upon which she was perched was separated by a half mile or so of open sea from the shore. It might as well have been a hundred miles, though, since she could not swim. If someone noticed she was missing, they would never think to look for her here. Diana heaved a bitter sigh. Even if they did, they would not come for her in a thunderstorm. To attempt it would be suicidal.

An object in the ocean beyond caught her attention. It looked like a bird beating its wings against the festering swells. Then she realized it was no bird. It was a human being.

It's Ivy.

The upsurge that had swept Diana out to sea must have claimed Ivy in its grip as well. Another immense wave erupted and carried Ivy away. Moments later, she disappeared.

Diana closed her eyes, trembling with cold. Ivy was young and strong. She might yet survive. But what chance did Diana have, stranded here in this remote spot in a thunderstorm? Had she saved herself, only to perish on these rocks? Had Morwenna won, after all?

An indistinct sound broke through the gale. Almost as though someone were calling her name.

"Diana!"

Was she hallucinating again? Diana opened her eyes. Incredibly, a boat was making its way across the storm-tossed sea, its sails straining against the fierce wind and pelting rain. A lone figure was at the helm.

The captain.

Diana burst into tears.

CHAPTER TWENTY-SEVEN

C APTAIN FALLBROOK DROPPED anchor and dove off the boat. Moments later, he emerged from the churning sea, clambered up the rocky crag, and knelt before Diana, who was still too exhausted to move.

His blue eyes were wild as he blinked back the driving rain. "Thank God I found you."

"How did you know where to look?"

"I'll explain later."

"Ivy tried to kill me. She killed your uncle, and Lady Fallbrook and Master Robert."

"I was beginning to suspect as much. Where is she?"

Diana told him.

"I must get you home." He reached for her.

"Wait." Her heart pounded. There was so much she wanted to say, so much guilt she carried. "I'm sorry."

"For what?"

"For suspecting you. I was out of my mind with fear. All the clues pointed to you. I didn't want to believe it. I wouldn't blame you if you never forgave me."

"I understand."

"Do you?"

"Diana." It was the first time he had called her by her Christian name. His tone, and the expression in his eyes, made her heart swell with hope.

"I know I hurt you. And I feel so awful because … I love you."

He swept Diana up into his arms and cradled her to his chest. "We'll talk about that later as well."

Diana wrapped her arms around the captain's chest and sighed with relief. Although she was drenched to the bone, freezing cold, and on an islet in the middle of the roiling sea, she had never in her life felt so warm or safe.

"ARE YOU SURE you're all right?" the captain asked.

"I am." Diana, wrapped in a blanket, sat on the sofa beside Captain Fallbrook in the blue parlor before a roaring fire. She had defied the doctor's orders and refused to spend another day in bed.

Yesterday, after Captain Fallbrook had brought her back to the house, Diana had told him everything she'd learned about Ivy. That morning, Ivy's body had washed up on the shore. Mrs. Gwynn had gone to pieces and was still sequestered in her room.

Miss Fallbrook, upon learning what had really happened to her father, stepmother, and brother, had been similarly besieged by grief. Later, however, relieved to know that her father had not been driven to take his own life, she had calmed down and thanked Diana for uncovering the truth.

"When I think what might have happened," the captain said, "if I had not gone looking for you …"

"You promised to tell me how that came about," Diana reminded him. "How did you know to look for me at sea?"

"It started, I suppose, when I went to see Mr. Wainwright yesterday afternoon. I was distraught by your accusation and needed a friendly ear."

Diana winced. "I'm so sorry," she began, but he pressed a silencing finger to her lips.

"We need not speak of it again. Wainwright helped me see things from your point of view."

Tears welled in Diana's eyes. She dashed them away. "I must thank him the next time I see him."

"He's a good man. I told him about Latimer, the scoundrel, how I had discounted your theory about the footsteps, but you had been right all along. I began to wonder what else you may have been right about. When I got home, Mrs. Gwynn came to me and confessed that Ivy was her daughter by my uncle. She said you had pulled it out of her—the fact that she and Sir Thomas had had a child together, even if she hadn't mentioned Ivy by name—and she didn't want me to hear about it from anyone else."

"Were you shocked?"

"About Ivy, yes. Not about the affair. That, I already knew."

"How?"

"I've been reading my uncle's journals. It is all in there. It's been going on for decades."

"Mrs. Gwynn loved him."

"Yet he recorded the affair matter-of-factly, not a word about love. He took terrible advantage of her." He sighed. "Anyway, at that point, I went looking for you and learned you were missing. The hall boy told me he'd brought you a note from Ivy. I found the note in your room. After discovering that Emma had not written it—she insisted that she'd taken your words about Mr. Latimer to heart and would never have considered such a thing—I grew suspicious. I immediately went down to Smuggler's Cave, where I found a lantern on the embankment."

"That was mine. I must have dropped it."

"Beside it lay a heavy fire poker that was wet with blood."

"Oh!"

"I presume that is the implement Ivy used to knock you out. I didn't know it then—but I feared something terrible had happened to you. The cave was flooded. I know how strong the tide can be. Something told me you had been carried out to sea, and I had to fetch you." There was a haunted look in his eyes. Diana wondered if he was thinking about his aunt and cousin, whom he hadn't been able to save. "I rigged the boat and set sail. When the storm blew up, I pressed on … and I spotted you on the islet."

"You risked your life to save mine," Diana responded with gratitude, for what must have been the dozenth time.

"I have sailed in plenty a gale," was his no-nonsense reply.

But Diana knew it had been dangerous.

"And I did not save your life," he pointed out. "*You* did that. You fought the sea and saved yourself. For a woman who cannot swim, you performed an amazing feat. How on Earth did you do it?"

Diana thought back to that moment when the ocean had almost claimed her. "I had help."

"Help?"

"Yesterday, when I was about to drown, I heard your voice."

He turned to her sharply. "What did I say?"

"You said: 'No. You cannot drown. Not today. Fight. Fight!'"

His eyes widened in astonishment. "I uttered those very words."

"When?"

"When I set out in the boat. I kept seeing you in my mind, struggling in the sea. Terror gripped me. I cried out to you aloud." He shook his head. "I was grateful no one was on board, or they would have thought me mad. And yet you heard me?"

"I did. And I answered."

"How? You were beneath the waves."

"I replied in thought."

"What was your reply?"

She told him.

"Now *you* will think me mad," he answered, "for I heard your reply."

Diana gazed at him in wordless wonder.

Gently, he brushed a tendril of hair from her forehead.

"'There are more things in Heaven and Earth, Horatio ...'"

Diana finished the quote from *Hamlet* with him. "'... than are dreamt of in your philosophy.'" They shared a smile.

After a moment, the captain said, "Thank you."

"For what?"

"For your courage, spirit, and dedication to a cause that I tried so many times to squelch. For insisting, despite my bull-headed opposition, to learn the truth about what happened to my family."

"I hope it has eased your burden?"

"It has. And there is something else." He paused. "One of my uncle's early diaries, from the year my parents died, was revealing. He wrote that sending his twelve-year-old nephew off to the Navy was the most difficult thing he had ever done, but he felt it necessary. Should he ever marry again and have a son, he said, I would not inherit Pendowar and would need a profession."

"You see, he did love you."

"It means a great deal to know that."

"If only there were some passage we could show to Miss Fallbrook so she would know the same."

The captain went quiet. "Actually, there is one. In the volume he kept a couple of years ago, my uncle mentioned an afternoon in the white garden, where he had come upon Emma sketching. He remarked in a positive way upon her artistic talent, and—uncharacteristically—he did so with affection and pride."

"I'm so glad." Joyful tears pricked at the backs of Diana's eyes. "Perhaps we can find a way to show just that page to her."

"We will." Taking Diana's hands in his, the captain urged her to her feet. The blanket slid from her shoulders as he gazed down at her with affection. "Diana, I cannot thank you enough for all that you have done since you came to Pendowar Hall. You have made an enormous difference in Emma's life. And mine. But that is not why I love you."

A sense of radiant lightness pervaded Diana's entire being. *He loves me.* She felt as if she were floating, weightless. "It isn't?"

"I love you because you are the best person I know. The most thoughtful, most intelligent, bravest, kindest, and most caring individual I have ever met. I cannot imagine my life without you."

"Nor I without you." She loved him for all the same reasons. She told him so.

"Do you remember I said I was unmarried because I hadn't met the right woman?"

Diana nodded.

"I have met her now."

"Have you?" Diana asked breathlessly. She couldn't help adding: "What about … all those other women I've heard of? One in every port?"

He smiled into her eyes. "Reports on that score have been greatly exaggerated. Only one woman holds the key to my heart. And I am looking at her." Holding her hands, Captain Fallbrook went down on one knee and gazed up at her. "Diana, will you do me the honor of becoming my wife?"

"Yes! Yes, Captain. I will."

He stood again, drew her close, and kissed her long and lovingly. "There will be no more 'Captain.'" He growled, briefly breaking the kiss. "From this moment on, call me 'William.'"

"Aye aye, Captain," was Diana's teasing reply.

They were kissing again when Diana heard someone discreetly clearing her throat.

Miss Fallbrook stood a few yards distant, her lips pressed with censure. "What does this mean? Please do not tell me that you two are in love?"

The captain and Diana exchanged a smile. He released Diana from his embrace. "We are, indeed. And you are the first to know: Miss Taylor … Diana … has just agreed to marry me."

"No! What are you thinking?" Miss Fallbrook cried. "Have you forgotten the Mermaid's Curse? Miss Taylor has nearly drowned twice. You cannot be together!"

"The curse—if there ever was one—is broken," insisted he.

Diana looked at him. "What do you mean?"

"All three criteria of the legend have been met. I pledged my love to you, 'a maid who comes from the sea,' which surely happened yesterday when you pulled yourself from the ocean. During the gale, I saw a series of huge waves rise to the very top of the cliffs. And ... look at the beach."

He beckoned Diana and his cousin to the window. Diana gasped in awe.

The coastline that curved away in both directions was thickly covered in heaps of seaweed.

As per the legend ... the beach had turned green.

CHAPTER TWENTY-EIGHT

"**D**EARLY BELOVED, WE are gathered here together in the sight of God, and in the face of this congregation, to join together this man and this woman in holy Matrimony ..."

Diana's heart drummed fast and thick as she and William stood, hands clasped, before Mr. Wainwright. Regal in his white surplice, the clergyman commandingly pronounced the opening lines of the marriage ceremony from the *Book of Common Prayer*.

The April morning sun shone in through the stained-glass windows, bathing the altar in its brilliant light. William looked impossibly handsome in his dark blue full-dress naval uniform embellished by gold epaulettes and cocked hat. His expression as he gazed down at Diana made her feel beautiful as well. And he had put the sentiment into words just before entering the church.

"Exquisite as a snowdrop, my love," he had pronounced, taking in her new gown of white embroidered silk and her rosette-trimmed lace veil, *"and I am the most fortunate man on Earth to have you as my bride."*

"I am the most fortunate woman to be your wife," Diana had answered. For in the three months since his proposal, they had grown even closer.

Diana's only regret was that her godmother could not be here. Two months ago, Diana, William, and Emma had traveled north to Yorkshire to pay Mrs. Phillips one last visit before she died. She had been too weak to rise from bed, but she'd been strong enough to enjoy their company, to wish Diana and William joy, and to thank Diana for all she had done while at Pendowar Hall. Although the truth had been painful to learn, it had meant the world to Mrs. Phillips to finally know what had really happened to her brother and his family.

The captain had told a partial truth to Mr. Beardsley and Mr. Wainwright, without revealing Ivy's parentage—that Ivy had admitted she'd forged the suicide note in a fit of temper towards her employer, and that she'd argued with Sir Thomas that morning on the cliff before he had accidentally lost his footing and fallen to his death. Ivy's death was portrayed as an accident as well, and the captain, wishing to spare her mother any further grief or humiliation, had remained mum about Ivy's other heinous misdeeds. After the parish constable had issued a new verdict in the baronet's death, Mr. Wainwright had approved the exhumation and removal of Sir Thomas's body to his family plot in the churchyard, an event which had brought further peace to his sister, daughter, and nephew.

Mr. Wainwright's voice drew Diana from her thoughts. She took in the beloved attendees standing beside her at the altar: her sister Athena, as maid of honor; Selena and Emma, her bridesmaids; and her brother, Damon, who had taken time off from his work in London to walk her down the aisle. On the other side, Lieutenant Commander Keating and two more of William's fellow officers looked on with poise.

Diana glanced at the congregation. They had kept the guest list small, and her heart swelled as she took in every fond and familiar face. Mr. Emity was dapper and dignified. Mr. Nankervis looked quietly pleased. Mr. and Mrs. Trenowden beamed. Mrs. Gwynn, who wore a mourning veil, sat teary-eyed, her lips trembling.

"Therefore," Mr. Wainwright was saying, "if any man can show any just cause, why they may not lawfully be joined together, let him now speak, or else hereafter forever hold his peace." He glanced up from his book and paused.

To Diana's joy, no impediment existed to prevent her union to the captain. Their hearts were knit together and would be always. They exchanged vows and rings. When Mr. Wainwright pronounced them man and wife and told William he may kiss the bride, the wedded couple came together in an embrace so sweet and fervent, it drew laughter and applause.

Afterwards, in the churchyard, Emma placed her bouquet of flowers on the newly erected grave of her father. A fresh spring breeze blew off the sea, infusing the air with its briny tang. The foxgloves and bluebells edging the yard nodded their heads as if in benediction of the ceremony that had just been performed.

Across the way, in a lovely spot beneath shady elms, a new play area was being constructed on William's orders, in memory of his aunt Sylvia and cousin Robert, and as envisioned by that boy's father.

In the church courtyard, while the captain conversed with his friends, Diana stood beneath the giant yew with Damon. Tall and handsome in his black clerical garb, he leaned down to kiss her cheek.

"My heartiest congratulations, Lady Fallbrook."

"Thank you, Damon." Diana beamed, so blissful that she wondered if what had just passed was real or a dream. "It means so much to me that you came."

"I would not have missed your wedding for anything," insisted he.

"Sometimes I think, *What if Mrs. Phillips had not asked me to come to Pendowar Hall?* William and I would never have met."

"God has a way of bringing us to the people we are meant to meet."

"I believe you are right."

"Diana." Damon's expression grew solemn as he took one of Diana's gloved hands in his. "Ever since you shared what happened that awful day at sea, it has made me shudder to think how close we came to losing you."

She bit her lip. "Perhaps I should not have told you?"

"I'm glad you told me. I want to know everything that happens to you … and matters to you." He let out a contrite sigh. "But it has opened my eyes to how remiss I have been. For the past few years, I have buried myself so deeply in my work, I have ignored my own family. If you had died that day, Diana, if we had never had a chance to speak again, my guilt would have haunted me forever."

"You have nothing to feel guilty about, brother dear." Diana had lived far too long with guilt and knew how corrosive it could be. "I admire your commitment to your congregation. I'm glad it brings you joy. You're here now and I'm thankful for it."

"I promise to be a more regular correspondent in the future. I love you, Diana."

"I love you too."

They exchanged a warm embrace.

As Damon moved off to speak to his friend Mr. Wainwright, Diana's sisters darted up before her, looking especially pretty in their matching white bridesmaid gowns.

"I adore your captain," Athena pronounced, brushing back an auburn curl that had escaped the confines of her upswept coiffure. "I can see why you fell in love with him."

"William is the sun and the moon to me," Diana admitted.

"And he is *such* a generous man!" Selena, a couple of inches shorter than Diana and Athena, had impulsively tucked a white camellia into her dark-blonde tresses. "We can never thank him enough for all he's done for us."

On their recent trip to Yorkshire to see Mrs. Phillips, William had made a point of visiting the property Athena had recommended as the ideal venue for a girls' school. Thorndale Manor, on the outskirts of a village called Darkmoor Bridge, had been on the market for four months without a single offer. The owner had just lowered the price and the captain, believing in Athena and Selena's proposal and considering the estate to be a sound investment, had purchased it on sight and given them a freehold to live there in perpetuity.

Athena and Selena, over the moon, had quit their posts as governesses and had just moved in to Thorndale Manor, where they would soon begin preparations for their future school.

"We are determined to make it a wholesome and nurturing environment where young girls can both learn and thrive," Athena declared fervently.

"It will be our life's work," Selena agreed, "and I can think of nothing more rewarding."

A part of Diana's being was envious of her sisters' new vocation—it was an enterprise they had discussed for years and had looked forward to pursuing together. But she reminded herself, she would still keep her finger in the educational world. She would oversee Emma's lessons for some years to come. She and William had hired a teacher to hold classes for local girls on weekday mornings in the Sunday School room at the village church, which Diana would oversee in between her duties managing the Pendowar Hall estate when he was at sea. And she had offered to help her sisters plan the curriculum for their new school and would provide whatever advice or assistance she could from afar. It wasn't the same as running the school with them, but it was the next best thing.

"The house is almost everything we could have wished for," Athena remarked with glee. "The previous owner left many of the furnishings, as he apparently moved to a much smaller place. Most of the servants have agreed to stay on and they seem to be good people. We are fortunate that your captain offered to pay their salaries for now."

"Hopefully, we'll be able to pay them ourselves when the new term begins in September," Selena added. "When we get back, we'll begin advertising for pupils."

"From what you've told me, Thorndale Manor is in such a desirable location, you will have your pick of students," Diana enthused.

"We hope so." Athena laughed. "Let us pray that prospective parents are not deterred by the strange history of the place."

"What strange history? Oh, you mean, the story that a murderess once lived there?" Diana recalled Athena mentioning something about that in one of her letters.

"It's not just a story. It's a fact. Some years ago, the nineteen-year-old daughter of the family who owned Thorndale Manor was convicted of murdering her betrothed, and she was hung at York Prison."

"Oh! How awful." Diana considered the implications of this. "Did the murder occur at Thorndale Manor?"

"No, at a neighboring estate," replied Selena.

"Well, you said it happened years ago. Thorndale Manor is under new ownership now. Most people, I believe, will see it as an intriguing piece of the house's history."

"That is our belief as well." Athena hesitated. "Although there is one thing that has us a bit ... disconcerted."

"What is that?" Diana asked.

Athena lowered her voice dramatically. "They say the ghost of the murderess haunts Thorndale Manor."

"Oh!" Diana couldn't stop her smile. "What rubbish."

"I agree!" Selena cried. "Every manor house in England seems to have a legend about a ghost. We didn't give it a second thought until ..."

Diana eyed her sister questioningly. "Until ...?"

Selena glanced at Athena, who gave her a silent nod as if to say, *go ahead*. "The night after we moved in to Thorndale Manor, we were walking down a hall when the strangest feeling came over us," Selena explained.

"What kind of feeling?" Diana asked.

"We sensed a sudden coldness in the air." Athena's shudder seemed involuntary. "And ... a presence. It was as if someone else were there, even though they couldn't have been. We were completely on our own."

Diana stared at them, then smiled again. "You're teasing me, aren't you?"

"No, honestly. We both sensed it," Selena asserted.

Athena averted her gaze and let go another short laugh. "I know what you'll say. It's ridiculous. And *it is*. We heard the legend about a ghost, and we let our imaginations run away with us."

Diana took that in. "Perhaps so. But on the other hand ... perhaps not." She had thought or been told that exact same thing too many times over the past few months about her own conjectures and knew better now than to question such a feeling. "It might not be a ghost, but there may be something else afoot. And you know our old motto ..."

Her sisters returned her smile. "Where there is smoke, there's fire," the threesome quoted in unison.

"Keep your eyes and ears open," Diana suggested.

"Excellent advice," Athena replied. "After all, we didn't call ourselves the Sisterhood of Smoke and Fire for nothing!"

"We should resurrect that old sisterhood," Selena mused, "but this time with a prefix."

"A prefix?" Diana glanced at her. "What do you mean?"

"Everything you accomplished here at Pendowar Hall, Diana, was done with such a bold and fearless disregard for risk. We must honor that and follow in your footsteps. Henceforth, I say we call ourselves the *Audacious* Sisterhood of Smoke and Fire."

"I love it," Athena cried.

The three women wrapped their arms around each other's shoulders in a circle, foreheads touching in a communion of spirits. "To the Audacious Sisterhood of Smoke and Fire," Diana said. "May we ever seek the truth and never back down."

"Hear, hear!" her sisters cried.

After which, they embraced each other while laughing.

Another hearty, familiar laugh caught Diana's ears, diverting her attention. Glancing across the churchyard, she caught sight of her new husband, and her heart swelled with love and pride. He was an amazing man. She could only count her lucky stars that fortune had showered such blessings upon her, and that he loved her as much as she loved him.

The thought, however, that he would soon be obliged to return to duty caused a sudden, wistful surge to rise in her chest.

"Diana? What is it?" Athena inquired.

"I'm just remembering how short my time is with my husband." Diana blinked back burgeoning tears. "His ship sails a fortnight after we return from our honeymoon."

"I'm so sorry! But," Athena reassured her, "you will have much to occupy you as the new mistress of Pendowar Hall."

"And who knows?" Selena smiled. "By the time the captain returns, you may be busy with a new baby."

Diana's cheeks warmed. "I pray that we are so blessed." Another thought occurred to her. "Oh! How shall I bear it? You are both so dear to me, yet you live at practically the opposite end of England."

"We shall have to make annual visits," replied Athena. "Alternately, you can come to see us, and we shall come to see you."

"An excellent notion!" agreed Selena.

After a sumptuous wedding breakfast in the dining room at Pendowar Hall, Diana and William descended the stairs in their going-away attire.

"How I shall miss you!" Emma threw her arms around Diana.

"Promise me you will practice your reading and writing, my darling Emma," Diana said, returning the embrace before pulling back smiling into Emma's eyes. "And draw, paint, and sculpt to your heart's content."

"I shall," Emma vowed.

"Be good while we are gone," remarked William. "And stay away from Smuggler's Cave!"

At the mention of that lonely place, a shiver raced down Diana's spine. "Yes, do," she cautioned. "Especially at high tide."

Diana's siblings and the small, gathered crowd showered the newlyweds with flower petals as they made their way to the waiting carriage. Inside the coach that would take them on the first leg of their journey to Portsmouth, where they would embark on a ship to Italy, the captain removed his hat and took

Diana in his arms.

"I can hardly wait to show you Rome and Florence," he murmured against her ear.

"I look forward to seeing them with you." Diana, who had never left England, was excited by the prospects before them.

"I wish we had more time. A month abroad is not long enough."

"It will have to do."

"It pains me to think that the moment we get back from Italy, I must leave again."

"If only we could spend every day of the rest of our lives together."

"If only. This is the first time I have contemplated a sea voyage with regret. But I will treasure every minute of shore leave when it comes. And you will do a magnificent job running Pendowar Hall in my absence."

"I hope so. I have so many worries."

"Such as?"

"How will the staff regard me now that I am no longer an employee, but the lady of the manor? What about the tenants? You have been so steadfast in handling their needs. Will I be up to the task?"

He tenderly gazed into her eyes. "You will. Your good sense and compassion will guide you. You have far more intelligence and skill, my darling, than you give yourself credit for."

Diana believed that now. Finally, she understood what Mrs. Phillips, Mr. Emity, and William had been trying to tell her. Yes, at Pendowar Hall, she had managed to avenge an evil, reveal a truth to a dying woman, help a struggling girl, and restore faith and a sense of honor to a gallant man. And yet, even if Diana had not done any of that, her worth, she now knew, was not determined by her accomplishments, her perceived failures, or by what others thought of her. She was worthy for simply being herself, a unique human being.

She had made a mistake when she had been a child, but it was time to forgive herself—and to forgive anyone who had ever hurt or wronged her. In so doing, a great weight had been lifted from her shoulders.

She had sometimes struggled, but she'd had parents and a godmother who had adored her. Two sisters and a brother who were incredibly dear to her. An occupation that had been fulfilling and brought her joy. A home in Derbyshire. And now a new home and future with a wonderful man whom she loved with all her heart. She was not perfect—no one was—but going forward, she would hold her head high and take modest pride in the person she was—and was becoming.

"I shall write to you every day, my darling," William promised.

"I shall do the same."

"Every time I put pen to paper or read your communications, I will see your beloved face in my mind. And I will hear your voice."

"It will be as though you are here beside me, instead of thousands of miles away."

"Yes. We will be united across time and space …"

"… in words and thought."

"We have done it before," he pointed out softly.

"Yes, we have."

He cradled her cheek in his hand. "Oh, how I love you, my dearest wife."

"I love you more than words can say."

William brought his lips to hers. As the coach carried them onward, they shared kisses imbued with all the tender affection in their hearts.

Each kiss was a promise for the future, a future so bright, it was certain to rival the very stars in the heavens.

Ever since I was a girl, when I discovered *Jane Eyre* by Charlotte Brontë in the school library, along with the novels of Mary Stewart, Daphne du Maurier, and Victoria Holt, I have been in love with Gothic suspense. I devoured the novels written by these authors, entranced by the thrilling atmosphere found in their page-turning stories, the clever twists and turns of the plot, the intriguing characters, and the romance—always the romance. Later, I became addicted to murder mysteries, especially the novels of Agatha Christie. As an author, until now I've mainly written historical fiction and romance. But I've been hankering to return to my first loves, Gothic suspense and murder mysteries, and to write a series set in nineteenth-century England, my happy place.

Many readers know I'm a huge fan of Jane Austen, but I also adore the Brontës. *Jane Eyre* is one of my favorite novels of all time. A couple of years ago, as I was rereading it for the zillionth time, I was intrigued by the character of Diana Rivers, one of Jane Eyre's cousins, with whom Jane takes refuge during the last part of the book. Diana Rivers and her sister—both strong, compassionate, intelligent women—were born into a well-to-do family but were obliged to become governesses when their father lost his fortune in a bad investment. I thought that was an interesting backstory for a character. In the final chapter of *Jane Eyre*, we are informed that Diana Rivers married a captain in the Royal Navy, "a gallant officer and a good man." I wondered: how did that romance come about?

And so, the idea for this novel was born. My heroine, Diana Taylor, becomes a governess at an ancient manor house, working for a brooding gentleman with "a past." A careful reader will find numerous "Easter eggs" and loving homages to *Jane Eyre* sprinkled throughout this book. (i.e., my introduction of Captain Fallbrook, whom Diana meets on the road, is a tribute to the scene where Jane Eyre meets Mr. Rochester—although the moment plays out very differently.)

In true Gothic suspense form, I sent Diana Taylor on a mission to solve a murder that puts her own life in peril. I wanted the pupil in Diana's care to present another mystery to solve—and so I made Emma Fallbrook dyslexic, a learning difficulty that was undiagnosed in 1849, when this story takes place. It wasn't until 1877 that German ophthalmologist Rudolf Berlin coined the term "dyslexia" to describe partial reading loss by some of his adult patients, but his speculation about its cause was incorrect. It would be another hundred years before dyslexia began to be better understood, and the educational psychology of the condition is still under debate today. I researched dyslexia extensively to present it as accurately and sensitively as I could. Any mistakes I made are my own.

The butler in the novel, Mr. Emity, is inspired by the Guinea-born British musician Joseph Antonio Emidy, (1775 - April 23rd, 1835) who was enslaved by Portuguese traders in his early life, later impressed into the Royal Navy, and eventually freed and discharged near Truro, Cornwall, where he became a celebrated violinist and composer. I was touched and moved by his story and hope that by melding his history with the character in this novel, I have in some small way honored the real-life Mr. Emidy.

I had great fun writing this novel, and I'm having an equally grand time plotting and writing the next books in the series. I hope you enjoy them. My goal, as always, is to write heartfelt, page-turning stories about strong, smart, sympathetic women and men who must rise above difficult challenges on the road to self-discovery, finding their soul mate, and falling madly in love.

ACKNOWLEDGEMENTS

Writing his novel has been a labor of love, and I am grateful to so many people for their help along the way.

I wish to thank my literary agent, Tamar Rydzinski, for believing in this novel from the moment of its inception and working so hard to find it the perfect home. Enormous thanks to Kathryn Le Veque for her faith in the book and for doing me the honor of bringing me into the Dragonblade fold. I'm thrilled to be a Dragonblade author!

Huge thanks to my editor, Amy McNulty, for her smart edits and thoughtful, insightful comments, which helped strengthen this novel immeasurably. I look forward to working with Amy on the upcoming books in the Audacious Sisterhood of Smoke and Fire series. Thank you as well to the entire Dragonblade team for all their efforts in bringing this book to press.

A heartfelt thank you to my beta readers, for generously taking the time to read early drafts of this novel and share their oh-so-helpful thoughts: Mimi Matthews, Karen Odden, Natalie Jenner, Susan James, and Laurel Ann Nattress (thank you for the mermaid bed!). And special thanks to my dear, lifelong friend Kimberly Yee, for all the long, late-night conversations on how to improve every aspect of this book. Thanks to my long-time medical research guru, Michelle Shuffett, for advice about the captain's injury. I love and appreciate you all!

And as always, thank you to my readers—those who've been with me from the start, and those who have discovered me for the first time with this novel. Writing books is my passion and writing Gothic suspense and mysteries has long been one of my ambitions. I'm delighted to share this new series with you!

The international and USA Today bestselling author of more than a dozen critically acclaimed novels of historical fiction and romance, Syrie James loves All Things English and is obsessed with the Victorian and Regency eras. (Fabulous gowns! Men on horseback! Country manor houses! Tea and finger sandwiches! Scones and jam! Sign me up please!)

Syrie loves to write about strong, brilliant, adventurous women who are ahead of their time and will stop at nothing to achieve their dreams, and the bold, irresistible men who crash headlong into their lives, and turn everything upside down forever. A research and story structure maven, Syrie is committed to writing page-turning books and taking her characters on challenging journeys of growth and discovery.

After writing romantic novels about Jane Austen and the Brontës (Syrie's favorite classic authors), a passionate version of Dracula, and a sizzling Victorian romance trilogy, she has gleefully turned her pen (okay, her computer) to writing historical murder mysteries set in the English countryside. This requires many research trips to England, the best perk on earth. A member of the Writer's Guild of America, JASNA, and the Historical Novel Society, Syrie has sold numerous scripts to film and television and her work as a playwright has been produced across North America and in New York City.

You will often find Syrie dressing up in one of her many Regency frocks and dancing the night away at a Regency ball or performing on stage as Jane Austen herself. When she's not writing or reading, Syrie loves to take long walks, eat delicious food, attend movies and the theatre, and play board games with family and friends. Syrie lives in Los Angeles a stone's throw from her grown children. She loves to hear from readers and can be contacted at www.syriejames.com.

Social media links:
Website: www.syriejames.com
Facebook: facebook.com/syriejames
Instagram: instagram.com/syriejames